3

This book is dedicated to the one woman who works as hard as I do to get one of these out. Not only does she have to proof read, she has to put up with me crashi8ng and burning every other day. Norma you're the best!!

Cover design by the enormously talented Amy Uhlenkamp
Editing by the word genius Heather Jones-Macke

5

The Yesterday Men

by

Dick Enos

Lou Anne McCally pushed in the cash drawer and picked up the bag with the money it. She sighed as she walked to the back of the store. Another night gone and no customers through the door. Mr. Biddle wasn't going to be happy. Many more nights like this and he'd start closing at four when the rest of the town shut down, and that would be a disaster for her pocketbook. After placing the bag in the safe, closing the door and giving the dial a good spin, she picked up her purse and jacket.

Clicking off the lights, she noticed how dark the store seemed. Through the window, on which the word *Variety* was emblazoned backward from this side, she could see the fog outside. Fog was nothing new this close to the swamp, but this one seemed even worse than usual. Normally the streetlight cast enough illumination for her to see her way through the store, but with the fog it seemed to be little more than a dying match.

No matter. She had walked past the glass counter and the racks full of sewing goods so many times that she could have done it with her eyes closed. As she moved back across the store, a cold chill running up her spine made her tremble. "Somebody must have just walked over a grave," she said offhandedly. Then she shook her head and smiled. "Yep, that'll make you feel good. Nothing like thinking a nerve spasm has something to do with a grave." She paused just before the door to put on her jacket. For a moment or two she thought she saw tendrils of fog slip under the door like ghostly fingers reaching for her. She buttoned her jacket and forced herself to laugh, hunting for courage in the sound. Then she pulled open the door with a bravado she didn't feel and stepped out into the night.

The fog seemed to close in around her. No sooner had she pulled the door shut and taken a few steps away from it than the doorway disappeared. Turning up the collar on her jacket, she set off quickly down the sidewalk, the *click-clack* of her heels echoing back at her from the dense wall of white.

By the time she'd gone two blocks, the moisture had soaked her coat and turned her hair to damp ringlets plastered to her forehead. Wiping the droplets from her face, she increased her pace, hoping to cover the six blocks to home in as little time as possible.

Suddenly, through the fog she could make out a picket fence running along the edge of the walk. She stopped, confused. There was no fence along the walk on the way home. As a matter of fact, there wasn't a fence on this side of the street till you got clear out almost to the end of Swanson.

"Damn it!" she cursed. "I must have missed my corner in the fog." She gritted her teeth and squinted into the fog. Well, she'd just have to turn around and go back. But... which way was back? Was the fence on her right when she stopped, or on her left?

A faint sound broke the silence of the fog. It was a skittering sound, like tiny hooves running over the pavement. She strained her ears to try and place where it was coming from, but it seemed to be all around her, and with every beat of her heart it was growing louder!

She spun wildly in the fog, seeking to find the source of the sound, but white was all there was. Then she heard the second sound. It was a gasping, heavy breathing. At first she thought that it was her own breathing she was hearing, but then she realized she was holding her breath.

A scream tore itself from her breast and she began to run, not caring in what direction, just running to get away!

Then suddenly the walk was empty. The only sign that Lou Anne McCally had ever been there was one lone shoe lying on its side in the middle of the walk.

Chapter 1

You just know when the phone rings in the middle of the night it's not gonna be good news. So when it started to ring at 2 a.m. I knew I was in trouble. When it hadn't quit by 2:30 I knew they weren't going to go away, so I rolled over to the cold side of the bed and dragged the receiver back to my ear.

The voice on the other end confirmed what I already suspected. "Captain, Captain, where have you been? I've been trying get a hold of you for the last half hour. Captain, this is Thelma, and I need your help!" As if I couldn't have recognized that cartoon voice, and the fact that she was talking at two hundred miles per hour.

"Just tell me where you are, Thelma, and I'll send Triple A."

"Captain, are you listening? Why would I need Triple A? I don't even drive. I need your help! Can you hear me, Captain?"

I scratched the back of my head and tried to wake up. The last thing I could remember was stumbling into bed about an hour ago after a flight back from Dallas. And I was having real trouble trying to make sense out of what she was saying.

"Captain? Aunt Sophie and Uncle Vince called, and they said my cousin Lou Anne has been kidnapped. They need you to find her!"

"Well you tell Aunt Vince to call the local police and have them look for her. They'll know what to do."

"It's Aunt Sophie and Uncle Vince."

I repeated it a couple of times inside my head to make sure that I got it right. Uncle Vince and Aunt Flo.

"I called Doctor Gallagher, and she said you'd be glad to help."

My tired eyes rolled back into my head behind their closed lids. Thelma had just played the Kate card, and there was no way to refuse her now.

Dr. Katherine Gallagher, head of New Mexico University's Anthropology department, was the woman I was in love with.

Thelma, five foot six and a hundred and eighty pounds of sturdy shoes, mousy brown hair and thick glasses, was her assistant. Her I could refuse anytime, but Kate? If Kate asked me to walk through fire, I'd drench myself in gasoline and dance happily into the inferno! So you might as well pass the gas can.

I sat up on the edge of the bed and rubbed the stubble on my chin. "Give me about 45 minutes or so, Thelma. Call Kate and have her meet us here."

She hung up, and I sat there wondering what Momma Steele's boy had gotten himself into this time.

*   *   *   *   *

The shower helped, but I knew that in a couple of hours it wasn't going to be a decent substitute for real sleep. I took a corner of my towel and wiped the steam off the mirror. I wasn't real sure about the face that was looking back at me.

Oh yeah, it looked a lot like me, but all of that youthful vigor I remembered so well seemed to have taken the last train out of town. There were gray circles under my eyes, and a couple of crows had left footprints around the corners.

It wasn't always this way. Not so long ago I came back from chasing Russians out of the skies over Korea with hope of testing jet planes. Yeah, I know, really safe job there. But that's what I wanted to do. Then my brother was killed, and when I went to find out what had happened I ended up involved in an alien plot to take over the world. Kate, her father, and I stopped them, but in the process we managed to blow up all their technical gear pretty much on purpose, so nobody else could get their hands on it. The Air Force wasn't real happy about that, and gave me my walking papers.

Well, I came back here, and with a good friend, my former crew chief, we started a small flying service, trucking packages here and there. And since then, every time somebody gets in trouble we have been off to save the world.

With a shave, shower, and fresh clothes I felt a little better, and my attitude improved a bit. But I knew if I stood in one place too long I was gonna be fast asleep again

Barefoot I padded into the kitchenette to make coffee. When we bought the air freight business, I moved into the small apartment behind the office. It's not much, but for a single guy like me, it's pretty much all I need: kitchenette/dining room/living room, a bedroom and a bath. And besides, it's all right next to the hangar, so I don't have to put on my shoes when I go to work!

I was just about to set the pot down on the stove when I saw headlights headed toward the airfield. Figuring it was Thelma, I lit the fire under the pot and went out to meet her.

If it was Thelma, then she'd come up a bit in the world. A long, black Chrysler pulled up in front of the building. As I walked out, the back window rolled down, and the barrel of a machine gun started spitting slugs at me.

I dropped to the dirt and rolled over behind a pile of empty oil drums, and bullets stitched a trail behind me in the dirt. Out of instinct I reached for the .45, but it was still locked in the safe in the back of the office.

Lead was pinging around me like rain drops, tearing holes in the siding and ventilating the drums. Franticly I searched around for a weapon, but the only things I could find were the rocks that Marie used as a border on her flower garden. I grabbed one about the size of a baseball and waited for the gun to sweep past me. I rolled out, hurled it, and rolled back. Bullets filled the space I'd just vacated, but I heard a loud thump from the rock connecting. Then I heard somebody cussing about the dent in his car.

A quick peek showed me a dent in the rear door of the car just below the window. I rolled back behind the drums and grabbed all the rocks I could hold. Then after waiting for his sweep again, I jumped up and let fly with a barrage of rocks like hailstones.

One of them was right on target and clipped the gunman in the head, and his tommy gun fell out the window.

Without even thinking I ran toward the car screaming and throwing more rocks. Rocks were bouncing off the car everywhere. The driver cussed again and slammed it into gear, and they streaked off just as I reached the tommy gun.

I was about to try a couple of shots at them when I saw another car coming up the road, and with the inaccuracy of the machine gun it wasn't safe to try. So I just stood there waiting for the car, machine gun dangling from my arm, watching the taillights of the Chrysler recede in the distance.

The taxi slid to a stop in front of me, the rear door kicked open, and a vision stepped out. Dr. Katherine Gallagher was the woman I was in love with. More smarts than a Harvard brain trust and more curves that a European racetrack, all stacked just a hair short of six feet tall. She had eyes like a summer's sky. Lips that were luscious and red, and were just begging to be kissed. Her auburn hair was down this morning and just brushed the tops of her shoulders.

She was dressed for traveling in a khaki skirt that stopped just above her knees, a blouse to match, and high, black leather boots.

She walked towards me, stopped, looked at the tommy gun, shook her head, and said snidely, "If you didn't want to pay the fare, then you could have just said so." Without waiting for an answer, she brushed past and walked inside.

I stood there for a moment, I think in shock more than anything, before I fumbled in my pants pocket and found a five for the driver. He never took his eyes off the machine gun. When the bill was in his hand, he was gone!

I was just about to follow Kate inside when I saw another set of lights approaching. Just in case, I brought the gun up and cocked it.

The cab slid to a stop and my partner Joey got out. The slight breeze brought me the scent of perfume. "I don't need to ask where you've been."

His dark face split with a grin that threatened to touch his ears. "I figured after that long flight back from Dallas I deserved some R and R."

"I just hope one of those R's was for Marie Ramón, or when she finds out you're going to need this." I held up the tommy gun for emphasis.

His grin got even bigger. "It was." Then he fumbled around in his pockets and looked at me pleadingly.

I handed him the gun and pulled another five out of my pocket. "Don't any of you ever carry cash?"

"Well, there was dinner and drinks…" He handed the gun back. Nodding to it he said, "I take it from that we're working again?"

I shrugged as I turned to go inside. "Thelma's coming, and she's got all the answers. Especially the one about why somebody just tried to kill me with this thing."

We were almost to the door, and Joey stopped. "You do know that they could have killed you anytime they wanted?"

I squinted an eye and looked at him out of the corner of the other one. "What are you talking about?"

"That's a .45-caliber machine gun, and it fires up to six hundred rounds a minute. It could have pretty much made scrap metal out of those barrels anytime. If you look at them and the building, you can see that they were all either above or in the dirt."

I stopped dead and looked back at him. "You think they were just trying to scare me?"

He shrugged his shoulders. "Well, you sure ain't dead."

We walked into my kitchen, and Kate was sitting at the table drinking coffee. I laid the gun down in front of her. "New toy?"

"Souvenir. One of the neighbor kids left it on the lawn."

Joey had poured himself some coffee and was sniffing the milk. "Is this milk fresh?" He shook the bottle like it would sound different if it were bad.

"I bought it just before we left. So your guess is as good as mine." Then I turned to Kate. "Any idea what this is all about?"

She shook her head and sipped her coffee. "Only Thelma knows."

"Well, she's late."

Kate looked concerned. "I know. She should have beaten me here. She's never late."

"Yeah, why would she be late? Ugly don't take no time. You just wake up and it's there." Joey bantered.

Kate's eyes narrowed, and I could almost hear the growl building up in her throat. I quickly stepped between them. "Try calling her, Kate."

She got up and walked over to the phone. As she passed Joey her elbow snapped out and caught him in the ribs, splashing his coffee on his shirt. A thin smile cracked her lips. "You're right, Joey, ugly is something you should know a lot about!"

I just threw up my hands. I decided it was safer to let them fight it out than it was to get in the middle of it.

I am pretty sure than none of us drew a breath as we waited for Thelma to answer. After a while Kate hung the phone back up. With a sigh she rolled her eyes. "Well, she could be on her way, or…."

"Or she's in trouble," I finished for her. "Joey, get the DC-3 ready to travel. Kate and I'll take the roadster and head into town. If she shows up before we get back, hang on to her!"

Chapter 2

The roadster was a little toy Joey and I had bought to play with: a '32 Ford coupe with the top, front fenders, and hood stripped off. A flathead V8 made it quick, and oversized tires all the way around made it stick to the road. It would do well over one hundred and twenty.

I backed out of the hangar and revved the exhaust a couple of times to let Kate know that I was ready. She came out, took one look, and started back inside. "No guts," I hollered over the engine noise.

She clamped her jaws together and came over and tried to open the door, only to find it wouldn't open. "Welded them shut for safety. You have to crawl over!"

"You do realize I'm wearing a skirt!"

I showed her my teeth. "You bet!"

Whatever it was that she said next I couldn't hear, because I was revving the engine and watching her cuss as she climbed over the top of the door. I got a nice shot of leg, and she slid into the seat.

WACK! She hit me as hard as she could in the shoulder. And believe me that was nearly as hard as any guy has ever hit me! "What's that for?"

"You know what that was for, you pervert!"

I dropped the clutch in, bouncing her back into the seat. By the time we hit the highway we were already doing a hundred.

Kate had one hand against the dashboard and the other was white-knuckled on the door. But I knew it wasn't the ride that was worrying her. It was Thelma. If she was late it meant almost for sure that she was in trouble. And if what had happened to me earlier was any indication, it could mean big trouble.

*　　*　　*　　*　　*

The open exhaust on the roadster made it roar like a jet, but Joey had come up with an answer for that. When we were a couple of blocks from Thelma's I pulled a lever, and baffles dropped into the exhaust, making it whisper-quiet. It wasn't practical to use them all the time because of the major loss in horsepower.

As I pulled up in front of the old brownstone, I spotted a familiar sight. There was a black Chrysler with a dent in the door and a cracked windshield sitting against the curb.

Kate started to climb out of the car and I stopped her, pulling her back into the seat. "That's the same car that was taking potshots at me earlier. So unless Thelma's hired some thugs to get rid of me, she's in trouble."

"So what do you want to do?"

I chewed on my lip for a bit while I thought about it. Finally I said, "Since going back home and back to bed isn't an option, here's what we'll do. I'll go around back and come up the fire escape. You go up the stairs and knock on the door. While they're distracted by you, I'll take them from behind."

"And I get shot in the crossfire?"

"Well, not if you stay out of the way."

She shook her head, climbed out of the car, and headed for the front door. Leaping over the side of the car I quickly caught up with her. "Kate, I...." I knew what I wanted to say, but the words seemed to be all tangled up in my tongue. Finally, out of desperation I asked, "Don't suppose you got a gun?"

She pulled up her skirt, giving me another nice shot of her leg and the little Browning automatic strapped to her thigh. I raised my eyebrows and asked, "You always wear that?"

"No, I take it off when I shower!" she snapped back. "It's the only way to be safe when you're around."

I took hold of her upper arm and pulled her against me, her full breasts touching my chest. "Well if you're gonna shoot me, I think you'd better do it now, 'cause I'm about to kiss you."

"I'll shoot you alright, but just not yet." Her lips brushed up against mine, and I felt my knees start to weaken. "Be careful, Rick," she whispered.

I kissed her again and said, "You too."

We pulled back apart, and she started for the front of the building again. "Give me about five minutes before you go in. That should give me plenty of time to get in place." Not waiting for a reply, I turned and ducked into the alley as she went up the steps.

The first jump I took at the fire escape missed, so I grabbed a garbage can, turned it over, and climbed on top so I could reach the ladder. It was flaked with rust that rolled off on my hands, and creaked loud enough when I pulled it down to make my heart stop. I stood there holding my breath, waiting for somebody to shout at me, but when nobody did I started my climb.

The ladder let me off on the first landing. When I stepped off it, it started to spring back up, but I was ready for it. And as quietly as possible I eased it back into place.

Keeping close to the edge of the treads to stop them from creaking and the hangers from bouncing against the wall, I made my way up to the third floor.

The fire escape landing on the third floor opened to the hallway window. As I looked in, I could see Kate just getting to the top of the stairs. I tapped lightly against the glass to get her attention. When she looked my way, I made motions to my wrist watch and showed her all five fingers. She must have understood, because she moved back down the stairs out of sight to wait.

You really have to appreciate the guys who designed buildings back around the turn of the century. They put in lots of ledges and facades that made my job way easier. Mine and a burglar's, I guess. Anyway, there was a nice foot-wide ledge reaching around to Thelma's window that was like a freeway for me. I stepped off the landing and onto the ledge and started around the corner of the building.

The one thing I hadn't counted on were the tenants that lived on the ledge. There between me and the window was a nest full of young pigeons, with two adults watching me like I was a giant cat. I got within about two steps of the nest when the first adult swooped at me. The other one wasn't far behind.

All I could do was cover up my head and hope they didn't put any dents in me as I slowly edged passed. The young ones were squawking and the two adults were diving at me, but I managed to get by, glad that I didn't have to come back this way. Two steps on the other side and they left me alone again. All I could do was hope I didn't traumatize them for life. I don't know if they have pigeon psychiatrists for that sort of thing or not.

I knelt down next to Thelma's living room window and dared a peek to see what was going on. That glimpse told me pretty much all I needed to know.

Thelma was sitting on the couch with her hands tied, and one of the thugs was sitting in the matching chair across from her, a gun lying in his lap. One with a bandage around his head was pacing back and forth in the room like he was waiting on a call.

Carefully I reached out and slowly began to ease the window up, hoping that the breeze wouldn't blow the curtains out into the room, thus giving my presence away. Then it was all taken out of my hands. Kate banged on the door. I was gonna have to buy that girl a new watch!

I shoved the window up the rest of the way as the thug with the bandage went to open the door, and I stepped into the room.

Unfortunately for me and my plan, there was a hassock under the window. One foot landed on the hassock and the other hit the floor, and I went down. As I fought to regain my footing, Mr. Bandage jerked open the door, dragged Kate inside, and threw her at me. We became a fun tangle of legs and arms.

Both of the thugs hotfooted it out the door and down the stairs. I could hear them going through the door, and I finally untangled myself and followed.

As I ran through the door, I called back over my shoulder to the girls, "Stay here till I come back, and don't let anybody in!"

\*   \*   \*   \*   \*

As I crashed out the door and onto the sidewalk they were just pulling away from the curb. Burning tires were filling the street with blue smoke. I snapped off a quick shot, and the guy with the bandage returned fire, sending me kissing the sidewalk.

I was back on my feet and running toward the roadster as they turned the corner. I jumped over the side and slid into the driver's seat, hitting the starter button as I did, and hearing the big engine roar to life. In a cloud of tire smoke of my own, I was in hot pursuit.

I took the first corner on two wheels, giving thanks to the gods at Firestone for my tires, and brought it quickly back under control. I could see them about four blocks ahead. I dropped out the baffles and stomped on the accelerator, and suddenly it was like a jet was in the street. The car leaped ahead and the gap between us began to close.

Driving with one hand, I fumbled with the other in the glove box and pulled out a pair of racing goggles. Once I got them on, I slowed enough to loosen the brackets on either side of the wind screen and folded it down. Then I stomped on the accelerator again.

The little Ford seemed like it wanted to fly, and I gave it its head. They were more than half a block away now, and the streets were just starting to wake up. Fortunately the traffic was still, so I had free reign and I intended to use it.

I was almost afraid to look down at the speedometer, figuring if I knew how fast I was going through town I'd probably scare myself.

Within ten feet of their bumper I brought the .45 up, and without aiming, I let one fly. It put a nice round hole in their trunk lid.

Before I could fire again, Bandage Head leaned out of the window and got even with me for my shot by sending one of his towards me. I felt it thump in the seat beside me. In quick succession I fired twice more, watching the back window disappear with one, the other punching a matching hole in the trunk.

The Chrysler tore around a corner, sending the rear of the car slewing across the street. I jumped even harder onto the roadster, sending it right behind them like a rocket. The edge of my bumper just caught their fender, and I started to spin them the rest of the way around. But the driver was better than I thought, and he pulled out of the slide, straightened it up, and shot off down the street again.

I had the accelerator down as far as it would go, and as I shot by the next corner a prowl car raced out behind me with lights blinking and siren blaring. "This is the police! Stop your car. You are under arrest!"

Suddenly it was a rock and a very hard place! I didn't want to defy the law any more than I already had, but I wasn't about to let them get away either.

I made up my mind, and I set the butt of the .45 on the dash, sighted down the barrel, trying to hold the car steady, and slowly squeezed the trigger.

The driver jumped about six inches into the air, slumped down into the seat, and the Chrysler slewed off to the left, clipping a lamppost with a front fender and coming to rest halfway up on the walk. The minute it stopped moving the man with the bandage on his head was out and running down the street. I slammed down on the brakes of the roadster, sending it screeching sideways, and even before it stopped moving I was out and over the side.

The guy with the bandage was fast! I was running flat out, my feet slapping the pavement like a goose taking off on a lake. My fingers were about to brush his collar when a bullet brushed passed mine and smacked into his shoulder. The momentum turned him from a running man into a rolling rock as he slumped down to the pavement. It all happened so fast that I had to jump over him to stop from tripping myself!

In less than half a step I turned around and was back kneeling beside him. I rolled him over onto his back to take a look. He was lucky. There was a lot of bleeding, but the .38 slug hadn't seemed to hit anything vital. I stuck my handkerchief over the hole to slow the bleeding. With my other hand I grabbed him by the chin and shook his head to get his attention. "Why have you been trying to stop us from heading to Louisiana?"

"Am I gonna die?"

I shook my head and squeezed his chin a little tighter, turning his face so his eyes met mine. "Not unless you lie to me, then you'll never get up off this sidewalk! Now who sent you to stop us?"

I had him scared now. "I don't know. My brother and I got a package in the mail with five thousand dollars in it and a note that said to delay you as long as possible from leaving."

I was going to ask more, but suddenly I felt a circle of cold steel against the back of my neck.

"Stand up very slowly with your hands behind your back. One wrong move and I'll put a bullet through your brain."

Slowly I straightened my legs and stood, trying not to make any threatening moves. I probably could have taken the gun away from him, but chances were real good that his partner, who was coming up the walk, would have shot me. So I just played docile and let him snap the cuffs on me.

After taking my driver's license from my pocket and picking up my gun from where I'd laid it on the walk, he led me over and sat me down against the building. "You just sit here and be good for a little while. The ambulance is on its way for your two friends. And as soon as the watch commander gets here we'll take you downtown."

So I sat there, my back against the wall, watching as the ambulance boys picked up the thug from the sidewalk and then pulled his partner out from behind the wheel of the car. As they loaded them up one of the cops walked over and sneered down at me. "Well, looks like you got off lucky this time. The boys from the meat wagon say that the one you shot in the car's gonna make it. So looks like you'll beat the homicide charge. But we've got enough other stuff to hold you till you're a really old man!"

I just sat there, not saying a word. Figured that was the best for me. If I opened my mouth I was liable to say something that would get me shot.

As the ambulance went screaming off to the hospital, an unmarked black prowl car slid into the spot that it had just vacated. The cop that got out was about my size, but the years were starting to tell on him. His belt was starting to disappear under his belly, and the hair showing under his cap had lost the color it had once had.

He hitched up his pants as he stepped up onto the curb, then he walked over and took my .45 from the cop that had it. As he crossed the walk to me, I stood up to meet him. "Sergeant." I turned around and offered him my wrists, and he unlocked the bracelets.

"I'd like to apologize for my men, Captain."

The sergeant and I had had dealings together a couple of times before. As a matter of fact, I pulled him out of the way of a bullet once. "They were just doing their job."

He handed me back my gun, and I slipped it into the holster under my arm and then rubbed my wrists to get the circulation flowing into my hands again.

Over by the patrol car, the two cops were fuming. One of them started across the sidewalk to complain to the sergeant, but he stopped him with a motion of his hand. He squinted a bit to read the officer's name tag. Like I said, the years were showing. "Officer Perry, don't get you shorts in a bunch. If the captain here has done anything wrong, he'll pay for it, but there's no need for him to be taken downtown in handcuffs."

That seemed to slow them down, but if looks could kill, they'd have needed another ambulance to carry my corpse away.

I hopped over the side of the roadster, and as I pressed the starter I called out to the sergeant. "I'm headed downtown right now. Want to tell them to have a steno standing by?"

He walked over to his car and reached through the window for the mic. He talked for a minute or so, and then he waved to me. I dropped the car into gear and left a little rubber behind as I spun out into the street and pull a U-turn to head downtown.

## Chapter 3

By the time I got done with the police the sun was well up, so I stopped and grabbed three coffees and donuts before I headed to Thelma's.

I knocked on the door. It opened a crack, and I found myself facing Kate's little automatic. I pushed the door against her and with my free hand grabbed her gun, taking it away from her, and pushed passed into the kitchen.

I sat the coffee and the rolls down and turned back to her. "First rule: bad guys don't show up with coffee and donuts. Second rule: don't ever let them get close enough to touch you." I spun the little gun on my finger like a Western star and handed it back to her butt-first.

Kate reached out to take it back, and suddenly I found myself flat on the floor. Kate was standing over me with a foot on either side of my chest, grinning. "Third rule: never underestimate the power of a dame!"

When I made no move to get up, her grin changed to concern. "I didn't hurt you, did I?"

It was my turn to grin. "Nope, I'm just enjoying the view!"

Kate blushed red, pulled her skirt tight around her legs, and stepped off my chest. "You beast!" She was still muttering as she walked over to the couch and sat down.

I climbed to my feet and got one of the coffees from the tray in the kitchen. After popping the top off the cardboard cup, I walked over and sat down across from them. "Now, who wants to be a good girl and tell me what this is all about?"

While Kate and I were fighting, Thelma had gotten into the donuts. She had a mouthful, and hid it behind her hand as she tried to talk around it and chew at the same time. "Shortly before I called you last night, my Uncle Vince called me and said that my cousin Lou Anne hadn't come home. And when they went looking for her all they found was one of her shoes."

I took a bite of my own donut and washed it down with a sip of the worst coffee I had ever tasted. "I thought you said that she had been kidnapped," I asked.

"Well, she wouldn't have just gone off wandering on her own."

I screwed up one side of my face and shook my head. "Doesn't mean she was kidnapped. Abducted, maybe. Kidnapped, no."

Thelma shoved the last bite of her donut in her mouth and brushed the crumbs off her blouse. "Semantics! She didn't go off on her own, thus she was kidnapped!"

I got up and walked out to the kitchen to wash the taste of the coffee out of my mouth. As I did I saw Thelma taking a sip of hers. I tried not to laugh as I heard her blow it out. "What is this? Are you trying to kill us?"

I swallowed a couple of glasses of water, and as I turned around Kate handed me a cup of fresh coffee. "I made it right after you left, thinking you might want some when you got back."

"As always you're a lifesaver." Then I hollered at Thelma in the living room. "They were the only place open close to the police station. Just eat the donuts."

"Did your uncle say anything about a note?"

Whatever it was that she said back I didn't hear, because I had stopped listening and turned my full attention on the eminent Dr. Gallagher. As I took the cup from her our hands touched briefly, and I felt the tingle all the way up my arm. Feeling it too, she blushed just a bit and took a deep breath.

I stepped closer, breathing in the soft scent of her and pulling her towards me, my own breathing picking up a bit. I could feel the heat rising up off her body. Less than an inch separated us, and as I made to take that last step I heard that voice again from the doorway.

"I said there was no note. Could that be bad?"

I stepped back and leaned against the counter top, trying to recompose myself and not let my frustration show. "Not necessarily…."

Kate walked out of the kitchen, and from behind Thelma she stuck her tongue out at me. "Is there any reason you can think of that somebody would take your cousin?" In the back of my mind, I was thinking that the cousin probably looked a lot like Thelma, and if that were the case, I couldn't see anybody wanting her. "You know—business rival, spurned boyfriend, crazed maniac?"

"Crazed maniac? You don't think—"

"No, no, no." That last one just slipped out. I tried to smile it all away, but Thelma wasn't having any of it.

"I assure you, Captain Steele, this is no laughing matter! My cousin has disappeared!"

And there were times that I wished I could. "I know Thelma, and it seems somebody doesn't want me looking into where she's gone. But that means that's just exactly what we're going to do!"

I couldn't move quite quickly enough in the small kitchen to get away. Suddenly she threw her arms around me and had me in a bear hug, wiping the donut crumbs from her face all over my shirt.

"Thank you, thank you, so much Captain Steele! I know I'll never be able to repay you for this, so thank you so very much!"

I tried to gently push her away, but she had a death grip around my waist and I couldn't figure out what to do with my arms. Finally I patted her on the back. "Probably better get packed, Thelma. Time's a-wastin'."

After she let me go and I could breathe again, I called Kate back into the kitchen. "I've got some information on the guy that took those shots at me that I'd like to check out before we go."

"What do you want us to do in the meantime?"

"Get your things together and head out to the aerodrome. I'll catch up with you as soon as I can."

She leaned forward and kissed me quickly on the lips. "Be careful."

"Hey, with a promise like that I might not even go."

Kate pushed me out the kitchen and into the hall. Then she slammed the door behind me. "Yeah, and I love you too!" I hollered through the wooden partition. Then I walked off down the steps. I heard the door open behind me, but I just kept on going.

*　*　*　*　*

Luckily for me the police hadn't seen me slip Bandage Head's wallet out of his pocket, or I'd probably be up on pickpocketing charges. In any case, when I was done with it I'd drop it in the mail anonymously, but for right now it was my only way to find out whether or not he lied to me.

The driver's license said his name was Will LeRoy, and the address was an old apartment building down by the rail yards, definitely on the wrong side of the tracks. So I fired the roadster back up and pointed it across town.

*     *     *     *     *

I stood across the street from the hundred-year-old building that stared at me like a freshly unearthed skull, its empty windows like eye sockets and its door a gap-toothed smile.

After a quick look around I stepped out of the shadows of a tumbled-down tenement and made my way across the street. I pushed through the warped door and into the vestibule, then paused and checked behind me to make sure that the coast was clear. The paper taped to the wall said Will LeRoy lived on the third floor.

There had be a security lock on the door at one time, but it looked like somebody had lost their key and used a crowbar to get in instead, and nobody had ever gotten around to repairing it. There was just an empty hole in the door and a big chunk gone out of the frame.

As I stepped into the building I was nearly overwhelmed by the smell. Cabbage, boiled potatoes and beets from meals eaten long ago, the sweat of the working man, and urine. It hung like a fog inside the building, making it almost hard to breathe.

Every city had buildings like this one. Places where the immigrants came to live until they died or found better. Places like this that the slum lords made their fortunes from, renting out hovels and never fixing anything. Entire families living in one or two rooms without indoor plumbing or sufficient heat. Today the immigrants were gone, replaced by those on their way back down, or those that never got a start on the road up. Outside a train rumbled passed and plaster dust sifted down from the ceiling.　　　I made my way up the stairs, so worn that they dipped in the middle, creaking loudly with every step. The handrail was polished black from all the greasy hands that had slid along its surface.

I heard noises behind some of the doors I passed, and once even the mournful wail of a baby, but nobody looked out into the hallway. For all they seemed to care, the building was empty.

The frame and the door to LeRoy's apartment hadn't been acquainted with each other in quite some time. Age and dry rot had sucked the life out of the frame, and there was nearly an inch gap between it and the door. I listened carefully to make sure there wasn't somebody on the other side, and when I didn't hear anything I took my knife and pushed it between the lock and the frame, popping the door open.

There wasn't much more to see on the inside than there had been in the hallway. Whatever they had gotten for delaying me they hadn't spent on furniture. There was a Murphy bed, which was messed like somebody had just gotten out of it, a scarred-up table, and two mismatched chairs. Just to make sure, I walked over and laid my hand on the bed first to make sure that it was cold and that somebody hadn't just jumped out of it. The sheets were so dirty I wiped my hand on the leg of my pants after touching it.

In the center of the beat-up table was some string and a piece of brown wrapping paper about the same size it would take to hold five thousand dollars. When I picked up the paper to read the mailing address I noticed it had funny smell, almost medicinal. The address was just a P.O. box with no return address.

As I scanned the room, I spotted a piece of paper over by the wall where the breeze from the door opening must have blown it. When I bent down to pick it up, I noticed something else;

a piece of the mopboard appeared to be loose, and there were dirty fingerprints on the wall around it.

I squatted down and with my knife pulled the board loose. Behind it was an open space in the wall. Hidden inside was the rest of the five grand and a faded brown photograph of two young men standing in front of a big white house. They were both dressed in clothes from the early part of the century, and there was a horse-drawn hay rake off to the side.

What was most amazing about the photo were the faces of the two men. Unless I missed my guess completely, they were dead ringers for LeRoy and the guy I shot. I turned it over, and on the back was scrawled *Will and Frank 1912*. If I had been drinking something, I'd have choked on it! As it was for a second or two I was having a hard time breathing. How could that be? The two guys in the photo were at their youngest, in their twenties, and the guys I'd tangled with weren't much older than that—forty years later!

I didn't have much more time to think about it. I heard cars squeal to a stop outside, and when I looked out the window I saw cop cars sitting against the curb. It was anybody's guess as to how they'd found out about the place. But however it was I wasn't going to hang around and ask.

Quickly I put the board back, slipped the photo and the rest of the cash into my pocket, and backed out the door. Already I could hear the police pounding up the steps, so I didn't have much time to make a decision on my choice of getaway.

Out the window at the end of the hall was a rickety old wooden fire escape, barely still hanging to the brick wall. I ducked out the window and started down, feeling it sway with the weight of my body as I did. I heard one of the cops yell, "There he goes!" punctuated by a slug drilling itself into the window frame.

I was about halfway down when I saw the first cop crawl out the window. Hoping to survive the fall, I braced my back against the wall and my feet against the steps and pushed. The bolts creaked and screamed. Then suddenly the wooden fire escape pulled free from the wall, and I was dropping through space to the garbage-filled yard below.

I landed on a pile of trash and a handful of boards from the stairs, but I didn't have time to even consider if I was hurt. I had to get out of there. I pulled myself to my feet and, with a quick glance over my shoulder to make sure I had slowed their pursuit, tore off through the yard. Two blocks later I was nearly out of breath by the time I'd gotten to the roadster, but somewhere in all the garbage and mud of the backyards I had lost the cops.

I climbed into the car and drove quietly away.

\*     \*     \*     \*     \*

As Steele drove away, the man who was watching emerged from the shadows and walked the two blocks to the tobacco shop. He made his way directly to the pay phone, deposited the right amount of change, dialed a number, and listened as it rang.

There were no pleasantries exchanged when it was answered. The man in the booth immediately began his report. "All efforts to delay Steele have failed.      The LeRoy brothers are in custody, and the girl is free. Any further instructions?"

The voice on the other end was almost monotonous in its response. "No. Let him come. We have already made provisions to be ready. You might as well come back too. It is nearly time for your next treatment."

The man hesitated a moment before he asked his next question. "What about the LeRoy brothers? What if they talk?"

The voice on the phone went from a monotone to a snarl. "They don't know enough, and haven't enough time left to be a threat." Then the phone clicked, and a dial tone filled the caller's ear.

The man in the booth returned the receiver to the hook, checked the change slot, and left the booth. As he passed the tobacco counter, he stopped and asked the man for a Corona cigar.

When the tobacconist handed him one from the humidor, he carefully clipped the end with a pair of scissors that hung from a chain on a button on his vest. Then he warmed it with a wooden match from the match can on the counter before sucking it to life.

With the cigar between his teeth and his thumbs hooked in his vest pockets, a trail of smoke following him, he walked out of the store and down the street to his car.

## Chapter 4

There was something depressing about the town. You could feel it the moment you first set foot on Main Street. It was like when the clouds cover the sun on your long-awaited picnic—that vague feeling of disappointment, of loss.

Maybe it was the fact that the streets were empty. Nothing moved except the flags in front of the city hall. Or maybe it was the starkness of the buildings; if it were a painting, they would have been blurry, indistinct shadows.

I took off my sunglasses and rubbed my hand over my eyes, trying to wipe the feeling from my mind. But when I was done it was still there. I looked at the others, and I could see by their eyes that they were feeling it too.

City Hall was the first building on the street. Its foundations were built so high out of the ground that it took six steps just to reach the doors. I screwed up my courage and with a deep breath put a foot on the first step. "The rest of you wait here. I'll go in and see if I can find a car to rent. Then we can go back and get our luggage out of the plane."

Kate shivered a bit and pulled her light jacket tighter around her as though she were cold. She forced a smile and nodded. I started up the steps, not knowing exactly what to expect.

From the looks of things City Hall must have been the oldest building on the street. It was red brick with cream-colored cornices to accent it. Carved into the brick above the door were the words *City Hall*, and then some roman numerals after it that I had long since forgotten how to read. And below that there was a slogan in Latin that I was pretty sure read, "Beware all who enter here!" But don't quote me on that.

Flagpoles stood on either side of the steps, one flying the American flag and the other the French flag. I guess that made sense. The French had always had more influence here in this part of the country than the British ever did.

As I reached out for the big brass handle on the door, I could have sworn I felt a spark jump off of it. But when I looked around to see if anybody else saw anything, nobody was looking. So after rubbing the imaginary electrical burn on the back of my hand, I reach out again, turned the knob, and pushed the door open. It gave out with a groan like the Crypt Keeper's. Kind of said City Hall didn't get a lot of business, or maybe it was cheaper than buying a bell.

A marble and wood counter about four feet tall stretched across the room to stop you from going any further inside. Around it the walls were lined with pictures of men in Confederate uniforms. Most were officers, but here and there an enlisted man turned up. It looked like everybody in town must have joined up when the time came.

Behind the counter there were four desks, but only one of them was occupied, and as the door closed the apparition rose up from her desk and floated across the room to the counter. Everything about her was gray—her hair, her skin, the dress she was wearing. If she had been any grayer, I could have looked right through her.

"May I help you?" Under all the ice in her voice there was just enough of a touch of Southern to say she was probably born here, went away to college, and came back to live the rest of her life.

I gave her my best Smilin' Jack look and said, "My friends and I were hoping that you could direct us to some place or some person that we could rent a car from."

Her gray eyes narrowed, and she seemed to x-ray my soul. "You're the people from that plane that I heard over the town, aren't you?"

I nodded, still showing her all my teeth. "Yes ma'am, we—"

The question must have been rhetorical. She cut me off before I could finish. Her eyes grew even colder and her jaw granite hard. A finger like a talon rose up from behind the desk to point at me. "There is nothing in this town for you or your kind! Get out of my office before I call the police."

I wanted to ask just what my kind was, but she turned her back on me, floated to her desk, and picked up the phone receiver. So with my tail tucked between my legs I made a beeline for the door.

I don't think I drew another breath till I was standing outside once more. I pretty much flew down the steps to the relative safety of the sidewalk.

"Well," Kate asked, "what did you find out?"

I ignored her and turned to Thelma. "How long have your aunt and uncle lived in this crazy town?"

Thelma shrugged the sandbags that passed for her shoulders and said, "Eight, nine years. My Aunt Sophie was born here, but went away to college and met my uncle. They only came back here after Lou Anne graduated. They thought it might be a nice place to retire."

I shook my head. "Well, it's not! It's Crazyville!" Then I told them what had happened inside. Before I could finish, Joey grabbed my shoulder and pointed down the street where a prowl car with his lights on was racing in our direction.

"I don't think unfriendly covers it, Boss."

The car skidded to a stop in front of us, and a man in a tan uniform rolled out of the driver's door. I can't really think of any other way to explain it other than *rolled out*. Wherever he was going his belly always got there first. I was willing to bet that it had been so long since he had seen his feet that he couldn't remember how many toes he had. His Mountie hat was pulled low enough to rest on his ears, and his eyes were lost behind mirrored sunglasses. Two could play that eyeless game. I slid my glasses back on. Glancing over I saw Joey doing the same thing.

He walked a bit like a man on the deck of a ship, feet spread sort of like he was afraid he was going to step in something. He had one hand on his gun and one hand on his baton. "I need to see some *i-dent-tif-a-cation*." He turned the word into five distinct syllables as he talked around the chaw in his cheek.

"And just who are you?" I asked.

"I would have thought that was obvious." He tapped the shiny shield pinned to his shirt with a fat forefinger. "I'm Vernon P. Tucker, Chief of *Pol-leese* in these here parts." He held out his left hand palm-up while his right loosened his gun in the holster. "I'll take those ID's now." He looked to Joey and said, "Yours first, boy."

Joey clenched his fist and started to step forward, but I quickly stepped between him and Tucker to stop him.

"Smart move. I won't hesitate to shoot either him or you. Now show me your papers!"

We pulled out our wallets and handed him our driving licenses and our pilot's licenses. As Kate and Thelma tried to hand him theirs, he held up a palm and stopped them. "That won't be necessary, ladies. I'm just interested in these two." He carefully studied our papers. When he was done, he tucked them into the pocket of his shirt and buttoned the flap. "I'll want to check these out with the wire service after I get back to my office. You can have them back when I'm done, or when you leave town." He flashed a grin. "Whichever comes first." Then his hand moved back down to rest on the butt of his gun. It was hard to tell whether it was a threat or a habit. "Now, what brings you to my town?"

I was about to answer when a long, black limo pulled in behind Tucker's car. A rather smallish man got out, round but not really fat, carrying a walking stick and dressed like an English lord in a tan tweed suit and cap. Long, grey sideburns and a full mustache covered his face, looking like they were leftover from the last century. He walked toward us with an air of authority. "Trouble, Tuck?"

Tucker nearly bowed before this little man. "No sir, Doctor. Just checking on these strangers."

The man he had called the doctor extended his hand towards me. "You must be Captain Steele. I'm Doctor Sharade. I talked to Thelma's uncle about your coming. I think you'll find he has a pleasant surprise for you."

"We were just getting ready to walk over there when the chief stopped us." Kate said.

The doctor seemed shocked. "Walk, Doctor Gallagher? Absolutely not when my car is at your service!" Then he turned to Tucker. "That is, if our fine chief of police has completed his investigation."

Tucker growled a bit under his breath, but what came out of his mouth was as sweet as candy. "Oh yes, Doctor. You know me, just being careful about who comes into town."

I held out my hand and just a sweetly said, "Then you won't mind giving us back our papers?"

He gave me a blank look like he had no idea what I was talking about. I was about to point out that they were in his pocket when the doctor beat me to the punch.

"I think I saw you absently button them into that shirt pocket of yours, Tuck."

Tucker reached up to his shirt pocket and reached inside, acting surprised. "Why, so I did." He took them out and handed them back. I could almost see his eyes narrow with venom behind his glasses. "I wouldn't want to inconvenience you folks in any way." In sounded nice, but it dripped blood. After handing them back he turned on his heel, climbed into his patrol car and sped away.

When he was gone, the doctor shook his head. "Vernon means well, but he's still just a small-town police chief and doesn't care much for having his routine interrupted." He swept his arm toward the car. "Now, shall we?"

The car was an old pallbearer car with the jump seats in the doors. The women took the main seat, the doctor and I took the jump seats, and Joey rode up front with the driver.

After we were all settled, the doctor took out an old briar pipe and stuck it between his teeth. Thankfully he didn't light it, but he must have read in my face what I was thinking. "It's an old habit, Captain. I seldom light it anymore, but I do enjoy having it to chew on." Then with a thin smile he said, "I hope you'll forgive the fine people of the town for their rudeness. Their luck with outsiders hasn't been the best—the British, then the Revolutionary Army, and finally Sherman. I hope you understand."

"Seems like an awfully small town for such a large hospital," Kate mentioned.

He reached up, clutched his cold pipe, and nodded in agreement. "True, but then it's not really for the residents. Oh, we handle the local emergency and birth a baby now and then, but for the most part it's a rehabilitation facility.

"After the Civil War it was used as a veteran's rehabilitation facility for Confederate soldiers. Then again after World War I. But by the end of World War II the government had finally gotten their own plan in place, and it was abandoned. I came here and opened the Cypress Glen Home for the Rehabilitation of the Aged."

"So it's an old folk's home?" I asked.

He shook his head. No, no, it's much more than that. It would be easier to show you than explain it to you." He was interrupted by the limo pulling up to the curb. "Oh, see, we're here already." He indicated a white, two-story wood-frame house.

At the sound of the car, the front door opened, and a male version of Thelma walked out onto the porch. Before I could even blink, Thelma was out of the car and running across the yard to throw her arms around him.

As I opened the door, I looked at Kate with a question in my eyes.

"What?" she asked.

Looking at them on the porch, I asked, "She did say her uncle, right? Not her father?"

Kate laughed as she climbed out of the car. It was a good sound after all that had happened in the last twenty-four hours. "Believe me, Rick. I've seen her father. That's her mother's brother."

I leaned back into the car as the doctor slid across to the backseat. "Thank you for the ride, Doctor. Maybe before we leave we can take you up on that tour."

He flashed me a smile. "Please do. I can use the company, not to mention I like to show off." Then he pulled the door shut and the limo sped off up the street.

The three of us made our way across the yard. As we stepped up onto the porch, he unwound himself from Thelma's deadly embrace and stuck out a ham for us all to shake. "Hi. I'm Thelma's uncle, Vince McCally. I want to thank you all for coming so quickly." His smile was big and warm, but quickly faded into distress. "Although, I'm afraid other than a visit from this one," he poked Thelma in the ribs and she giggled like a six-year-old, "I'm afraid you've made a wasted trip."

It was my turn to look even more confused than usual. "How's that, Mr. McCally?"

He opened the screen door and ushered us in with one big hand. "Please come inside and I'll explain. After we had stepped inside, he looked up and down the street nervously as though to see who might be watching.

For the first time I noticed three of his neighbors had stopped what they were doing and were busy gawking at us. Maybe they were just nosy, but I was picking up a bad feeling from the way Vince was looking at them.

The front door opened to an either-way hall. Go left and you go to the dining room and kitchen. Go right and you go to the living room, and straight ahead would take you up to the second floor. The furnishings fit the house. Nothing fancy or too elaborate, just the kind of things people collect after years together. Comfortable chairs and a couch in the living room, a worn but treasured dining room set—the kind of place even a stranger could call home.

As the screen door closed he called toward the kitchen. "Sophie, they're here. Come out and see Thelma and meet her friends." Almost reluctantly the woman called Sophie came out of the kitchen and into the dining room.

Sophie had the look of a woman who'd grown too tired to ever catch up again, a woman that every moment of life weighed too heavy on. Her once dark hair had grown grey, and lines etched the years onto her face. Her skin was pale, almost colorless, her blue eyes lifeless. When she moved, it wasn't really a walk, but more of a shuffle.

She crossed the room and lightly kissed Thelma on the cheek without any sign of real affection. The hand she held out to us was a dead fish on a stick that protruded from her faded housedress.

"Sophie, this is Captain Steele, Doctor Gallagher, and the captain's partner, Joe Washington." She offered each of us a weak smile, but that was it. No "hi," no "how are you," no "thank you for coming." All she did was look up at Vince and in a flat voice say, "Have you told them yet?"

Vince shook his head. "No, I really haven't had the chance yet. Why don't we all go into the kitchen and I'll make some coffee, and I can explain." That ham flew out again and was already ushering us toward the kitchen, so the best we could do was go with the flow.

I followed Kate through the kitchen door and had to slam on the brakes to stop from tripping over her. But Thelma and Joey didn't make it, and slammed into my back. What had stopped her so abruptly was sitting at the table staring off into space, an untouched cup of tea sitting in front of her.

From Thelma's and Kate's reaction I could only assume this was the missing Lou Anne. Then seconds later I knew for sure when Thelma squealed and pushed me out of the way to run over and throw her arms around the girl. The girl at the table didn't move. Not even under Thelma's assault did her expression move from the blank stare she was wearing.

They had told me that Lou Anne was two years younger than Thelma, but this girl at the table looked ten years older. She was thin, almost anorexic. Grey flecks dotted her brown hair.

I looked to Vince and could see the sad resignation on his face. "She just showed up at the door this morning, minus one shoe, but for the most part no worse for wear."

Kate walked over to the table and knelt down next to the girl, taking her wrist in her hand to check her pulse. As she moved her arm up from her lap, a bandage on the inside of her elbow became visible. "What's this, Vince?"

Sophie stepped up and pulled Lou Anne's arm from Kate's grasp. "Doctor said she must have caught it on something during her confusion."

Kate reached out for the girl's wrist again, but Sophie pushed herself between. There was suddenly fire in her eyes. "The doctor said she'll be fine!"

"But she's nearly catatonic!"

"We called the doctor—a real medical doctor, not an anthropologist that thinks she's one. He said that she was in shock from the trauma of getting lost. He said she will recover in a few days!"

Kate pleadingly looked to me, and all I could do was shrug. Vince saw the look and tried to defuse the situation. "We called the doctor just as soon as she showed up this morning, Doctor Gallagher. He checked her out thoroughly and said physically she was fine. The only injury was that wound on her arm."

Kate backed off a couple of steps, but Sophie held her ground between Kate and Lou Anne, her arms crossed over her chest and her mouth a thin, determined line.

"Vince," I asked, "do you think you could drive Joey and I out to pick up our luggage from the plane?"

Sophie's head swiveled toward me like a snake with a new target. "There is no need of you to stay. Lou Anne is back. If Vince had listened to me in the first place, there would have been no need of you to come here at all. But now there is no need of you to stay!"

I gave her kind of a guilty look and raised one shoulder in capitulation. "Yes ma'am, I realize that, but it's getting rather late now, and we've been up all night. So if you wouldn't mind, we'd sure appreciate a chance for a little rest before we head back. I promise you we won't be any trouble, and we'll be out of your way first thing in the morning."

Uncle Vince jumped in to help save me. "They won't be any trouble, Sophie. And besides, it'll give us a chance to visit with Thelma a bit before she goes back. Heck, it might even help Lou Anne recover having people around."

Sophie sighed. "That's fine then, but first thing in the morning…."

Vince walked through the kitchen and out the back door. "I'll bring the car around front."

I motioned toward the front door with my head, and Kate and Thelma followed us into the dining room, out of ear shot of Sophie. "I want you two," I said in a low voice, "to stay here and keep a close eye on those two. See if you can find out a little more. Maybe get a better look at that arm. And Thelma, I need you to tell Kate everything you can remember about your aunt. Joey and I'll be back as soon as we can."

"Are we really leaving in the morning, Captain?" Thelma asked in a worried voice. Behind the thick lenses of her glasses I could see the concern in her eyes.

I shook my head. "We're not leaving here, Thelma, till I know exactly what's going on."

Joey had the curtain pulled aside and was watching the neighbors. "They're still out there, Rick, eyeballing the house. I get the feeling they don't like us being here very well."

I walked over and laid my hand on his shoulder. "You sure it's us? Or maybe just you?"

His brown eyes narrowed and his lips scrunched up. "And what do you mean *me*?"

"Maybe they've never seen a black man before," I ribbed him.

Flatly he said, "Or maybe they're thinking about hanging one."

Neither of us laughed.

Chapter 5


As Rick and Joey drove off with Vince, Sophie took Lou Anne upstairs for a nap, and Kate and Thelma settled into the living room. When she was sure Sophie was out of earshot, Kate moved over onto the couch next to Thelma. "Has your aunt always been like that?"

Thelma's myopic eyes blinked a couple of times behind her thick lenses. "Like what?"

"I don't know—cold, unfeeling?"

"I really don't know, Kate. Since they came back here, I haven't talked to her very often. Usually it's Uncle Vince that I talk to, and he's never said anything about her changing. I know she was very glad when Lou Anne came to live with them again.

"I mentioned coming to visit a couple of times, but Vince always said that it was a bad time. So I've never been here."

Kate kicked off her shoes and curled her long legs up under. "Why did they come back?"

"Sophie got sick, and the doctor here was the only one who could save her. After she got well they just stayed. Then last year Lou Anne kind of hit on hard times and came back here, too. She's been working in the five and dime since then."

With the sound of Sophie's footsteps on the stairs, the girls fell silent. Sophie came into the living room and stiffly asked, "Can I get you anything?" Her tone said that just by being there it was an imposition.

Rather than incite her, both girls just shook their heads no. Sophie nodded and went into the kitchen.

After she was gone again, Kate got up and walked across the room to peer out the window. Outside the neighbors went about their chores, always keeping an eye on the McCally house. "This town is really starting to give me the creeps. Have you noticed there aren't any dogs? Not once since we got here have I heard a dog bark."

Thelma came across the room to join her. "Or kids. No bicycles left in the yards. No swing sets, nothing."

Kate shivered with a sudden chill. "Like I said, it gives me the creeps."

\*     \*     \*     \*     \*

It was pretty quiet in the car as we drove through town. Joey was in the front with Vince and tried to engage him in conversation a couple of times, but all he was getting were monosyllabic answers. Finally he gave up and just sat staring out the window as the town went past.

Vince seemed distracted by something, but it wasn't his driving. We were the only vehicle on the road. Not even the usual milk truck crossed our path.

As we turned off onto the dirt road that led to the plane, Vince stopped the car. Putting it in park, he turned sideways in the seat so that he was facing both Joey and me. New lines of worry creased his face, and after a moment of thinking about it, he finally let go. "Contrary to what my wife says, we—or at least I—desperately need your help."

Joey shrugged his broad shoulders. "I kinda thought that's why we were here, but everybody keeps trying to run us off."

I put my hand on the back of the front seat, and leaned forward. "What is it exactly that you need, Vince?" I was tired of playing around and wanted a few straight answers.

Vince looked down and his eyes got watery. "That woman in the kitchen isn't my daughter. Oh sure, it might be physically, but all the things that made her Lou Anne are gone. That's just an empty shell."

I raised one shoulder. "Your wife says the doctor said she was in shock."

"Look, I was a medic during the war. I've seen all kinds of shock, from guys getting their legs blow off to the guys that watched things happen and couldn't stop them. And what she's got ain't it!

"When she disappeared she was tanned, happy, even a bit of a smart ass. Now she comes back almost catatonic? Flakes of gray in her hair? Something was done to her while she was gone, and I want to know exactly what it was!"

I shrugged. "Actually, we would too. Somebody tried to stop us from even getting here, and I'd like to know why."

Vince looked shocked. "Tried to stop you? What...?"

I told him what had happened since he called Thelma to report Lou Anne gone. When I was done, he looked shocked. "I had no idea this thing was that big. I just thought it was a family thing."

I leaned back in the seat and toughed up my jawline. "How about you tell us a bit about this family thing, and why you're here in Crazyville to start out with."

Vince nodded his pumpkin of a head. "You're probably right; it does go that far back." He took off his glasses and laid them carefully on the dash, and washed his face with his hands. When he was done, his naked eyes looked tiny and far away.

"It was almost thirty years ago when I met Sophie. She was the most beautiful woman I had ever seen. I was working behind the soda counter in an Atlanta drug store, jerking sodas and trying to finish up my pharmacy degree."

*   *   *   *   *

It had been a slow morning, and it was giving me a bit of a chance to catch up on my studies. I'd pulled over the tall stool and had my books spread out on the end of the counter when she came through the door. I guess I was so intent on what I was doing that I didn't hear the bell above the door, and didn't notice her until she was standing right across the counter from me. When I did, I nearly fell off the stool.

A lone shaft of sunlight was breaking through the window, covering her in gold and giving her a halo effect. Everything about her sparkled, despite the homespun way she was dressed.

Trying to stand up and getting my foot caught and nearly falling brought a snicker from her lips. It was like a music I'd never heard before.

Turning red and trying to regain my composure, I grabbed my rag to wipe off the counter in front of her, only to knock over a jar of straws. This time she didn't snicker, she just plain laughed.

Climbing up onto the stool and sitting down, she said, "How about I sit down before you knock the building over trying to help me?" Her eyes were the most beautiful blue, and they sparkled like Christmas lights.

I grinned like a fool and asked if I could get her something.

She looked up at the menu and gave me kind of a confused look, like she didn't really know what she was looking at. I solved the problem by grabbing a soda glass and tried to give her my best soda jerk performance. I nearly dropped the glass as I spun it in my hand. Finally filled, I sat it down in front of her.

I waved away her objections with my rag, knocking over a napkin holder, which got me another giggle. "The soda's on the house, but the floor show costs extra."

She laughed again, and then got a little more serious. "Can I ask you sort of a foolish question?" There was an accent in her voice that I couldn't quite place. Maybe a bit of Louisiana Cajun mixed with something else.

I gave her a grin, and leaned down with one hand under my chin to look into those beautiful eyes. "I'm not married, I'm in school, clean, and I can cook. Anything else you'd like to know? I can get a note from my mother that says I'm really a nice guy."

This time she didn't laugh. "Thank you for that, but it's not really what I was looking for right now. What I wanted to know is where I'm at."

I pointed to the name on my hat. "Fisk's Drug Store, Miss, at your service!"

She shook her head. "No, no, not that. I mean the city."

I kind of thought she was funnin' me a bit, and that there was a punch line comin'. But for her I'd take anything. "Miss, this is the great city of Atlanta, Georgia. The biggest city in the South!"

She smiled weakly and offered an explanation for her question. "You see, I walked into the bus station with a handful of cash and asked for a ticket as far as this would take me."

She was a runaway, but now she was my runaway, and I wasn't about to break that spell. After all, how many women that looked like her were going to smile like that at a man like me?

Over the next couple of weeks I helped find her a job, a place to live, and fell deeply in love with her. Once in a while I'd ask about where she came from, and she'd go all secretive. So finally I stopped asking, and even after a while stopped worrying that one day the police would come and drag her back to whatever hell she'd run away from.

I graduated from school and worked my way up to my own drug store, and then a chain of drug stores. Lou Anne was born. Your typical American family.

Yeah, there were moments. Sometimes in the middle of the night I would wake up to find her staring off to the west like she was listening to something only she could hear. I'd say her name, and she'd snap out of it and come back to bed. In the morning she'd tell me she didn't have any idea what I was talking about.

Thelma and her family were always around then. My sister's husband was some rising muckety-muck in the government, and he looked into Sophie's background. But he said he couldn't find any trace of her—almost like she didn't exist. I told him that she was here now, and that was all that mattered to me. It caused a quite a rift between us.

Then she got sick. It didn't happen all at once; it came on kind of slow. At first she started dropping things and stumbling when she walked, and we just blamed it on her getting clumsy in her old age. But then her hair started to gray, and her memory began to fade.

One night I woke up, and she was staring off to the west mumbling to herself. "Damn you for this! You could have just left me normal, but you had to make me one of you! And now I'm dying!"

I got up out of bed and put my arms around her. This time she didn't pretend. There were tears streaming down her cheeks, and I hugged her tight to me. "I'm sorry, Vince. I never thought this would happen. I need to go home."

The next morning we loaded up our things into the car and came here to check her into the hospital. Almost immediately she began to recover. When I was sure she was going to be alright, I went back and sold out my business and came back here to retire. Dr. Sharade said that it was something genetic, and that it happened to a lot of people that were born here. Said that if we'd waited much longer he couldn't have saved her.

*    *    *    *    *

"From the day I brought her home from the hospital, she's been pretty much the way you saw her today. But she's alive and she's with me, so I don't care.

But I can't let that happen with Lou Anne. I want you guys to find out what the hell is going on and stop it!"

Wow! It had been quite a story. And I was even more confused than I had been before. But I was also more determined than ever to find out what was behind it all. I looked at Joey, already knowing what he would say. "We'll do what we can, Vince."

"Thank you, thank you both!" He shook our hands, then putting his glasses back on, he dropped the car into gear and we sped off up the road.

Chapter 6

There was no wind as I unlocked the door to the plane. It was deathly still. Motes of dust hung unmoving in the air. There was no sound, not even the buzz of insects or the chirping of the birds. Out of the corner of my eye, I thought I caught a flash of red moving in the corn, but when I looked closer nothing moved.

Joey walked over to the door, and I handed him a pistol. "Keep a pretty close eye on things."

"Did you see something?"

I shrugged. "Nothing I can confirm. Just an edgy feeling in the middle of my back."

From somewhere he had found a long piece of grass with a fuzzy head on it, and he was chewing on it like a hillbilly. Grinning around it, he blew across the barrel of is pistol. "Hell, I've had that feeling since we first walked into town. But don't worry. Sheriff Joey is on the job. Nothing'll get by me."

The words were barely out of his mouth when a rock the size of a baseball skidded across the top of his head and folded him up like a cheap accordion. I yelled for Vince as I dropped down beside him and a meteor shower of rocks rained down on us. "Vince! Incoming! Joey's down!"

I looked off toward the cornfield and approximately twenty men suddenly appeared, each with a bag of rocks, and they were throwing like Bob Feller at the World Series!

I grabbed Joey and pulled him back under the plane to at least stop the rain of rocks from above. Now all we had to contend with were the line drives. I was bleeding from five or six hits, but luckily none of them had hit me in the face. Some smart thinking on Vince's part pretty much cut off the rocks. He pulled his car between him and us. The men didn't stop throwing, they just stopped hitting us. I could hear them thumping against the plane and could see the windows in Vince's car shatter.

I pulled open the door, and with Vince's help we managed to get Joey pulled into the car. Then I smelled it. There was smoke rising up from the grass in front of the plane. "Take Joey and get out of here!" I almost had to scream to be heard over the sound of the rocks.

"What about you?"

I slammed the back door on the car. "I've got to get the plane out of here, or I'll lose it. If I make it, I'll bring it down on that strip behind the hospital. Now get out of here!"

As I jumped back into the plane and fought to get the door shut, Vince stepped on it, bending forward trying to peer through the broken windshield, and the car spun rock and dirt and took off up the road.

I ran up the incline to the cockpit and slid into my seat. The sound of the rocks was like antiaircraft fire outside. And the flames were rapidly creeping toward the plane.

There wasn't time for the check list. I primed the mags, checked the mixture, and hit the Kaufman. A bang like a loud gunshot followed, a trail of smoke rose up from the right engine, and the prop began to turn. Without waiting to see if the engine caught, I repeated the procedure with the left.

My luck was holding, and I was rewarded with a roar coming at me from both sides. I feathered the left, throttled out the right, and started to bring the big bird around. As my nose turned toward the field, a rock spider-webbed my windscreen. It was followed by a second and a third, turning the glass into an opaque piece of warped glass.

I knew once I hit speed going down the road it was going to end up in my lap like a drunken girlfriend, so I decided I had to take care of it now. I looked around for something to beat it out of the frame with, but the best I could do was my foot. So, wasting precious seconds, I climbed out of the seat and, using my boot, kicked the windscreen free. Almost immediately the cabin filled with smoke, and I started coughing as I slid back into my seat.

I brought the nose the rest of the way around, centering it up with the middle of the road. There were a pair of goggles in the map compartment, and I slid them over my head so at least I could see. I slammed the throttles as hard as I could, saying a silent prayer under my breath that the DC-3 was as tough as I thought it was.

I started gaining speed. The tail came up, and it looked like I was going to make it. Then suddenly a line of men appeared across the road in front of me. Good gawd! They were like suicide bombers! No matter what it took they were going to try and stop me from getting away.

I reached up to pull the throttle back, but a glance at the speed indicator told me that even if I wanted to there was no way that I could stop in time. All I could do was try and force the throttles further ahead, jerk back on the wheel, and hope.

The scream of the engines deepened. It felt like I was lifting the front end of a boxcar filled with lead, but the gear left the ground. The minute it did, I hit the lever to retract it. I knew that if I had to come back down, there wouldn't be enough left of any of us to scrape into a mason jar. A fusillade of rocks hit the front of the plane as it started to lift.

I closed my eyes, leaned down to stay out of the wind, and gritted my teeth!

\*  \*  \*  \*  \*

When I opened my eyes again, the wind was hitting me in the face like I was on a motorcycle at a hundred miles an hour, and the plane was headed almost as straight up as a DC-3 could. I eased forward on the stick and leveled it off. Then I started to check for damage.

Everything was green on the right side, but I was picking up a smoke trail off the left, and the oil pressure was looking a little low. I suppose those little bastards got just lucky enough to hit an oil line. I shut down the fuel booster pumps, trimmed the flaps, and turned my nose toward the hospital.

Out the window I could see a fire truck racing to where I'd been. At least whatever their plan was didn't include burning down the town.

Out behind the hospital there was a nice long strip of mowed grass to set the '3 down on. I dropped my nose and hoped that invitation from the doctor included my plane.

I felt the tail wheel touch and slowly started to bring the nose down until the gear hit. It was a lot smoother than the last spot I'd sat down on, and so far a whole lot less rocky. With the gear on the ground I pulled the throttle back and hit the brakes to bring the big bird to a stop. Just before the end of the grassy strip, I leaned on the right brake and hit the power on the left engine to bring it around in case I needed to make another swift takeoff. I shut everything down, ran through my checklist, and did a quick interior damage report. Other than a possible broken oil line on number two, a shattered windscreen and some dents, I guessed that it survived the whole affair probably better than I did.

As I jumped down from the door, I noticed that a small crowd of nurses and interns had gathered at the side of the runway. They were probably all curious about who the big dignitary was that had just landed in their backyard. So, like the true celebrity that I was, I waved to the crowd. Unfortunately, after one look at me the crowd gave out a groan of disappointment and headed back inside the hospital.

The only person that stayed was Dr. Sharade. He stood waiting for me with his hands in the pockets of his white lab coat and his pipe clenched between his teeth. As I approached, he shook his gray head. "When I asked you to stop by for a tour, I expected you to come by foot or by car. Although I must admit for a few short moments you broke the boredom of my staff. Now all I need to do is get them back to work again."

I looked at him a bit sheepishly and dug the toe of my boot in the grass. "Well, that wasn't my intention, but the landlord where I had the plane parked decided he wanted his ground back. So I had to make a bit of a hasty retreat."

He turned back toward the hospital, and I had to quickstep to keep up with him. He walked fairly fast for an old man. "Was that the same person who tore your shirt? Or is this a new trend?"

"I, uh, got it caught on some rocks." About that time Vince's car came streaking around the side of the hospital and skidded to a stop on the rock driveway. "Speaking of rocks, do you think you could take a look at Joey's head? He hit it on one of the same rocks that tore my shirt."

Vince's car looked a lot worse from this side. This was the side that was facing the rock throwers. The windshield was broken, and there were numerous rock dents in the doors and fenders. As we got to the car, Vince was just helping Joey out.

The doctor's jaw line grew tight and his mouth became a thin line as he looked at Vince and the car. Sounding like a reproving parent, he said, "Does Sophie know what you've been up to, Vince? I'm pretty sure she wouldn't approve."

Vince just looked down at the ground and remained silent.

The doctor took a glance at Joey's head and then turned for the hospital. "Bring him inside," he said gruffly. "I'm not putting stitches in his head on the lawn."

I put one of Joey's arms over my shoulders, and Vince did the same. We half carried, half dragged Joey into the hospital after the doctor.

Sharade led us down a short hallway and into a greyish room that reminded me of a cell. A cot was against one wall, a sink to wash your hands, and single window with wire glass. If it hadn't been for the blood pressure cuff hanging from a hook, the tray of instruments ready to be used, and the glass-fronted cabinet filled with bottles of pills and strange liquids, it could have passed quite easily as a cell.

The doctor walked straight to the sink and started washing his hands. "Sit him down on the gurney, and one of you will need to hold him. This is going to hurt." His hands clean, he settled onto a stool with wheels and rolled himself over to the cabinet and took out a brown bottle marked as alcohol and some gauze pads. Then he pushed himself back over in front of Joey.

He poured alcohol onto one of the pieces of gauze. "Hold him now." He took the gauze and began mopping up Joey's cut with it. It was all I could do to stop him from jumping right up off the table every time he wiped over the open wound.

Something in the doctor's manner had changed since we were out at the car. Maybe it was because he was working on Joey, but she seemed harder, almost cruel. I looked questioningly at Vince over the doctor's head, but all he could do was shrug.

Sharade reached up with his thumb and forefinger and pulled the cut open. It wasn't long, but it was deep. I could see the bone underneath.

"See that," Sharade pointed out. "If he were a white man, he'd probably have a broken skull."

I felt Joey tense up on the table, but I did my best to cover it up. I was starting to get the feeling that Dr. Sharade wasn't real fond of black men.

He handed me a piece of gauze and told me to hold it over the cut while he got his sutures ready.

"You're going to give him something for the pain, aren't you?" I asked.

The doctor looked at me like I was crazy. But then in resignation he nodded, and he wheeled himself over to the cabinet again and took out a syringe and a vial of clear liquid. When he had it filled he squirted the liquid into Joey's cut. "That's just Novocain, just like the dentist uses. It'll take a couple of minutes for it to work, and then he won't feel anything."

That sounded like the perfect time for me to take a quick look around, so I plastered a stupid look on my face and, dancing from one foot to the other, asked, "Is there a bathroom while we wait?"

The look I got back was one I'd seen on my father's face a thousand times when I was growing up. It was a look of exasperation. "It's out the door and to your right. You can't miss it. There's a sign on the door." Then he turned to Vince. "If you want to be a part of this so bad, get over here and make yourself useful. I want you to hold the boy."

The word *boy* made me cringe. I hoped it was just a figure of speech, but what I'd seen in the last few minutes told me it probably wasn't. I just hoped Joey could go on playing possum till I got back.

As the door closed, I turned left instead of right. I wanted to see if I could get some kind of idea about what was actually going on around here.

I knew this had been a plantation house originally, but from the sheer size it was more like a mansion. And when they had first decided to convert it to a hospital, they must have nearly gutted it. The portion that I was standing in now would have probably been the kitchen area. But instead it was now a hallway lined with doors on either side. And at the far end I could see a nurse's station centered so they could watch both this hallway and what I was guessing was its twin on the other side.

Each of the doors to the rooms had a ten-by-ten window, glassed in with wire glass again. It was almost like they were afraid their patients were going to escape. Inside they were carbon copies of the room I had just left.

The first couple of windows I looked through were empty rooms, but with the third I hit pay dirt. On the cot in the room an old man, apparently on his last legs, was lying with an IV, the needle almost bigger than the aged arm it was inserted into. Even from the window I could see that his breathing was shallow and irregular. I tried the handle on the door, but it was locked.

I moved on down the hallway, looking in more windows. Two more were occupied by old men, but the third surprised me. The cot in that room held a young man, probably in his mid-twenties. From what I could see from the window he looked like he was in pretty good shape. The ever-present IV was there again, but I couldn't see any reason for it.

I was about to try the door, even though I knew it was going to be locked, when I heard thunder in the hallway. "Hey, what are you doing there? This is a hospital, and you're in a restricted space!" I looked down the corridor to see a tank dressed in a white uniform and white shoes rolling on me like Patton against the Germans.

My first instinct was to run, but I fought it down, knowing that if I did she'd never let me get out of here alive. So, untangling my tongue I blurted out one word. "Bathroom?"

I swear the hallway floor was shaking as she got close. A pincer reached out and with a steel grip grabbed my upper arm and began to drag me back down the hallway in the direction that I'd come from. All the time she was lecturing me on restricted space, bothering patients that were critically ill, and what a lowlife I was.

When we got to the door marked as the bathroom where I was supposed to have gone some minutes ago, she hurled me against it. "There's your bathroom—now use it!"

I started through the door but she must have thought I wasn't moving fast enough, because she reached out with a giant ham, or maybe it was a full side of beef, and slammed me in the back, propelling me through the door like a rocket and depositing me on the tile floor inside.

Slowly I picked myself up off the floor and took a quick look around. It was your standard bathroom: two urinals and two stalls. None of that mattered. What did was a pebbled glass window that opened inward and upward. It had a 90-degree lock on it, and I pushed it just far enough to one side that the window would open, but unless they looked closely they wouldn't notice that it was unlatched. I was coming back, and I was going to find out what was going on in those rooms that was so important they had to lock the doors.

Flushing both the urinals, I washed my hands and stepped back into the hallway. The nurse hadn't moved since I went inside. She was standing there with feet spread and her arms crossed over the giant hills on her chest.

I just kind of squeezed by her and escaped into the exam room.

The doctor was finished with Joey and was washing up his hands. He tossed a suspicious look over his shoulder at me but didn't ask where I'd been. Vince was still holding Joey upright on the cot.

As he was drying his hands, Sharade walked over to the glass-fronted cabinet and took out a small bottle filled with white pills. "If he has any pain, just give him one of these. Be careful with the dose," he warned. "More than one and it might be quite some time before he wakes up." Now that he was done working on Joey, his attitude seemed to have gone back the other way.

I took the bottle from him and reached for my wallet, but he stopped me with an open palm. "Don't worry about it. This time it's on the house. His own doctor can take out the stitches in a few days."

I thanked him again, and then Vince and I scooped Joey up off the cot and went back out the way we had come.

As we cleared the building, the glaze cleared out of Joey's eyes and he was fully conscious again. "That doctor's a real son of a bitch! All the time you were gone and when he thought that I was out of it he was berating Vince here about being with us, and saying how the two of us were just going to cause trouble for him and Sophie."

"That right, Vince?"

Vince nodded. "Yeah, he was pretty tough on me, but nothing that I hadn't heard before. It was the same kind of speech I got from the welcome wagon right after I moved here."

As we loaded Joey into the car, I looked back and saw the doctor standing in the window watching us. I waved, but he just turned away. Kind of had the feeling that our welcome was starting to wear out.

## Chapter 7

As the car was pulling out from behind the hospital and back onto the street, across town a boy just barely out of his teens was leaning back in his chair and propping his feet up on a desk. The suit he had on was expensive, but the way it fit his thin frame said that it had been cut for a more mature man.

He wiggled a bit in the chair till he was comfortable, then he reached into his pocket and pulled out a big, black cigar. He stripped the wrapper off and cut off the end with a pair of silver scissors attached to his vest with a finely braided silver chain. He snapped a match with his thumbnail and gently rolled the cigar in the fire to warm it. As he did, the sun glinted off the gold band with the red script that read *Carona*. Satisfied, he tucked the cigar between his teeth. Lighting a second match, he held it till the sulfur was burned off and sucked the cigar to life. Clouds of blue smoke enveloped his head.

Suddenly his peace was interrupted by the jangling of the telephone on the desk. For a long time he let it ring, squinting at it from time to time like he was trying to wish it away. When that didn't work, he finally took the cigar from his teeth and picked up the phone.

There were no pleasantries exchanged from the other end of the phone, just an angry, gruff voice. "Your little rock-throwing incident did nothing more than make them even more resolved to stay. Now they're sure something is going on that they need to look into."

"It was Vernon's idea. He said to try and drive them away without shooting them."

The voice at the other end got even angrier. "And since when do you work for Vernon?"

"Well, I thought—"

The voice cut him off before he could finish. "I don't pay you to think! Or for that matter Vernon either." He went on for quite a while, till he finally wore out his tirade. Then he gave instructions to pass on to Vernon before hanging up.

As the boy laid the receiver back in the cradle, the door opened and Chief of Police Vernon Tucker walked in. He blew a cloud of smoke at the chief. "That was the boss on the phone, and he's not happy. Here's what he wants you to do...."

\*     \*     \*     \*     \*

When we got back to the house I had Vince drop me off in front. Joey got my drift and stayed in the car to ride around back to the garage and keep Vince busy while I talked to Kate.

Kate was pacing the floor. Worry lines creased her pretty face. As I came through the door a smile broke across her face, and she ran over and into my arms. "Rick!" She wrapped her arms around my neck and started burying my face with kisses faster than I could catch them.

Laughing, I lifted her up off the floor and spun her around in my arms. "Is that any way for a lady to act?"

She kissed me again. "Nobody ever said I was lady!"

I held her close and mashed my lips against hers. Breaking the kiss, I sat her feet back down on the floor. "Where have you been? I was worried sick!"

I took a deep breath to calm the fire inside me, and unwound myself from her. With one of her hands in mine, I walked over to the couch.

When we were both settled I told her what had happened at the plane, and then later at the hospital. When I finished, she stared off into space a long time before she spoke. Finally she said, "This is way bigger than a simple abduction, isn't it?"

I nodded my head. "I'm afraid so. Whatever it is that's happening goes clear to the core of this little town, and I'm pretty sure that core is rotten!"

She turned and looked at me like she was hoping for answers. "What now?"

I dug at my cheek with my tongue while I thought about how to answer her. "Well, I'd like another look at what's going on at the hospital. And I've got a special mission for you."

Her head tipped back, and the blue pools of her eyes looked down her nose at me suspiciously. "What kind of special mission?"

I scrunched my eyes shut like you would if you were about to be hurt, and I said, "I need you to go to the capitol—"

I didn't even get the rest of it finished before she was off the couch, calling me names and stamping her pretty foot on the floor. "RICK STEELE! You sneaky, scaredy-cat—"

I put up my hand to stop her. "Hey! Hey now! Wait till I finish!"

"Oh, you're finished already, Captain! You are not just sending me off so I'm safe and you don't have to look out for me! I'm as valuable a part of this team as you or Joey, or... or... THELMA! I can probably shoot straighter than either one of you, and I know I can outthink you both!"

I was gonna wait for her spring to run down, but as tight as she was wound I'd be here all night. So I reached out with the toe of my boot and caught her right behind the knee with enough force to send her falling into my lap. The minute she landed I mashed my lips against hers to shut her up. I held her that way till I was sure she was out of air. Then I let up.

"Now," I said, looking down into the most beautiful blue eyes I had ever seen, "are you gonna shut up and let me finish?"

Her mouth was a thin line, so tight I almost couldn't see her upper lip. "If I have to! But I don't have to like it!"

"There are things I need to know about this town, the hospital on the hill, and the doctor. And there's nobody else right now I trust to find them out for me."

She pulled back a bit and eyed me suspiciously. "You don't trust Thelma?"

"No, I wholly trust Thelma, and she's busy enough being our inside man here with the family."

"And Vince?"

"He's married to Sophie. That gives whoever is behind this a way to make him do exactly what they want. So I think the less he knows the better." I held up a stop motion as she tried to interrupt. "Just stop and think before you say it. In this part of the country Joey is not real well-welcomed. So chances are that if I sent him, I'd either find him hanging from a tree or get pieces of him back in a box. That leaves you, my one and only."

As she was climbing up off my lap, the matter finally resolved in her head, Joey and Vince came back inside.

"Vince, I need another favor."

He rubbed his chin with one hand. "Let me see. So far your favors have cost me the glass and paint job on my car, nearly got me killed, and forced me to lie to my wife. What is it this time? Want me to shoot one of my nosey neighbors?" A big grin broke across his face. "How could I refuse after all that fun?" He glanced around at the empty house. "Where's Sophie?"

"She and Thelma went shopping for groceries," Kate answered.

Satisfied, he turned to me. "So, what's this next favor?"

"I need to borrow your car so Kate can take it into the capitol for parts for the plane. And while she's there she can get the glass and dents fixed."

His grin got even bigger as he handed the keys across. "I just don't see how I can lose with a deal like that."

I took the keys from him and passed them over to Kate. "Come on, I'll walk you out."

As we walked out to the garage, I told Kate what I knew about Sharade and the hospital. "It's not much, but I hope it's enough to get you started. Surely somebody there in Archives will be able to help. Check with the newspapers, too. Might be something there."

She nodded as she slid into the seat and pulled the door shut. I leaned in with both hands on the window sill. "I don't have to tell you to be careful. I'm hoping that nobody will even know that you're gone, but just in case." I pulled the automatic from under my arm and handed it to her. She stashed it in the glove compartment, slamming it shut with a bang.

"I don't know how you can carry that under your arm like that. If I tried it, my blouse and bra would be stretched clear down to my knees. Takes nearly two hands to pick the thing up."

"But if you have to shoot somebody, they don't get back up. Don't hesitate to use it if you have to. Shoot first, and we'll sort the whole thing afterward." Then I leaned in and let my lips mingle with hers for a long moment.

The fire rose back inside me again, and I wanted to pull her out of the car and ask her to stay for just an hour or so more. But I knew that hour would never be enough. I needed her beside me forever. As I looked into her eyes, I could see that she knew what I was thinking. There was a sparkle in her blue eyes, and a red flush to the soft skin of her throat.

Pulling back outside, I slapped the window with my hand. "You better go."

She nodded. She stepped on the starter and the car roared to life. As she slipped it into gear she called back to me out the window. "Don't go getting yourself killed before I get back here, you big lunk! I've got plans for you!" Then she was driving away down the street.

## Chapter 8

As Kate sped up the street, she watched Rick dwindle in the mirror till he was out of sight. It made her feel good knowing he watched until he couldn't see her anymore. It showed just how much he cared, and how much he would miss her when she was gone.

Rick Steele was an easy man to love. In the last couple of years he'd saved her life more times than she could count. He even saved her from becoming the bride of a demon once! That made her shake her head. She wasn't even sure she believed in demons, yet one of them tried to run off with her soul.

But Rick wasn't the only one saving lives. More than once she had pulled his bacon from the fire, too. With her off on her way to the capitol, that worried her just a bit as she turned off the road from town and onto the main highway. But as long as Joey was there, he'd be right there beside Rick, watching his every move.

She accelerated the battered Desoto up to a nice, even sixty and let it cruise there. That made the ride pretty comfortable and gave her plenty of reaction time.

The sunlight glinted off the spider-webbed cracks in the windshield and made her squint. She made a mental note that at the first service station she needed to pick up a pair of sunglasses. Wouldn't do to have crow's feet all around her eyes when she finally got Rick to ask that question she'd been waiting on.

Glancing down at herself in her dirty khaki skirt and boots, she made another mental note that before she tried to find anything out she was going to need something a little more businesslike to wear.

Kate was about ten miles or so up the highway when she noticed for the first time that she wasn't the only car on the road anymore. Nothing unusual about that; after all, this was a state highway. But just to make sure, she slowed the big car down to a crawl, waiting for him to catch up and pass. Instead, the car behind her slowed down and maintained the same distance between them.

Just in case that was just a coincidence, she downshifted into second gear and poured on the gas, pushing the car up to about eighty miles per hour before backing off. The car behind her stayed exactly the same distance away.

"Looks like I've got myself a friend," she said out loud to herself. She reached over with one hand still on the wheel and popped open the glove box and took out Rick's automatic. She tucked it between the cushions so she could just drop her hand on the butt and pull it free.

It was probably really pretty country that she was driving through with all the fields of tobacco, corn and cotton, but now her attention was being spent elsewhere. She was driving with one eye on the mirror and one eye on the road.

As she got closer to the city the traffic began to increase going both directions, but like a hound on the scent the car behind her never faltered. It steadily maintained the half a mile or so that had separated them since Kate first noticed it.

It was time to think of a plan. She couldn't be sure that they were going to be satisfied with just following her. Sooner or later they were going to make their move. And Kate wanted to make her own move first.

Kate swung the DeSoto out into the other lane just enough to peek at oncoming traffic around the truck that she was following. She pulled back to avoid an approaching car, but after it was gone the road was clear. She pushed the accelerator down hard against the floorboard, and like a lumbering beast the big car began to pick up speed, charging toward the rear of the truck. Just before the two would connect, she turned the wheel hard to the left and shot out into the other lane.

Up ahead, a car just topping the hill was approaching her. As if it would help, she pushed even harder on the gas pedal, urging the big car to go even faster. At the last instant her bumper cleared the front of the truck, and she jerked back into her own lane. The car going the other way went by with its horn blasting out a warning.

Kate's heart was beating fast, sweat was beading on her brow, and her ears were still echoing from the angry blare of the horn. Biting her lower lip, she leaned closer to the big steering wheel, pushing all her weight against the accelerator pedal. Ever so slowly, the speedometer crept upward. 70... 80... 85 miles per hour. The front of the car seemed almost weightless, and a tiny rocking from side to side began as it skimmed over the roadway's surface.

Her hands were white-knuckled as she fought to keep the steel beast in her thrall. The armpits of her khaki blouse were brown with perspiration. In the rearview mirror she saw the other car weaving in and out of oncoming traffic trying to catch her. Her last maneuver must have made up their minds for them, and now they knew they couldn't wait much longer to stop her. They were making their move.

Suddenly another player entered the game as big, silver drops began to splash against her cracked and dented windshield. Within seconds it became a full-fledged downpour, and her view through the crack was looking out of a submarine. With reluctance she took one of her hands from the wheel and reached out to the center of the dash to the wiper switch. Then with a silent prayer she turned the switch and hoped that after all the damage they still worked. Kate was rewarded with the slow crawl of the blade across the glass, and the breath she was holding hissed out between her teeth in a sigh.

It was nearly twilight now, and combined with the storm it was rapidly growing dark outside the cocoon of her car. She needed her lights, but an idea was dawning, so she left them off. She was nearly invisible to the car behind her.

She flexed her stiff fingers on the wheel, one hand at a time. There was a cramp starting in her leg from holding the gas pedal tightly to the floor. She tried working her knee without lessening the pressure, and that seemed to help some. If only it would hold off till she put her plan into action.

Kate tried to beg a couple more mph's out of her car, but she knew it would never be enough. The other car was lighter and faster than hers was, and on the straightaway it would rapidly overtake her. What she needed was a car between her and them, a hill, and a side road. She shook her head. Why not just wish for wings to fly away from them—that was probably just as likely.

But it's been said that God smiles on little kids, idiots, and women with bad guys in pursuit! There, less than a half a mile in front of her, was just what she was looking for. A car in her lane was slowly crawling forward in the rain. Blinking her lights and honking her horn, she raced up on him, and he did just what she hoped he would. He slammed on his brakes and brought his car to a screeching halt.

Kate waved as she shot by. He should slow traffic down long enough for her to make the turn just on the other side of the hill, according to the sign. That half a second should give her time to get far enough down the road that they wouldn't see her as they shot by. And by the time they realized she wasn't in front of them, she could be miles away.

With a grin of triumph on her face, Kate topped the hill, started back down the other side, and reached out to step on the brake pedal. Suddenly, her world was going sideways. Or at least the DeSoto was. The combination of the rain, the speed she was traveling, and the old, worn tires was too much for the car. It lost its grip on the road, and the rear slewed sideways, stretching across both lanes.

Desperately she fought to regain control, but the steel hulk of a car had other ideas. Almost with a mind of its own it decided that it had suffered enough at her hands. It and the laws of physics were in charge now, not the small, pink human.

With all the slop on the road the DeSoto played its final card. The tires on the driver's side found the only dry spot on the oil- and rain-soaked highway. The tires stopped their sideways skid, but the momentum carried the right side up and into the air. The car began to roll like a log going downhill. The roof of the car came down to meet Kate's head, and blackness folded over her.

\*     \*     \*     \*     \*

Kate's head hurt. The pain was like a blinding light boring into her eyes. Then she realized it was coming from a flashlight being shined at her from outside the car. She wasn't exactly sitting in the car anymore. Her feet were up and over the back of the seat, and her head was in the floor next to the pedals. When she tried to move, everything hurt so badly that she gave it up as a bad idea and lay just where she was.

The light probed through the car again, and a voice asked, "Is she still alive?"

The flashlight wielder waved it across her face, and she tried to stop her eyes from blinking behind their lids. "Yeah, I thought I saw her eyes open a minute ago. But it looks like she's passed out again."

"So what are we gonna do with her? If she'd have just died we wouldn't have had to worry about it. But no, she had to go and survive! We weren't even supposed to try and stop her, just follow her, but you were afraid she was going to get away. Now look where we are."

Suddenly the flashlight went away, and Kate heard a smack like the sound of flesh hitting flesh.

"Owww! Wadya do that for?"

"'Cause I'm tired of listenin' to ya talk. Now get that door open and get her out of there. I'm gettin' wet!"

Kate heard the door scream on its hinges as they pried it open, and rain started to fall inside the car.

"Hey, look at this—the dame was armed!" *He must have found Rick's automatic,* she thought.

"Wow, you didn't tell me she was half naked! She's got a really nice set of gams!"

*Half naked?* Kate wondered what he meant. Then she realized from the way she was lying her skirt was closer to her head than her knees. She wished she could pull it back down, but with the pain and her playing possum, there was no way.

A crude hand reached in and swung her legs down off the seat, lingering longer than necessary on her ankles. It was all she could do to stop from screaming as he started to pull her free.

"Give me a hand, will ya? For such a good-looking broad she sure is heavy."

As they pulled Kate free of the car, she no longer had to worry about pretending. The pain of being moved sent her into the warm, comfortable darkness again.

*     *     *     *     *

When I got in the house, Thelma and Sophie had come back from the store. Vince was in the kitchen helping her with dinner.

I grabbed Joey and Thelma and took them out on the front porch where we could talk without being overheard.

"Where's Kate?"

I gave her a quick rundown of the afternoon's adventures and told her that I sent Kate into the city for information on the doctor. "Speaking of which, did you learn anything from your aunt Sophie while the two of you were on your shopping trip? Her mood seems light years different than it was before."

Thelma sat down in the swing, her big feet barely reaching the floor. Joey went over to lean against the house where he could watch the window, and I parked my but on the railing so I could see the door.

Thelma took off her glasses and polished them on her shirt. Without them her eyes looked tiny, almost like two BB's. "Just before we left, she got a phone call. It was about the same time that you were flying over the town. All she did was say hello, and then it was like she went into a trance.

"I tried to get close enough to hear what was being said, but either they were talking too low or nothing was being said. When she hung up she was just like she is now."

I looked at Joey, and he kind of tossed his head to one side a bit. "Huh. That's it?"

She shrugged back at him. "That's all there was. I know earlier she was really worried about Lou Anne, but none of that's changed. Maybe she's finally realized we're here to help."

I shook my head. "I don't think so. But I do think she knows a lot more about what's going on than she lets on. And she's not telling anybody."

"Even Thelma's uncle?"

"Even Vince. And while we're talking about him, we need to keep him out of the loop from here on out."

Thelma put her glasses back on, and the big eyes were back. "You mean you don't trust Uncle Vince? I assure you he's one of the most honest men I've ever known!" she protested.

"And maybe he is, but he also loves his family very much. And I'm pretty sure he would throw us to the wolves if it meant saving them. So from here on out, we're not telling him any more than is absolutely necessary."

Thelma tried to cross her legs tailor-fashion in the swing, but her chubby thighs just wouldn't let her. Finally she slid out to the edge of the swing where her feet would reach the floor if she tipped the swing back. It was a bit like watching a flea circus—not something you really cared to see, but damn you just couldn't turn away.

"I did kind of get the feeling that this had all happened before, not to Lou Anne, but maybe others. The people in the store seemed to know everything that was going on, and didn't seem upset by it."

I turned and looked across the neighborhood. It looked a lot like a million other small towns all across the country, except for one thing. "Have you noticed there's no school here?"

They both looked at me like I was crazy. "Maybe they bus the kids to another town? Lots of places do that now."

"What kids?" I turned back around and looked at them, waiting for their reaction. I could see it beginning to dawn on them. "Yep, not a bike, not a trike, not even so much as a swing set. There aren't any kids in this town. How many people do you figure live here from the number of houses we counted when we flew over?"

"I don't know," Joey shrugged, "fifteen hundred, maybe two thousand?"

"Exactly! How do you get two thousand people in a town and not one kid? Not even a crying baby. And for that matter, there aren't any animals either. No birds or dogs or cats. It's almost like a movie set."

Joey was about to say something, but Vince came to the door and announced dinner, and we filed back inside.

Chapter 9

Kate returned to consciousness slowly. She was stiff, and tiny aches and pains reminded her that she was at least still alive. And sitting in a chair? Well, not actually sitting in a chair—tied to a chair. Her arms were thrust through the slats in the back and her wrists tied. Each ankle was tied to a leg.

Her chin was resting on her chest, and there was a crusty, stiff spot of what she guessed was blood on her right temple, another leading downward from her lip. Whoever it was that had tied her hadn't taken the time or maybe made the effort to gag her. That meant he was pretty sure there was little chance of her being heard.

Wherever she was it was pitch dark, and the air was heavy with the smell of damp earth. It made the air thick and hard to breathe. Her fingers were numb from the ropes cutting off the circulation. Wriggling them helped some, but they still felt as thick as sausages.

For some strange reason her shoes were gone, and her feet rested on the bare floor. She could feel the cold through the bottoms of her feet. It made her shudder with the chill.

For the first few seconds after she awoke, Kate didn't move and was hardly even breathing. Rick had always said, "If you wake up in a strange place, always take stock of your surroundings before you do anything. It might save your life later."

That's what she did now. She strained her ears to listen for any kind of sound. When there was only silence, she softly spoke her own name, listening for it to bounce back off the walls and let her know how big the room was. When no echo came back she decided the wall must be dirt, absorbing the sound. That was consistent with the damp earth smell. She was probably in a basement or some kind of cellar, more than likely the latter from the dirt floor and walls.

With her surroundings catalogued as well as she could, she started to take stock of herself. The chair she was tied to was wood. She could feel it against her legs and her wrists. A kitchen chair from the feel. She tipped her body back and forth on the seat, listening to the glue joints creak as she moved. It sounded old and rickety. With her numb fingers she did her best to feel the slats in the back, and thought that if she had to she could break them and pull her arms free.

She remembered that the two men hadn't wanted her dead yet, but how long would that last? It was time to come up with a plan. There in the darkness, Dr. Kate Gallagher put her mind to work on her escape!

*     *     *     *     *

Dinner was roast beef, and the dinner conversation was a far cry from the way things had been this morning. Sophie was the perfect host, making sure that everybody had enough meat, except for Thelma who stuck with the mashed potatoes. But somehow it just didn't feel real. Her smile seemed like a mask she was wearing over her real face.

"Vince tells me you had a little trouble this afternoon when you went out to your plane. Nothing too drastic, I hope."

It was a good thing the forkful of potatoes was on its way to my mouth rather than in it. Otherwise I might have spit the whole thing clear across the table. I quickly looked at Vince, but all I got was a "What do you expect?" look. So I turned to Sophie and said, "Yes ma'am, we did. A group of men came out of the cornfield and pelted us with rocks."

She wiped her lips on a napkin and shook her head. "Even here we occasionally have trouble with hooligans. I can't imagine what it must be like in the city. Did you report it to the police?"

"No, we didn't, ma'am. We had no way to identify the men, so we felt it wouldn't do any good. Your husband's car suffered some damage in the incident though. Kate is going to have it taken care of in the city."

She turned that cold smile on me again, and waved it all away with a hand. "That old car was ready for the junk pile anyway. We so seldom use it. It's like a relic from another age."

The rest of the meal was pretty much just small talk, Sophie occasionally chiming in about something totally unrelated.

When dinner was over, I volunteered Thelma and myself to clean up and do the dishes. After a short argument Sophie relented and said that they would wait for coffee until we were done. Then she, Joey, and Vince retired to the living room.

After the kitchen door closed and I had the water running to fill the sink, I turned around and leaned back on the counter. "I need you to do a couple of things for me, Thelma. One of them is really easy, but the other one may be the hardest thing I've ever asked you to do."

Thelma just stared back at me blankly, her eyes slowly blinking behind the thick lenses of her glasses. Then, almost as though she came out of a trance, she shrugged her slanting shoulders. "Whatever you need, Captain."

I shook my head and turned up my lip a bit. "Better wait till you know what I'm asking." She tilted her head off to the side, and the blank look was back. It felt a little like I was talking to an owl.

I took a deep breath and said, "I need you to spy on your uncle and aunt. I want to know everything there is to know about them—past history, current. Absolutely everything."

The blank look didn't change this time when she spoke. "Okay, so what's the hard thing you want me to do?"

It was all I could do to stop from bursting out laughing. I walked over and threw my arm around her shoulders and hugged her. "Thelma, you're a brick!"

Her eyes blinked a couple of times, and she asked, "Is that a good thing, sir? Being a brick I mean."

This time I did laugh as I hugged her again. "Yes it is, Thelma. A very good thing."

I walked over to the sink and started working on the dishes. She followed me to dry. As I soaped a plate clean I explained the rest of what I wanted. "I need you to go down to the library and track the history of the town and the hospital."

Taking the plate from me to dry, she said, "I thought that was what Dr. Gallagher was doing in the city."

I nodded as I washed another plate. "It is, but sometimes little facts never make it to the big cities. Small-town libraries are just chucked full of secrets the rest of the world never knows."

She pursed her lips and nodded. "Yes sir, I see what you mean. I'll do my best."

I just nodded and soaped up another plate. I knew she would. And I hoped I wouldn't get dishpan hands from this.

*   *   *   *   *

We were all sitting in the living room finishing our coffee and making small talk when the doorbell rang. It seemed kind of unusual in a town like this and at this time of night, so when Vince got up to answer it I kept an ear peeled to listen.

I heard a clipped Southern accent ask if he was Vince McCally, and if he owned a grey DeSoto. By the time he finished saying DeSoto, I was out of the chair and standing right behind Vince.

The accent belonged to a man wearing jodhpurs and knee boots, and holding a motorcycle helmet under one arm and an open note in his gloved hand. A Sam Browne belt cut across his chest, holding up the big gun on his hip, and there was a big, gold star pinned to the left breast of his Eisenhower jacket. His dark eyes rolled up to meet mine as I approached. "What is it, Officer? What's happened?"

He snapped his notebook shut and eyed me suspiciously. "And you are?"

My jaw line was tight. Something had happened to Kate, and I wanted to know what it was and wanted to know now! "Who I am doesn't matter. What's important is what's happened!" I said impatiently, taking another step forward.

His free hand dropped down to causally rest on the top of his holster, his finger fumbling a bit with the flap. "It happens to matter to me. Now who are you?"

My body tightened up like the bow string on a violin that was pulled too tight. My hands became balled-up fists. But before I could do anything really stupid, Joey came up behind me and laid his big hand on my shoulder. It was there to calm me down, but also to hold me back if necessary.

"We're good friends of Mr. McCally's, Officer. And a friend of ours was driving the DeSoto." Joey's deep, rich voice was calm, but under the calm I could feel the fear. "Can you tell us what's happened?"

"Yes," Vince asked, "Please tell us."

Looking me over carefully, he removed his hand from the top of his holster and flipped open his notebook again. He read directly from his notes. "At 7:20 PM this evening a passerby reported seeing a 1939 DeSoto sedan, grey in color, with broken windows and a smashed-in roof, sitting about 100 yards from Highway 12 in a clump of weeds."

Inside my head there was a roar like the ram jet on a crusader, making it hard for me to hear. Sweat was rapidly soaking my palms, and I wiped them on the legs of my pants. *The driver? Where was the driver?* I wanted to scream it out loud, but I closed my eyes, took a deep breath, and as calmly as I could I asked, "Any idea how it got there or what happened?"

He nodded, the light glinting off his closely cropped hair. "It appeared the driver tried to make a right hand turn at a high rate of speed without considering the weather conditions, and lost control of the car. Our estimates figure the car must have rolled at least ten times before coming to a stop."

High rate of speed? In a steady downpour? Kate was in no hurry, and had no reason to speed. That meant somebody was chasing her. "And what about the driver?" I was almost afraid to hear his answer.

He flipped over a page in his notebook. "No sign of the driver. There was some blood in the car, but not enough in our estimates from any type of major trauma."

The breath I'd been holding slid out over my teeth like escaping steam as I waited impatiently for him to finish his notes. "We searched the entire rollover area, but no signs of a body. So we're guessing the driver must have ridden it out."

"Any sign of footprints around the car?" I asked curtly.

Joey's hand tightened on my shoulder to remind me to remain calm.

The patrol officer looked kind of helpless as he shook his head. "I'm sorry. The rain washed away whatever evidence there might have been."

I ground my teeth together, and without opening them I asked, "Any witnesses or other cars in the area?"

He flipped his book open one last time. "One driver did report seeing a late-model two-tone blue Ford parked on the road in that vicinity around the time of the accident."

"And you checked all the hospitals?"

His jaw line grew hard this time, and I could see his teeth grinding to match mine. "Look, Mister—"

"Actually, it's Captain. Captain Rick Steele."

"Despite the fact that you seem to think we're all just hick cops here, Captain Steele, we are very efficient at our jobs. That is the reason for the delay in us reporting the accident. We wanted to make sure that we had left no rocks unturned before we came to you. So yes, we did check all the hospitals, and no accident victims were reported from that area in the last 24 hours. Now if you'll excuse me, I have a family waiting on me for dinner." He spun on his heels to go, but Vince stopped him.

"Where is the car now, Officer?"

"Our impound yard in the city," he called back over his shoulder as he walked off the porch. Seconds later he was sitting astride his motorcycle, kicking it to life. And then he was gone.

I scrubbed my hands over my face, feeling the day's stubble and the tiredness of my eyes. Inside I was buzzing like a hive of bees ready for the attack. Turning to Joey I said, "They've got her! And we don't even know who the hell they are! I should have never let her go!"

Joey tried to calm me down, but I wasn't having any of it. When he reached out, I slapped his hand away. "And we don't even know who they are!"

I stalked back toward the living room, but Thelma and Sophie were standing in the door. Sophie was still wearing that disconnected smile, and that seemed to make me even angrier. Thelma's muddy brown eyes were wide, and her mouth was hanging open. "What are you going to do, Captain?"

I looked at her, and the words were out of my mouth before I could even think. "I'm going to get her back! What the hell do you think I'm gonna do?" I said, taking a metaphorical bite out of Thelma's rather large derriere.

I turned to walk away but Vince was right behind me, and suddenly I felt penned in with no sense of escape. All I knew was I had to get out, and I had to get her back. I lashed out with a roundhouse punch, but Joey was there to block it. And as he did, he slid his other hand under my swing and open-palmed he caught me right in the chest, knocking me backwards.

My knees buckled and I landed hard on the floor. Then I heard Sophie start to scream.

It wasn't me she was screaming about. Lou Anne was standing on the last step, her arms hanging down and blood pouring from the open cuts on her wrists.

Vince and Thelma ran to help her while Sophie continued to scream, her hand pressed to her cheeks in horror.

Vince scooped Lou Anne up into his arms and carried her past the screaming Sophie to the couch. Thelma followed with a couple of towels she'd grabbed from the kitchen. As Vince went by us, he told Joey to call the doctor and that the number was on a pad by the phone.

Sheepishly over my tantrum, I got up off the floor to see if I could help. Vince and Thelma had the towels wrapped around her arms, trying to slow the bleeding.

Gently I took Sophie by the arm and led her over to the armchair and got her to sit down. She had finally stopped screaming, but her eyes were still wide with the terror she was feeling. Tears were streaming down her thin cheeks in rivers, and sobs racked her body.

Joey came back into the living room. He was the only truly calm one at the moment. "The doctor is on his way." Then he turned to where I was kneeling beside Sophie, trying to calm her down. A small smile sneaked across his lips. "You done throwing tantrums now?"

I looked over at Vince and Thelma, and then back to Sophie. "Yeah, I'll be okay. I think this crazy town is getting to me."

He nodded. "Getting to all of us, Boss."

It was about then that the doctor hustled into the living room, his black bag clutched tightly in his hand.

## Chapter 10

Sharade pushed everybody but Thelma and Sophie out of the living room. Then he knelt down bedside the couch and slowly unwrapped the towel from one arm. Looking at the cut, he shook his head. He wrapped the towel back around it and dug in his bag for a suture kit.

With Thelma holding the wrist, he unwrapped it again. He wiped it clean with a pad and alcohol and began stitching the cut shut.

Joey's eyebrows pulled down together as he watched. I stepped between him and the others with my back toward them and mouthed, "What?"

He shrugged his broad shoulders and very softly he said, "How many doctors carry a suture kit in their bag?"

"Didn't you tell him what it was all about when you called?"

Joey shook his head. "Didn't give me much of a chance. He answered the phone, and when I told him who it was he said he'd be right here. It was almost like he was waiting for me to call."

I rubbed my hand across my stubble. "Maybe we're building too much into this. It could be all country doctors carry that stuff in their bag."

"I suppose you could be right."

I turned back toward the living room, and the doctor was just finishing up the other wrist, wrapping it in gauze. He stood up creakily from where he had been kneeling and walked stiffly out to the porch.

As Vince and Sophie hovered back over to Lou Anne, I followed the doctor outside. He was just lighting his pipe as I walked out.     "So is she going to be okay?"

He puffed on his pipe a bit before he answered. "She should be, but I'm going to have to take her up to the hospital for a transfusion."

"Any idea why she did what she did?"

He shook his head. The light from inside reflected off his eyes, making them like two tiny pinpricks of light. "Whatever it was that caused her to run away in the first place has manifested itself again. It's not uncommon in cases like this for that to happen. If I were a psychiatrist maybe I would have some answers, but all I am is a country doctor who's more used to treating old people.

"For now we treat her physical ailments, and when she's stronger we'll find a way to treat her mind."

Sharade was quiet for quite a while. The only sound on the porch was him sucking on his pipe. He seemed to be thinking something over. Finally he said, "Your being here isn't helping. It just adds turmoil to the family that it doesn't need."

I really wanted to say that we were asked here to try and solve some of that turmoil, and that right now the woman I loved might be dying, but for the first time tonight I held my tongue. I just didn't feel that I could trust the doctor that far.

He seemed almost to read my mind, and he grew steadily angrier. He took his pipe from his mouth and poked me in the chest with the stem. "This town has been fine all these years without strangers stepping in. And it will go on being fine long after you're gone."

I reached out and pushed his pipe away from my chest with my index finger. "Joey and I'll be gone first thing in the morning."

He slid the pipe back between his teeth. "And Thelma? What about her?"

"She's going to stay and visit a while longer."

That seemed to satisfy him, and he calmed down. He went back into the house.

I could hear him explaining what he was going to do, and then something about giving Sophie a sedative. When he came back out Vince was with him, carrying Lou Anne, and Thelma was following. She stopped as she was going by.

"I'm going with the doctor to look after Lou Anne. Sophie is too upset, and Vince needs to stay here and look after her." Then she gave me one of those big conspirator's winks, meaning that she was going with him to have a look around.

I hugged her so I could whisper in her ear. "Be careful. Joey and I are leaving in the morning, so you're on your own till we get back."

She hugged me harder than I wanted and said, "I will. Bring Kate back safe!" Then she let go and followed them to the car.

A few minutes later, Vince came back in and helped Sophie up to bed. When he came back downstairs he went over to the sideboard and pulled out a half-gone bottle of bourbon. Holding it up by the neck he asked, "You guys want a slug of this? It's been kind of a rough night!"

Both Joey and I shook our heads. We were going to need to be icy clear in the morning.

Vince took down a water tumbler and poured it halfway full of the amber liquid. Looking at the light through his drink he said, "Sophie wouldn't approve, but damnit, I need something to calm me back down. This whole thing is starting to drive me crazy." He raised the glass to his lips, and when he sat it back down on the table it was empty. He picked the bottle up, hesitated for a moment, then he put it away. Turning back around he said, "I'm going to go up and sit with Sophie. The house is yours."

I walked across the room and laid my hand on his shoulder. "Joey and I will be gone with first light to find out what happened to Kate."

"Probably a good idea. The doctor's not real happy about you guys being here. Says it's not helping Lou Anne's recovery."

"Yeah, he told me that too. Thelma's going to stay and help look after the women till we come back."

Vince nodded his head. "Yeah, that'll be good. I know the girls really like having her around." He looked at me, solemn and a bit downcast. "I'm really sorry for all the trouble this has caused you. And I hope that Doctor Gallagher is alright."

He looked at the floor and shook his head is resignation. "If only I'd waited, Lou Anne would have come back on her own and none of this would have happened."

I reached out and squeezed his upper arm. "But you still wouldn't have had any answers, Vince."

He didn't look up. "Maybe I don't care about the answers anymore. Maybe I just want my life to get back to normal."

I grabbed both his upper arms and shook him just a bit to make him look up at me. "And what if it happens again? What then? Or maybe not to you but to somebody else, and you know that you had the chance to stop it? How will you feel then?"

He pulled free of my hands and retreated up a couple of steps. "Maybe that'll be their problem then and not mine. I've got to look after my own. My girls can't take any more of this. DAMNIT! My daughter nearly died right here in the living room, and my wife's nearly catatonic! What more do you want?"

He shook his head and balled up his fists, and for a moment I thought he might come back and take a swing at me. But instead he turned and started up the stairs again. Over his shoulder he said, "I just want it over, and I want you two gone in the morning!" Then he disappeared up the stairs.

As Vince went upstairs, Joey looked at me and said wryly, "Well, I see you've worn out your welcome again, and poor Joey has to find someplace new to vacation." Shaking his head he walked into the living room and settled into the big chair. He took off his boots and put his feet up on the coffee table. "I'm going to catch a nap. Wake me up when you're ready to go." Two heartbeats later he was fast asleep.

I walked out onto the porch, envying Joe's ability to sleep anywhere, anytime. He said he got it from being an enlisted man. You learned to sleep when you could.

He hadn't seen a lot of fighting, but what he had seen was some of the fiercest in the war. He was one of the lucky ones who escaped unscathed, or at least unscathed in body. I still remember the first time I ever saw him….

\*     \*     \*     \*     \*

I brought my F-86 Sabre down and felt it bounce just a bit as it hit the runway It had started running uneven about halfway through my patrol and forced me to turn back. Now as I brought it in, it damn near fell out of the sky!

I taxied it into the flight line and leaned on the brakes to bring it to a halt. Seemed the only time it moved fast anymore was on the ground. On my last couple of encounters I'd barely slid away with my butt intact.

I was just climbing out when I heard a voice holler at me. "Hey, BOSS!"

That stopped me dead. I wasn't a big stickler for rank, but I wasn't used to being called "Boss" either. I dropped down onto the tarmac and saw a lone black soldier standing at the edge of the concrete. With my index finger I pointed at the silver bar on my shoulder. "That's Lieutenant Boss to you."

He flashed me a big grin full of white teeth and said, "Well Lieutenant Boss, how do you manage to keep that crappy-ass airplane in the air? My momma's got a vacuum runs better than that. Probably flies better than that, too."

He proceeded to tell what was wrong with it and what to do about it, but he lost me right after he mentioned the first injector. What I knew about airplanes was that you gave them all the speed you could and they flew. Throttle back and you fall out of the sky. So he might as well have been speaking Korean.

I didn't know if he was right or wrong, and besides, it wasn't my job. If he had any idea what was wrong with the plane he could take it up with the crew chief. He was still talking when I walked away.

It was about midnight when I finally left the Officer's Club and headed back toward my tent. I was just about there when I heard a rather loud commotion coming from the airfield. I should have just gone on, but I never was one for keeping my nose out of other people's business.

As I came up to the flight line I spotted two MPs, well worse for wear, with a black man between them. Each one of them had a hold of one of his arms, and he was still struggling to break free. I figured that if he did, they were going to look a lot worse than they did now, and that wasn't good. They stepped into the light, and I recognized the soldier from this afternoon.

There was a new big, purple bruise forming on his forehead and a trail of blood trickling down from his lip.

It looked as though he had gotten his punches in, too. The one MP's eye was swelling shut, his uniform nearly torn to shreds. The other was in just as bad of shape. His lip was swollen and his nose was pushed a bit to one side. 'Course, maybe it was already pushed to one side. I think it might have been a requirement for MPs.

Stepping into the light so they could see my rank, I asked, "What's going on here, Officer?"

The one with the ripped shirt and swollen eye was the first to speak. It came out with that twang that only comes from Mississippi. I could see now that he was the ranking MP. "We caught this shine trying to sabotage one of the airplanes, sir. When we tried to stop him he decided to get tough with us!"

I watched the black man's glare grow fiery at the use of the word    of the word *shine*, but for the moment I let it go by. "Is that what you were doing, Corporal? Trying to sabotage my airplane?"

He tried to shake his arms free and nearly made it until the MPs set their feet and grabbed his arms with both hands. So now in all of that he found his grin again. "No sir, Lieutenant Boss, I was trying to fix it. Just like I told you earlier. Then these two crackers jumped me from behind."

One of the MPs started to bring his nightstick around, but a look from me stopped him. "I think we can do this without that, Officer. Right, Corporal?"

The corporal nodded and stopped struggling. I motioned for the cops to let him go. "Did you go to the crew chief like I told you?"

He nodded. "Yes, sir I did, but he told me to get the hell out of his office. He said, and I quote, 'I don't tell you how to march, you don't tell me how to fix my planes!' When he said that I knew he wasn't going to do anything about it, and that meant most likely if you took it up again you weren't coming home. So I took it on myself to fix it."

There was something about this big black man that made me want to believe him. Maybe it was his grin or his attitude. I don't know. I just felt I could trust him. "Tell you what, Corporal. I'm gonna make you a deal. You finish up what you're doing. In the morning I'll have my crew chief take a look at it, and if he can't find anything wrong with it, you and I will take it up for a ride. If I don't come back neither do you. Deal?"

He nodded and hit me with the grin again. "Yes, sir!"

Keeping his back to the corporal, the ranking MP walked over to stand beside me, his mouth close to my ear. "You know, sir, a lot of these coons have been going over to the other side. I don't think you should trust one of them. It's not like they're real Americans like you and me."

My smile got a little stiff and I leaned into him. "One more word out of that Southern fried chicken-eatin' mouth and I'm personally going to push your teeth down your throat. Now, I want you to stay with him until he's done. And if I hear that you abused him in any way…."

He squinted his one good eye at me, and I got a chance to see his teeth gnash together. But when he spoke there was a salute in his voice. "Yes, sir."

I felt pretty good as I walked the rest of the way to my tent. I might be dead in the morning, but right now I felt pretty good.

The next morning I took my time. I had breakfast, wandered around a bit, and finally about 8:00 I made my way toward the flight line. My first stop was the crew chief's office.

Les Martin had been the crew chief since I got to Korea. A tall, thin Irishman with pale skin and freckles the same color as his hair all over his face and arms. He was a damn good mechanic. There wasn't a jeep or truck that ran better anywhere in the war. But with jet engines he had a bit of a problem. As long as it was something simple he was okay, but a big problem meant it was easier to buy a new plane!

He was standing in the middle of the hangar wiping his hands on a rag when I moseyed in. He always seemed to be wiping his hands off, sort of like he got them into something once he didn't like and couldn't get it off. He stopped wiping long enough to give me a halfhearted salute. "Morning Lieutenant, sir. Something I can do for you?"

I brushed off the salute and said, "Yes there is. I need a favor." Then I proceeded to tell him about what had happened yesterday afternoon and last night.

He took off his cap and, still holding it in the air, scratched his head with a finger. "You know Lieutenant, I heard something about some black guy in the infantry that's supposed to be some kind of mechanical genius. But didn't take much stock in it. After all if he's a genius, what's he doing in a fox hole?"

I shrugged one shoulder. "Couldn't be because he's a black man, could it?"

Les pulled a pack of Luckies from his pocket and, after offering me one, which I refused, lit one for himself. After a couple of big draws he nodded and said, "Maybe you're right. Seen some pretty smart black guys, but they just don't get the chance to prove it."

"This one's gonna." I said.

We walked down the flight line to where my Sabre was sitting. The two MPs were asleep on some crates. I snuck up on them and kicked one of the packing boxes, scaring them.

They both leaped to their feet, hustling around like two of the Three Stooges. "I take it he didn't try to get away?" I asked sarcastically.

Both their heads wobbled on the ends of their necks like one of those toys you can win at a carnival. "No, sir!" they said in unison, almost like a vaudeville act. It turned my stomach just a bit. The two of them could beat the hell out of a black man, but knuckled under to a white guy.

I pushed past them and over to the Sabre. The corporal was sitting under the wing up against the landing gear. He scrambled out from underneath and made an attempt at attention before I waved it away. "Did you get it done, Corporal?"

"Yes, sir, Boss. I mean Lieutenant Boss." The grin was back.

"You mind if I have my crew chief take a look?

He shrugged his shoulders. "That was our deal, wasn't it?"

Les held out his hand and the corporal grasped it firmly. "Les Martin."

"Corporal Joseph P. Washington. I left the cowling off so you could take a look."

Les walked around to the front of the jet, and his head and hands disappeared first in one side then the other. When he came back, silver dollars wouldn't have covered his eyes, and he was shaking his head in disbelief. "I've heard about some of those changes, but never had enough knowledge or skill to try any of them on my own. That's really beautiful work!"

"That's nice, but will it fly?" I asked.

Les shook his red head again and preformed that scratching maneuver again with his cap. "Fly? It should go like a rocket!"

"Well then I guess I get to see up close and personal just what it'll do. Get her closed up and I'll take it for a ride."

I pulled down the step and climbed up to the cockpit, but when I got to the top, Corporal Joseph P. Washington was already there. "And just where the hell do you think you're going?"

He grinned, and I was starting to wonder if it ever went away. "I'm goin' with you. Like our deal said."

I popped the latch on the canopy, pushed it back, and slid into the seat. "This is a coupe, Corporal, not a sedan. I haven't got room for a giant. Besides, if I die up there I want you left alive to feel sorry about it!"

I think I could see every one of his teeth, and there was a twinkle in those brown eyes to go with it. "It'll fly alright. It's just whether or not you've got the skills to handle it."

"You do know I have a gun, don't you?"

"You wouldn't shoot me, Lieutenant Boss. You gonna need me to keep this thing in the air."

\*　　\*　　\*　　\*　　\*

Needless to say it flew. It flew like nothing I had ever piloted before. I pulled a few strings and got him out of the infantry and assigned to me as my crew chief and mechanical instructor on the base. Best I could do for the man was get him his stripes. And when the war was over and I came back here to test jets, he came with me. This man with more education than I could ever cram inside my tiny little skull became my friend. The best friend I had in the world. And now I was about to take him out and make an attempt at getting him killed again. Some friend I was! Shaking my head, I settled down on the porch swing.

## Chapter 11

Hospitals can be scary places in the night. The lights were turned down so low that only the feeble night lights were there to fend off the darkness. The only sounds were the moans and groans of the patients, like the constant beating of the wings of the Angel of Death hovering above.

Yes, hospitals are scary places at night, when you trespass where you don't belong....

\*     \*     \*     \*     \*

The ride to the top of the hill had only taken a couple of minutes. When Sharade pulled the car into the small ambulance bay in back, there was a nurse and a large man dressed in white waiting. The man looked a bit like a prize fighter who had lost one too many battles. His ears were cauliflowers and his nose was making a right turn towards his face. The nurse too was a big woman, and from his description earlier, Thelma deduced that it was the woman that Rick had tangled with earlier in the day.

As the car stopped they came over to meet it, pushing a metal gurney. The nurse opened the back door and the big man scooped Lou Anne out of the backseat and laid her carefully on the cart. She seemed pale and limp, almost like she was already gone.

As they pushed the cart through the double doors, Thelma turned to follow. But Sharade's hand on her arm stopped her. "I need you to come with me for a short time, Thelma. Ramona and Hooker will take good care of Lou Anne. It will give them a chance to get settled in."

Reluctantly Thelma followed the doctor across the garage and through another smaller door. As he escorted her down the hall he chattered away with small talk, but then he finally got to his point. He asked, "So how long have you been with these people? Captain Steele and company, I mean? Are you close to them?"

Thelma pulled her bushy brows together. "They're like my family. We all look out for each other."

Sharade paused and looked into her eyes. "That's not what I saw. When I was watching they seemed to treat you more like a servant. Even the black man seems to rank above you!"

She glared right back at him. "There's no ranking here. We're all equal. Everybody has a right to a decision. Nobody bosses the rest of us. Doctor Gallagher is like a sister to me!"

"But they decide to go after her and leave you behind? How many times has that happened?"

Thelma shook her head, denying what he was saying. "No, they left me here to look after Lou Anne and Aunt Sophie."

His voice took on a condescending tone. "Yes, yes, of course. You're right, I just misinterpreted what I was seeing."

For a moment her eyes behind the thick lenses seemed far away as she mulled over the things that Sharade had said. Could he be right? Was she really blind to what was going on around her? She shook her head to clear it and pushed the thought away.

Dr. Sharade just smiled and continued on down the hallway. He had planted a seed; now all he had to do was let it germinate!

\*      \*      \*      \*      \*

The path they were on led Thelma to an empty exam room where the doctor had her climb up on the gurney. "I need to take a sample of your blood and cross match it to Lou Anne's in case we run short. Our blood supplies have been depleted some over the last week or so, with what turned out to be a major accident on the highway. We've had to do a couple of emergency surgeries."

Thelma felt a bit like she was in a trance. The things that Sharade said just kept surfacing in her mind. Absentmindedly she held out her finger for a stick, but the needle that the doctor took out of the cabinet was way too big for that. She pulled her arm back. "I thought you said a type and cross match?"

He gave her his best bedside manner. "I did, and normally a stick would be enough. But with Lou Anne's weakened condition we need to test for viruses and bacteria. That takes more blood than a simple stick."

Reluctantly she rolled up her sleeve and extended her arm again, only to quickly withdraw it once more as the doctor pulled a syringe from the cabinet and filled it from a small vial. Eyeing him suspiciously once more she asked, "What's the syringe for if this is a blood draw?"

Sharade fussed a bit and gave her his beaming smile. "Simply a bit of Novocain to take away the sting of the larger needle."

She shook her head and flashed him a smile of her own. "I think I can handle the pain of the stick quite well without the Novocain." This whole procedure was setting off alarm bells inside her head, but it was for Lou Anne, so she didn't jump up off the exam table.

The doctor laid the hypo back down on the instrument tray. "It was just something to make you feel more comfortable."

Thelma's smile was still there, but it was a bit harder. "Could we just get this over with so I can go and check on Lou Anne?"

"We'll be done in a jiff,' he said as he wrapped a tourniquet around her arm. Thelma's vein bulged out clearly as the blood tried to force its way back past the rubber band tied around her upper arm. With one push the needle slid in, a drop of blood appearing almost immediately on the end of the needle.

He slid a piece of clear rubber tubing over the needle and hooked the other end to a small valve on a sterile bottle hanging from a hooked stand. Then, satisfied with his connections, he removed the thick rubber band, and the blood began once more to flow down her arm. Only this time it ran through the hose to the bottle rather than returning to her heart.

She lay on her back on the table, watching the thick, red fluid fill the bottle. For a moment as she watched, panic started to set in that he would take too much, but when she tried to rise, his hand was on her shoulder pinning her back. Thelma was no weakling, but Sharade was much more powerful than he looked. He held her down quite easily with his one hand.

Finally when the bottle was nearly full, he turned the little valve off and the flow stopped. He removed the tubing, and then pulled the needle free from her arm. After pressing a piece of gauze and tape on the now-seeping hole, he patted her affectionately. "You're going to be a bit dizzy for the next while. So I want you to stay here and rest for the next hour. When it's up, I'll send Ramona in to take you to Lou Anne."

Thelma nodded sleepily and watched Sharade leave the room.

The minute the door clicked shut, Thelma rolled off the exam table and nearly went right on over onto her face! Sharade hadn't been kidding about the dizziness. The room was going round and round like a high-speed carnival ride.

Focusing on her feet, she tried not to watch the room spin and made her way slowly to the door. A sigh of relief escaped her lips as her hand closed on the door handle, and she was still standing. Slowly she turned the knob only to find it locked.

Carefully Thelma settled down on her knees till the knob was even with her face. Then reaching to the back of her bun, she pulled a bobby pin free. Dragging it through her teeth to scrape off the rubber tips, she bent it straight and went to work on the lock. After a couple of seconds she heard it click free. "Thanks, Uncle Lou," she said to herself in a whisper. "I'll try and be there when you get out next year."

With the door unlocked, she settled down onto her butt and slowly took off her big shoes and socks. Without the shoes her feet seemed surprisingly small. She remembered how much noise her boots had made on the floors on the way in, so she wasn't going to take any chances of them giving her away. And without the shoes, the socks had to go. Combined with the slickly polished wood floors, her socks and her dizziness made for a deadly combination.

Crawling back across the room to the exam table, she set the shoes and socks next to it. That way if they were found, they'd think she had taken them off for comfort. Her whole plan right now was that if she was caught, it was the fault of the dizziness that she was suffering from. Not exactly an iron clad alibi, but better than nothing.

Still on her hands and knees, which was easier than walking right now, she crossed the room to the door. Reaching for the handle, she caught it on the second try and pulled herself to her feet. A wave of nausea swept over her, and only her sheer will helped her from tumbling right back down to the floor and onto her derriere.

Taking a deep breath, she held it till the wave passed. After a quick look out to make sure the hall was clear, she stepped out. It felt a little like stepping out on another planet. The near darkness of the hall, the cold of the floor against her bare feet, the up and down motion of the floor from her vertigo. Adapting to a motion that wasn't really there left her walking like a drunken sailor. With one hand on the wall for balance, she wove from side to side as she walked. Thelma quickly discovered that it was easier to maintain what little balance she had if she kept one eye tightly closed. A low laugh escaped her throat. She must look a lot like a pirate now, weaving from side to side with only one eye. It's a good thing nobody was around.

None of this was making any sense to her—the confusion, the dizziness, and the nausea. She had given blood before, and it had never been like this. Had Sharade somehow drugged her? Was there something on the needle he had used? She tried to remember, but everything up to when she got off the exam table was rapidly becoming a blur in her mind.

Thelma looked around the hallway, trying to remember how she got here and why she was here. Her perceptions were shifting. One moment it was like looking through a telescope backward with everything in the distance, and the next it was all in crystal clarity.

She pushed herself on down the hall. "Think, Thelma, think!" she told herself. "You need to find somewhere to try and get your thoughts together. You're here for a reason!" That thought made her giggle. Maybe it was for a reason, but she couldn't remember what it was, and if she couldn't remember was there really a reason?

An image of Rick floated across her clouded mind. She felt her heart beat faster as she thought about him. Why couldn't he feel about her the way he felt about Kate? Didn't she have just as much to offer? Maybe even more? But no, he had to chase after the pretty Dr. Gallagher. Didn't she work just as hard? Didn't she do everything he asked? "Why, Rick? Why?" Suddenly she realized that she had said that out loud, and her hand flew up to cover her mouth as she gasped and looked up and down the corridor to make sure that she hadn't been heard. She was still safe. She was the only living soul in sight. She giggled again, thinking of herself as a ghost floating up and down the hall.

She started her stumbling walk down the hall again, one hand still pressed to the wall for guidance. Thelma hadn't gone more than a step or two when suddenly the wall gave way, and she found herself tumbling into space!

\*   \*   \*   \*   \*

As I sat on the porch thinking about Joey to try and keep my mind from going crazy over Kate, thick fog rolled in. It seemed to creep over the buildings of the town, blotting them from sight like a giant white slug devouring them an inch at a time. Soon it had covered the entire town, the streets, and had rolled right up to the edge of the porch.

Fog's a funny thing. If you stare into it you start to believe that you can see through it. That's the only explanation I have.

I was sitting there on the swing looking out into the fog and suddenly it was like I was seeing right through it. Where the white cloud had covered the town, buildings began to appear, but not the familiar structures that the fog had blotted out. These were different, older styles, and between them was a town full of people going about their daily business. They were as clear to me as they would have been if it were noon.

Buggies traveled up the streets; ladies in long dresses and men in frock coats walked on wooden sidewalks past stores and other businesses. Children played in yards just off the center of town.

In disbelief at what I was seeing, I rose from the swing and started across the porch. But as I walked toward the steps, unable to take my eyes off the street, I accidentally kicked the milk box. The clang in the silence was like a cannon shot. As I froze, so did the people in the fog. In mid-step they stopped what they were doing and turned to stare at where the sound had come from.

I could feel the pounding of my heart making time like a wall clock. I felt embarrassed that I had disturbed them. Yet, at the same time, how could that be? How could they hear me, yet I couldn't hear them? For that matter, how could they even exist?

For one hundred beats of my heart they watched me. Then as suddenly as they had stopped, they returned to doing what they were doing before I interrupted them.

I watched for what seemed like a very long time. I remember once checking my watch to see what time it was, only to notice that it had stopped.

Finally the fog began a slow retreat, and the people of the street began to fade. I rushed off the porch to try and see more before they were gone, but with every step the fog retreated faster. By the time I got to the street, both the people and the fog were gone.

Standing there looking up the once-more familiar street, I told myself that I had imagined the whole thing. Then I spotted something that hadn't been there before the fog! I rushed out and picked it up. It was a child's toy, a hand-carved slingshot like the kind boys from the last century would have carried in their back pockets.

It was smooth and warm in my hand. I pulled the sling back a couple of times to test the action as I walked back up to the porch. It was a really beautiful piece of workmanship, a piece any ten-year-old boy would be proud to own. Just before I started back up the steps to the porch, I turned around and held it into the air. "I promise," I said to the street that wasn't there anymore, "I'll take good care of this." Then I slipped it into my back pocket.

I walked up onto the porch and settled down into the swing again. Suddenly I was very, very tired, unable to hold my eyes open. The minute I sat back down, I drifted off to sleep.

Chapter 12

Thelma sat on the floor, stunned from her fall. It hadn't been the wall that had moved, but an unlatched door. Now she was sitting in the stairwell. Again she giggled, but held her hand over her mouth to suppress it. Using the stair rail as an aid, she pulled herself to her feet. As the giggles passed, she forced herself to focus on where she was going.

If there were any secrets to be uncovered, it would be downstairs. People never hid things in their attics. *I don't even have an attic!* she thought. And then the giggles started again, but this time she stopped them before they were out of control. Gripping the handrail, she eased herself to the first step. Her chubby toes looked tiny and miles away as she looked down. Slowly and carefully she slid her foot across the cool concrete and out into open space. Her grip on the rail became white-knuckled as she eased her foot down onto the next step.

After testing her footing, she slowly lifted her other foot and moved it out. As her heel cleared the step, something in her controls seemed to go haywire, and her whole body pitched forward into space. Her free arm windmilled backward like it was trying to blow her back onto the landing. But it would have taken a jet engine to stop her fall. Her hand came loose from the rail and her pudgy body pitched forward into a roll.

Her head hit the first step, and her butt and legs came up over the top, dragging her forward. Thelma's momentum picked up and suddenly she was a snowball thundering down the slope. But instead of smooth snow to roll in, it was concrete steps that were jabbing her back and banging her head as she rolled.

Thelma's hands skimmed the wall as she rolled, looking for a grip, and her legs churned the air before they were crushed under her in the next orbit of her butt. It felt like the fall would go on forever, but evil Mr. Fate had other things in mind when he built this stairway. He put in a landing and reversed the direction. She hit the wall fully face-on!

Stars filled her narrow field of vision, and she tasted blood in her mouth. Through the pain she fumbled around    and found her glasses. Luckily she had kept her face turned far enough inward that they had stayed on her nose right up until she hit the wall.

As she sat there on the floor, her crazily messed-up emotions took a right turn. She was in pain now, bleeding, and just felt that she couldn't take any more. She had tried, but she'd failed. Tears streamed down her cheeks to mix with the blood that was running from her split lip. Rick had asked her for something simple, and she'd screwed it up! Just like she'd screwed up everything else in her life.    She was becoming just what her father had said she'd be. A failure. She remembered what it was like when she came home and told him what she'd decided to do.

"Going to work for *who*? Thelma, you speak seventeen languages! You have four PhDs and you want to play assistant to a professor of anthropology at New Mexico State? Have you lost your mind?" He held up his hand, stopping her from speaking. "That was a rhetorical question. I don't need an answer. I'm sure you've lost your mind!"

She'd tried to explain, but he wouldn't listen. And even after she proved herself in the field of anthropology, he still wouldn't have any of it. Now she was sitting at the bottom of a stairwell, drugged out of her mind and bleeding, and she was about to agree with him.

Would Rick have let himself get caught with a hidden needle? Even Joey wouldn't have let it happen. But Thelma, oh no! He leaves her behind to do a little covert looking around and what happens? She gets messed up right away! She was almost out of time, and she knew there was no way she could get back before they caught her! So the whole thing was going to be a waste if she didn't get up off her fat duff and find something out. At least then it would be worth something, unless they killed her and she never got the chance to tell anybody.

Still sitting on the floor, she inched her way over to the next flight of stairs and swung her legs over. Drugged or not and in spite of what her father had told her all those years ago, she was still one of the most resourceful women in the world. If she couldn't manage to walk down the last flight, she could slide. Slowly with one hand on the handrail to control her speed, she slid her butt over the edge and dropped to the next step. Except for the bruises on her bottom, and it must have been nearly solid purple by now, this was a safe method of going down steps— at least safer than rolling! And amazingly faster.

Within just a couple of minutes she was on the bottom. Taking a deep breath, she pulled herself to her feet and carefully walked away from the steps. One pudgy hand on the wall like before, she managed to reach out and pull the door open.

The other side of the door was like another world. Pipes stretched across the ceiling, some carrying water and steam to other parts of the hospital, and sewer lines carrying away the waste. It was like a maze. Pipes, wires, and single light bulbs hung down every few feet or so to keep the darkness back.

The air was heavy with humidity and smelled a bit like boiling water. Wrinkling her nose against it, she pushed on down the dimly lit hallway. As she passed, she opened the doors to see what was on the other side. She uncovered numerous workrooms, closets, and rooms filled with unknown mechanical devices whose sole purpose seemed to be to make loud and scary noises.

But the doorway in the middle of the hall stopped Thelma in her tracks. For a moment she thought it was the drugs again making her hallucinate. The air in the room was cool, almost cold, and smelled slightly of age. In the dim light she could see a painting hanging from the wall, and across the back wall hung a well-worn version of a Confederate battle flag. Even in the dim light she could see the frayed edges and the dark spots that she suspected were blood. Next to it a tailor's dummy stood, and on it was an officer's uniform. And next to the flag was a picture of President Jefferson Davis shaking hands with a very familiar face. The man he was clutching hands with was none other than Dr. Sharade!

Thelma's mouth came open to gasp at what she saw, but instead she felt a prick in the back of her neck. Her knees collapsed from under her and she hit the floor like a rock.

\*    \*    \*    \*    \*

Kate had no idea how long she had been sitting tied in the dark. She suspected that she might have a slight concussion from the crash because she had been fading in and out. But she did know it had been long enough that her butt and her ankles had gone numb where they were tied from not being able to move. She tried to wiggle a bit now, but there just wasn't room. And she was thirsty. Whatever she had done to her nose in the accident had swelled it shut, and she'd been breathing through her mouth. Despite the damp air, her mouth and tongue were like leather.

She started pulling on the center slat of the chair but wasn't making much headway. Oh it was wiggling, but not enough to pop out. At the current rate, she was going to be here for a hundred years if she had to wait till she got the slat out.

Kate cursed, and if she could have she'd have stomped her foot. But the chair and the rope pretty much stopped that tantrum from happening. It was just as well, because right about then she heard the approaching of voices and saw a thin line of light appear across from her. It was the first sound she had heard since she was imprisoned, and she wasn't sure at first that it was even real. Then she recognized the voices as they got closer. They were the two men that had taken her from the car wreck.

Suddenly it was like sunrise. A white hot star burned into Kate's brain that even her eyelids couldn't seem to stop. The light was from the men's flashlight, but after all the hours in total darkness it was a knife in her brain.

Gradually the pain eased, and her eyes became accustomed to the light again. But to stop her from seeing the faces of her jailers they kept the beam pointed directly into her eyes. Behind it they were just two shadowy figures. Kate knew them anyway. She recognized them from their voices and from their smell.

The bigger of the two smelled of cigar smoke and had an educated Southern drawl. The smaller one smelled of whiskey. He too had a Southern drawl, but it sounded less educated and cruder than his companion's.

The leader said, "Welcome back, ma'am." She could almost see him reaching up to touch the brim of an invisible hat. "I was hopin' that you hadn't succumbed to your injures from the crash. They didn't look serious, but doctorin' is somebody else's job. I'm just here to make sure people go where they're supposed to."

Kate struggled against her ropes, making the chair bounce. When she tried to speak, it came out as only a croak.

He seemed to understand and told his companion, "Give her a swallow out of that flask you're always hiding in that hip pocket of yours."

Staying out of the light, the smaller of the two men walked over and pushed her head back, opening her mouth, and poured something down her throat. It burned like fire all the way to her belly and sent her into a fit of coughing. After a minute she recognized the taste as whiskey.

Surprisingly, when she stopped coughing she found she could speak again, raspy as her voice was. "Who are you?" Why am I here? What's going on?"

The man with the light laughed at her, "You know why you're here. Your meddlin' beau, his darkie, and you have been messin' in places where you don't belong. We've been doin' what we're doin' fer a long time, and don't need no help from some outsiders. Least of all yer kind."

"And just exactly what is my kind?"

"Damned Yan—" Whatever it was he was going to say, and Kate thought the word was probably *Yankees*, he managed to catch himself before it was all the way out. "You damned city folk!" Whatever courtesy had been in his voice was gone. There was a hard edge to his drawl now. "Don't really matter much anyhow. You'll all be dead soon enough. First that sky jockey and his buddy, then you!" He used the flashlight and gestured to his companion. "Check her ropes. We've wasted enough time down here."

The one who had poured the whiskey down her throat walked over behind her and jerked painfully on the ropes that had her hands tied. Then he came back around front to check the ones holding her ankles. Kneeling down, he ran his hands over her ankles and up her calves, letting his grimy fingers linger on her soft skin. His face was so close Kate could feel his fetid breath against her face.

As he started to rise from the floor, using Kate's thighs to push himself up, she lashed out with her head. It caught him right in the bridge of the nose, and she had the satisfaction of hearing the cartilage crunch as she felt the warm spatter of blood on her thighs where he had pulled her skirt up. But the instant she hit him, she almost wished she hadn't. Lightning exploded in her head to remind her of her concussion.

It was followed by more pain as her captor leaped to his feet and backhanded her. He was about to do it again when the bigger man stopped him. "Enough!"

"But she busted my nose, Major!" he whined.

"Y'all best shut yer damned mouth! I don't care what she busted. Get yerself outta here and get cleaned up."

Through the stars she was seeing, Kate watched the man leave. But the big one wasn't done yet. He walked over and stood directly in front of her, for once his light pointing at the floor instead of her eyes. "He got what was coming to him, ma'am, so I don't care what ya did. But real soon the time's gonna come when the boss turns him loose, and I ain't gonna be able to stop him then. So I hope you enjoyed yer little moment." Then without waiting for a reply, he turned and walked out.

But that one instant when the light was out of her eyes, Kate got to see the room. She'd been right; it was a root cellar. Along one wall were shelves packed with mason jars of canned goods. Against the other wall was a potting table. The whole room was about six feet by ten feet, and she was pretty much right in the middle. Then the lights went out and it was dark again.

## Chapter 13

As she sat there in the darkness listening to the sound of them leaving, she studied the picture her mind had snapped of her surroundings. The potting table was on her right, the door straight ahead, and on her left the shelves full of mason jars. "That would probably be the most fruitful choice," she told herself. Then she cursed under her breath. She must have hit her head harder than she thought if she was resorting to crummy puns like that.

She pushed it out of her mind and went back to the problem at hand. The shelves were only a couple of feet away, but with her tied to the chair it might as well be a million miles. She could always tip the chair over, but then she'd just be lying on her side and still couldn't reach the shelf.

Kate leaned forward, putting her weight on her feet, trying to lift the chair and duck-walk across the room, but she was tied too tightly and the chair was too heavy. Finally she decided that the only way she was going to get herself and the chair across the room was to hop the chair.

The ropes around her ankles were just far enough up that she could hook her feet around the legs of the chair. Then with her hands holding the seat, she threw all of her weight up and into the air. The chair came up off the floor a couple of inches and moved a couple of inches to her right.

"Grrrr!" she growled. "Not that way, the other way!" She stopped complaining for a minute and thought about it. Gravity and momentum, that's what she had to worry about. *I have to get it to move left when it comes back down. That should mean if I lean to the left, the chair should go that way,* she thought. *But not too far, or I'll end up falling over.*

So like an artillery officer she planned her next hop. *Up into the air and lean left.* The chair moved a couple inches to the left this time, putting it about back where it was when she started. She was almost jubilant, but she quickly reminded herself that she hadn't gained anything yet. So it wasn't quite time to celebrate. So she set herself and got ready to hop again.

It took four hops to get across the room. By the time her chair thumped up against the shelf, she was nearly exhausted. Even in the cool damp of the cellar she was sweating. She could feel it under her arms, and her auburn hair was plastered against her forehead. And the pain was back, tearing at her brain.

Dr. Katherine Gallagher was not the kind of woman who was given to despair. The accident, the concussion, and being imprisoned here in the dark were almost too much for her. It had been a long night and she was rapidly nearing her breaking point. She felt tears start to roll down her cheeks, and she clamped down on her lovely lips with her teeth. "Come on, Kate!

You don't know when they're coming back! You have to get out of here. Rick needs you! Joey needs you! You can cry later. Right now you've got to get loose!"

She took a deep breath and picked up the chair again and spun it in the air like a top. As the chair turned a couple of inches she forced a smile, and sarcastically she said, "Gee, if I get this right I could take this show on the road!" The chair came up and spun one last time, the back banging into the shelf.

Stretching out her fingers she managed to grip one of the jars. Holding it by the top, she brought it down and slammed it against the shelf. All she got for her trouble was a thump. All the years in this damp cellar had made the wood soft, and it wasn't hard enough to break the jar.

Growling again and trying to stomp her foot, she cursed. "Can't anything go right when you're tied to a damn chair?"

With her fingers alone, she moved the jars into place behind her. One by one she pulled them over till the shelf was stacked full clear to the edge. Kate tried to blow her hair out of her face, but between the blood and the sweat it wasn't going anywhere. She picked up one of the jars and swung it against the others. This time it was enough. She heard the crash of breaking glass and suddenly the room smelled like pickle juice, and the jar in her hand felt almost weightless.

Fumbling around with the glass, she found the edge and went to work on her ropes. The first thing she cut was her wrist. "Great, now I'll bleed to death before I get loose." But after a couple of tries she got the rhythm right and began to saw on the ropes. It seemed to take forever, but at last she felt the strands part, and her hands were free!

For the first time in hours she brought her hands back around in front of her and laid them in her lap. Cursing the darkness again, she felt the cuts on her wrists. They were bleeding, but not pumping, so she hadn't cut any arteries. With a half-numb finger she tore a couple of strips off her skirt and wrapped them around the cuts to try and staunch the bleeding. Then she went to work cutting her ankles free.

As the last of the ropes fell away, she pushed herself to her feet and promptly fell facedown into the dirt. Her feet and ankles felt like somebody was sticking a thousand pins into them, and the circulation was restored. "Real smart, Kate! Sit in a chair all night without moving and expect to get up and walk away?" She pulled her body back across to the shelves again and opened jars till she found one that smelled like peaches. She drank the juice and ate the fruit with her bloody fingers. "Probably a good thing it's dark in here," she quipped. "I really don't want to know what's on my hands!"

*　　*　　*　　*　　*

I was cold and I was stiff from sleeping in the swing. I checked my watch and it was working again. Or had it ever really stopped? I had been sitting on that swing for most of the night. Off in the distance I could see the first ray of dawn crossing the horizon.

Walking across the porch I stretched to throw off the stiffness in my back and in my arms, and I nearly stumbled over the milk box again. Yeah, I faintly remembered tripping over it when the fog and the people....THE SLINGSHOT!

I shook my head as I walked down the steps, feeling my empty back pocket. There weren't any people or fog. I had dreamed the whole thing. Yeah, that's what it was—a dream. I turned and walked back into the house. It was time to wake up Joey and get this thing in the air.

*     *     *     *     *

Thelma's eyes fluttered open. She was staring up at a white ceiling, albeit a fuzzy white ceiling without her glasses, but a white ceiling all the same. She was lying in a warm bed with the covers pulled up to her chin. She smiled a half smile and snuggled down even deeper into the bed. Then suddenly she sat bolt upright. She wasn't supposed to be in bed! If anything she should be lying on the floor of the lower level.

The big nurse got up from her stool and walked over to push her back down into the bed. "Easy there, honey. You had quite a night. So y'all just lay back." Then she reached out and pulled the cord for the call light.

As she lay back down, Thelma took a quick look around the room. It was a typical hospital room. On the other side Lou Anne was lying quietly, gray like death, with tubes running in and out of her arms. The hiss of the oxygen machine filled the air.

Just as her head touched the pillow, the door opened and Dr. Sharade bustled in. Before even saying a word, her took her wrist and checked her pulse. He patted her wrist as he laid her arm back down on the bed. Pulling up the stool the nurse had vacated, he sat down, a worried look on his face. "You gave us quite a scare last night. Charlotte came back to the exam room to get you, and you were gone!" He paused and gave her a tired smile. "We get a little upset around here when we lose a patient. Do you remember any of what happened?"

At least for now, Thelma thought that it was best for her to keep the truth to herself. "Not really. I remember suddenly having to pee and walking outside the room. Then it's all just kind of a blur. I remember wandering and wanting to find my way back, but every turn was the wrong one," she lied.

Sharade's smile seemed to grow less tired and more sincere. "Well, don't worry about it then. No harm was done."

Thelma raised herself a bit up off the bed and looked across the room at her cousin. "How is Lou Anne? Is she going to be alright?"

The doctor turned and looked at the silent girl. "It was a pretty scary night for her too. But I think the crisis has passed, and recovery should begin soon."

Thelma looked at the tape on the inside of her arm. "Did you have to use some of my blood for her?"

He followed her eyes down to the inside of her elbow and shook his head. "No, that was from a couple of injections we gave you to stimulate blood building, and one for tetanus for the cut on your forehead." He patted her hand again. "Now why don't you get a couple more hours of sleep before breakfast."

She returned his smile. "Could I have my glasses? I like to keep them close. I have a very hard time seeing things clearly without them."

Sharade nodded and took her thick spectacles from his pocket and handed them to her. "I picked them up off the floor from where you fell last night. Luckily they weren't broken."

"I always carry two pairs just in case, but my second pair is with my luggage in the plane."

He looked sheepishly at the floor. "Sorry to tell you this, Thelma, but probably in the next few minutes those will be well beyond your reach. Rick and Joey are about to take off and leave you behind."

118

Her smile faded, and inside a funny feeling began to build. It was almost like either a hint of jealousy or maybe even anger at them leaving, and she didn't understand why. But then her eyelids felt very heavy, and she drifted back to sleep.

\* \* \* \* \*

The sun had just crossed the horizon as Joey and I finished up our preflight checks. The grass was wet with dew sparkling in the new sun.

"Ready to roll, Boss," he said as he slid into the copilot's seat.

"Gonna be a cold and windy flight without a window." I was wearing my goggles, a fur-lined flight jacket, and my gloves.

Joey grinned and reached out and tapped the window on his side of the cockpit. "Mine's just cracked. I should be cozy over here."

Shaking my head, I hit the starter on number one, and got a nice, loud gunshot-like pop. There was a thin trail of smoke from the exhaust, and the fan began to slowly turn.

I waited for the oil pressure to come up. I hit the button and exploded the cartridge on number two and watched the fan on it begin to turn. They were both a little rough at first, but as the oil thinned down they began to smooth out to a nice purr.

Joey was reading me numbers as I stepped on the rudder, feathered number one, and poured the power to number two. Slowly at first we started to move, and the big bird began to turn. It wasn't very elegant to watch on the ground, but in the air it was a thing of beauty, like an albatross or a condor.

As I straightened the nose up on the grassy strip we were using for a runway, I set the flaps and pushed the throttles forward. The purr moved up to a roar, and like a fat man losing weight as he ran we began to roll, picking up speed with every turn of the wheels.

When we were flashing past the hospital, Joey touched my arm and pointed. Sharade was standing just outside the backdoor, pipe clenched between his teeth, watching us leave. "Guess he just wanted to make sure we were really leaving!" I hollered at Joey over the noise of the engines and the wind rushing through the cockpit. He just nodded back.

I pulled back on the stick and we seemed to leap into the air. There's really nothing like it. The closest thing I can think of is when you're a kid, and you're riding your bike as fast as you can and you fly off the top of a hill, airborne for just those few seconds. Only here, those seconds last forever.

I trimmed the flaps and leveled off, keeping it closer to the ground than normal to stay out of as much wind as possible, and so we didn't freeze.

Joey poured me a cup of coffee from the thermos. As he handed it to me, he leaned in and yelled in my ear. "Should have poured some of Vince's bourbon in that to keep the ice out."

I nodded and laughed, wriggling my cold fingers inside my gloves to keep the blood flowing.

"I'm going in back to get a blanket," he yelled. "Anything I can get you?"

Stiffly I shook my head. I could use a little more heat on my feet, but there wasn't any of that hiding in the back of the plane.

As he turned and left through the cabin door, I turned my thoughts back to Kate. I was pretty sure that she was still alive. Otherwise, whoever had her would have made a point of letting us know that she was dead. That didn't mean they were going to keep her alive forever.

The moment she became useless to their plan they'd eliminate her. I just had to find her before that happened! But who the hell were they? And why?

Joey came back through the door, his face almost as white as mine. I took off my headphones and asked him what was wrong.

He shook his head. "We didn't buy a big, new wall clock to hang on the side of the plane, did we?"

I screwed up the corner of my mouth, trying to figure out what he was talking about. But before I could ask, he went on. "I think you better have a look in back, Rick."

He slid into the copilot's seat, and I climbed out of mine. "Where?" I asked as I handed him my headphones.

"Fourth brace back after the hatch. You're not gonna like it!"

Chapter 14

I walked to the back of the plane, and there it was just like Joey said—a one-by-one-foot metal box bolted to the strut with some really big bolts. There were aluminum shavings all over the floor from the holes being drilled in the strut.

With trembling hands I carefully lifted the cover off. I almost wished I hadn't. Under the cover there were six sticks of dynamite wired to three round dials. One of the dials was a clock, set for exactly thirty minutes from now. The other two were altimeters. One was set at 500 feet, and the other one at 1,400 feet.

Taking a deep breath, I set the cover down on the deck and walked up to where the intercom headset was hanging.

Slipping on the headset and adjusting the microphone, I called Joey. "Better keep it between 600 and 1,200 feet, unless you want somebody trying to decide which leg is yours and which leg is mine after the crash."

I heard him suck in a deep breath. "You're saying it's a bomb, right? And it's set to blow at either 500 or 1,300 feet?"

"Well," I said, "fourteen hundred, but I'm not one to quibble over a hundred feet. Oh, and one more thing… it also has a timer set to blow up in about thirty minutes."

I could almost see him wiping his face with his hand. "Pretty thorough, aren't they?"

"Yep."

"So what are we going to do?"

"Well, I was kind of thinking that it was time you and I dissolved the partnership. I just don't think people like you," I told him.

"That may be right, but it doesn't help us much with our current dilemma. Besides, who says I want to own a broken-down freight company with a crazy white pilot."

Since there was enough cord on the intercom I walked back over and looked down into the bomb again. "You know I could just bail."

"You could," he sputtered, "if I didn't own all the parachutes now."

"So you're saying that I should probably try and do something about the bomb?"

"That would probably be my suggestion."

I hung the headset on the bolts holding the bomb and walked back further into the plane to get the toolbox. The spot where it was normally bolted was empty. I went back to the bomb and put the headset on again. "Remember I told you they were thorough? They took the toolbox too."

The plane hit a spot of rough air, and it bounced a bit. "Hey!"

"Sorry, I'm supposed to design planes, not fly them," he replied. Then he asked, "How tight are the bolts?"

"Well, let's see. If I were Superman or maybe you, I could just twist them off with my fingers. But unfortunately I'm just a poor, weak white guy. So I'd have to say, REAL DAMN TIGHT!"

"Well, I'm kind of busy right now flying my new airplane, so you're probably going to have to work this one out for yourself."

"And just how long is your new airplane going to stay in the air if I don't get this problem solved?" I started searching all over the back of the plane for any kind of tool. I did manage to find a hammer, but didn't figure beating on the bolts that held a bomb to the side of the plane was such a brilliant idea.

The static crackling in my ear for a second cleared. "Rick? You still there?"

"And just where would I go?" I snapped back.

"Then you don't want my help?"

"Yes, darling, I want your help. As a matter of fact I can't think of anybody else's help I could want more right now."

His voice was a little sheepish when he came back to me. "I know where there's a pair of clamp-on pliers."

I glanced at the bomb. I could almost hear the time ticking away over the roar of the engines. "Where? Or is it a secret?"

"Well, it's not in a real good place."

"In a couple of minutes it's not gonna matter if it's a good place or not." I informed him.

"Port rudder cable under inspection panel R."

I started walking toward the rear of the plane, and suddenly my headset was jerked off as I ran out of wire. I had to backtrack and put it back on. "How do I find R?"

I heard him snicker a bit as he told me. "R stands for *Rear*. You can't miss it."

I laid the head set down on the floor and followed the floor panels back till I came to the one with the handholds on it. I lifted it out and laid it aside.

It was dark in the open hole, and I lit a match to see what I was looking at. It was like a junction box where wires come together, only this was bigger and it was filled with cables instead. They were constantly moving back and forth as Joey kept us on course.

On the one cable where there would normally be a cable clamp was a pair of clamp-on pliers instead.

I scrabbled quickly back across the floor and picked up the headset. "Okay, I found it. Now what's gonna happen when I take it loose?"

"It's gonna get real hard to steer," he answered. "If it starts to drift to starboard, we'll just have to go with it. No more left turns."

I nodded that I understood before I remembered he couldn't see me. "Okay. I'm going to go back and take them off. I'll let you know when I get them off."

"Don't worry about that. I'll know the minute the cable pulls free. I'll start flying in left-handed circles."

I laid the headset down again and crawled back across the floor to the hole. I dropped my feet in so they were on either side of the cables and reached down in to feel for the releaser on the pliers. I squeezed the lever and the tension popped them free. As they did, I fumbled to get a grip on them, but I missed and they fell to the bottom of the compartment, under the cables.

It was starting to look like fate had it in for either me or Joey on this flight the way things just kept going right! Lying down on my belly, I reached into the dark hole, feeling with my fingertips for the pliers and all the time trying to keep my arm out of the way of the cables.

Despite the chilly temperatures, I was starting to sweat as my fingers brushed up against the pliers. I gently pushed them over to the edge of the hole where I could slowly work them up the side until I could get a better grip. As I pulled them out of the hole and stood up, the starboard cable let go and snapped like a rubber band pulled too tight. If I'd still been down there I'd have probably lost an eye, just before I was blown to hell. Then to top it off I felt a gust of wind catch the plane, and it shifted sideways.

I hurried back over to the headset and got it on. "Joey, are you all right? Can you hold it?"

"Not much to hold, Boss. We're just sort of going in circles. Great big circles. You might want to hurry though, if you can. I gotta pee."

"Well try and hold it."

"You mean the pee?"

"No, the plane. I've got to get the bomb loose, and a smooth ride would help."

I could hear his grin as he came back. "I'll see what I can do. But hurry up."

Yeah right, working with a bomb and he tells me to hurry up? What's he think, I'm napping back here?

A couple of steps carried me to the bomb. I needed both hands to adjust the pliers, so I put the headset back on. I wound them tightly and clamped them down on the nut and pulled. "Ughhh!"

"I hope that was the nut coming loose."

"Sorry, buddy. That was me trying to move this thing. They tightened them as tight as they could, and then burred the threads to make sure they didn't come off." I started my search around the cabin again. I got lucky this time, and over against the bulkhead was the piece of pipe we used to tighten the tie-downs. I could use it as a cheater bar to give me more leverage. The timer was staring back at me like an evil eye. It reminded me that I had just less than eight minutes left to get this thing loose and out of the plane.

I slipped the pipe up over the handle of the pliers and leaned on it with all my weight. With a groan the first nut broke loose and turned. I picked myself up from the deck where I'd fallen when it suddenly came loose, then quickly reset the pliers. This time it moved much easier.

As I dropped the first nut down on the deck, the timer dropped under the five minute mark. At this rate, with two bolts to go, I was never going to make it.

My hands were slick with sweat, and there was blood dripping from my torn knuckles. I could feel the cold against the wetness of my shirt, and my mouth was full of cotton.

The second bolt spun lose easier than the first one, or maybe I was just getting better at it. Maybe this would open up a whole new career: Rick Steele, Bomb Unscrewer!

Both hands were busy now, each one spinning off a nut. As soon as one fell to the floor and I had a hand free, I pulled the mic up and called Joey. "I just about have it free. Take it up to about 1,200 feet and hold it there."

The deck suddenly tilted out from under my feet, and I grabbed the bomb for support. Luckily my fingers in the middle of it didn't do any damage. As the plane leveled out again, I twisted the last nut off and the bomb pulled free of the brace. "Joey! I've got it! I'm going to toss it out the door! The minute I say go, head straight for the moon!"

"Yes, sir! Just make sure you don't go out with it!"

Carrying the bomb in my arms like a newborn, I said, "Thanks for the vote of confidence."

I undogged the door and leaned into it as hard as I could with my shoulder. The best I could do against the wind was about six inches, not enough to get the bomb out!

Then I remembered the pipe. Unfortunately it had rolled away when Joey took the plane up to 1,200 feet and was now lying against the back of the plane. The face of the clock said that I had less than a minute to go.

I think I wanted to cry. But instead I ran towards the back of the plane. I forgot the intercom cable again and nearly strangled myself as it pulled tight and jerked off my head. I scooped up the pipe in my left hand and flew back to the door, grabbing the intercom headset as I did.

I stuck the pipe in the partly opened door, trying not to look at the timer on the top of the bomb as it slid passed thirty seconds.

Pushing my weight against the pipe, I forced the door open and pushed the bomb towards it with my foot. For a second it caught, and then with one last push it fell free and tumbled outside the plane.

I hurled myself across the plane, screaming into the headset as I did. "Now!"

Suddenly the nose of the plane went up, and I lost my footing and went tumbling backwards into the plane. As I crashed my head against the bulkhead, I heard the bomb go off outside. The darkness settled over me.

## Chapter 15

Slowly I opened my eyes and looked around. My head hurt and I could see light through a hole in the side of the plane, but I seemed to be alive. Although I wasn't real sure of that when I tried to stand and the deck did a quick dance under my feet. I could hear the faint voice of Joey yelling for me over the intercom headset a few feet away.

Bracing myself, I eased over and picked it up and put it on. "I'm here, Joey. What's going on?" I was wincing against the pain in my head, and I'm sure he could hear it over the mic.

"If you're done blowing holes in the side of the plane, I could use a little help up here. This thing is bucking like a bad horse, and I'm having a little trouble keeping it steady." The plane bounced again to punctuate his comment.

"I'm on my way."

I stumbled my way up front and pushed open the cockpit door. Joey's knuckles were nearly white he was gripping the wheel so hard, and his big ears were turning red from the cold. It was frosty enough I could see my breath. If my head hadn't hurt so much I would have laughed.

I slid into the seat next to him and pulled my goggles back into place. When I took my hand away, it was covered with blood from my forehead.

He took one look at my bleeding head and said, "I thought the bomb went off outside the plane?"

I showed him my teeth, but I'm guessing it was a pretty feeble attempt at a grin. "It did. It was your flying that did this to my head." I took the wheel back and dropped us down to about

500 feet, where it was a little warmer so we didn't freeze to death. It felt a little like trying to fly a tank. I pulled back on the throttles a bit, cutting our speed, and that helped. It lightened up on the wind a bit too.

Suddenly, he was a lot more serious. "Are you okay to fly?" As it warmed up, he stopped shivering and the color started to come back in his ears again.

My grin got better this time. "I have to be if I want to survive the rest of the day. But I need you to do me a favor."

He raised his eyebrows. "Sure. What is it?"

I held up the clamp-on pliers. "Could you put these back on the rudder cable until I can get a real mechanic to take a look at it?"

He started to explain about why the pliers were there, but my grin stopped him and he jerked them out of my hand. "I can re-clamp it, but I can't pull it tight. That needs to be done on the ground."

I nodded. "I'll take whatever I can get."

A few minutes later he was back up front, and he looked almost as scared as he had when he found the bomb. "Looks like you cut it really close."

I was a tough guy now that it was over. "As close as I could and keep my fingers. No sense in hurrying."

He slid into the other seat and wiped icy sweat from his forehead. "Wheeew. I gotta find a safer job!"

*     *     *     *     *

It was a little rough bringing it down onto the tarmac. It kept pulling to the left and didn't want to stay level. It was probably one of the worst landings I've ever made with the wheels still on. But after severely jarring my teeth and making my head hurt even worse, I got it on the ground and slowly taxied over to the hangar. The mechanic took a look at the plane and asked if we'd just flown back from a war someplace. Joey told him we'd been in a meteor shower, and he seemed to believe it, so who was I to deny it.

After that I was a little leery about having him fix the plane, but he was the only mechanic around so I didn't have much choice. And he said he could have it done by tomorrow. So we left him to it and went into the terminal to see if we could rent a car.

A few minutes later, after dragging Joey away from flirting with a cute brunette desk clerk, with keys in hand we headed out for the parking lot.

The dusty, weed-filled lot was empty except for a fifteen-year-old Ford with a crumpled fender and a broken driver's side window. Joey's grin put in an appearance as I walked around the heap checking it out. "You should feel right at home. Looks just like your airplane, right down to the broken window."

I gave him a growl and grabbed the door handle to pull the driver's door open, only it wouldn't move. I threw my weight into it, and it still refused to move. Finally I put my foot against the fender for leverage and stretched. With a groan like the Crypt Keeper's door it gave in and pulled open far enough for me to get in.

Joey was still grinning as he opened the other side. He stuck his head in to take a look around and immediately pulled it right back out.     He looked a little green around the edges as he said, "Oh my god! This car smells like cheese!"

He was right, it did smell like cheese, but it was all we had. I slid into the driver's seat, onto upholstery that was more springs than padding, and reached out to pull the door shut. Of course it refused to move. Giving Joey a pleading look I asked, "A little help here."

Joey walked around the car and put his shoulder into the door. With a groan from the door and one from Joey, he managed to push it most of the way shut before it stuck tight. Looking at me through the six-inch gap he said, "That's as closed as it's gonna get, Boss."

I shrugged my shoulders. "Well at least I can't fall out."

Shaking his head, he walked around and climbed in beside me. He reached for the handle to roll down the window and started complaining again. "There's no winder on this window! I think this whole car's a trap!"

"Right, a trap put here in the middle of this empty lot just in case we ever came to town!" I turned the key and stepped on the starter. For a moment nothing happened, and then at last the engine began to spin. It fired and banged and a cloud of smoke rolled out of the exhaust. I reached out to roll down my window, but just like Joey's, no winder handle. With a sigh I slipped it into gear, let in the clutch, and we jackrabbited out of the lot.

\*    \*    \*    \*    \*

In the dark cellar Kate sat on the floor against the shelves, eating fruit and drinking juice. Twice she'd found beans instead of fruit and had thrown those against the other wall. After all the time she'd spent tied in the chair, her legs felt like lifeless sticks, and she massaged her ankles and calves to get the blood flowing again. She was feeling a little better, and a plan was beginning to form in her mind.

She ran her fingers through her tangled mass of auburn hair and felt the lumps on her skull for damage. It was hard to tell here in the darkness, but nothing seemed to be too drastic. The waiting was going to drive her crazy, but she didn't see any way around it. She needed the element of surprise for her plan to work and pounding on the door, even if they could hear her, wasn't going to give her that. So with her belly fairly full and her energy levels back up to about normal, she made herself comfortable and began her wait.

\*     \*     \*     \*     \*

Sharade walked into his war room and sat down at his desk. Behind him on one wall was the worn and torn battle flag of the Confederacy, and on the other wall were mementos and pictures from the long ago war. It was here that he felt the most comfortable. He was surrounded by the musty smells of yesterday and his beginnings. It felt like he was home again.

Taking out his pipe, he tamped it full of tobacco, lit it with a wooden match, and leaned back in his chair. Time flowed backwards around him, and the wall shimmered and disappeared....

\*     \*     \*     \*     \*

The horse was covered in lather, his long tongue hanging out the side of his mouth and his eyes wide with fear and exhaustion. He needed rest and water, but what he got instead were the colonel's spurs digging deep into the meat of his flanks and pushing him even harder.

With a quick glance back over his shoulder, the colonel could see that none of the other horses or their riders were in any better shape than his. It wouldn't be long before one of them went down.

Then, almost as though by command, the horse carrying Corporal Quinn stumbled and rolled forward, head down, flanks in the air, hurling the rider off into the tall grass where he lay still.

Reluctantly the colonel reined in his own horse, turning to face the oncoming riders. "One of you check on that man. If he is alive, the one with the strongest horse take him aboard and follow." As the others watched, he pulled his pistol from his belt and shot the fallen animal in the head.

One of the men rode off to check on Quinn, and the colonel turned his horse forward again and spurred it to a run. The others quickly followed suit. Off in the distance he could just make out the tree line and what he figured would mean safety. But behind them almost the same distance he could see the dust of the pursuing Union troops.

Colonel Sharade and his men had been on the run now for nearly four days, hardly being able to pause long enough to water the horses or even for the men to urinate. But they were used to that. A soldier often had to pee when he could and where he was. Like their horses, they were nearing the end of their endurance too.

Looking back, maybe robbing that bank hadn't been the best of ideas. But they were short of supplies and even shorter on funds, and they sure as hell weren't going to get any more from the Confederacy. If what they'd heard a while back was true, Lee, that coward, had surrendered to Grant at a place called Appomattox and the war was supposed to be over. Well maybe for them it was, but not for Sharade and his men. When they had signed up they had vowed to fight till the last man, and that was just what they were going to do.

So he and his men had begun a guerilla war against the Yankees, hitting them and running, blowing up bridges to slow their progress, and killing as many as they could when they could. Unfortunately war wasn't cheap in the cost of supplies or in men. His troop of twenty-five was down to twenty. Nineteen if Quinn hadn't survived. He glanced back to see if any of the men were riding double, but with the dust it was hard to tell.

It should have been just a simple robbery. Just a small town bank, most of the men still off in the service. Walk in slow, leave two men outside, grab the money, walk out and ride away. Then that damn clerk had to act like it was his own money and go running after them screaming about the robbery. That brought the Yankee patrol down on them.

Jacobs was the first to go. He'd fallen with a bullet tearing out his belly even before he had gotten to his horse. Dolridge and Morris had made it to their horses, but Yankee bullets had caught them in the back as they rode out of town, leaving the saddle bags of money headed in the wrong direction aboard a riderless horse. Now four days later they were riding nearly dead horses, headed for the swamp and what they perceived as safety.

Sharade heard a noise behind him, but as he turned to look, his own horse buckled beneath him. Suddenly his world slowed to a crawl. His horse dropped forward, both front legs folding under. The colonel threw all his weight to the left and jerked hard on the reins, trying to keep the horse's head up to stop him from summersaulting, and kicked his feet free of the stirrups. The horse went sideways and he leaped clear. After a quick roll he was back on his feet, his revolver tight in his hand.

One of his men reined to a stop and extended his hand to Sharade, offering him a ride. The colonel promptly shot him between the eyes and pulled him off the horse. Seconds later he was in the dead man's place and riding like the wind for the swamp again. The Confederacy had greater need of officers than enlisted men.

*     *     *     *     *

By the time we got to the state police headquarters, I was pretty much nuts. It might have been because the heater in our car was on full blast and wouldn't shut off-. It could have been because of the exhaust rolling up inside the car trying to suffocate us. But mostly I think it was Joey's constant complaining about the windows that wouldn't roll down. I was so crazy by the time I stopped the car that I forced open the door with both feet, walked over to the flagpole with the nice ring of painted rocks around the base, and picked one up. I took the rock and proceeded to break out all the side windows in the car. When I was done, I gave Joey a satisfied look, tossed the rock back and said, "Now you won't have to worry about whether they roll down or not."

Joey tipped his head a bit to the side, nodded and showed me all his teeth in a grin. "Thank you very much. Now I'll be fine as long as I can survive your driving."

Shaking my head, I walked up the steps and into the building. The desk sergeant let us inside his wooden corral and pointed us to an officer at the back of a herd of desks. As we approached he stood up to greet us, and for a second I felt my blood run a bit cold.

Ten years ago we had shot people dressed like him. From his shiny knee-high boots, passed his neatly pressed gray wool jodhpurs and his tunic with its Sam Browne belt across it, to his pencil-thin mustache and his slicked-back hair—if this were Germany he would reek of Gestapo. Instead what we got was a country accent and a warm, dry handshake that he even shared with Joey.

After seeing that we were comfortable, he settled back behind his paper-strewn desk and leaned forward on his elbows. "Now, what can I help you two gentlemen with?" Not waiting for an answer, he shuffled some papers around and picked up a thin manila folder. Laying it on top of the pile he opened it and took out the single piece of paper it contained. "You're here about the accident last night, I take it."

I didn't know whether to answer him or wait for him to do it himself. So I just sat back and watched for the next act to start.

Laying the paper back down on the folder, he reached down and pulled a pack of Luckies and a silver Zippo lighter from his drawer. There was a half worn-off Marine Corp symbol on the lighter. My opinion of him might have crawled up half a notch.

As he lit his cigarette, he seemed to be waiting for something and I took it as my cue to talk. "We were hoping that maybe there was some new information that your patrolman hadn't had last night."

He exhaled a cloud of smoke in my direction and picked up the single sheet of paper from the file again. He carefully studied both sides as though something might suddenly appear, and when it didn't he let it flutter back down to its nest on the desk. The hand with his cigarette was doing some fluttering of its own in the air next to his head. He was holding the butt between his first and second fingers, clear out by the tips, while the rest of his fingers worked the air. It looked a bit like a bird on fire trying to get away. My opinion slipped back to where it was when we first met. He tweaked his mustache with his other hand and flatly said, "No."

I wasn't sure if that meant no news, or no he wasn't going to give it to me. I was about to ask which when we were interrupted by the arrival of the desk sergeant. "Captain?"

Out of habit, I answered the same time he did. "Yes?"

The desk sergeant looked at me, reddened a bit and said, "Beggin' your pardon, sir, I meant Captain Hays."

"No problem." I passed the ball to Hays with an open palm.

"Sir, there's a lady at the desk wantin' to know if the woman in the accident last night is okay."

Joey and I were out of our chairs and scrambling like the Three Stooges at a free buffet when Hays reached out and caught each of us with a hand and pushed by. "Excuse me. This is my office and I'll do the questioning."

So we backed off a couple of inches and followed him up front.

Chapter 16

Even over the sweat of his horse, Sharade could smell the swamp as he neared the trees. The aroma of rotting vegetation and stagnant water was unmistakable. Normally it might have turned his stomach or made him wrinkle his nose, but today it made him smile. It was the smell of freedom.

He leaned in close to the horse's head like a jockey would and jabbed again with his spurs, not that it did any good. This horse had traveled too far and too hard. He was on his last legs and nothing was going to make him go any faster than he was right now. Not far behind he could hear the hoof beats of his men.

Suddenly almost as if from thin air, the first of the trees sprung up around him. The ground grew soft and spongy and his horse faltered. He reined to a stop and leaped from the saddle. Hitting the ground he reached out with his pistol and whacked the horse across its flank, forcing it away and giving it its freedom.

A quick look around located cover, and two steps later he was on his knees behind a fallen cypress tree. He pulled his hat low and cocked his pistol, waiting for the arrival of the Yankee patrol. All around him his own men were seeking cover and readying for a fight. The air was thick and humid, almost like they had stepped off into another world. The dampness was already seeping through the thin material of his uniform pants.

For less than a blink of an eye he let his fatigue surge over him. His eyes drifted shut and he took a deep breath. Then the thunder from the approach of the patrol snapped him back awake.

Their horses were covered in lather and wheezing, but nowhere near as beaten as his had been. Even with the dust and dirt, the uniforms the Yankees were wearing were in far better shape than Sharade's and his men's. They were ragged, mismatched, and filthy. His men looked more like a band of refugees than the last of the Confederacy.

The young lieutenant stopped his troop with a raise of his hand, and sitting high in the saddle peered into the perpetual twilight of the forest. The colonel could see his eyes squinting as he searched for a sign, his horse dancing around with the smell of swamp and danger in his nostrils. Sharade closed his left eye and sighted down the barrel of his pistol, putting his mark on the center of the Yankee's chest, waiting to see what his next move would be.

After what had seemed like forever, the Lieutenant settled back into his saddle, and Sharade drew a breath. The next second would tell whether they would live or die today.

The lieutenant took off his hat and wiped the sweat from his forehead with the cuff of his gauntlet. Then he called into the trees. His voice had that northern twang the colonel had come to hate. "I know you're in there, Johnny Reb, but you're not worth wasting the lives of my men on. Sooner or later you'll have to come out of that swamp, and when you do, the rightful government of this country will be waiting for you!" Then he put his hat back on, signaled to his men, and they rode off the way they had come.

Sharade's finger tightened on the trigger of his pistol, tempted to put a bullet in the Yankee's back. But instead he eased the hammer down. He turned and slid down the side of the tree, landing on his butt in the wet grass. He sat there for a long time, legs splayed, pistol in his lap. Even over the stench of rotting vegetation he could smell his men. The stink of sweat, urine, and feces—the aroma of the Confederate Army. He took out the last of his tobacco and tamped it into the bowl of his badly worn pipe. With the flick of a wooden kitchen match he managed to get it lit, and for a few second the smells of the swamp and his men were gone. With his eyes closed he was sitting on his own front porch once more, one of the darkies cooking dinner and the hands just coming in from the field. For just a second he was free, and then the voice of his major tore into his revelry. "Colonel, the men are asking what are we gonna do now, sir"

Slowly he opened his eyes and stared down his outstretched legs. The major was standing directly in front of him, and without looking up all he could see were the major's boots. The toe of one of the boots was out, and he could see his foot moving around inside. Suddenly it struck Sharade as funny, and he began to laugh.

One by one at the sound of his laughter, the remains of his troop came out of their hiding places and gathered in a semicircle around him. Even though they had no idea what he was laughing about, it was contagious. Soon they were all laughing, slapping each other on the backs and hee-hawing like braying donkeys.

Suddenly he felt sick and stopped laughing. Moments later the rest of the men slowly stopped, still not knowing why they had laughed in the first place. Sharade slowly pulled himself to his feet to face the major.

The major pulled the ever-present stub of a cigar from his mouth and asked again, "What now, sir? Do we ride back out now that the Yankees have gone?"

Sharade scratched his beard and felt his fingers smash something amidst the hair. Damn lice! He reached into his pocket and took out a ragged piece of oil cloth, and kneeling down used the fallen tree for a desk. "According to my calculations, we should be about here." He stabbed a spot on the map with a dirty fingernail, then traced a line across the paper. "If we head due east from here, we should cross through about six or seven miles of swamp. On the other side is a small town called Cypress Glen. We should be able to relax and resupply there."

The major didn't say what he was thinking, but stared back the way they had come. Even without words the colonel caught his thoughts. "I'm afraid that if we go back that way, the Yankees will be waiting, and we're in no shape to take them on in a head-to-head fight. No, the quick trip through this end of the swamp will be best to keep us alive."

Sharade folded the map back into his pocket and took charge of the troop. "I need a couple of you to find us something to eat. Another couple, find fresh water and something to carry it in. When we get into the swamp, there'll be plenty of water, but very little of it fit to drink. And the rest of you gather all the dry wood you can find so that we can have a fire tonight. It might be the last time for a couple of days that we're dry." As the men started to walk away, Sharade called the major back.

"I need you to set one of the men up as a lookout. I wouldn't put it past the Yankees to try and sneak back up on us."

The major looked down at his worn boots, hesitating over what he had to say. Finally he spoke. "There's some talk, sir, about what happened out there. They all saw you shoot Jensen, sir. What do I tell them when they ask?"

Sharade pulled himself up to his full height and straightened his tunic, trying to look once more like a soldier despite the circumstances and the shape of his uniform. "You tell them that the man responsible for their lives decided that it was in their best interests that I survived. It is unfortunate that Jensen had to die to assure that, but those are the fortunes of war. If they have anything further to say on the matter you tell them to come to me, and they can discuss it with the barrel of my .44. I am an officer in the Army of the Confederate States of America! The survival of the Confederacy is my primary and most singular purpose. I would shoot my own mother, God rest her soul, if it were necessary to protect my government!"

\*     \*     \*     \*     \*

When we got up front there was a rather plain-looking woman in a head scarf, long coat, and sturdy shoes waiting nervously for us. From the way she was fidgeting I was guessing she wasn't used to spending much time in the presence of so many policemen.

The captain gave her the same toy-factory molded smile he had used on us. Briefly it brought a smile to her face, but her fear stole it away again.

"Good morning, ma'am. I'm Captain Hays. How may I help you? Would you like a seat?" He motioned her towards the bench along the wall with his hand.

That rich Southern drawl of his didn't seem to help calm her down much. She scuffed her shoes against the floor a bit and kept her eyes pointed down. She shook her head. "No, thank you. I was just wondering about the lady in the accident last night. If she was alright and all. I was coming home, and I was a couple of cars behind when it happened. By the time I got up there, the two men were helping her out of the car."

My heart was pounding like a trip hammer, and all I could do was stop myself from shaking her to get the information she had. With an air of calmness I really didn't feel, I asked her, "Did you see what kind of a car it was, ma'am?"

She shrugged her thin shoulders inside her coat. "My husband pays attention to those kinds of things. I just know what color they are. Why, is there a problem?"

"Oh no, ma'am. We just want to find the two men and thank them for all their help. It seems they didn't leave any information when they left the woman at the hospital. So anything you can tell us about the car would help us find them."

That seemed to reassure her, and the smile sneaked back to her lips, making her look a little less worn. "Oh yes, I understand."

Hays must have been feeling left out, because he decided to play cop again and elbowed me out of the way. "Anything you remember, ma'am, would help us immensely."

She nodded and thought for a moment, and then she said, "I remember it was red on the bottom and white on top."

"Anything else? Maybe something about the men?"

"No, nothing about the men." She shook her head. "It was raining really hard, and they just looked like two very wet men. I couldn't leave my window down for very long. One of them came over after they put her in the car and said she was going to be fine." She hesitated for a moment before she went on. When she did, she wrinkled up her nose. "He smelled like whiskey. And talked with a really thick accent."

"Like a foreigner, ma'am?" I asked.

"No, more like him, only thicker." She pointed at Hays.

"Anything else?"

For the first time Joey spoke, and that deep baritone of his took her a bit by surprise. She smiled and said, "You sound just like that fella on the radio, that Armstrong fella. Are you related?"

Joey shook his head and tried to smile. "No ma'am, we're not." Then he tried to pull her back to the subject. "Anything at all you can remember about the car? A sun visor? Anything?"

Suddenly her face lit up. "It had one of those things my husband likes so well, but I don't understand why. Just seems like a place to catch bugs to me."

"Thing?"

"That shiny strip up over the top."

All the lights just came on. A late-model Ford Crown Victoria in red and white! These boys traveled in style.

Touching her lightly on the shoulder, Hays directed her towards the desk sergeant again. But before he could lead her away, I reached out and clutched her hand. "Ma'am, I want to thank you very much for your help. The lady from the accident is going to be just fine."

She squeezed my hand warmly and gave me a genuine smile. "I'm just glad I could be of help."

I squeezed her hand again before letting her go. "You have been a great deal of help."

As she walked away with the sergeant, I turned to Hays. "Joey and I are going out to the accident site and have a look around to see if we can pick up anything else. But before we do, I'd kind of like to take a look at the car."

Hays nodded. "It's parked out back in our impound yard. Just follow the sidewalk around the building and tell the officer at the gate I said it was okay."

I started out the door after Joey, but he called me back. "Steele?"

"Yeah?" I asked.

The nice was gone out of his voice, and the tough cop was showing through. "Remember, this is still a police operation, and if you find anything I want to know about it. I don't want you taking the law into your own hands. Understand?"

I tossed him a half salute and a smile I wasn't feeling. "You betcha, Captain." I pushed through the door before he could say any more.

Joey was waiting for me on the sidewalk. He gave me that knowing look of his and asked, "He give you the talk?"

I nodded and squinted one eye. "And I promised him that if we found anything we'd be sure and let him know." I started around the corner of the building, expecting Joey to follow. After a couple of steps I realized I was all alone. I stopped and turned around. He was still standing where I left him. "What?" I asked.

He looked down at the walk, then looked back up. The grin he had been wearing a minute ago was gone. He scratched his chin and shuffled around a bit before he spoke again. "You sure you want to do this?"

I shrugged my shoulders. "I don't see how I can't. I need to know how bad she was hurt, and this looks like the only way."

"It could also scare the hell out of you!"

"That's a chance I have to take."

It was only a few short steps from the corner of the building to the gate of the impound yard. I could see the car from the gate, and it made me stop dead still.

I know Joey must have told the cop at the gate who we were, but I don't think I heard a word of what they said. I remember the gate sliding open, and I walked in like a zombie. I hadn't realized just how bad it had been.

Both front fenders had been mashed back into the tires, and the hood was gaping open. A puddle of fluid was slowly running away from under the engine like blood from an open wound.

The corner of the top on the driver's side had been pushed down to where it was nearly touching the fender. All the glass that had been left from the rock attack was gone. The driver's door hung agape and weirdly askew from the force it had taken to   open it amidst the twisted metal. I grabbed it with both hands and pulled it open the rest of the way so I could see the interior.

The inside was pretty much a reflection of the outside. The steering wheel was bent into a lopsided oval where she must have collided with it, and it was a good six or eight inches further back into the passenger compartment than Chrysler had ever designed it to be. There was a Kate-size dent in the dash, and traces of red ran down towards the floor. The rear seat had come loose like they do in rollovers and was wedged between the seat back and the roof. I reached in and gently touched the dash where her head had hit, almost like I could feel her there.

On the other side of the car, the glove box hung open and empty. I looked under the seat and behind it. No sign of the .45.

Joey had come up behind me while I was looking. "They were probably already armed."

"Well if they weren't, they are now." I kicked the door shut with my foot and turned away from the twisted hulk. "Come on, I think I saw a hardware store down the street. They should have what I need."

"What do you need a hardware store for?" he asked.

"Gonna buy new windows for the car!"

*　　*　　*　　*　　*

The bell over the door announced our arrival, and the old codger in the green apron looked up from behind his cash register. He was bald, and his teeth were long gone. For a second I wondered which brush he threw out first. "Can I help you boys?"

"I sure hope so." I pulled open my jacket and showed him the empty holster under my arm.

He gave me a knowing look and pointed us to a glass counter in the back of the store. Behind it on the wall were a couple of shotguns and a Winchester, like Gary Cooper won the West with. Or at least he did on film.

The old guy took his keys, unlocked the doors, and pulled out a couple of guns and laid them carefully on a cloth he had stretched out on the counter. One was a .38 Police Positive with the long barrel, and the other was .32 automatic—a lady's gun.

I looked at both of them and shook my head. "I was kind of hopin' for something with a little more stopping power."

He nodded like he knew what I meant and reached down under the counter again. This time he pulled out a foot-by-foot wooden box with *US Army* stamped on it in big, black letters. Before he opened it, he looked both ways like he thought somebody might be looking. When he was sure it was safe he lifted the top off the box.

Nestled inside the box in a bed of excelsior was a brand-new, still covered in Cosmoline, 1911 Army Colt .45 automatic! He handed me a rag and I reached into the box, lifted it out, and began wiping it clean.

"Issued that to me back in the war. Didn't even have a chance to clean it up before they signed the armistice. So I just packed it up with the rest of my stuff and brought it home with me. Been sitting in that box waiting for the right guy to come along. Looks to me like you might be him."

I popped the empty clip out and laid it on the rag, and then began disassembling the rest. "Got a gun cleaning kit, Pops?"

He reached around behind him and picked up a tin box with guns painted on the lid and handed it to me. Within a couple of minutes I had it cleaned and reassembled. It felt almost as good in my hand as the one I had sent with Kate. I set it gently back on the counter. "I need two boxes of cartridges. One of steel-jacketed slugs and one of hollow points."

He took two boxes off the shelf behind and set them next to the gun. I opened the hollow points and filled the clip. "I hope these aren't as old as the gun."

Toothless cackled at me. "Nah, I got a couple of customers that use these in their rifles. That keeps them pretty well used up."

I slammed the clip home and slid it into the holster. When I pulled my hand back out of my jacket, my wallet was in it. I took out my pilot's license and my permit to carry. He pushed them back across the counter at me. "Don't need none of that stuff. I trust you. Besides, that gun really doesn't exist anymore. The Army recorded it as destroyed right after the war, melted down for scrap."

So I picked them up and pushed two one hundred-dollar bills across the counter. He greedily picked them up and tucked them in his shirt pocket.

As I turned to go, he said, "I sure wouldn't want to be the guy you're lookin' fer. Got a feelin' when you find him he ain't gonna be breathin' long."

I showed him my teeth, but there wasn't any humor in my smile. "Count on it, Pops!"

* * * * *

The colonel was miserable. From the waist down he was soaked from slogging through the brackish water. His boots were full of water mixed with grains of sand. Every step was agony, but the alternative of crossing this swamp without his boots sent chills up his spine. Most of his men had chosen to go without, and the few times he had seen their feet lately they were like hunks of raw meat. The skin on his hands was peeling away in great chunks from the constant exposure to the water.

It had been days since they last saw dry land. The best they could do was to possibly climb out onto the knees of a cypress tree, or possibly one of the small, grassy hummocks.

The sun and the bugs were a relentless team, one burning their skin red and the other feasting on the roasted flesh. Fortunately he had kept his hat, and what little help it gave stopped the sun from burning his brain to a dried-out crust. The faces of the men without hats were twisted in the agony of approaching madness.

What should have been only a two-day trek, according to the map, had become endless days of burning sun and nights filled with fog and predators in search of a meal. The only explanation could be that since his map was drawn the tide had risen, pushing more water into the swamp and changing the landscape. Now the only question was if they would survive long enough to reach the other side.

Colonel Sharade rolled his swollen tongue around behind his teeth, looking for even the tiniest drop of moisture to lessen his thirst. Water supplies had run out days ago. Some of the men had tried drinking the green, slime-filled muck that passed for water only to heave up what little remained in their guts.

Hope was gone. The buoyancy of their spirits that came after they escaped the Yankees had faded like the fog in the morning sun. Command was becoming harder. The encroaching madness of the men made it hard to make them listen. But he knew that he was their only chance. Without him they would wander here in this piece of hell until they fell of either starvation, thirst, or as the prey of one of the denizens of the swamp.

Behind him he heard one of the men scream and, before he could turn, the sound of a hammer falling on wet powder. As he slogged back to his men, one of them, Cyrus he thought, was screaming and crying, clutching his leg in the thigh-deep water.

"What happened?" he asked, though he was almost sure of the answer.

"Snake bit him as he was walkin'."

He grabbed the crying soldier by the shoulder and shook him, trying to quell his sudden panic. "Where, boy? Where did he bite you?"

The boy Cyrus, the colonel was sure of it now, calmed down. His breath was still coming in great gulps like a drowning man's, but at least between breaths he could speak. "Feels like just above my ankle, sir."

Quick action was the only chance they had of saving him, but even then Sharade wondered if it was worth the effort. "A couple of you men pick him up and carry him over to that cypress and get him out of the water. Keep that bit leg down to stop the poison from rising too fast."

Three of his men grabbed Cyrus and carried him over to where the roots of the tree were above water and laid him across it. The colonel followed. Pushing them out of the way, he took his belt off his holster and tied it above the wound, pulling it tight. He held out his hand palm up and asked, "Who's got a knife?"

One of the men laid an oversized hunting knife named for some frontiersman in his hand. He used the tip to put two crosses over the wounds. Then he bent close, putting his lips to the first fang mark, and sucked the poison out. Twice more he worked the first wound until the blood ran red and thick, spitting out the venom each time. Then he did the same to the other one. After spitting the last time he loosened his belt and laid his hand on the scared boy's shoulder. "I think you'll be alright now, son."

He turned and half swam, half walked over to another stump and climbed up onto the perch to get out of the water. Then he pulled off his boots and flushed the sand out of them.

While he was dipping his left and pouring the water out, the major came over. He stood in front of him and saluted.

"We're pretty much out of protocol around here, Major. What was that salute for?"

"For saving that boy's life, sir."

Sharade wiggled his toes before slipping his boot back on. Oddly, he thought that he was going to have to get new socks when this was over. Leaning down close so only the major could hear him, he said, "The boy's gonna die, Major. Not from the venom, but he's gonna die. He had an open wound below the water level. The first time he steps off that tree, it's gonna get infected. He'll be dead within four days."

The major looked at him astounded. "Then why did you go to all the trouble to try and save him?"

Sharade's yellow teeth showed through his scraggly beard. "Because the men believe in me. And if we're gonna get out of here, I need them to follow me. And now that they believe I care about what happens to them, they will. Now find yourself a stump and get up out of the water for a rest. I want to try and get a little further before the night comes."

\*     \*     \*     \*     \*

There wasn't much to see at the site of the wreck. Just a lot of torn-up ground, tire tracks, and footprints from the police.

I got out of the car and walked back to the skid marks on the highway and starting walking slowly forward, reliving the crash in my mind. I heard her slam on the brakes, felt the wheel tear from her hands as the DeSoto started its sideways skid. I could see her fighting to regain control. Then suddenly it began to roll, and the car became a 3,500-pound hulking coffin, traveling at sixty miles per hour, Kate rolling around inside it like a ball bearing inside a tin can. Hopefully after the first rotation she went unconscious and her body limp, rolling with the gravity and saving her the pain.

I closed my eyes and rubbed my temple with my fingers. It helped the vision to fade, but Kate's imagined screams were still there. When I opened my eyes, Joey was staring at me.

"You all right?"

I shrugged one shoulder and tossed my head a bit. "I guess. I was just thinking about what happened."

Suddenly the flat of his hand hit me in the chest. "Damn it Rick, that's not gonna do either one of you any good. Yes there was an accident, and yes she probably got hurt, but she also got taken hostage! So wrap your head around that. None of the rest of this is gonna matter if we don't find her and get her back!"

I smiled a thin, sad smile. As usual, he was right. There'd be plenty of time for self-pity after I found her. But I had to find her first. Then suddenly like a light coming on I got an idea, and the corners of my mouth turned up a bit further.

Joey narrowed his eyes. "You've got an idea, don't ya?"

I let my smile widen into a grin as I nodded my head. "Yep. I do." I turned all the way around, studying the country. "That Ford of theirs is going to stick out like a sore thumb in this country. And if they thought somebody could identify them, they wouldn't want to go any further than they had to. So I'm betting they're holed up somewhere fairly close. So what say you and I go for a drive in the country and see what we can see?"

Chapter 17

We'd been driving around the countryside for a couple of hours, and so far we hadn't seen anything more than cornfields and tobacco. And between the heater that wouldn't shut off, the sun beating through the windshield, and the cheesy smell of the car, I was about three minutes away from losing the breakfast I wished I'd had this morning.

I'd thought that having Joey drive might shut him up for a while, but he was in a chatty mood, and nothing I could do or say would shut him up. He complained about the car, the road, the fact that he was hungry. Anything he could think about came out of his mouth. After a while I just tried to tune him out, but it was like the buzz from a beehive.

I had my hands crossed on the sill of the window with my head resting on top. When I talked it made my head bob up and down like one of those kid's toys. It didn't help my stomach, but I was just too discouraged to move. "You know, I think you talk more than Thelma!"

Then suddenly I sat straight up in the seat. "Stop the car!" Then I changed my mind. "Don't stop the car, but slow down!" On my side about fifty yards off the road, in a tumbledown shed so old the wood had turned grey like an old man, the rear taillights of a brand-new red Ford were sticking out.

Joey's voice was barely a whisper as he asked, "Is that it?"

Not really wanting to take my eyes off it as we went by, I turned and gave him a look of disbelief. "How many brand-new red Fords do you figure are in a county like this?"

His eyeballs rolled off into the corners of his eyes and his face scrunched up like he was figuring, but I didn't give him a chance to answer. I waved my index finger at him. "You say anything but one, and I'm gonna black your eye!"

It was his turn for a look of disbelief. He held up his index finger and pointed it to his cheek. "Maybe you didn't notice, Boss. My skin's already black!"

"Well, actually more of a brown, but you know what I mean!" I can't begin to explain the weight that it felt like had been lifted off my shoulders. No she wasn't free yet, and no I still couldn't be sure that she was still alive, but for the first time since I watched her leave in the DeSoto, there was a chance!

I waved Joey on down the road away from the farm. "Take the first right you come to, drive up a ways, and stop. That should put us parallel with the house."

Joey nodded and looked over at me. "I take it you have a plan?"

"Sort of, and this cornfield is gonna be a big part of it."

Joey pulled the car up alongside the road and we climbed out. "So just what is your plan, if I might ask?"

I pulled out the .45 and checked the clip as I walked toward the corn. "We're gonna use this corn as cover and sneak up to the house on foot."

"Seems like a lot of people are using cornfields for cover these days." He rubbed the pale bandage on his forehead.

"Yeah, but we're not using rocks!"

\*     \*     \*     \*     \*

It was all I could do not to run through the corn. The long leaves kept reaching out and grabbing at my clothes, and occasionally taking a bite out of the back of my hand or my cheek, but I was totally oblivious. My gut was telling me that it was only a short while before Kate was in my arms again, and I wasn't going to let anything get in my way.

A couple of rows over I could hear Joey cussing the corn and me. It was a little tougher on him. With those broad shoulders of his it made a lot tighter squeeze in the rows. And being taller he had to spend most of his time bent double, while all I had to do was duck a bit to keep my head down.

Up ahead I could see the rows begin to change direction, and if I remembered what I knew about cornfields from the few times I went pheasant hunting, that meant that we were nearing the edge of the field.

I hissed at Joey and the cursing stopped. I dropped down to my hands and knees and began crawling toward the edge of the field. Joey followed my lead. I held up my finger to my lips for silence, and he nodded. Slowly we began to inch forward, trying not to disturb the corn as we moved. Above us a slight breeze rustled the leaves, helping to keep us covered.

As I inched forward, hardly moving at all between the stalks of corn, I disturbed a rabbit. He took off like a shot and nearly made me pee my pants. I could hear Joey snickering, and I hissed at him to shut up.

On my elbows, like back in boot camp, I pulled myself forward till only one row of corn stood between me and the yard.

The house wasn't in much better shape than the shed. It had the same grey color. The open porch across the front had given way on one corner and leaned dangerously. Through the grime-covered windows I could see the faint glow of a light, and from somewhere inside there came the sound of a radio playing. The grass around the house and the shed was more than a few weeks overdue for a cutting, but not tall enough to hide in.

I motioned for Joey to follow me and I crawled back into the corn. When I was sure we were safe, I stopped and turned to face him.

"Looks pretty dead, Boss."

I nodded. "If the lady was right, there are only two of them. And with the car here, I'm guessing both of them are too." I crawled forward a bit to where I could see again, studying the situation. When I crawled back to Joey, I was grinning.

"Gonna need a distraction, and I've got the perfect one."

Even before I could go on his face wrinkled up in pain. "You're gonna do somethin' bad to the Ford, aren't you?"

I nodded, still grinning. "You betcha! I'm gonna make my way over to the shed and set their car on fire. You stay here and watch the house. When they come running out, we'll pick them off! If anything happens before I get the fire started, don't hesitate to shoot. Remember, they have at least my .45 and probably more."

Joey rolled over onto his side and pulled his old Colt from his belt. After spinning the cylinder, he pulled out a box of shells and sat them beside him.

I shook my head. "You expecting an army? Or has your aim gotten that bad?"

He showed me all his teeth in a grin. "That's just in case."

"Remember, don't underestimate these guys. They had a hand in trying to kill us at least twice, and whatever they've done to Kate."

We clutched hands, and I made my way back far enough that I thought I couldn't be seen from the house before I climbed back to my feet. Staying in a tight crouch, I took off through the corn again. This time I moved just as fast as I could. I didn't want to waste any time.

When I got to where I figured I was behind the shed, I dropped back to my knees and crawled to the front of the corn. Then I lay there and waited for my breath to catch up with me.

As I looked out, I could see the dark patch that was Joey. He flashed me the okay sign.

I lay there on the ground smelling the dirt and listening to the rustle over my head. There was about eight feet of open space between me and the entrance to the shed. The minute I moved, I was going to be a wide-open perfect target.

I considered my options. I could wait for dark, but by then who knows what could happen to Kate. Or they might suddenly decide to leave.

While I lay there trying to make up my tiny little mind, I watched an ant climb up onto my hand. I blew him off, but another quickly took his place. I repeated the measure, but another ant came right back. I kept blowing them off and they just kept coming back.

That pretty much made up my mind. If they could be relentless against something as big as me, I could chance an eight-foot run through open ground. Besides, I was starting to itch from the anthill I was lying on.

I grabbed a quick look around and a deep breath, and I shot out of the corn like a rocket. I was going so fast that even if they had looked, I doubt they could have seen me. All there would have been was a streak! I flashed around the doorway to the shed and dropped down onto the dirt floor beside the Ford.

As I caught my breath I heard the screen door slam, and I wiggled myself around to where I could see the house. A short man in a dirty tee shirt and without any shoes was standing on the front porch holding my .45.

From inside the house a gruff voice with a deep Southern accent hollered at him. "What the hell are you doin'?"

He called back over his shoulder through the screen. I thought I saw something out here."

The second man came to the door and pushed the screen partway open. "There ain't nobody out there. Hell, there hasn't been but one car in the last two days, and that was some old farmer's beat-up heap."

He shook his head. "I'm tellin' ya, Major, I seen somethin'."

"Something from that damn 'shine you're always drinkin's what it is. Now get back in here and play cards. The colonel should be calling soon to tell us what to do with the girl."

Reluctantly he took one last look around and finally went back inside.

My mind was awhirl with sudden facts. Kate was still alive! And their boss was somebody called "the colonel." With the back of my hand I wiped the sweat from my forehead. Careful to stay out of the way of the door, I climbed to my feet for a look around.

Sometime in the past it must have been used for a machine shed. Scattered all around were bits and pieces of rusted metal that I had no idea what their purpose had once been. Nothing I could really use for what I was about to do. Then in the far corner I found just what I needed. Piled amongst the debris was a stack of old, rotting gunnysacks.

Sitting down on the floor next to the pile, I took one from the top and began to tear it in long, thin strips. When I had half a dozen, I picked them up and crawled back to the rear of the car.

After checking to make sure that nobody was watching, I rolled under the car and pulled myself over to where my head and arms were under the back bumper. I reached up and pulled the license plate down and unscrewed the gas cap. Then, after sticking a rock under the plate to stop it from snapping shut, I began to feed the burlap strips down the fill pipe and into the gas tank. As I did, I crossed my fingers that they had at least half a tank.

A couple of minutes later, I was rewarded as the first drops of gasoline dripped off my improvised fuse. I started to climb out from under the car, but another quick idea grabbed me and I stopped. I felt across the tank until I found the fuel line, then I took my foot and kicked it till it broke free of the tank and gas started to spill out onto the ground.

I climbed out from under the car and rolled a couple more strips of burlap in the puddle under the car and strung them out toward the back with the other fuse.

Now came the tricky part. I had to light the fuses without being seen, make sure they were burning, and still have enough time to get out of here before the whole thing went up.

I crept out of the shed on my belly and around to the back of the car. Everything at the house was quiet. So far, so good. I popped a kitchen match with my thumb, shielding it against the breeze until it was thoroughly afire and touched it to the burlap hanging from the tank. As the first yellow fingers of fire licked down the burlap, I lit the other fuse. Then I climbed to my feet and without even thinking of cover took off at a run for the cornfield.

As I hit the third or fourth row, I heard the whoosh from the puddle of gas catching fire, and seconds later I was flying thru the field, with parts of the shed chasing me, as the gas tank caught and the whole thing exploded.

I quickly pulled myself out of the dirt, and with gun in hand I turned and sighted on the front door of the house. I was just in time to see the shoeless man come running down off the porch and into the yard. He had what looked like my .45 clutched in his right hand. As I watched, I stood there holding my breath and hoping Joey would wait before firing. He did, and seconds later the other man came running out.

I sighted down the barrel of my pistol and squeezed the trigger. The bullet went wide, catching him in the shoulder and spinning him like a top. But before he could start to fall, I adjusted my aim and pulled the trigger a second time. I watched him bounce back, and the second shot hit the mark.

While I was bringing him down, Joey had done a little better and dropped the first man with one shot. I drew a bead on the front door, and stood silently waiting and listening for any sign of movement. There was only the roar of the blaze and the soft rustle of the corn.

*     *     *     *     *

The rumble and the shock of the explosion shook the cellar and roused Kate from her stupor. Slowly she opened her eyes, but that was no help. The darkness was too complete. Death himself could have been sitting just a few feet away, and she wouldn't have known it till his talons raked the life from her soul.

'Course, his eyes had best be better than hers, or he'd never find her. Death crawling around on his hands and knees while she stood right beside him. That thought made her giggle like a school girl. *I'm starting to lose it*, she thought. She shook her head, but that only made it hurt, and when she rubbed her temples she got the sticky from her fingers all over her face. No matter how you looked at it, it was a lose/lose situation.

Gently she eased herself to her feet and staggered the few short steps to the door. With her ear pressed to the door, she could hear some kind of commotion above in the yard. It sounded like shots, but she wasn't sure.

Kate pounded on the door, but with no more strength than she had it was little more than a soft thump. She tried yelling, but her voice was so hoarse that even she could barely hear it. She slumped down to the floor beside the door, tears streaming down her face. It just might be her only chance for a rescue, and nobody would ever find her.

In her despair, her mind and the darkness began to play tricks on Kate.

Gradually the room began to lighten, and across from her she could see her father in his white lab coat working at his bench, his glasses pushed up on his forehead, and surrounded by bits and pieces of electronics. "Daddy?"

At the sound of her voice, her father turned. His face was young, a just slightly older version of her own, the way he looked right after her mother was killed. He beamed a smile at her, but she could still see the sadness in his eyes. "Just get home from school, Kitten?"

She shook her head. "No, Dad. I'm all grown up. And I'm trapped in a cellar."

Professor Gallagher laid down the tool he was using and walked over and sat down beside her. He seemed visibly older now, more the age he was when she last saw him. The sadness of loss was gone from his eyes, and there was a new sparkle of adventure. Rick had done that for both of them.

"Trapped, huh? Well, I'd just bet then that Rick is moving heaven and earth to find you. He's probably on his way to save you right now."

A tear raced down her cheek. "I don't think so, Dad. He might be in too big of trouble himself."

He reached out with a calloused hand and patted her gently on the knee. "Well, honey, then you just might have to save yourself. You're more than capable of that, you know."

Kate seemed to draw new strength from his smile and the touch of his hand. For the first time since they dragged her down here, she felt powerful enough to help herself.

The Professor rose to his feet with a groan of old bones and offered her his hand to help her up. "Probably should get ready now, Kate. Somebody's coming, and you should be ready just in case it isn't Rick."

His hand was warm in hers as she pulled herself to her feet. Then she reached behind her and took the heaviest jar she could find off the shelf. She might lose this battle, but she was going down fighting.

When she turned back around the cellar was empty and dark again. Her father, if he had ever been there, was gone.

She pressed herself to the edge of the door, the heavy jar like a club in her hand.

Suddenly, like a white-hot explosion of fire, the door opened, flooding the cellar with light. A shadow stood in the door, and blindly she struck out, feeling the jar collide with flesh. Through slitted eyelids she watched as it tumbled to the floor.

Giant hands seized her from behind, and she began to kick and struggle. A weak scream escaped from her throat!

\*　　\*　　\*　　\*　　\*

I lay there in the dirt peeking out of the corn, the sights of my .45 pointed at the door. Well, actually they were pointed to just the left of the door to compensate for me not having time to set them after I bought the gun. I'd gotten lucky. Any other time it could have gotten me killed.

Yeah, all those dumb thoughts were running through my head as I counted time and watched the house for movement, hoping maybe that somebody else wanted to stick their head out and let me add another hole to it for them.

When I figured it had been long enough, I stood up and waved Joey in. He shot out of the corn and plastered himself against the worn siding at the corner of the house to watch the door. Then it was my turn.

My heart pounding and my face scrunched up in anticipation of feeling a bullet tear through me, I ran as fast as I could, zigzagging my way across the yard and up onto the porch. Once there, I pressed myself against the side of the door and turned to bring Joey the rest of the way in. He was sitting on the edge of the broken-down porch, laughing. Between gasps for breath he asked, "Just what the hell was that?"

Through clenched teeth I hissed, "That was me trying to keep from getting shot! Now get up here—Kate might be inside!" That sobered him back up, and he came across the porch to stand beside me.

"Now what?" he asked.

"I go in low, and you go in high, and we take out whatever baddies are still waiting for us."

I eased open the screen door and he crashed into the room, expecting trouble. But there was only silence.

We were standing in a living room filled with worn furniture that smelled of cigar smoke, and the table had been pulled out of the kitchen, a deck of cards strewn on the top.

Straightening up, I motioned him towards the kitchen, and I worked my way back to the lone bedroom. I was just about to ease the door open when he called me. His voice had an urgency in it. "Rick, you better come out here."

When I got to the kitchen, he was standing with the curtain pulled back from the pantry. I could see two pairs of feet sticking out. One glance was all I needed to know they were dead, and it didn't look like death had been quick or pleasant. I felt less bad all the time about shooting the two in the yard. "It must be the farmer and his wife."

Joey nodded solemnly. "Probably took them by surprise after they picked up Kate."

I felt sick to my stomach as I turned away from the pantry. But as I did, I caught a glance out the back window, and my hopes shot up again. There was a beaten down path of grass leading from the back door to a storm cellar. I took off at a run, calling back over my shoulder as I crashed out the back door. "I know where she is!"

I was nearly to the door on the storm cellar when one of those giant hands plucked me right off the ground and into the air. "Hold it, Rick! This could be a trap."

Floating there in the air in his grip, I looked at him in disbelief. "Come on, Joey. You've seen these guys. They may be evil, but when it comes to smarts… they're not the Red Chinese."

He shook his head and me with it. "They may be thugs, Rick, but they've been damn smart about what they're doing. And they've managed to stay ahead of us at every step. So be careful!"

He was right. I let my own enthusiasm for rescuing Kate get the best of me, and I forgot my smarts.

I knelt down by the door and ran my hands carefully around the outside edge, looking for any sign of a wire or a booby trap. Finding nothing, I looked up at Joey and he shrugged. So, very slowly I lifted the door, watching all the time for any signs of tampering. I didn't find it until I had the door all the way open and flopped back. Even then I almost missed it.

A hair-thin wire ran along the second step. On either side of it were what looked like two WWI hand grenades with the wire tied to the pins. If I had gone charging down the steps, my ankle would have hit the wire, pulling both pins and blowing me and whoever was with me into little tiny pieces.

Carefully, I used my knife and sliced away the twine that bound the one grenade to the step. I rolled the wire up around it, and then cut the other side loose and tossed them off into the yard. Looking at Joey, I smiled. "Guess you stopped me from making one hell of a noisy entrance."

He grinned and said, "That's what you pay me for, Boss."

The inner door of the shed had a two-by-four across it, Fort Apache style, locking the door. "Now who locks a storm cellar on the outside? Trying to keep the fruit jars from escaping?"

I lifted the board and stepped into the darkness. Suddenly the back of my head exploded and I slumped to the floor.

## Chapter 18

As the stars faded from behind my eyes, I opened one to see if I was still where I'd been before somebody decided to reshape the back of my head. I was. I was on my knees in the dirt of the cellar floor. Gingerly I reached up and felt the back of my head, almost afraid of what I might find. My hand came away wet and sticky, but it wasn't blood. It smelled like pickle juice. Somebody had hit me in the back of the head with a jar of pickles. Dill, from the taste of it.

A second later when I got the other eye opened, I became aware of all the commotion going on behind me. There was lots of hissing and screaming, and I wondered where Joey had gotten a cat to fight with. But when I turned around I could see it was Kate. Or at least I thought it was Kate. Her normally perfect auburn hair was frizzed out like a clown's, and it was clotted with blood and what looked like small bits of fruit. She was minus her shoes and most of her skirt. Joey had her around the waist, holding her up off the floor, and she was tearing at his face with her nails and kicking him in the shins with her bare feet.

I reached out and grabbed one of her arms. Then in my most commanding voice I said, "Kate, stop."

In mid-swing her other arm stopped, frozen in space. Slowly she turned toward me, and for a moment the madness in her eyes cleared. There was relief there as she softly said, "Rick?" Then she collapsed in Joey's arms like broken doll.

I felt for her pulse, and even with her unconscious it was racing. "We need to get her to a doctor right away. And we can't get caught here." Outside I could hear the sounds of a siren drawing closer. One of the neighbors must have seen the smoke and called the fire department. "Can you carry her?"

He nodded and scooped her up in his arms like a baby. "What about you? She hit you awfully hard with that jar."

I ran my hand over the back of my head again, and accidentally got some pickle juice in it from my hair and winced with pain. "I'll be alright. Just get her to the car."

Without another word he nodded and headed up the steps. I hung back and looked around the cellar, trying to imagine what she had gone through, and how she must have thought that when we didn't come, we'd abandoned her. Looking around down here now made me glad we'd shot those two. It saved me from having to do it all again, which reminded me of something I had to do before I followed Joey into the corn.

I ran up the steps and around the corner of the house into the front yard, and I turned to stone. I'd come back out here to pick up my .45 from the guy who had it, but he was gone and so was his partner. The grass was still matted where they had lain, but they were gone. I didn't have much time to think about what could have happened, since I could see the fire truck getting closer. So I followed Joey's lead and took off into the corn.

\*     \*     \*     \*     \*

Joey had Kate loaded in the backseat and already had the car turned around by the time I got there. I slid into the backseat to hold her. I gently brushed her matted hair from her face and picked out some of the twigs and fruit imbedded in it and tossed them to the floor. I felt an ache as I looked into her bruised and battered face. There was a big purple spot on her forehead where she must have hit the wheel.

Her blue eyes were moving behind her fluttering lids in half-consciousness, and her arms flailed a bit but nothing like before. I tried to hold her down without doing any more damage to her arms or legs. The marks from the ropes and the cuts from her getting free were deep crimson, like a side of fresh-cut meat. I could feel the anger growing inside me again. "Joey, the bodies were gone!"

He slammed on the brakes, nearly throwing us out of the seat. "What?"

"They were gone. I went back around front to get my .45, and they were gone."

For the longest time he just sat there staring at me over the seat. Then he turned back around and let the clutch out, and we started back down the road. "I'm goin' home, Boss. I don't want any part of dead men that get up and walk away."

"I know, Joey, I know," I said softly.

I glanced out the window, and we were going past the farm. The firemen had the fire out and were rolling up their hoses. There was little left of the shed but a pile of smoldering ashes with the blackened hulk of the Ford sitting in the middle of it.

By the time we'd gotten a couple of miles down the highway a patrol car went screaming by, headed for where we'd come from, his lights and siren going. Joey caught my eye in the mirror and said, "Looks like they found the bodies."

I nodded. "Knew they would sooner or later."

"At least they'll get a decent funeral now." What he didn't know was that I suspected they had been shot with my gun. And that made it as personal as what they had done to Kate. The score against them just kept getting bigger all the time.

Kate whimpered in my lap, and I brushed her cheek gently with my finger to try and calm her. She wasn't struggling as much now, but I didn't know if that was good or not.

Joey glanced back at the sound and asked, "Is she going to be alright, Boss?"

"I wish I knew, Joey." Times like this I usually relied on either her or Thelma to tell me how bad things were, and now I had neither.

I sat there in the backseat of the car, looking at all the trauma that was evident on her face, feeling the pain tear at my guts. Without so much as a second thought I had sent her into danger, and this was the result! The beautiful, vibrant woman that I loved, the woman whose smile would brighten a room, was lying in my arms battered, beaten, and maybe dying.

I could stomp my feet and rage at the men that did this, but in the end it was really me that was to blame. Me, the big tough cookie who carries a gun and swaggers around like John Wayne. Me, the one who sends helpless women into danger.

Kate whimpered again, and I looked down and saw her eyes slowly flutter open. This time the madness was gone. Softly she said, "It's not your fault, Rick," and she tried to smile with her swollen lips. Moments later her eyes slid shut again, but there was no more struggling. Now she was simply sleeping. All the damage was still there, but for the first time since we had taken her out of the cellar, there was calmness.

I felt a smile of my own break across my face. "She's gonna be okay, Joey! She's gonna be okay."

\*     \*     \*     \*     \*

When we got to the hospital Joey went to get help. He came back with two attendants and a nurse. They loaded Kate up on a gurney and covered her with a sheet. She looked so pale and helpless as they wheeled her inside, and I felt that old fear come back.

I followed a few feet behind, but at the double doors marked *EMERGENCY WARD* one of the attendants stopped me. "Far as you go, Bub. It's authorized personnel from here on."

He was bigger than me and could probably pound me into paste, but I was willing to chance it. "Well, I'm giving myself the authorization! Now get out of my way."

His hand came up to push me away, and I balled up my fists and was ready to go town on him when one of Joey's big, brown hands reached out and stopped me.

"That won't help anything, Rick. Rules are rules. Besides, I think there are probably papers for you to fill out."

The attendant nodded and pointed to the waiting room. "Just take a seat in there, and we'll find you when we know anything."

I wasn't happy, but I did what they said. I went over to the desk where a hawk-nosed nurse with a bun under her winged cap was sitting.

After I gave her all the information I had, I went into the waiting room and fell into a chair next to Joey. He was having a bit of a tough time himself. The rest of the waiting room was filled with white faces, and they were busy giving him the "What the hell are you doing here?" look.

There was a coffee machine across the room. I fumbled in my pocket for change. Raising my eyebrows in question I asked, "You want coffee?"

He nodded. "Sure would, but I think they might object if I went and got it." He nodded his head in the direction of the farmers on the other side of the room.

If I hadn't been so tired, I'd have done a Bojangles and *Amos 'n' Andy* walk to the machine. Instead I just shook my head and pushed my way through the other people without a word. I dropped my nickels in and came back with two cardboard cups filled with steaming, black goo.

After giving Joey his, I settled back into the chair and gently sipped at the stuff in the cup. It tasted pretty much like it looked—like thin tar. But it gave me something to do with my hands.

As I stared into that circle of darkness, I thought about Kate. Her hitting me in the back of the head with the pickle jar was nothing new. As a matter of fact, the first time I met her she had knocked me out. I woke up tied to a chair in her father's apartment with my own gun pointed at me.

I'd never know a woman quite like her before. Oh, there had been plenty of women; I was a pilot after all. But nobody like her. She was smart, beautiful, and could be as tough or even tougher than I. And she was, most of the time. Yet she knew when to back off and let it look like I was running the show. She saved my life a couple of times, and more than once I returned the favor.

And I think I fell in love with her the first time I saw her. It was all the little things that made Kate Kate—her stomping her foot when she got mad, her smile lighting up the room as she came in, and her biting sense of humor.

Suddenly a shadow fell across me, dragging me back from my revelry. The first thing I saw was a pair of worn work boots standing in front of me. I started to work my way up past the dungarees so old and worn that they were more white than blue, to the flannel work shirt hanging half out of the pants, and the grizzled face, unshaven and lined with too many days out in the weather. "Do something for you, Pops?"

His jaw was set firm as he said, "Yeah, you can take your darkie and get out of this waiting room. You may not have noticed the sign, but the rest of us did. The coloreds' waitin' area is down the hall."

Now that he mentioned it, I could see the sign beside the door. I got up out of the chair and pushed passed him. I walked over, tore the sign down, and threw it in the middle of the room. "Not anymore it's not. This hospital's just been integrated."

I thought at first he was actually going to try it. I was kind of hoping that he would. I wanted to take my anger out on somebody, and this room full of farmers would do real fine. But instead he just stood there seething at me for a minute. Then he gathered his people together and they quietly left the room. I walked over and picked up the sign from the floor and tossed it in the trashcan next to the coffee machine. When I turned back around, Joey was watching me. "You know, Boss, I could have left."

I shook my head as I crossed the room. "And why should you? What makes them right and you wrong just because your ancestors came from someplace else. If we all saw it that way, we'd need waiting rooms for Swiss guys, Italians, and British guys. Hell, all we'd get done is the building of waiting rooms. This is the twentieth century, and it's time they got used to it!" I dropped back into the chair beside him. It was all he could do to hide his grin.

"Sure set those farmers movin'."

I sat there for a bit, but I was feeling awfully antsy, and the tar I'd been drinking didn't help. Finally I couldn't take it anymore, and I went out to the desk to see if there was any news. The group of farmers was sitting in the hallway on folding chairs.

The hawk-faced nurse was still behind the desk and from the look I got, she thought I was the scum of the earth. When I asked her if she'd heard anything, she just gave a sneer and a shake of her winged cap.

Guess I had that coming for messing with their status quo, but someday they'd see that I was right. Or maybe some people never would.

On the way back to the waiting room, I tried to peek through the little windows in the double doors, but all I got for my troubles was a really great view of the empty hallway.

I came back into the room to find that we weren't alone anymore. A white couple was sitting next to the coffee machine, and over in the corner was a gray-haired black man. Joey was grinning like a Cheshire cat. "Friend of yours?"

He shrugged his shoulders. "He was looking for the waiting room, and this is a waiting room."

I slumped into the chair next to him and leaned forward with my head in my hands. "Before you start the revolution, give me a chance to get Kate out of here."

A couple more people moved in and out of the waiting room, and a few poked their heads in, but it all became pretty much routine. People would come and sit with us till their name was called, then they would disappear behind those double doors to never be seen again. Or at least not by us.

Finally an unbelievably thin man in a white lab coat came through the door and called my name. Both Joey and I jumped up so fast he looked at us in confusion till I said, "I'm Steele."

The look I got in return was mostly pure suspicion. He glanced down at the clipboard he was holding and said, "I'm Doctor Redmond. I have a couple questions if you don't mind."

It was all I could do to stop from grabbing him by the lapels and shaking the answers out of him. But for once I held what little temper I had. "What questions?" After all, it might be something concerning Kate's condition.

He narrowed his eyes at me, studying me from head to toe. If first impressions meant anything, I was in real trouble. I crawled through a cornfield, rolled around under a car, shot a guy and started a fire. Oh yeah, and ran a bunch of locals out of the waiting room. Yep, I could see already I was gonna be the next governor. He glanced at his notes again and then said, "You said the cause of the trauma was a car accident. But the ligature marks on her wrists and ankles seem to indicate otherwise. Can you shed any more light on what happened?"

I decided to be honest with him. "Well, ya see, Doctor, there wasn't a box for being held captive in a cellar, so I just went with the next best thing."

His jaw dropped down on his chest, and he began to stutter. "Well, then the police have to be notified at once!"

I wrinkled up my nose and shook my head. "Nah, they already know all about it," I lied. "Matter of fact, they were the ones that sent us here." Sooner or later I was going to have to tell Havs about it, but the longer I waited, the longer I got to stay out of jail, so it was just easier to lie. And I let a bit of my temper loose. "Enough questions! Is she going to be all right?"

He looked down at that damn clipboard again, and I wanted to tear it out of his hands and read it for myself, but I knew that whatever information was on it was written in Doctor, and only a handful of nurses and a few druggists could manage to translate it.

"She has a mild concussion," he read, "two cracked ribs, various bruises and abrasions, the ligature marks from the ropes on her wrists and ankles, the lacerations from cutting them off, and what appears to be a large, purple beet stain around her mouth."

"And?"

"And," he continued, "she should be fine in a couple of days, all except for the beet stain, which in my estimation should take about a month to wear off."

I'm pretty sure that I deflated like a balloon with a hole in it, and everybody in the room could hear the rush of air out of my body. The hype and the tension just seemed to flow out and left me almost trembling. The cardboard cup in my hand had gotten crushed just a few minutes ago in a fit of anger, and I turned to drop it into the trash.

The doctor pointed at the back of my head with the eraser-end of his pencil. "You really should let me take a look at that cut. Looks like it could use a couple of stitches."

"Sorry," I answered, shaking my head. "I've got to see Kate."

"Doctor Gallagher is asleep! And rather than have you come charging in and waking her, take a few minutes and let me have a look at that. Besides, as your doctor, I'd recommend it."

"And just when did you become my doctor?"

"About thirty seconds ago when I appointed myself. I'm not sure you two can make those decisions on your own." He tore a sheet of paper off his prescription pad and wrote an address on it. "Besides, you two need a decent, clean place to stay." He handed it to Joey. "This is a nice place. Not too upscale."

He pointed that pencil at me again. Gonna bust it and the clipboard! "They even take crazy white people like your friend. So after you check on Doctor Gallagher, give it a look-see."

Joey took the paper, and after stuffing it in his pocket raised his eyebrows in question. It was like a cheap mime show, but the doctor understood and said, "Room three, and don't wake her up!"

Joey gave him a big grin, showing all those white teeth, and said, "Yes, suh," using his dumb black man voice and shuffled off down the hall. I knew what he was doing. A rather non-intelligent black man in the South draws considerably less attention than the genius that he really was.

The doctor held open the double doors and indicated for me to precede him. "And I do hope that gun you're wearing, Captain Steele, has the safety on. I'd rather not have my emergency ward shot through with holes because of your negligence."

Seems he was a little smarter than my first estimate. He had spotted the bulge under my arm and knew what it was right away.

He walked a bit ahead of me, still talking and expecting me to follow. "I'm taking it for granted that you two must be some kind of investigators, private or otherwise. That's the only reason I don't have the police swarming all over the building. That and the fact I checked on Doctor Gallagher."

He led me into a small exam room and indicated for me to sit on the wheelie stool. Then he rolled a second one up behind me and sat on it. I winced as he pulled on the edges of the cut with his fingers, and then I heard him sniffing behind me.

"Do you realize, Captain Steele, that the back of your head smells like pickle juice?"

"Yep. That's what was in the jar she hit me with."

"She?"

"Kate."

"Why would Doctor Gallagher hit you…?" He stopped and held up his hand. "No, never mind. I probably know too much already."

\*     \*     \*     \*     \*

In his war room, Sharade pushed away from his desk and at the same time pushed the visions of the past away. He rose, and after closing the door from the outside, carefully locked it. Then, feeling safe, he returned upstairs.

But the past wasn't to be denied. Behind the door, like the flickering film of an old motion picture, what had been was again….

\*     \*     \*     \*     \*

The colonel's command was over. The endless days of nothing but swamp and twilight had seen to that. What the brackish water hadn't claimed, the bugs and unknown beasts had. Only seven bearded skeletons remained of what had once been his glorious troop. The major and Corporal Caleb, along with Private Tucker, were still relatively alive. The Carny brothers were carrying each other, and it was doubtful they would both survive the next rising of the sun. LuPon was showing signs of the fever that had killed so many.

Suddenly the colonel stumbled, his foot hitting something submerged below the murky surface. He tumbled down to his knees, expecting the water to come rushing over his head and this time claim his life. There wasn't enough strength left in his tired limbs to fight his way back to the surface. But the muck his knees landed on was nearly a foot higher than the bottom his feet had been slogging on less than a moment before. He forced his eyes to focus in the dark, and he thought he saw land emerging from the water like a beach.

Feeling much as Noah must have felt when he awoke to land, he forced his parched lips apart, and a scream tore from a throat that had grown unaccustomed to making sounds in the last few days. "Land! There is land!"

From somewhere blood and power flooded into his wobbly legs and he forced himself forward. In the darkness the water fell away, and the ground rose to become solid beneath his feet. For the first time in what seemed like weeks, he was standing on solid ground.

His world began to spin, and he tumbled down into the darkness.

Chapter 19

As the doctor stitched the back of my head, he must have been stopping the ideas from leaking out, because suddenly one crossed my mind. Between winces I asked, "Hey Doc, you know anything about the Cypress Glen Home for the Rehabilitation of the Aged?"

He stopped what he was doing and leaned around my shoulder to look at me. His eyes were narrow with suspicion again. "Why? What does that have to do with you?"

Suddenly my own guard came up, and I decided to lie again. "Well, a friend of ours has relatives in Cypress Glen, and I thought we might take Kate there to recover."

He walked around front to stand with his feet defiantly placed and his arms crossed on his chest. "If that's what you're planning, I refuse to release her to you."

Seeing the way he felt about it, I figured I was on the right track. So I made a change in tactics and decided to trust him. "You've been pretty square with me, Doctor, so I'll square up with you. You're right about us being investigators, and right now it's the Cypress Glen Institute that we're investigating. I thought with you being a doctor you might know something about it, and it looks like I was right. So spill."

He pulled his wheelie around front and sat down again, relief mixing with something else on his face. "It was about thirty years ago, right after I finished up my residency. I was working the night shift here in the emergency ward when a patient was brought in by rural ambulance. He was in his mid-forties or so, but nearly totally depleted of blood and very near death. His family said that they had taken him there to rehab after having broken his leg in a fall. When they went back to check on him they found him in this condition, and immediately called for an ambulance and had him brought here. No matter what I did, he died several hours later.

"The really incredible part was that I could see no reason for his massive blood loss. Other than his broken leg, which was healing quite well, there was no reason for his anemia." He ran his fingers over his close-cropped graying hair.

"I was still new enough at the doctor business that I hadn't grown used to the fact that in some cases, people are going to die no matter how good a doctor I am or what I do. I followed up on everything, right down to the autopsy. There was no reason for his blood loss. So I began an ethics investigation.

"I even went to Cypress Glen to investigate the hospital. What I found was a quaint little hospital in a quaint little town. The people there seemed to think that elderly doctor was a god. When it was all over and done, I barely got out of town with my life."

"You mean they threatened you?"

"Not physically, but the police chief told me that if I were to continue my investigation in the town, I would most likely find myself in one of his jail cells on a slander charge. So as quickly as I could I packed up my luggage and left the town."

All seemed pretty familiar to me. "So you just gave up after that?"

He shook his head. "Probably should have. But nope, I was still young and self-righteous. I filed a complaint with the state medical board. I gave them everything I had about the night the patient came in and his condition. I told them that in my opinion I felt that the doctor's negligence was the direct cause of death.

"For nearly six months, I heard nothing. Then one day I got a summons in the mail to appear before the board. I went expecting to testify as to the information about Sharade and the institute. What I got instead was a very stern warning about wasting the board's valuable time.

And that if I continued on the path I was currently on my own license would become subject to a very intense review. I had no choice but to let it go."

I raised an eyebrow. "So you figured that the institute had some very powerful friends?"

He shook his head in defeat. "I really don't know anymore. All I know is that if I wanted to go on practicing medicine, I had to mind my own business."

"Wow! It looks as though nothing has changed in the last twenty years. We seem to be running up against the same type of resistance. Do you remember what that doctor's name was?"

His mouth was a grim, hard line as he nodded his head. "Oh, I'll never forget it. It was Nathan Sharade."

It was my turn for my jaw to drop and my eyes to turn into saucers. "What?" I stuttered. "Are you sure?"

"Like I said, I'll never forget it. It's pretty much burned into my mind as if it were done with a branding iron. Nathan Sharade."

My head was going round and round. The numbers just weren't adding up. Thirty years ago and the elderly doctor's name was Sharade. Maybe it was his father. "Do you remember what he looked like?"

"I only met him twice while I was there. Once when I first went up to the hospital, and then when the chief of police, a man named Tucker, threatened me with incarceration."

I suddenly felt so dizzy that I had to grab my head to keep it from falling off my neck. "Sharade is a rather stout man with whiskers, smokes a pipe, about sixty to seventy years old?"

The doctor nodded. "That would have been him. And the chief of police was tall with a pot belly that hung over his gun belt."

I felt my stomach leap into my throat, and I was nearly physically sick. The wheelie stool didn't seem capable of holding me, and if it weren't for the doctor I would have fallen.

The doctor reached out and grabbed my shoulder to hold me up. "Are you all right, Captain Steele?"

I took a deep breath and tried to get control of myself again. After a couple of seconds my stomach stopped rolling, and I was able to speak again. "He's still there, and still practicing."

The doctor looked at me like I was crazy. "He can't be. From the age he was when I was there, he would be nearly one hundred years old! It must have been his father."

I sucked on my teeth for a second, trying to decide what I was going to tell him. "No, I don't think so. And the reason I don't is that Tucker is still the chief of police!"

It was his turn to be shocked. "That's impossible!"

I shook my head. "Lots of things here are impossible. We were attacked by a cornfield full of kids, yet there are no kids in the town. I shot a man today, and yet he got up and walked away. Now you tell me that the same man that is running the institute was running it then, and the chief of police is still the same man. Impossible doesn't begin to cover it!"

The doctor moved back behind me and finished stitching up my head. He gave me a few more small pieces of information while he worked, but nothing that helped confirm one way or the other what was going through my head.

Somehow after he finished I managed to find my feet, and with my head still swimming with all the things he had told me, I pushed my way out of the exam room and down the hallway to Kate's room.

Joey was already gone, and she was still sleeping. So I pulled a wooden chair up as close to the bed as my knees would let me, sat down, and took her pale hand in mine. It was easier now that I knew she was going to be all right, but it still hurt. I still blamed myself for everything that had happened to her.

Holding her hand in mine, I crossed my arms on the bed and laid my head down on top of them. As I lay there watching her breathe, my vision blurred and I slipped away.

*     *     *     *     *

Joey walked out of the hospital and took a deep breath, sucking in the smells of the city. Despite the exhaust fumes and the soot, it made him feel better than the antiseptic smell of the hospital. Hospitals just gave him the willies. Too many times people he cared for had spent their last days withering away in one.

The sun had gone down while they were inside, and the cars were just starting to turn on their lights. There was a cool dampness in the air, the kind that would fog the windshields of the parked cars before morning. He made his way across the parking lot to their rental car. He took out the key and opened the trunk. After making sure that nobody was watching him, he slipped off the revolver and holster that he was wearing and laid it carefully in the compartment. The he slammed down the lid. After he made sure a second time that nobody else was around, he put the keys under the floor mat for Rick if he needed them.

Finished with his business in the parking lot, he walked slowly over to the bus stop. He would have liked to have taken the car, but that was just asking for trouble. An old beater like that with a black man driving it was like waving a red flag in front of a bull. The police would have been on him before he had gone a mile. This wasn't home. Here in the Deep South he was like an alien in his own country—the same country his people had fought and died for in the last two wars. But here none of that mattered. What mattered was the color of his skin.

Reminders of it were everywhere, just like the sign in the waiting room. Whites only! Without Rick there to defend him he was liable to get himself into big trouble if he forgot that. Any excuse would bring the police down on him, and he'd be off to jail. They boasted that their conviction rate for black men was 120%. Nobody got away.

He walked down to the bus stop and leaned against the pole holding up the sign. He was tired and wished that he could use the broad bench sitting there, but that wasn't allowed. So instead he put his back against the iron pole and tried to make himself as comfortable as he could.

Any other day he might have noticed the car that crept past a block up the street and pulled to the curb, but tonight he was just too tired.

Inside the car, five burly men were watching Joey. The passenger in the front turned to the driver and asked, "You sure that's him?"

The driver nodded. "Matches the description we got to a tee. Great big coon, buzzed hair, wearing an old army field jacket. That's him alright. Ain't two of 'em like that."

The passenger shivered inside his suit a bit as he watched Joey. "Big 'un like that could be hard to take down."

"Nah! I ain't afraid of no coon. Besides, I got this." He reached into his pocket and took out a leather-wrapped cosh. Slapping it against his other palm and making a smacking sound, he said, "This sap'll bust even that bowling ball he's got for a head."

He turned and looked at the men in the backseat. "Squint, I want you to get out here and distract him. While he's busy with you, me and the other boys will roll up and jump him. Got it?"

Squint was a former boxer, and his eyes were so buried in scar tissue that they looked like tiny points of light looking out from under the brim of his hat. "Gotcha, boss." He opened the car door and stepped out, starting towards Joey.

Squint had that rolling walk that came from too many years in the ring. It was a kind of a left-to-right swagger, always trying to keep his keep his weight on his forward foot ready to throw a punch, the leather of his shoe soles making clicking sounds against the concrete.

At the sound of his approach Joey looked up, but that was about as far as it went. It was just a man walking down a city street.

As he came abreast of Joey, Squint pulled a crumpled cigarette from his pocket and stuck it between his lips. "Hey boy, got a light?"

At the use of the derogatory term *boy*, Joey felt a fire light inside of him. But he pulled it quickly back under control. The man could have used a lot of terms worse than *boy*. Nonetheless he answered without even searching his pockets for a match. "No, suh, I don't. Sorry."

The man nodded and reached his hand into his own pocket again, but instead of emerging with a match it came back out holding an evil-looking snub-nosed revolver. The pulps called it a Bulldog Special because of its short, stubby snout. His lopsided lips smiled, and he spit the cigarette to the pavement. "Never mind, boy. I don't want one right now anyway. I'd suggest you stand real still, or one of these bullets is gonna find out whether your blood is really yella like the say." Then he whistled, and Joey heard a car start up somewhere down the street.

Joey's eyes narrowed on the gun, taking into account how it was being held and the man's stance, picking the time for his move.

A dark sedan screeched to a halt behind him, making the decision for him. Joey leaped forward, his left hand catching the gunman's wrist and pushing it up even as it went off. His own right fist sailed towards the man's belly, sinking in nearly up to the wrist and folding him over double.

Squint had never been much of a fight, taking far more punishment than he ever dealt out. The only fight he had ever won had been fixed. But he had always thought of himself better than he was. So that and the fact that he'd always been told that all black men were cowards, Joey's movements took him totally by surprise. By the time it dawned on his dim brain what was happening, Joey's knee was turning his nose to paste. Like a balloon with a hole, he slipped to the sidewalk.

From the minute he threw the first punch Joey had been moving forward, and even now after dropping Squint he went over the top, gaining momentum and about to break to open ground. But before he could make that next step, three of the men from the car leaped on him, their weight dragging him towards the ground.

He let them pull him down, compressing his legs like giant springs. Then he released them. The men flew away like they had been shot from guns, tumbling in every direction. What he hadn't counted on was the last man. As he turned to run, he stepped forward and directly into the path of the swinging sap.

Quickly he jerked his body to the right, and the leather and lead weight missed his head but caught him on the shoulder, and he felt his arm go numb.

Squint picked that moment to find his tiny wits and start to his feet, grabbing Joey around the waist. As he fought to break free again, he accidentally stepped into the path of the leader's second swing, and the sap came down on the side of Joey's head with a wet smacking sound. Darkness flooded over him, and he slumped to the sidewalk.

## Chapter 20

I awoke to someone gently running their fingers through my hair. It wasn't a sensation that I was used to feeling, so I lay with my eyes closed for a few more seconds, enjoying it.

When I did open my eyes, they met the sparking blue of Kate's looking back at me. "Hi ya, handsome."

I wanted to look over my shoulder and see who she was talking to, but figured out that she must mean me. I smiled my lopsided grin as I raised my head. I could feel the finger marks in the side of my face from lying on my hand, and my sleeve was all wet with drool.

"You're kind of cute when you sleep," she said, "like a little boy."

I stretched, trying to twist the pain out of my back from being bent in a U all night. "Things are kind of backward this time. Usually I wake up to you sitting next to my hospital bed."

"Well, I thought maybe it was my turn."

"Kate…" I started, but she held up a finger to stop me.

"I already know what you're going to say, so don't. None of this is your fault. You didn't force me to go. I was the one that made that choice. So if anybody is to blame, it's me."

"As much as I love your logic, I don't agree with it. But I promised myself we wouldn't argue over it."

She smiled in agreement.

"If you feel good enough, do you think you could tell me what happened after you left Vince's?"

"Sure. What I can remember, anyway."

Turned out she remembered quite a lot. I heard about the accident, them pulling her from the car, and then her waking up to the nightmare she went through in the cellar.

When she was done, I filled in the blanks for her with our side of the story. Some of it, like the bomb on the plane and the gun fight outside the farm, I skimmed over fairly quickly.

As I finished up I could hear people starting to move around in the hall, and the sun was creeping in the window.

For the first time since I'd opened my eyes, I felt a wave of panic sweep through me, turning my insides to ice. My watch said it was nearly six in the morning. Joey should have come back a long time ago.

Without saying anything I jumped up, checked her nightstand, and then rushed out into the hall to find the nurse. She was at the desk giving reports to the new shift coming on.

I couldn't wait for her to finish, and I was forced to interrupt her. The look I got said she wasn't used to being interrupted.

"Yes, what is it?" If I hadn't already been half frozen inside with fear, her voice would have done it.

"The man that was with me yesterday—I need to know if he left any message, or came back at any time last night."

She shook her head. "Nobody left anything for you."

"Are you sure?" I was almost begging, hoping that maybe she had forgotten.

"I'm certain that if a giant colored man had left a message for you I would remember it. I'm not in the habit of forgetting things like that."

As I walked back into Kate's room, the look on my face made it obvious something was wrong. And she asked me about it. "What is it, Rick? What's happened?"

"Joey's overdue. He left here to get us a room, and he hasn't come back."

"Maybe he was as worn out as you and decided to take a nap before he came back," she offered.

I shook my head. "He'd have found some way—a note, a phone call, whatever—to let me know what he was going to do."

Even without a mirror I knew my face was a grim mask. "I'm afraid he's in trouble, Kate. For him, this is hostile territory."

She reached out and laid her hand gently on my arm. "Rick, black people get along fine here every day."

"Because they were born here. Joey's not one to take what happens here lying down. So if it's not the police, it's Sharade's people. Whichever it is means that he's in trouble."

Kate started to get out of bed, and I stopped her. "Where do you think you're going?"

"You're going after Joey, and I'm going with you."

I took her slim shoulders in my hands and looked deep into her blue eyes. "Sorry, Kate. You can't. The doctor says you need complete bed rest for the next couple of days. When I find anything out I'll be back. But for right now, this is the safest place for you to be."

Her lip came out in a pout, but she knew that I was right, and she settled back down into the bed. I leaned in and kissed her gently on her purple lips. "I'll be back as soon as I can." I turned to leave and got almost to the door before I came back and took her up in my arms and mashed my lips to hers. "Kate... I—"

She stopped me with another kiss. "I know, Rick. I feel the same way. Now get out of here and go find Joey." I pushed myself away to follow her advice and floated to the door. As it closed behind me I took one last long look.

It took some cajoling and a five dollar bill, but I finally got the doctor's home number out of the nurse behind the desk. Then I went down to the pay phone in the lobby and dropped a nickel.

The phone rang for a long time, and then the doctor's groggy voice filled my earpiece. "Hullo?"

"Doctor, this is Steele. I need the address of that hotel you sent Joey to last night. He never came back."

Whether it was my tone or the simple fact that he was used to being awakened with emergencies, his voice cleared up right away. He gave me the address, and I scratched it down on a scrap of paper I had wadded up in my pocket.

I thanked him and was about to hang up when he asked. "Is there anything I can do, Steele?"

I thought for a second and nodded like he could see me. "Keep an eye on Kate. If they've gotten Joey, then they probably know where she is."

"You want me to bring the police in on this?" he asked.

I ran my hand over the stubble on my face, thinking. "Technically, I'm still wanted by the state police. So if you can do it without dragging my name into it, go ahead."

I could almost hear the wheels going round in his head. "Tell you what. I'll tell them it's a domestic thing and that her husband has threatened her, and that I'd feel a lot safer with an officer on duty. How's that?"

I nodded again. "That'll work. Thanks, Doc."

"I want to see Sharade stopped almost as much as you, Steele. Good luck."

I hung up the phone to break the connection, then I dropped another nickel in the slot and dialed the number of the cab company on the ad hanging above the phone. I didn't know the city, and didn't have the time to spend driving all over looking for an address. So the quickest way was by cab.

It wasn't long after I stepped outside that a yellow Checker pulled up, and I slid into the backseat. The driver turned halfway around and asked where to. I gave him the address and he turned the rest of the way around to face me, almost doing a double take.

"You sure that's where you want to go?" he asked. "You know that's up in Coon Town!"

I looked up and let him see the hardness in my eyes. "You gonna take me? Or do I have to find another cab?"

He held up his hand in surrender. "No, I'll take ya. I just wanted to make sure you knew what you were getting yourself into. After all, if it's a hooker you're looking for, I can get you a good clean white one. You don't need to mess with that dark meat."

I reached up and grabbed the collar of his jacket, pulling his head towards my face. I spoke to him very slowly and very clearly, showing him all my clenched teeth. "I'm getting real tired of the garbage I keep hearing in this town. I'm hiring you to drive this cab to where I want to go, not advise me on what I should be doing with my life. Do I make myself clear?"

"Yes, sir, you do," he answered nervously.

I let go of his collar and tossed a fifty down on the seat next to him. "Then get me there as fast as you can."

The driver let in the clutch, and in a squeal of tires and a cloud of exhaust smoke we tore off down the street.

I settled back into the cushions and tried to make sense out of this whole thing. We were called in when Thelma's cousin went missing. By the time we get here she's back, but there's no explanation for where she's been or why a once happy girl is almost catatonic.

And when we decide to find out why, the whole town seems to come up against us. Kate is taken prisoner, and beaten. Joey and I are shot at. And now I find out that the doctor that's looking after Lou Ann might be over a hundred years old.

Surely whatever secret he's fighting to hide can't be his age, could it? And why does it seem like for such a small operation that his reach is enormous?

Trying to think it through didn't seem to help. All it did was make my head hurt. So instead I watched the town pass by out the window.

The hospital had been built back in the days when the neighborhood had been fairly affluent. Well, that all changed during the depression. All that money went away, and they were forced to open their doors to the general public. That caused a change in the neighborhood. Places where once graceful, old, rich houses once stood were filled with business that catered to the hospital and its patrons—eateries and taverns, medical supply houses, and gas stations. All the things you might need if you were coming here to see a patient, or be a patient.

As we drove on, the neighborhoods began to change. Gone were the supermarkets and the big stations. Instead it was mom and pop stores and one or two pump stations. Then the houses started to get shabbier, and the color of the people changed. You could feel the hunger and see the despair in every face along the street. In some places windows were boarded over, the money to replace the glass gone for food. People forced to live in squalor simply because of the color of their skin. It turned my stomach!

*    *    *    *    *

Slowly Thelma opened her eyes.

Her head was pretty fuzzy, and she wasn't real sure what was going on. She knew she was in the hospital, but she couldn't remember why.

Lou Anne was in the other bed, looking pale as death. If it weren't for the slow rise and fall of her chest, Thelma would have sworn that life had long since left her.

Thinking as hard as she could, she was able to clear away some of the fog. Or at least clear enough that she could see around the edges. She and that nice Dr. Sharade had brought Lou Anne to the hospital after her accident.

Lou Anne had needed a transfusion, and Thelma had volunteered her blood. The doctor had tested her blood to see if it was a match. And after finding out that it was, he had taken some for Lou Anne. After that, things were just a jumble.

There was something stiff and tight on her forehead, and Thelma raised up her hand to see what it was. There was a bandage above her eye, and looking over at the side table she could see a crack in one of the lenses in her thick glasses.

*Yes*, she thought, *that makes sense. I remember falling down and hitting my head. But I don't really remember anything after that. There was something that I was supposed to tell someone or something I was supposed to do, but I don't remember what it was.*

She was still puzzling over it minutes later when the door opened   and Dr. Sharade came in. The pudgy man's smile made her feel warm and safe inside. He even reminded her of her father. If only that nagging voice in her head would go away.

"Good," he said, beaming a smile at her. "You're finally awake. You had quite a nasty bump last night. Do you remember any of it?" He took Thelma's wrist and counted her pulse while he was talking.

Thelma shook her head and tried to hide the blush she was feeling at his touch. "No, I don't. Everything is pretty fuzzy after you transfused Lou Anne with my blood."

He put his stethoscope in his ears and listened to her heart through her gown. "Probably just as well. Falls can be scary things, and sometimes it's best when the mind blocks things like that out. We can just be grateful it happened on this side of the stairs and not the other. Otherwise you might have been really hurt instead of just a bump on the head." He smiled a grandfatherly smile at her.

Thelma returned his smile. "I didn't break anything, did I?" she asked.

"No, just a dent in my door shaped like your head." He picked up her broken glasses from the nightstand. "Although, it looks like these are going to need some work. Did you bring a spare pair with you when you came to visit your uncle?"

Thelma screwed up her face while she thought about it, but that made her head hurt, so she stopped. "There should be another pair in my luggage. Maybe you could have Uncle Vince bring them up when he comes to visit Lou Anne."

"Good. Good idea. I'll call him later and ask him to bring them up."

The door opened behind him, and the burly nurse came in carrying a covered tray that smelled of breakfast.

"Looks like your breakfast is here. After you're done eating we'll get you up and walking again. Can't have those muscles getting stiff."

Thelma gave him a smile and pulled the cover off the tray. There was a plate of bacon and eggs underneath. "Yummm," she said. "I just love bacon!"

\*     \*     \*     \*     \*

As the door to Thelma's room closed, Sharade turned to Tucker, who had been waiting to report. "Does she remember anything of last night?"

The doctor shook his head. "No, the venom always works."

Chief Tucker sucked on one of his teeth. "That was really careless. If anybody knew what she found, that could blow this whole operation."

Sharade's voice hardened. "Don't you forget who's in charge here, Tucker." Then a plastic smile settled on his face. "Now tell me what's going on with Steele."

Tucker took off his Mountie hat and scratched his head with his index finger. "After the bad news we got before, it seems that the boys are back on track. They've taken the Negro and know where the girl is, and are preparing to recapture her next."

Sharade's lips were smiling, but his eyes weren't. "It's about time. There have been way too many screw-ups. In all the years we've been here we've never faced this kind of trouble. I'm starting to wonder if you boys aren't getting senile."

\*     \*     \*     \*     \*

In the middle of all the squalor stood the hotel like a fortress against the creeping blight. Around it the neighborhood crumbled, but it stood like a beacon, the neon of its sign blinking out a message of refuge for the tired.

Not knowing what I was going to find, I gave the cabbie another ten and told him to wait. He didn't look happy about it, but I think I had him scared enough that he wasn't going to run off with my money.

I walked up the short flight of steps and pushed through the pebbled glass door into the lobby. It was old and worn, but from what I saw around me it was well taken care of. A once proud staircase, now showing the hundreds of feet that had climbed it, wound off on one side of the lobby, and in the back corner a single elevator stood waiting. In the lounge area two redcaps, both black men old enough to be my grandfather, were idly playing a game of checkers. Must be their slow season.

A thirty-foot marble desk stretched across the back of the hotel. Behind it a tired-looking black man was sitting with his feet up on a small writing desk reading a two-day-old paper. He didn't look up till I cleared my throat. Then he leapt to his feet like he had been shot out of a cannon, his paper flying in pieces to the floor and his chair rolling over backward.

On his way to the desk he jerked down his red vest and attempted to make himself look presentable. "I'm sorry, suh. I didn't hear you come in. Ol' ears don't work quite like they did."

I gave him a smile with half my mouth that pretty much said, "It's okay for now."

"If you're lost, suh, I can give you directions back to the better part of the city."

"This is the Reynolds Hotel, isn't it?" I asked, and when he nodded that it was, I said, "Then I'm not lost."

He eyed me suspiciously, and even without saying it I heard it in his mind: *Cop!* And right away what little cooperation he was going to offer started to melt away.

Leaning forward with both palms on the desk, I looked him right in the eye. Whatever it was he saw in mine must have scared him a bit, because he trembled. "I'm looking for a rather big black man—short hair, wearing an old army field jacket. He was supposed to check in here sometime last night."

He just shook his head. "Nobody like that checked in here." It was right there behind his eyes. *And if he had, why would I tell a white man?*

I didn't trust him. But the only way I was going to get the truth was to put the fear of God in him. With a quick move I reached over the counter and grabbed him by the front of his red vest. The two playing checkers heard the noise, but when they started to get up I pulled my jacket back far enough for them to see the butt of my rod sticking out, and they went back to their game.

The desk clerk's eyes were big and round, a tiny bit of spittle running down from his lip. "Look, I know how you feel. White people have given you a raw deal, and you don't like 'em. Well, down here neither do I. That black man is my friend, and I suspect he's in trouble. And if he is, I'll tear this town apart to help him. You understand?"

He managed a feeble nod, and I let go of him. He immediately moved back out of my reach. "I ain't lying to ya, suh. Nobody checked in last night." He pointed to the registration book. "You can see for yourself."

I spun the book around and looked, but my eyes weren't seeing it. I already knew the man wasn't lying to me. He was too scared to try it again.

I let my breath out in a whoosh and tossed a five on the counter for his trouble. There was a pay phone in the corner, and I decided it was time I made that call I'd been putting off.

I pulled the folding door shut and dropped a nickel in the slot. I took the number from the card in my pocket and dialed. It rang a couple of times, and then a voice said, "State police."

"Yeah, let me talk to Captain Hays. Tell him it's Steele."

There was a buzz of conversation in the background, then a couple of clicks, and for a second the line went dead. Then Hays' voice came over the line. "Steele. I was wondering when you'd call. Seems we have a lot to talk over. Not the least of which are the bodies of a farmer and his wife with holes from a .45 just like that one you bought this morning."

"Yeah, well, we can do all that some other time. Something else has happened, and I need your help."

"That's what you said before, and I got left sitting here on my thumbs while a farm burned and somebody killed a farmer and his wife. As far as I can see, you should be a wanted man."

"Look, Hays, cut the crap. Joey's been taken by the same people that had Kate earlier, and I need your help to find them."

Suddenly there was a commotion behind him. I heard him put his hand over the mouthpiece, muffling the sound. When he came back on the line the smartness was gone from his voice, replaced by a cold, grim horror. "Something's just happened. Where are you, Steele?"

I gave him the address, and he said he'd send a car. He was gone before I could ask him what had happened, but it didn't sound like he was coming to arrest me. It sounded more like he needed my help with whatever was going on.

I could feel eyes on me as I crossed the lobby, but I just ignored them. It wasn't till I was just about to the door that it mattered.

As I reached for the door, a big black man in a twenty-year-old pinstripe with no tie stepped in front of me. His thick lips were drawn back over his teeth, and yellow eyes were glaring. "You got no right to come down here and make trouble. Makes me think you got no manners." His big hand came up, catching me in the chest and shoving me back.

"I think maybe we should teach you some before you go back where you came from." He did something with his other hand, and a knife flicked open.

I let out a sigh. It was starting to look like the whole world had a dose of crazy in their morning coffee. I held up my hand, palm out. "Look, bud, you're probably right. I was a little hard on the poor guy behind the counter, and I apologize. So why don't you just get out of my way and I'll leave, and you can tell all your fiends how you scared off the big, bad white guy."

I watched his muscles tense under his jacket, and I knew what was coming next. He had the knife loosely in his right palm, thumb on top. More than likely that meant a slash motion rather than a stab. As I watched I saw it move just slightly off to the right, signaling the beginning of the sweep.

The knife started towards me, and my hand flashed behind it, catching him on the wrist. I spun my shoulder in towards him, and at the same time that my shoulder collided with his chest I brought my knee up and pounded his wrist down on it.

A scream escaped from his lips and echoed across the lobby as the bones in his wrist broke, and the knife slipped to the floor. I spun out of the hold and smashed his nose all over my fist. He dropped like a stone.

I reached down and, after putting my boot on the blade, twisted the knife up and broke it off. Then I walked back to the desk and laid it and ten dollars on the counter. "When he wakes up you take him to the doctor and get his wrist fixed. And you be sure and tell him that I could have just as easily killed him if I wanted to. He needs to be a little better judge of character."

This time nobody moved or even breathed as I crossed the lobby.

\*     \*     \*     \*     \*

By the time I paid off the taxi and sent him on his way, the patrol cruiser was screeching to a stop at the curb. The cop on the passenger's side in front jumped out and opened the back door for me. "Captain Hays says you're supposed to come with us, Captain Steele."

I slid into the backseat, and he closed the door behind me. As soon as his butt hit the vinyl we were off again the way they had come, the siren wailing and the red gumball making us look like a winning slot machine. I tried to question the two up front, but for all I got you'd have thought they were mute.

As we raced across the city I started to recognize the route. It was the same one I'd taken with the cab to the hotel. We were on our way back to the hospital, and I felt icy fingers playing music along my spine.

\*     \*     \*     \*     \*

The outside of the hospital was chaos. Police cars, both city and state, blocked the sidewalks, and cops in gray and blue were going in and out like they meant business. Our car bumped up over the curb and onto the walk to join up with the rest. Maybe in a crisis they had to keep the streets open, so everybody got to park on the sidewalk. Made sense to me; after all, in the movies people that were panicking were always in the street.

My escorts climbed out and came around to let me out of the back of the car. Then with one in front and one in back they ushered me into the building through the emergency entrance. I could feel my blood slowly turning to ice in my veins.

If the outside had been chaos, this was total pandemonium. Nurses and patients were huddled in the waiting room, crying. A line of bullet holes I'm pretty sure the decorator hadn't insisted on were stitched across the wall from what looked like probably a tommy gun, and the stiff, unmoving legs of a nurse were sticking out from behind the desk.

While I was taking all of this in, Hays, looking haggard, suddenly appeared, and before I could so much as move he had my gun out of my holster and was handing it off to one of his officers.

I started to protest, but he wasn't listening. "Take this back to HQ and have them run ballistics on it."

With a nod the aide took my gun and disappeared into the crowd.

Suddenly, like a ton of bricks falling on an idiot, I knew what had happened. I hit Hays like a linebacker, knocking him out of my way, and took off down the hallway at a dead run, calling her name, all the time hoping that I was wrong.

When I got to her room, I knew that I wasn't. The doctor was sitting on the floor nursing a gun-sized cut on his forehead. I slowly pushed the door open and had to step over a blue-suited officer. Otherwise the room was empty. Kate was gone!

Head down in despair, I walked across the room and felt the rumpled sheet with my fingertips. They seemed to still feel warm to my touch like she had just gotten out of bed. I picked up her pillow and held it to my face, drinking in the scent of her. Hays came up behind me while I was standing there.

"About half an hour ago or so two men, one of them with a Thompson, came in and shot up the place, killing two nurses and that cop out there by the door. Luckily they just pistol-whipped the doctor. She was what they were after. And they were willing to kill anybody who got in their way."

I tossed the pillow back on the bed and tried to push past him, but this time he was like a stone wall. "No more games, Steele. Too many people are dead, and I don't have any explanation."

I nodded, making up my mind. Walking over to one of the wooden chairs, I turned it upright and sat down, indicating he should do the same.

After he settled across from me I told him everything. He sat there quietly, taking it all in, not even interrupting. When I finished, his jaw was tight, and I wasn't sure if he was about to explode. Finally when he spoke his voice was almost flat, emotionless. "And you decided not to tell me any of this?"

I shrugged my shoulders. If I was going to be honest with him, I was going to have to go all the way. "I wasn't sure how far Sharade's influence reached. I didn't know who I could trust."

Then suddenly from the door a blubbery voice boomed. "Captain Steele, you're under arrest!"

## Chapter 21

From the brim of his peaked cap down passed the metal and brass buttons on his jacket, sliding down the razor-sharp crease of his pants to his highly polished shoes, the man who had just come in the door was shiny. There was nothing else you could call him. In the sunshine he must have looked like a star walking down the street. But underneath that shine he was blubbery fat. It oozed out around his cuffs and up over the collar of his shirt. It was like Jell-O stuffed inside a suit. His face was ruddy red, and his nose was a blob stuck on his face with a bit of clay.

Behind him came his escort—two patrolmen almost as shiny, their guns drawn to stop anybody from stealing his brass buttons. That or they'd lost their way to the O.K. Corral.

A fat finger at the end of a fat arm came up and pointed at me like the hand of God after Adam, and the blubbery voice filled the room again. "Arrest that man!"

The two gunslingers started my way, but Hays jump up between us. "On what charges, Chief Inspector?"

His piggy little eyes narrowed. "The murder of one of my patrolmen, and now that I've gotten here, the possible death of a second."

"And what makes you think that he did it?" Hays asked.

"I got a tip shortly before this fiasco that Officer Bowen was killed with a .45 just like that man carries." That finger came up again and pointed my way.

Trying to look my most innocent and friendly, I pulled my jacket back to show him my empty holster. Then Hays had to go and ruin it all.

"We have his gun out being tested by ballistics right now."

I have to admit, Hays was doing okay. And I was still managing to stay out of the way of the patrolman with the cuffs. Then his officer came back with a paper sack. From the way he was carrying it, I figured it wasn't his lunch.

Hays reached into the sack and took out my gun and laid it on the bed. Then the trooper handed him the report. When he finished it, he wasn't smiling. Turning to me, he slowly shook his head. "You lied to me, Steele, and probably have been lying all along." He held up the piece of paper for me to see. There were two pictures of bullets on it, and from what I could see with a quick glance, they matched perfectly. Looking over at the bed, I knew why.

"That's not my gun, Hays. Well, it is my gun, but it's not the gun I had. Somebody pulled the old switcheroo"

The steam engine was blowing again. "How much more of this are you going to listen to, Hays? Nothing that comes out of his mouth is the truth. Put the handcuffs on him, and we'll take him to jail."

Hays actually looked apologetic. "Sorry, Steele. If you'd have been honest with me, maybe I could have done something. But now all I can do is turn you over to them."

I felt the rage rising in me. "You turn me over to them, and I'll be found hanging from the bars of my cell by a bed sheet."

Hays took another step towards me as he drew his gun. His back was toward the inspector and the patrolmen, so I was the only one that could see his face. His left eye winked, and his lips said, "Run!"

I reached out and grabbed the long barrel of his revolver and pushed him back into the others as I did. Then I turned and leaped for the window. In less than a heartbeat I had it open and was going feet-first over the sash. But I must not have been as fast as I thought, because one of the patrolmen managed to get off a shot that creased the wood next to my hand as I was going over.

As I was rolling into the bushes below, I saw Hays blocking the window and heard him say something about me stealing a patrol car. Moments later, fat boy and his men came running out and piled into cars to chase me.

I lay there under the bushes for a while, in part to make sure they didn't come back, but also to try and figure out what my next move was. I was free, more or less, but to do what? Not a clue as to where Joey was.

Deciding that it was safe enough for now, I climbed to my feet and started around to the back of the building. Maybe there I could manage to steal a car and find someplace to hole up till I figured out what to do next.

I edged carefully around the corner of the building and nearly fell over an idling cruiser with its back door open. Hays was sitting in the backseat. "Get in," he ordered, "before those blue-suited clowns come back."

I slid in beside him and pulled the door shut. The minute it latched we were moving. These troopers weren't much for waiting for a guy to get settled. I shook my head at Hays in disbelief. "You want to tell me what's going on?"

He shrugged a shoulder. "When the chief inspector showed up, I figured something was fishy. Then when my man came back with a different gun, I was sure somebody was setting you up."

"You knew it wasn't the same gun?"

His eyes narrowed and his lips twisted wryly. "I am a cop after all. A long time ago I was trained to notice things. I saw the wear on the grips and the slide right away. The gun I gave to him was nearly brand new."

I nodded and handed him back his pistol butt-first. He took it and swung it open and began to slide five bullets into the cylinder. I sat back in the seat in shock. "You mean I took an empty gun?"

"I always empty my gun before interrogation. It stops me and a lot of innocent people from getting killed."

I settled into the corner of the seat. "So, what now?"

"Well, you said your rental is still in the lot, so that means your friend must have taken the bus or at least intended to take the bus. I thought we'd cruise over and have a look around."

"What about the city police?"

"At least for a while they're off chasing a stolen patrol car. And pretty soon they'll be tired of that and get back to sitting in the taverns waiting for a call."

The radio in the front squawked, and Hays leaned up over the seat to listen. After a minute or so the driver handed him the mic, and he rogered the call. When he sat back he said, "Probably didn't get much of that, did you?" He squinted one eye. "Takes a little practice to pick out what they're saying over the static. It'll get better someday."

He paused to light a Lucky and filled the car with smoke. "What they said was that a lady reported a fight between five white men and a black guy at the bus stop up the street from the hospital. She said they loaded him up in a black or dark blue sedan with *RI* on the plate and took off."

"Did they investigate?"

The look I got said it all. "This is the south, Steele. Do you honestly think the city police force is going to waste their time chasing down a lone black man beaten up by five white, upstanding citizens?"

"Well, at least we got a description of the car and a partial license number," I said hopefully.

He shook his head. "Every plate in this parish starts with *RI*, and do you have any idea how many black or dark blue sedans there are around here?"

While we were talking the driver had pulled to the curb a couple of car lengths from the bus stop to make sure he didn't disturb anything that might be left. I was pretty doubtful about finding much this late.

Hays seemed more optimistic. "If there's nobody at the stop, the bus doesn't stop. So hopefully anything that might have been dropped will still be here."

I moved slowly down the sidewalk, carefully checking the grassy edge first. I could see the scuff marks of the struggle in the scraggly grass, but nothing that would help me. After I'd gone almost twenty-five feet, I turned around and started back, this time on the curb edge. That's where I found it.

It didn't look like much lying there close to the curb in the street. It was just a small clump of dirt like what you get caught between your heel and the sole and can't seem to scrape off. But it was the composition that was important. I picked it up, and it felt greasy and smelled like oil. Climbing up off my knee, I handed it to Hays. "Do you have any idea what this is?"

Hays took the lump out of my hand and held it up to his nose. "That's *adober*."

"What's *adober*?"

"Back in the thirties, when concrete was so expensive, they came up with a process where they packed the dirt and then covered it with oil to seal the floor. Nearly all the warehouses in town have floors like that."

Suddenly a smile split my face, and I slapped him on the shoulder. "I think we've got our clue, Hays—that and the car. Now all we have to do is find it."

\*    \*    \*    \*    \*

So after about five hours and a gazillion warehouses I was starting to lose that enthusiasm I'd picked up. I don't think ever in my life had I looked at more rundown buildings and more rats, at least of the four-legged variety. Even with the other car checking half of them it seemed endless.

About sundown, when we were just about to give up, we got lucky. We were on Canal Street headed to the next address on our list when we saw a dark sedan shoot by on the cross street. It might have been just a fluke, but we stayed just far enough back that we could see where he went. And sure enough his passenger got out, opened the sliding door on the warehouse, and the driver pulled the car inside. Hays had his driver pull into a nearby alley, and I opened the door to get out. "I'll need that gun of mine you're holding, Hays."

"Just what do you expect to do, Steele?"

I'm going in there to make sure they don't get away while you get the rest of your men here. And make sure it doesn't go out over an open band, or we'll have every cop in the city here."

Hays shook his head. "This is my job, Steele, not yours. I should be the one going in."

It was my turn to shake my head. "'Fraid not, Hays. If this all goes down wrong, nobody takes responsibility for any of it but me. Now, do I get my gun back?"

This man just couldn't say yes. He shook his head again. "I can't give it back—it's evidence. You shoot somebody with it, and it's proof positive you killed the rest of them." He reached under the seat and pulled out a snub-nosed .38, a detective special. "This is the best I've got. I know it's a peashooter compared to what you're used to, but it's my throwaway. In other words, it's untraceable."

I took the gun but wasn't real happy about it. It had nowhere near the stopping power of my .45. "Bullets?" I asked.

He handed me two speed loads of five each, and I stuck them in my jacket.

"That should give you enough ammo to kill everybody in there. But don't. I'd kind of like a chance to verify some of your story."

I nodded, pushed the door shut, and had turned to head off down the alley when he called me back. "Steele, be careful." In the quickly dying light I could see the concern in his face. Maybe up until now he'd figured this all was just kind of a game, but reality was rapidly setting in. Time to roll the dice and hope it doesn't come up snake eyes!

\*     \*     \*     \*     \*

The colonel lay on top of the hill in the tall grass and looked down on the small town nestled in the valley. He wished he still had his field telescope, but, like most everything, the swamp had eaten that too. Here was just what they had been looking for. A smile twisted his cruel mouth. Finally he and his men could resupply, and maybe even find a few new recruits to swell their depleted ranks. And even if they didn't want to enlist, their nation was in trouble, and he, being the last commander, had the right to press into service whomever he needed.

Leaving one of the Carny brothers to watch the town, he turned and slithered back through the grass to the other side of the hill where the rest of his men were waiting.

The major rose as he saw the colonel's approach. "Is it what the younger Carny said it was?"

The colonel nodded. "Might be even better. Looks like it's mostly a farming community, so we shouldn't have much trouble. We'll wait until after dark when everyone's inside, then we'll move in. Send the other Carny up to spell his brother."

He walked over to a scrub tree where one of his men was sitting with his back against it. Under the deep red of his sunburn LuPon looked pale, and even though sweat was running from his forehead he was shivering with cold. The colonel knelt down and touched his wet forehead with his hand. LuPon's flesh was burning hot. The colonel offered him a weak smile. "By tonight we'll get you everything you need, Private. You just hold on a little longer."

Private LuPon tried to smile through his shivering. "Yes, sir, I will. I know you'll get me through this just like you got me through the swamp."

The colonel patted him reassuringly and walked back over to where the major was squatting. "I don't think LuPon will see much passed sundown. Even if he does I suggest we

211

leave him here until later. Then we can send the Carnys after him." Then he changed the subject to something more important. "What do we have left for working firearms, Major?"

The major pulled out his own pistol and spun the cylinder. "Just the two sidearms, suh— yours and mine. But even then I can't promise that the ammunition will fire. I worked very hard to keep it dry, but after that many days in the water, even if it doesn't look like it, it's sure to have gotten damp."

"Then I would suggest our first stop tonight be the general store. There at least we should be able to rearm to take on the rest of the town."

Night came, and LuPon still lived on. Leaving him where he was, the colonel gathered the rest of his men around him and started over the hill. The Carny brothers were waiting when he reached them. Quietly he outlined his plan, and then they set off down the hill.

Even close-up the town was nothing special. Seven or eight clapboard buildings formed the main street itself, with the houses set further off the path. It couldn't be more than two hundred people all told.

The general store was easy to spot. It was the largest of all the clapboard buildings. As the others waited impatiently and guarded his back, he used the butt of his pistol to knock the padlock from the hasp on the rear door. Then with his shoulder against the wood he pushed the door inward.

A plethora of aromas flooded his nose as the door swung inward. Fresh fruits, new material, oils—so many that his mind was nearly overwhelmed. Turning, he could see that his men were too.

Suddenly without thought of safety or stealth, they pushed past him and into the store. The Carny brothers found the bin of apples and started gobbling them up like they had never tasted anything so wonderful. Disgusted with their behavior, the colonel walked over and pulled them from their feast.          "You have had nothing but wood rats and gators for over a month. Your stomachs will not be accustomed to such rich food. Eat only one, or I promise you they will be coming back out of both ends of your body within mere minutes."

Reluctantly the two moved away from the bin, but he failed to notice that their pockets were already filled to bulging with the red fruit.

The major was behind the store's counter, a small oil lamp lit to provide light as he searched the shelves. His mouth, like that of the brothers', was salivating, but he knew other things were more important. After a short search he found what he was looking for. He took a long, thin box marked *Gun Cleaning Kit* from the shelf. He set his lamp on the counter and proceeded to break down his pistol. With deft fingers he carefully cleaned and oiled each piece. Satisfied with the way it looked, he reassembled it and filled it with fresh ammunition. Then he began his real quest.

In a wooden box he found just what he was looking for: cigars. He took one out and ran it under his nose, relishing the scent. He bit the end off, spitting it on the floor, and with a blazing match sucked the fine smoke to life. For the major his world was right again; he had fresh ammunition in his gun and a fine cigar between his teeth.

For the colonel, on the other hand, it was fresh clean clothes that he sought. He found a new pair of gray trousers on the shelf, and after pulling off his ruined boots he unbuckled what was left of his pants and kicked them away. In the light of the lamp his pale legs looked like two sticks peeled free of bark hanging from beneath his blouse. Shortly his shirt and undershirt joined the pile of clothes. A new broad-brimmed hat replaced his army-issued Stetson. With the fresh clothes the colonel was whole again. He would have preferred a bath to go with them, but there wasn't time for that now.

His men, with the exception of the major, who was now cleaning the colonel's own gun, were milling about the store, opening boxes and playing with the women's things on the shelves and making crude comments to each other. In a corner of the back room he found the corporal. He was sitting on the floor, back against the wall, sipping on what he suspected was a bottle of sacramental wine. The toe of his new boot caught the bottle, sending it flying across the room. Enraged at what he was seeing, he turned and stormed back into the front of the store.

It was at that same instant Elisha Biddle, proprietor of the town's fine general store, was sliding his key into the lock of the front door to investigate the light that he had seen flashing behind the drawn shades of his store. He pushed the door open, the small bell above it sounding.

Without thinking, the major's hand flashed to his gun, and it delivered its deadly cargo into the kindly Mr. Biddle.

\*    \*    \*    \*    \*

As I left the patrol cruiser and started down the alley, I looked in disgust at the revolver in my hand. Maybe for self-defense it was okay, if the guy happened to be strangling you. But otherwise it was just for show.

I worked my way down the alley, trying not to be seen by anybody. We were close enough to the river now that as the sun went down everything felt cool and clammy, and the brick streets started to shine with moisture. Probably will be a fog rolling in later.

Whoever had used the warehouse last hadn't been real careful about what they had done with their stuff. Packing cases and pieces of machinery were strewn around the building, giving me plenty of cover while I cased the building.

The warehouse itself was an old wooden building built sometime around the turn of the century, back when using shingles for siding was all the rage. It was about sixty feet wide and I'm guessing about one hundred fifty feet long. Not quite big enough to play football in unless you had a team of midgets, but big enough I guess for a band of crooks to hide out in.

Most of both sidewalls were windows. Back at the time it was built, lighting was at a premium, so sunlight was the answer for everything. But with the dawn of electric light that all changed, and now somebody with a big brush had covered them in black paint. After all, you couldn't have people peeping in your windows and watching you if you were a gang hiding out.

Luckily for me they must not have paid the painter much money, because he did a lousy job. The brush streaks were wide, and in a lot of places he had run low on paint. That gave me plenty of places to peep, and that's just what I did.

Inside, the building was fairly well-lit by hanging ceiling fixtures. I could see four men sitting around a makeshift table made from a packing crate. A fifth man was on the phone over by the far wall. Whoever he was talking to must not have been telling him what he wanted to hear. He was pacing back and forth as far as the phone cord would let him, knuckles white around the receiver.

I couldn't get close enough to hear even his side of the conversation, but I sensed it probably didn't mean sunshine and roses for Joey. So hoping nobody moved for a while, I stopped watching them and made my way around to the back of the building.

My first thought was to try the rear door, but I gave that up after finding that it was padlocked with giant nails going through the wooden frame for extra protection. So instead I found a convenient pile of packing crates that made a nice little ladder up to the roof. Nope, I still didn't have a plan, but I knew for sure I wasn't going to get by either ground entrance.

I climbed up the crates and onto the edge of the roof. It was one of those corrugated things, and with what little light I was getting from the street I could see numerous skylights breaking its rippling surface. Before going any further, I sat down on the edge and pulled off my boots and my socks. It was going to be hard enough trying to stay quiet while walking across the metal surface, and the weight of my boots wasn't going to help. And that damp I had mentioned before was settling. For us rooftop types that meant slip and slide, so barefoot was the way to go.

I tried to use what passed as stealth for me, and it didn't take me long to make it up to the skylight I had chosen for my entrance. It was an easy pick; I used the one farthest from the front entrance.

I sprawled out next to the glass and peered down inside. What I saw pretty much made my blood boil. They had strung a rope up through the rafters and tied it around Joey's wrists. Then they pulled him up off the floor until only his toes touched. After that, from what I could see in the reflected light, they proceed to use him for a punching bag.

Gritting my teeth, I tucked my new tiny gun in my belt, pulled my knife from my pocket, and went to work on one of the panes of glass in the window. It was slow, tedious work scraping out the glaze so I could pull the pane. After a couple of minutes I had gotten it sufficiently loose to get my knife up underneath and pry it free. Carefully I lifted it out and laid it beside me on the roof, only to my horror to watch it slide slowly down the roof and tumble into the abyss.

I stuck my ear into the hole, listening to see if the thugs had heard it, but they were way too interested in their card game. The one I had assumed was the boss slammed the phone down, letting out a stream of profanity. "They're not coming for the shine for a couple hours yet. They said we're to wait till they call with instructions."

One of the men at the table slowly got up and walked back to where Joey was hanging. Without warning he delivered a vicious right to his midsection. I heard the air rush from Joey's lungs as his body became a tetherball swinging out and back. I drew a bead with the .38, but stopped myself from pulling the trigger. From this distance I might miss, and all it was going to do was alert the others.

"You hear that, coon? You get to be our guest for a while longer."

He made ready to swing at Joey again, but one of the guys from the card game distracted him. "You playin' cards or not?"

Joey's body swung toward him, and he took the flat of his hand against Joey's face and pushed him away, making him swing like a pendulum, the toes of his shoes dragging trails in the hard dirt of the floor. "Yeah, I'm coming." Turning, he walked back to his card game and resumed his seat.

I knew now that even with the extended deadline they weren't going to leave much of Joey for their mysterious employer to pick up, so I needed to work fast. Also, my watch said that it had been over half an hour since I left Hays, and I knew he'd be getting antsy.

With the pane of glass out of the skylight I could reach down inside and free the latch. Then it was just a matter of lifting it slowly enough to stop it from scratching like an old lady who'd just lost her purse. When I'd gotten it open far enough I slid under and let my body slowly slide down, knees to elbows, elbows to fingers, till I could find a footing in the rafters.

There was a nice thick beam running right under my window, and I dropped down on it. Suddenly behind me I heard a skittering noise, and as I turned to look I saw behind me the biggest brown rat ever on the beam, nearly as large as a small dog. Whether I was blocking his way or simply invading his territory, he didn't like it and was willing to go to war over it.

With both my hands holding on to the crossbeam over my head I waited for him to charge. He was incredibly fast, and I barely got my feet up before he rushed me. With a skill I knew I couldn't pretend to imitate, he spun around on the beam. Even from the five feet that separated us I could see the yellow of his fangs as he snarled at me and the cruel sparkle in his beady eyes.

He tensed to move, and I tensed to counter. Suddenly he was flying towards me as fast as his four feet could propel him. I sucked in my breath, waiting till just the last second. Then I kicked out with my bare foot, catching him just under the forelegs and turning him from your regular brown rat into a flying brown rat. He must have sailed about ten feet before he tumbled into the dark at the back of the warehouse. I heard him screech as he landed, and so did everybody else. Two of the men at the table leaped to their feet with guns drawn. A third told them to sit down, saying it was only rats chasing rats. They both stared off into the darkness, then finally settled back down.

Okay, with the rats out of the way I had to find a way down. Following the beam I was on led to a catwalk that circled the perimeter of the warehouse almost like a guard-walk in a prison. The only reason I could think of it being there was for the boss to watch the employees. As I got closer to the wall I could see that there was a rickety staircase leading down to the floor.

Breathing a sigh of relief to be standing on something over four inches wide, I dropped down onto the catwalk, never taking my eyes off the group playing cards. I felt like I'd been making enough noise to raise the dead, but unless they were pretending, they hadn't heard a thing.

Slowly and carefully I made my way down the creaky staircase to the dirt floor. Hays had been right about the composition. It was packed dirt covered with oil. The only difference was we referred to it as *adobe*, and with his accent he had called it *adober*.

Once on the floor, travel was quick and easy. I raced over to where Joey was hanging, and with the help of a chair I cut him loose and eased him to the floor. He was pretty bruised and beat up, but as I got him down his one eye opened, and he smiled with swollen and split lips. "Took ya long enough. Figured real soon I was going to have to take them on again by myself!"

"Yeah, well, traffic's a real bear this time of day. And the birds ate all your breadcrumbs, Hansel."

He passed out again, and I laid him carefully on the floor. Now it was payback time!

## Chapter 22

After making sure Joey was still breathing, I made my way towards the lighted end of the warehouse. When I'd managed to get within about fifteen feet I stopped and pulled the .38 from my belt. Trying not to sneer, I pointed it over their heads and pulled the trigger. Inside the empty warehouse it sounded bigger than it really was, and the effect was pretty much immediate. The four at the card game leaped back, rolling onto the floor and pulling their guns from under their jackets. Four sets of eyes rolled in my direction. "Alright, that's far enough. Everybody just lay your guns down, and we promise not to put any extra holes in you." I was trying to sound way more confident than I felt and was hoping that Hays and his men had heard my shot.

It was looking like my battle was nearly won when the dirt by my bare right foot exploded into a small crater and set me to hopping on one foot. Then I heard the man who had been on the phone and had just shot at me holler, "It's only one man. Shoot him!"

Suddenly the air was filled with bullets, and I was rolling across the floor as they tore streaks out of the dirt behind me. Taking half a second, I tried to right myself enough to use the .38. I pulled the trigger and watched it kick up dirt two feet in front of my target. I cursed Hays, and without taking time for another shot I rolled up into a crouch and raced for the side of the building.

The box I leaped behind was too small and too light to protect me, but it was all that was close. I lay there behind it as the bullets stitched their way through it and into the wall. The only thing that stopped me from becoming cheese was their anger and lousy shooting. I poked my head out for a quick look and snapped off a shot. I was rewarded with the sound of somebody cursing me, and I watched him tumble to the floor. One down, four to go.

At last I could hear the sound of pounding on the outside door. Pounding, but no cops rushing in with guns ablazing. Then suddenly it turned into total chaos. One of the windows shattered, and a tear-gas bomb flew inside. It exploded in the middle of the room, and within seconds it was hard to tell who was who and where anybody was.

Mostly by feel I worked my way back over to Joey. Picking him up under the arms, I dragged his giant form back as far as I could out of the fray, behind the cover of some boxes. Then I positioned myself in front of him to protect him. Tears streaming from my eyes and hardly being able to catch my breath, I sat there with my pistol in my lap waiting for anybody to get close.

At least as the warehouse filled with vapor, the goons stopped shooting for fear of hitting each other. I heard a commotion off to my right and heard one of them call, "This way!" Then, other than the banging on the door, silence fell across the giant building.

Suddenly I heard the door crash in. The opening let a breeze flow through, and the tear gas started to dissipate. What I assumed to be cops came rushing into the building, but other than me and Joey, I was pretty sure that it was empty.

I heard someone coming toward me, and I cocked the .38. Slowly they approached till I could see the toes of a pair of shiny shoes through the fog. I knew who they were connected to, and I wanted to scream. Could this day get any worse?

The chief inspector was standing in front of me, a gas mask covering his face. As I watched he took off his hat and pulled it down to let it hang around his neck. "Well, Steele, I should have known." He gave me his fake smile. Then he reached down and took the gun from my hand. He spun it open and dumped the slugs out on the ground.

"Where's Hays?" I asked. "I've got a man here that needs an ambulance."

The inspector walked around me and used the toe of his shiny shoe to lift Joey a bit. "Nah," he said. "The black boy looks like he's gonna be dead in a couple of minutes." Then he turned and called back into the remaining cloud. "He's over here, boys."

Pushing myself to my feet, I faced him eye to eye. "Where's Hays?"

He gave me that politician's smile again. "Captain Hays is outside being questioned by some of my men. I haven't decided whether to file charges against him yet or not. After all, I believe he's been aiding and abetting a known criminal."

I shoved my face up close to his, right up until his gas mask was touching my chest, making him step back. With my teeth clenched I said, "I don't know how deep a hold Sharade has on you, but if anything happens to that man on the floor, nothing, absolutely nothing, will stop me from tearing the life out of you with my bare hands."

He was about to squeal for help when a tall figure stepped out of the darkness and shoved a pistol in his back to stop his retreat. "I don't think we'll have to worry about that, Steele. The ambulance is on its way," Hays said.

I felt my body go nearly limp. I thought I was going to have to take on the chief inspector myself and carry Joey out of here. "Where the hell have you been, Hays? I was nearly eaten by a rat and shot full of holes!"

He pulled the inspector's hands behind his back and clicked on the cuffs. "The chief here had me and my men detained."

I could hear the siren wailing outside and figured it was the ambulance. I knelt down to check on Joey, and his eyes opened again and he tried to smile. "Take it easy, pal," I reassured him. "Your ride's almost here."

Hays pushed the chief over to one of the crates and had him sit down so that he could watch him. "What now, Hays?"

He shrugged one lean shoulder and fished a Lucky out of his pocket with one hand. "The chief here is going to take a couple days of vacation, courtesy of the state, till you get this thing cleared up. Then I think probably jail time. But right now, it's all on you."

I let out a deep sigh. No pressure there. "As soon as they get Joey loaded and on his way to the hospital, I'm going to go after those goons and see if I can find their connection."

Suddenly the phone at the other end of the warehouse started to ring, and I took off at a run to answer it. I snatched it from the cradle, and in a voice as close to that of the gang leader as I could, I answered it. The voice on the other end was a little harsher than when I heard it last, but it was the same voice.

"The men are on their way," Sharade said. "Have the black man there for pickup immediately."

"Yeah, okay. Give me the address again just to make sure I don't screw up. I'm tired of looking after this shine! If I get stuck with him much longer, I'm gonna have him made into a pair of shoes—black ones!" Then I laughed, hoping that I wasn't overdoing it. But when I heard him chuckle I knew that I was right on the money.

He gave me the address and said my money would be there waiting.

"If you ever need any more 'pickups,' let me know."

He said he would and then hung up. When I turned around, Hays was standing behind me.

"What was that all about?"

I grinned. "A little business deal with the master of this whole thing. He's sending people to pick up Joey, and I'm gonna be there to deliver!"

*     *     *     *     *     *

There was a slouch hat and one of the kidnapper's jackets hanging on a nail next to the phone. It was going to help me pull this thing off. I was tearing the insides of the pockets out when Hays asked me what I was doing. "This way I can keep my hands in the pockets and look really causal, and hopefully get as close as I can and still keep my guns in hand." I pulled off my flight jacket and handed it to him, replacing it with the new jacket. I put my hands inside the pockets, and using my fingers for guns, I drew them out of my pants without taking my hands out of the jacket. "Surprise!"

Hays just shook his head. He handed my leather jacket to one of his troopers and told him to put it in the car. "And where are you going to get these guns to pull out of your pockets?"

I gave him my grin. "First of all, evidence or not, you're gonna give me back my .45. We'll worry about what kind of charges Brass Buttons and his crew have against it, and me, later."

"And secondly?" he asked.

"I need one of those long-barrel .38s that you guys carry. No more of this detective special junk. I don't get that close. Nearly got me killed!"

Hays stuck out his jaw in indignation. "Well, it was supposed to be 'just in case,' not 'because I got it.'" He turned to another trooper and sent him out to the car after my automatic.

When he came back with it and handed it to me, I pulled a loaded clip from my back pocket and shoved it home. Instead of nesting it back under my arm, I put it in my pants pocket. Hays handed me his revolver, and I did the same with it on the other side. Then I checked my watch. Nearly time to go.

As I walked over to the kidnapper's car sitting in the middle of the floor, Hays stopped me before I could get in. "Aren't you at least going to tell me where this meeting is?"

I shook my head and slid into the driver's seat. "I can't take the chance on any interference this time, Hays. You mean well, but the bottom line is you still have laws to follow. If you don't know where I'm at, you can't do anything about it."

"And what are you going to do when the city police hear the shooting and show up?"

I shrugged. "I'm kind of hoping there won't be that much shooting. Or even if there is, I'll either be dead or gone by the time they get there." I pulled the car door shut and started the engine.

"Can you get the door for me?" I asked through the open window, meaning the overhead.

Hays walked over and pulled the chain up himself this time. He was standing by the open door as I backed out. As I came abreast of him, I stopped. "Just in case, Hays, I want to thank you for all you've done. I wouldn't have gotten this far without your help."

He looked a little embarrassed and ran the side of his index finger along his mustache. Then he nodded. "Be careful, Steele."

I nodded in return and backed out into the darkness.

*　　*　　*　　*　　*

I let the big car glide to a stop. The meet was supposed to be out on the pier, but I wasn't going to drive out there. In case of trouble that would leave me trapped with only one way off.

I climbed out of the car for a look around. Out in the middle of the river I could see the lights of one of the big barges moving slowly toward the coast. Occasionally its mate sounded a call with its horn, and it answered back.

The air was cold and damp, and I turned up the collar of my stolen jacket to keep the chill away. The river air smelled of diesel fuel, crude oil, and algae. I wrinkled my nose. Real soon it was going to smell of cordite, sulfur, and death.

It seemed that at every move, Sharade and his bunch were just one step ahead of me. This was my chance to catch up. If I could shorten up his crew at this end, it would help when I went to get Kate and Thelma back.

I stood there, leaning against the car and looking up and down the street. The buildings across from me were deserted, their dark windows looking down at me like sightless eyes. About a block away a streetlight burned, but the glass was so dirty from diesel exhaust and coal smoke that it gave out barely enough light to puddle beneath it.

There was a slight breeze blowing, and behind me I could hear the lap of the waves against the shore. It was the kind of sound that should relax a man. But there was no relaxing me. My nerves were as tense as an over-wound rubber band. I'd have felt a lot better if Jocy had been there, but I think that had been part of their plan all along. If they couldn't manage to kill me, they were going to take away my allies and try to demoralize me, hoping to break me. What they didn't know was that they were making me even more determined to bring them down!

I heard the hiss of rubber against the damp paving stones. A big sedan rolled around the corner and stopped in the middle of the street, leaving its headlights on. The front doors opened and two men climbed out. They stayed behind the lights, so they were little more than silhouettes.

I stuck my hands further in my ripped-out pockets, loosening the .38 and taking the safety off my automatic. I walked around the rear of the car and up onto the sidewalk, trying to get out of the lights and to where I could see them better. I was only a couple of steps over the curb when the one I'm guessing was on the driver's side yelled for me to stop.

"That's far enough. We want you where we can see you." That was a little contrary to what I wanted, but I stopped.

If it hadn't have been for the streetlight they would have been nearly invisible in the darkness. Now I could only hope that my moving had done nearly the same for me. I squinted my eyes, blocking out as much of the light as I could, trying to pierce the shadows. But when the silhouette on the passenger side spoke, I might as well have not wasted the effort. I had heard those sweet, syrupy tones before in his bedside manner.

"I want to thank you for coming, Steele. It saves us the trouble of hunting you down. I'm guessing you didn't bring the black with you. From what Tragg said, his men had been rather hard on it. That is unfortunate. Even an animal shouldn't be made to suffer."

"If you knew it was me all along, Sharade, why come?"

Even with the shadows I could see him holding out his hands, palms up. "To speak to you one last time."

I snorted a bit in disbelief. "One last time? Why, Sharade? Are you going to kill yourself?"

His chuckle was evil, and I felt my blood run a bit colder. "No, Steele, I have come to kill you!" He slid his hands into his pockets, and I wondered for a moment if he knew my trick. He was pacing a bit beside the car, and I used the distraction to move a little closer to the edge of the pier and further into the dark.

"I must admit," he began again, "you have been a very resourceful adversary, something I haven't had in a long time. But my amusement with you has waned. It is time to bring this cat-and-mouse game to an end."

I cocked an eyebrow. "And you think that killing me is going to bring all of this to a halt?"

He chuckled again. "You're the one who doesn't follow the rules. You can't be bought or coerced. All admirable qualities, but also most annoying. With you out of the way, I can easily take care of the rest."

I was almost starting to believe him. "You won't stop Joey so easily."

"Your loyal friend, always coming to the rescue. Well, Captain, this is Louisiana, and he is little more than one more black man here amidst thousands. Every day in this state black men disappear, never to be seen again. Do you think that one more will be an exception? I don't believe so."

The guns were out of my pockets now and hanging at my sides, my hands damp against the grips. My mind was in a whirl, trying to piece together Sharade's plan. I could see both of them well enough to know that neither of them was holding a gun. Sharade's hands were behind his back, the way he stood when questioning a patient. I quickly scanned the buildings across the street. Nothing had changed there. No sniper had suddenly appeared. Behind me was only water.

Sharade's hands came back around front, and he seemed to be holding something in his right hand. Suddenly I knew. All along he had intended to kill the men who had taken Joey, and I had walked right into their trap. The car was loaded with explosives, and Sharade was holding the detonator.

"Goodbye, Steele!" If I had been looking, I might have seen his smile in the darkness as he pushed the switch, but I was way too busy running to look.

Suddenly behind me the world exploded, and a giant hand reached out and slapped me upwards off the ground into the air. At that moment, time came to a near stop. I was able to see things more clearly than ever before. Pieces of flaming debris joined me on my flight, hunks of wood from the railing along the sidewalk filling the air like the arrows of a hundred Indians, and the water reaching out to claim me in its icy grasp. Then suddenly something hit me, and the world faded away.

Chapter 23

Even before the dust and debris had settled, Sharade and his driver were back in the car. As he started the auto, he asked, "Where to, Colonel?"

Sharade held up his index finger, correcting him. "Remember, it's *Doctor* now."

The man behind the wheel nodded. "Sorry, sir. After an operation like this it seems like old times, and I forget."

Sharade smiled, pleased with himself. "It did go very well, didn't it?" he asked rhetorically. "Take us home, Major. I'd rather not be caught here and have to talk to that buffoon of a chief inspector." He crossed his hands over his stomach and settled back into the seat.

"What about the black man, sir?" the major asked as he swung away from the curb and started to accelerate.

Content and drifting off to sleep, Sharade managed a smile. "We can take care of him anytime."

"And the women?"

"Thelma is working out very well. The other one is too headstrong to be controlled and will only be trouble. So we will use her for food!"

*　　*　　*　　*　　*

Even as the explosion was tearing through the waterfront, a block away Hays was dropping the sonic listening device he'd been monitoring the conversation with and started running down the street. He reached the spot where the car had stood as the other sedan turned the corner. He tossed off his gun belt and boots and hurled himself into the water below what was left of the pier, trying to avoid the flotsam created by the explosion.

There was little evidence left to mark the passage of Steele through the dark, murky surface—only a ripple moving off toward infinity. His body cleaved the surface, carrying the trooper down into the depths. Even during the day the polluted water would have let little light penetrate much beyond the surface. Now, in the darkness, it was like swimming through oily sludge.

On his first trip to the bottom he came up empty-handed, breaking the surface and gasping for air before diving below for a second time. It was only by sheer luck that he felt something brush by him, and he reached out to grab it. It was a human arm, and so even was the buoyancy that for a moment he thought that it had become detached from its owner. But gritting his teeth and finding strength he didn't know he possessed, he pulled it towards him, feeling the weight and knowing that there was a man attached to it. Swimming upwards, he dragged Steele's limp form to the surface.

As stroked toward the shore, pulling Steele's body behind him, he could see that his driver was already there waiting to help him out of the water. He handed Steele's arm to the driver, and then, with him pulling and Hays pushing, they managed to lift him onto the shore.

While Hays caught his breath the trooper rolled Steele onto his belly and started artificial respirations, pulling back on Rick's folded arms like chicken wings. In the distance the sound of a siren wailed. Hays raised an eyebrow in question, and the aide said, "I radioed for the Rescue Squad while you were running down the street, sir. Didn't figure we had a second to waste." Almost as though on cue, the red Cadilac ambulance skidded to a stop. Two men piled out and quickly began removing equipment from the back.

The men from the rescue squad trundled their pulmotor down the hill on its two-wheeled cart, leaving deep trails in the sand. While one of them set up the breathing device, the other took over the artificial respiration for the trooper.

Lying on the ground, his head turned to one side while they worked on him, Steele looked dead. The oily water had plastered his hair to his forehead, and the wound from the debris was still slightly oozing dark crimson blood. His eyes were half open, his skin chalky grey, and his lips and fingertips were slowly turning blue. It made Hays shudder. He hadn't known Steele long, but in the short time that he had, he'd come to admire his courage. With his loyalty to his friends and his determination, he was the kind of man they created the word *hero* for. He was the kind of man Hays himself strived to be, but for Steele it just seemed to come naturally.

To the rest of the world it always looked as though he was charging headfirst into trouble, but, even if he was, there was always a plan. Maybe not the best plan, but always a plan. Now looking at him lying there, Hays wondered if all that had come to an end.

The first of the rescue men had his device ready to go, so he helped his partner roll Rick over. He fitted the mask over his mouth and nose, hooking the elastic strap around the back of his head. There was a hose like one from a vacuum cleaner that ran back to the box containing the oxygen tank. The medic made a few final adjustments, opened the bottle, and began to turn the crank. The effect was startling. Rick's chest began to rise and fall almost as if he were awake.

They ran the pump continuously, checking every few minutes for a pulse. Finally they stopped cranking, and the movement in Rick's chest stopped. The medic by his side took off the mask, and, after checking for a pulse, rose, shaking his head. "Looks like we've lost him. Nothing else we can do."

Hays walked over and knelt down where the medic had been. He was frustrated and angry. It couldn't end like this. Heroes were supposed to go out in a blaze of glory, not from a simple drowning! In a moment of rage, he brought his fist down in the middle of Rick's silent chest. "Damn it, Steele! You can't do this to me. You can't make me the one responsible for letting you die!" Again he hit him, and almost as if Rick heard him, he began to cough and spit water.

Immediately Hays slid his arm under Rick's shoulders and rolled him over on his side to get the water out of his lungs. The two medics were standing back watching, amazed. He held Rick up till he stopped coughing and then laid him back down. As he did, two city police cars with sirens screaming skidded to a stop on the street above.

Standing up, Hays grabbed the arm of one of the medics and said, "Get your stretcher and load him up. Cover him up like a dead man. And if anybody asks, tell them you did all you could, but you couldn't save him." Hays took off his blanket and used it to cover up Rick's face. Then he called his aide over.

"Go up there and see if you can't keep those metro boys from coming down here. I don't want them finding out he's still alive."

As his aide went up to slow down the local police, Captain Hays helped the men from the rescue squad get Rick loaded onto the stretcher and back up the bank. When they were loading him into the back of the ambulance, one of the cops walked over and pulled back the blanket to take a look at Rick. Fortunately he was lying as still as death, and the grey, sallow color hadn't left him yet.

The cop shook his head and covered him back up. "Nothing like a drownin' to make a man sick. Just lucky he wasn't in the water any longer, or the fish would have gotten him."

Hays shoved the stretcher home and then followed the attendant to the front. "Take him to the receiving morgue at Central Hospital. Tell the attendant there to call down Doctor Redmond, and have him take care of the body."

"Yes, although I can't see what this is all about."

"You don't worry what it's about. You just do what I asked, and I'll explain it later."

"And what about our report?" the other one asked.

"Just fill it out like you would for any other dead body." He glanced into the back where Steele was lying. "We all three know he was dead when you got here. Anything that happened after that was just chance."

The driver shifted into gear and let in the clutch, and the big station wagon rolled away. After a couple of feet he hit the lights and siren, and then he floored it, spewing dirt and gravel in his wake.

As they pulled out, the cop walked over to where Hays was standing and said, "In kind of a hurry for carrying a dead man."

Hays shrugged his shoulders. "Maybe it's their coffee break time." Then he changed the subject. "You want to write up what happened? 'Cause I'm getting real tired of standing here in these wet clothes."

The cop nodded and took a notebook from his back pocket. Flipping it open, he stood poised with pencil in hand. "What was the victim's name?"

Hays looked out across the water. "The man who died here today was Captain Rick Steele. He was caught in an explosion of unknown origin, thrown into the river, and drowned."

*　　*　　*　　*　　*

I remembered the explosion, and flying through the air headed towards the river. After that it all got kind of weird and fuzzy. The next thing I remembered was floating underwater, and there was a body hanging limply in the murk beside me. I reached out to touch it, but every time I got close it would move away, like two magnets with the same poles facing each other.

I knew I was underwater, but for some crazy reason I wasn't drowning. Matter of fact, I wasn't even holding my breath. Suddenly behind me there was splash, and another swimmer dove by. He seemed to be looking for something. Not finding it, he had to go back to the surface to catch another breath. I wanted to tell him about my really wild secret way of not breathing, but I couldn't make myself heard.

When the swimmer came under the next time, I realized that he was looking for the floater. So I used my crazy antimagnetic thing to push the body in his direction. He managed to find his arm and pull him along to the surface and then the shore.

Tired of being underwater, I decided to follow and see what was going on. I started toward land and realized that I didn't have to swim; I could just kind of walk my way to the shore.

As I got there, the swimmer, and now that he had his head out of the water I could see that it was Hays, was handing the body's arm to his aide, and together they managed to get him up on shore. As I floated up out of the river, I watched as they laid the body on its belly and started artificial respirations on it. It was looking pretty sad for the guy on the ground. From what I could see, he was pretty much a dead duck.

I hollered at Hays as I stepped onto the sand. He looked my way for a second, but didn't say anything back. I just took for granted he was worried about the dead guy. The trooper was working really hard on him, but it didn't look like it was doing much good, so I just kept my yap shut and watched.

It wasn't more than a couple of minutes after we got out of the water that the rescue squad pulled up. They didn't seem to be in much of a hurry. I'm kind of guessing they realized the same thing that I did, that this guy was set for the Big Sleep and nothing they could do was

235

gonna save him. But they were getting paid, so they unloaded their equipment out of the back of the station wagon and drug it down over the bank. I could hear them cussing about why guys always have to drown at the bottom of a four-foot bank instead of a nice, sandy beach with girls in swimsuits around. I was pretty sure Hays didn't hear them, or he'd have read them the Riot Act. From the look on his face, this guy was a friend of his.

The smaller one of the Mutt and Jeff pair took over for the trooper while the other one went to work setting up their thing. I'd seen one once before after a fire, but couldn't remember what it was called. And from what I did remember the guy they were using it on died anyway.

Hays' aide brought him a blanket to keep him from getting too cold in his wet clothes. I was kind of thinking maybe I should have gotten one too, but then I realized I wasn't cold at all. And for that matter, I wasn't even wet anymore.

I stood there beside Hays, watching the rescue guys work and really wanting to ask a couple of questions, but for once in my life keeping my mouth shut instead of letting it run wild.

The guy on the pulmotor—yep, just remembered that—got done adjusting his dials and tapping his gauges. He dragged the hose with the mask on it down to his partner, and then helped him roll the near-stiff over. And for the first time I was going to get a look at the poor guy's face.

I moved over to get a good look, and suddenly a scream was ripped out me. I felt dizzy and nauseous and weak. I sank down to my knees in the sand, noticing for the first time I wasn't leaving any marks. *The face on the body was mine!* My gawd, I was dead!

I got hold of myself well enough to crawl over there and try urging them on. "Work harder! Turn the crank faster! That's me—you have to save me!"

I pushed on my stomach, pleading with myself. "Come on, Steele, breathe! You remember how! You've been doing it since you were a little baby. Try it, damn it! Just one breath! In-out, in-out! Do it for me!"

But the body on the ground, that poor dead soul that was me, wasn't trying. He was just lying there like a lazy lump. I stood up and kicked him in the side with my ghost foot, but the repulsion we had for each other just knocked me over backwards, and I landed on the spiritual seat of my spiritual pants in the sand.

I sat there with my head in my hands, feeling sorry for myself and regretting all the things I had done since I was a kid. Or the stuff that the dead guy on the sand had done. Since he wouldn't do what I wanted him to, I was disassociating myself from him. If he wanted to stay dead that was fine with me. I didn't need his pruned-up self. I'd just go on alone. Probably for the better anyway. Bullets would go right through me. And I wouldn't have to pay taxes. Hell, I bet I could even fly without a plane!

I thumbed my nose at my body. He shouldn't have gotten himself caught in the explosion in the first place. I wouldn't have.

Suddenly the two rescue guys stopped working and looked at each other. The one who'd been doing the artificial respirations shook his head, and the other one agreed. He stopped turning the crank and walked down to his companion. "Nothing left to do. He's gone."

I jumped up from the sand screaming. "No, you can't just leave him! I didn't mean what I said—you have to try some more. He's my best friend, next to me. Heck, he is me." I raced over to their pulmotor and tried to turn the crank, but it kept sliding through my hand. I tried to push the big guy back to his machine, but I couldn't touch him. Finally with tears streaming down my face, I sank down in the sand next to my body.

Hays walked slowly over and settled down on the other side of my body. From the look on his face, he was feeling every bit as bad as I was. If I ever got the chance again, I'd tell him thank you for that. I didn't know that he liked me that much.

Then I changed my mind. Hays reached out and slammed his fist down on my chest. I reached out to try and stop him as he did it again, but his fist went right through my wispy hands. I couldn't understand why he was feeling bad for me one moment, and beating on my dead body the next!

Suddenly my chest hurt, and I felt like I wanted to throw up. Ghosts don't throw up! Oily, scummy water was pouring out of my mouth, and I wasn't sitting up anymore, I was lying on the sand. I was back in my body! I wanted to scream and shout, but all I could do was puke up brown water. Then I couldn't feel even that anymore. I slipped slowly into the sweet realm of unconscious.

## Chapter 24

Elisha Biddle was a quiet family man who enjoyed people. That made running a general store perfect for him. It gave him the chance to do what he loved best: talking and gossiping, and making money at the same time. There was more news about the town in his store than any newspaper would have had room to print.

He'd always been a rather lucky man, finding fortune where it fell. He met his wife on a chanced blind date, and they had hit it off immediately. Two months later after a quick courtship they were married and armed with a wagon full of supplies as they headed west from his native North Carolina. He had heard there was a boom out west and decided to follow his nose.

That nose had led him here to the tiny town of Cypress Glen. It wasn't much of a town yet, just a collection of farmers, but they were in need of a store for supplies and he was there to provide. After fifteen years and two kids, it was like heaven. And best of all, he felt better than he ever had in his life. Even his wife showed no sign of the years they had spent together. Since coming here neither of them, or anyone else in the town for that matter, had spent so much as a day down with a cold. Yes, for Elisha Biddle, Cypress Glen was pretty much a paradise. But as he pushed open the door of his general store, that was all about to change.

As the door swung shut the bullet caught the dear Mr. Biddle just slightly above his eyebrows, right in the middle of his forehead, and the force of the impact sent his now lifeless body tumbling back through the glass on the just-closed door. He landed with a hard thump he didn't feel on the wooden boardwalk outside.

The colonel was just coming from the back of the store when the major shot Mr. Biddle. He snatched the gun from the major's hand and angrily hurled it to the floor. "Damn it man, what part of be careful do you not understand?" He didn't wait for an answer; the wheels inside his head were already assessing the situation. Turning to the rest of his men, he started issuing orders.

"You men each grab a new weapon and as much ammunition as you can carry. I want you to go from house to house and rouse everybody in the town and bring them here in front of the store. I don't care how you do it, by gunpoint or subterfuge, just bring them here. But, and this is a direct order, *do not* kill anyone unless it is absolutely necessary! And if you do, your excuse had better be a valid one, or you're liable to end up just as dead!"

Armed with fresh weapons, the ragtag group of soldiers stepped through the broken glass and over the body of the once-pleasant Mr. Biddle to complete their orders. The major was the last to leave. He picked up his revolver from where the colonel had thrown it, replaced the spent load, and started to follow the others out. With one leg through the door, he paused. "Do you want to explain your plan, or am I to be like the rest of them now—a mindless fool?"

Still angry over the shot that had forced his hand before he was ready, the colonel glared back at him. "Just do what I tell you. We'll discuss this later."

Nodding his acquiescence, he stepped out the door and stalked off down the street. The colonel stood, watching him go. That was the burden of command, something that he must not forget again. No matter where they reached in rank, enlisted men would never be more than animals wearing fancy collars.

The colonel propped open the door and dragged the body of Mr. Biddle back inside the store and out of sight. It wouldn't do for the good citizens of the town to realize too soon what his plan was.

After dragging Biddle's body back into the store, he picked up his revolver, carefully loaded it, and then slid it into the new leather holster hanging at his side. Then he took down a double-barreled scatter gun from the rack. Not a choice weapon for a gentleman, but desperate times called for desperate measures. After loading it and filling his pockets with shells, he grabbed a wooden chair from the half circle around the potbellied wood stove and carried it outside onto the boardwalk to wait for his men. The colonel didn't have long to wait. Even as he was setting down the chair, one of the Carny brothers was coming back with a family of four in front of the barrel of his gun. When they got to where the colonel was sitting, he calmly rose and took off his hat to the lady. She, like her husband and their children, was only half dressed, as though they had been pulled from their very beds. Shortly after, more residents began to arrive.

Some of the men were starting to protest their treatment, but a quick look at the colonel's shotgun stopped that.

It didn't take much over an hour before the twenty or so families of the town were milling around in the street in front of the store, corralled in by his men.

The colonel rose to his feet and loudly cleared his throat. When no one responded, he pointed his shotgun into the night sky and pulled the trigger. Some of the women screamed and a few of the men grumbled, but the crowd fell silent.

Having done its job, he sat the shotgun next to the chair and turned to address the crowd. "Ladies and gentlemen, I wish to apologize for the necessities of my actions tonight. But as good sons and daughters of the Confederacy, I'm sure you will understand why I have done what I have done."

Somewhere in the crowd a voice called out, interrupting him. "The Confederacy is dead! The war ended nearly a month ago!"

The colonel's glare met the man eye-to-eye, and before he could speak again the major pushed his way through the crowd and clubbed him down. No one else in the crowd said a word.

Satisfied that he wouldn't be interrupted again, the colonel continued. "Contrary to what that hooligan said, the Confederate States of America is alive. Though injured by the foul tactics of the likes of Sherman and Grant, this war is not over, and it will not be over till no son of the South still stands!"

The crowd grumbled, but nothing was said. So he changed his tone and his tactics, trying to sound more fatherly than soldierly. "My men and I intend to finish this war. Any of you who would like to join us of your own free will are welcome. And as much as it pains me, I am forced to tell you that if you do not, I will be forced to conscript you. But that is a few days in the future. Let us talk about our current situation.

"I have to get word to the war office that I am still alive and active. Seeing no telegraph wires leading into town, I must send a rider to the capitol. That means we will be partaking of your hospitality for the next few days. I do hope that will not disrupt your daily routine any more than necessary. But there will be disruptions, and of course a new set of rules for the duration of our stay.

"First of all," he continued, "I'm afraid that I must ask you to temporarily give up all your firearms." There were murmurs of protest from the crowd, and the colonel held up his hand to stop them. "This for both your protection and that of my men. In a short while one of my men will begin a house-to-house search for guns. You will be given the choice of cooperating with them or having them invade your property unescorted. Personally, for your sake, I hope you will cooperate."

With his hands locked behind his back he began to pace up and down the boardwalk. "Secondly, I ask that you all help provide my men with food and shelter while we remain here in your town. We are not asking for anything special, just three square meals a day and a roof over our heads till we are ready to move on. Until that time, consider this general store my headquarters until we leave."

In the middle of the crowd a woman spoke up. "Have you talked to my husband about this? Does he know what you're doing?"

The colonel took off his new hat and peered into the crowd. "And you are, ma'am?"

A tall, thin woman in a nightdress and bare feet pushed her way to the front of the crowd, clutching her robe around her. "I'm Charlotte Biddle. My husband and I own that store you're standing in front of."

The colonel took a deep breath, considering just how to explain to her what had happened to her husband, when suddenly a voice from behind him said, "Does anybody know how my door got broken? And why are all you people in the street?"

*　　*　　*　　*　　*

I opened one eye very carefully and glanced around the room. I was lying in a hospital bed, with a giant mummy sitting next to me keeping watch. The first thing I thought was that this wasn't heaven. That meant either I was alive or they had hospital beds in hell just like on Earth, and they used giant black mummies to guard the people from running away.

I closed my eye and tried it with the other one. Nope, nothing changed. Still in a hospital bed. I reached out and poked the mummy with my forefinger. When he yelled, "Hey, quit it," I was pretty sure that unless he was dead too, and being a mummy he just might be, I was alive.

I opened both eyes at once this time and looked at the mummy. "So, Karloff was busy?" I asked. "And I got stuck with the mummy stunt double?"

That was all I had time to say because he scooped me up out of the bed and tossed me around in the air. "You're alive, boss! You're alive!"

I fought my way out of his grip and managed to get my bare feet on the floor. "I won't be if you don't knock it off," I complained. But looking at that big, ugly grin under all those bandages was well worth it.

Climbing back onto the bed, I asked, "What day is it?"

Joey got a little more serious. "You've been out three days, boss. Hays and the doctor weren't sure you were ever coming out of it. They said you were dead!"

The sudden exertion had tired me out, and I lay back onto the bed. I looked over at him, trying to decide just what I was going to tell him. Finally I decided on straight out. "I was dead, Joey. I saw the whole thing."

Joey backed up a step and made a cross with his fingers at me. I shook my head at him. "I think that's for vampires."

His eyes were big and round, and I wasn't sure if he was putting me on or not. "My great-grandma used to whisper stories about people like you, people back from the grave that had to eat living flesh to survive." He held one bony, black finger up in front of my face. "Does that make you hungry? Would you like to take a bite outta that?"

I scrunched up my face while I thought about it for a moment. Finally I said, "Nah, I'm pretty much a white meat man myself." We both broke into laughter, and hugged each other.

We both said at the same time, "I thought I was going to lose you." Then we laughed again.     When we both finally ran out of feeling good, I got serious again. "What's happened while I was out? What's the situation?"

Joey pulled his chair back over and sat down. "Well, according to all the papers, you died in that explosion. Hays thought for now, and considering the shape you were in, that was the safest bet."

I nodded my agreement. "Besides, it gives us a bit of an advantage when we finally strike against the hospital."

"I take it you've got a plan?"

I shrugged one shoulder. "At least the beginnings of one. Right now, though, I'd kind of like some breakfast. I'm starved."

That weird, scared look crossed Joey's face again, and he pulled his chair back a couple more feet. I scrunched up one cheek in kind of a wry look and shook my head. "No, not you, you big scaredy cat. Just some plain ol' bacon and eggs would be fine." Then I grinned. "Maybe with a side of damsel for desert."

After stuffing myself as best I could on hospital food, the doctor came in to check on me. He was pretty much as amazed as Joey, but without the zombie thing. "It really is remarkable, Steele. When they brought you into the morgue and called me down, I figured you were done for."

"You know, Doc, people are always saying that about me. Then when they least expect it, I turn up again." Then I changed the subject. "When can I get out of here? I've still got friends out there in trouble that are counting on me."

"Even as remarkable as your recovery has been, your body is still pretty weak. Let's give it a couple of days, and then we'll see."

I didn't care much for his answer, but there wasn't much I could do about it. I jerked a thumb towards Joey. "What about the mummy there? When can he leave?"

It took him a second to get the joke, and then he smiled thinly. Need to work on that sense of humor of his. "Joey's free to go any time. Most of what he's got left are just bumps, bruises and abrasions."

Joey looked at him with a pained look on his face. "You sure, Doc? I gots me some mighty bad hurtin' goin' on."

The doctor shook his head. "First of all, you can drop the dumb black man act. I know you have a degree in engineering, and that you're probably smarter than both of us. Secondly, if you're afraid I'm going to toss you out before I do this one…." His turn to use the thumb, and it was pointed at me. "Neither one of you are really here, so how can I throw you out?" Then he turned back to me. "I'll be back to check on you this afternoon. Don't get out of that bed for anything but the bathroom. And when you do, make sure he helps you. Don't want to have to fix a broken nose along with everything else."

As he walked out the door, I thought that maybe he was starting to get it.

The doctor wasn't gone more than a couple of minutes when the door opened a second time, and Hays blew in. He was ear-to-ear smiles. "The doctor called me earlier and told me you were awake. I thought I'd stop in and see how you were doing."

Before he got settled in the other chair I stuck out a weak hand, and he took it. "You saved my life, Hays. Those two whacks on the chest started everything working again. I don't know how I can ever thank you."

Hays looked bewildered. "How did you know…?"

I gave him a grin. "Long story. If we all get out of what's coming up next alive, I'll tell it to you."

He fumbled with his hat a bit, not really meeting my eyes. "Speaking of which, the city police department has issued a warrant for Joey and wants a full autopsy done on your body."

"That sounds like the chief inspector talking. I thought you had him under wraps?"

"I did, but I couldn't hold him forever. Word came down from the commander that I had to let him go. When I explained what had happened, he said that I had overstepped my bounds, and if formal charges couldn't be filed I had to let him go. I'm currently on probation, awaiting the results of an investigation."

I winced at that. After all he had done for me, that hurt almost as much as the pain in my chest. "So what now?"

He shifted around in his chair, leaned forward, and looked over his shoulder before he spoke. It was a gesture I had seen him use numerous times before he said something important. Must be the paranoia from working for the state. But at the same time it must be contagious, because I saw Joey do the same thing, and we were the only people in the room. "Ever since the explosion," Hays began, "I've had a surveillance team on the hospital." He reached in his pocket and took out his notebook. "Seems there's quite a daily crowd of customers there. Almost a line at times, all made up of the locals. They all come back out sporting one of those little round bandages like they put on you for polio vaccinations. You know what that's about?"

I shook my head. "A few ideas, but nothing concrete yet. What else?"

He checked his notes again. "Had a body come out of there yesterday."

Suddenly my blood ran cold, and I clenched the sheet up in my fists. "What kind of body," I asked, afraid of the answer.

"Seventy-five-year-old man. Died of acute anemia and massive dehydration."

"The old man I saw in the room with the IV in his arm," I mumbled.

"What's that?"

I just shook my head. "Nothing. Go on."

He flipped his notebook shut. "That's all, other than a lot of packages marked as medical supplies being shipped out. All in the same size box, all very carefully packed."

"I don't suppose your boys got their hands on one of those packages?"

He shook his head. "I thought about that too, but not without starting a ruckus. And remember, my men aren't really there anyway."

A germ of an idea was starting to grow inside my head. "Can I count on you for a little more help?"

Hays gave me kind of a goofy grin. "In for a penny, in for a pound. What do you need?"

"We're gonna need a car, a fast car, and someplace that Joey can work on it without anybody knowing about it."

"What are you cooking up now, Steele?"

There was no humor in my grin. "I'm gonna get us one of those shipments, and we're gonna find out what's in it."

Hays stood up and set his chair back against the wall. Putting on his hat, he said, "I'll let you know this afternoon where the garage is. I'm guessing you'll want a full array of tools?"

"And a cutting torch and a welder."

He stopped as he went out the door. "And I don't get the car back?"

"At least not in the same shape."

As he left, Joey pulled his chair closer, and he and I began to scratch on a piece of paper.

*    *    *    *    *

It had been nearly a week since she had been taken from the hospital by Sharade and his crew. Despite the rough treatment she had suffered, Kate had continued to recover. At least this time there were lights in her prison, and she was fed at regular intervals. Once she even thought that she had caught a glimpse of Thelma in the hall, but when she had called to her, Thelma, or who she thought was Thelma, had ignored her.

She had to guess what part of the hospital she was in. Only by the high humidity and the warmth of the wall did she know that she was somewhere near the boiler room. It was just a brick room with a door, a single light, and a metal cot. The heavy door was locked on the outside. After the first day she had kept her spoon from her evening meal and had begun to work on the mortar and brick around the door. It was probably a fool's errand, but having something to do stopped her from going crazy, when she had the energy that is.

When she awoke from being brought there, she found a subclavian catheter line in her chest. Her first instinct was to tear it out. But just as she was set to pull it free, she realized that it was plugged directly into an artery in her chest. If she pulled it free, the chances were excellent that she would bleed to death before anybody found her. She racked her mind, trying to decide what it was they were injecting or were going to inject into her.

On the third day she got more answers than she ever wanted. Sharade and a burly attendant had appeared at her door with an ultimatum. Either she cooperated or they would withhold her food and water until she was too weak to protest.

Finally, despite her misgivings, she was forced to agree. The orderly had entered first, and under his instructions she was forced to lie back on the cot while he secured her hands and legs with webbed straps. Once it was safe, Sharade entered and attached tubing and a bottle to the line in her chest. Then slowly he began to draw the warm blood from her body.

When the beaker was full, he replugged the line and turned to go. Kate called him back. "You gonna tell me what this is all about?" she asked weakly.

Sharade held the bottle up for her to see. "Your blood keeps a very dear friend of ours alive. And in turn, he keeps us alive. Be grateful that I'm only taking a pint and leaving you time to recover. I could draw it all at once, and there would be nothing left but a bloodless husk."

Kate shivered at the thought of what he was doing with her blood. What kind of a friend could he possibly be keeping alive? A vampire? That was just silly. She didn't believe in vampires, but what else could it be? Was that the secret they were hiding here? Could they all be some form of vampire?

Kate settled back on her cot, weak as a kitten, as the attendant released the straps.

Twice since then Sharade had been back, and she was no closer to an answer than she had been before.

*　　*　　*　　*　　*

Thelma came into the living room, plopped down on the couch, and kicked off her shoes. With a heavy whoosh of breath she raised up her feet and settled them on the top of the glass coffee table. In the reflection on the glass she could see that there was a new run in the back of her white stockings, the second pair she'd ruined this week.

She was tired, but she felt better than she had in ages. It was so nice to be back here living with her aunt and uncle and helping to look after Lou Anne.

When Lou Anne had first had her accident, and Uncle Vince had called and asked her if she would come and help for a few days, she had been hesitant at first. After living in the big city for so long, she wasn't sure she wanted to come back to small-town America. But now, after all these long months, it felt like home again. Even if Dr. Sharade could be a real bear sometimes. And besides, they weren't real busy at the hospital right now. There were only four patients. Oh yes, she corrected herself, five if you counted the mysterious crazy woman downstairs. Why just the other day she had suddenly called out to her when they brought down her meal. She had even known Thelma's name. That sent a shudder down her spine.

What if she escaped and came looking for her? Uncle Vince and Aunt Sophie could be in danger, not to mention poor Lou Anne who was catatonic in her hospital bed. Maybe tomorrow she should speak to Dr. Sharade about that. But for now she was just going to relax and enjoy the evening.

Finding herself nearly nodding off, she got up and walked into the kitchen. Warm, delicious aromas were drifting from the oven. As usual, Aunt Sophie was at the sink, dressed in her apron doing dishes. Thelma kissed her lightly on the cheek. "Mmmm, what smells so good?" she asked.

Sophie took her hands from the wrist-deep dishwater and peeled off her yellow rubber gloves. Walking over to the oven, she opened the door and peeked inside. Satisfied with what she saw, she said, "We're having your Uncle Vince's favorite, pork chops and kraut."

Thelma rubbed her rather ample stomach. "Mine, too." After walking to the coffee pot, she poured herself a cup and settled down at the table.

"How was work today, dear?" Sophie asked, sitting down across from her.

Thelma blew carefully on her coffee before taking a sip. When she'd set the cup back down she said, "Nothing too busy there, but it's vaccination time again. So there's plenty to do. You'll want to make sure that you and Uncle Vince don't forget."

Sophie shook her head. "Just me, Thelma. Remember your Uncle Vince in an outsider. He doesn't get the vaccination."

She nodded knowingly. "I had forgotten. It's really too bad that he never accepted the way of life. But I guess everyone has their own way."

Sophie got up and refilled her own coffee cup. When she sat back down she asked, "So tell me, what's exciting at the hospital? Any new gossip from the people coming in for vaccinations?"

Thelma thought for a minute, then she shook her head. "Not really. Although, we did get in this crazy woman a couple of days ago. The doctor says she's really dangerous, and he's keeping her in a locked room downstairs."

That piqued Sophie's interest, and she leaned forward a bit. "Is she from around here?"

"No," she answered, shaking her head and realizing for the first time she'd forgotten to take her starched cap off. "She's from the city. I peeked at her file. Says she was some kind of doctor once. Can you imagine that? A doctor gone crazy?"

Sophie just shook her head, thinking about what the kindly Dr. Sharade would be like crazy. The thought of it made her shiver.

*     *     *     *     *

After three days on my back in a hospital bed, I was starting to go stir-crazy. I hadn't seen Joey since I sent him off to work on the car, and Hays must have been busy someplace else because I hadn't seen so much as a mustache hair from him. When the doctor stopped coming to see me, I figured that either I smelled bad or the world had ended while I was asleep. The best I could say was the food kept coming, and while lying there in bed I kept working my muscles to try and get my strength back.

Needless to say, when the doctor showed up on the morning of the third day, I could have kissed him.

He had me walk across the room, listened to my heart, and used one of those little tubes you blow in to check my lung capacity. All the while the only comments I was getting from him were "Hummm, uh huh, I see." Typical doctor speak.

Finally I settled on the end of the bed and asked, "Well? Do you let me out, or do I have to escape?"

Laughing, he said, "Don't start planning your big break out. I'm going to parole you. But you have to promise me you'll take it easy."

I gave him my most sincere look. "Absolutley, Doc. I'll make sure Joey does all the heavy shooting."

The smile faded from his face, and he was the solemn old doctor again. "You're going after them, aren't you?"

"I don't have any choice, Doc. They've got Kate, and they've got Thelma. Even if they weren't two of my favorite people, I couldn't leave them there to die. Travel with me and nobody gets left behind."

He stood up and patted me on the thigh. "Just be careful. He's one dangerous man. And he's already managed to kill you once. Not sure we can get you back a second time." As he got to the door, he paused. "I'll tell Captain Hays you can leave."

About an hour later Hays showed up with two grocery bags. One had my clothes in it. He had even managed to find my flight jacket from when I took it off at the warehouse.

I was just buckling my pants when he handed me the other bag. Inside was my shoulder holster, and nestled very nicely in it was a .45 Colt. I laid the holster on the bed and took the automatic out. I pulled the slide back to check the action and popped out the clip to make sure it was full. Everything was in perfect working order.

When I raised an eyebrow at him in question, he said, "It's the one you bought before all this happened. I've got a trooper sitting in a cell, trying to decide whether he wants to talk or not about what he was doing with it."

I slid the rig over my shoulder, tied the lanyard to my belt to stop it from dragging, and then I put the gun to bed. I felt whole again. "Shall we?" I asked, motioning toward the door.

Hays nodded, and then he said, "We can't go out the front, though. The inspector still doesn't trust us, and he's got people watching the doors. So at least until we get out of here a ways we're going to have to take a ride in a laundry truck."

So with him in the lead we made our way to the back of the hospital, through the kitchen, maintenance, and finally laundry, where there was a truck backed up to the loading dock. We climbed into the back with all the dirty laundry, and Hays yelled for the driver to take off.

The smell of urine, blood, and feces was almost overpowering. As I settled onto what seemed to be a reasonably safe bag of laundry, I said, "What, was the garbage truck busy?"

Hays, trying to stand as we bounced out of the lot, gave me a wry smile. "Nah, this was my first choice. I thought I should show you how the other half lived."

"Other half died, maybe."

At least the ride wasn't long even if it was memorable. A couple of blocks from the hospital, we pulled into an alley and jumped out. Hays had a cruiser waiting for us. As I walked to the car, I sniffed my jacket collar. "You know I'm never gonna get that smell out."

"Steele, I think that smell's been in that coat since World War II."

I climbed in one side, and he got in the other, giving the driver our destination. The driver turned around and gave me a big grin. "Glad to see you're okay, Captain Steele."

I raised an eyebrow in question, and Hays said, "Bill's the one who kept up the respirations after I pulled you out of the river."

I stuck my hand up over the seat, and he clasped it warmly. "Thanks, Bill. I really appreciate it." He gave me that big grin again. Then he turned back around and dropped the car into gear, and we were off.

Chapter 25


The garage was on the poorer side of town. It wasn't quite in the slums, but the building across the street might have been. It was surrounded by abandoned buildings and homes that hadn't be occupied by paying residents for at least the last decade. Roofs were tumbled down, and the weeds in some places were higher than a man's head.

From the outside, the garage matched the rest of the neighborhood. That is unless you looked a little closer. Then you could see the new solid roof under the old torn shingles and the battered siding that was just a facade.

As we got out of the car, I glanced at Hays suspiciously from the corners of my eyes. "What is this, some kind of secret government facility?"

"Well, not quite. But sometimes our patrol cars take a bit more tuning than the state allows, so we set this place up to do it at."

I pushed the door open and stepped into the most fully equipped garage I had seen since Joey's workshop. Three of the walls were lined with benches and tools. In the middle of the floor there was a grease rack and a pit. All of it spotless, right down to the floor.

Joey was looking a bit haggard, but at seeing me his eyes lit up, and that big grin of his split his face. He grabbed me around the waist and spun me through the air.

When I managed to squirm out of his grasp, I told him, "You make one move to kiss me, you big ape, and I'll put a bullet right between your eyes."

That just made him grin even more. "Glad to see you're back to normal, boss." Then he walked over to the wall and flipped on the overhead lights.

It sat like a diamond in the middle of all of that light, a diamond without the shine. It was a 1950 Ford, painted flat black with all the chrome removed. It was like a shadow in the middle of the room.

Like a proud father Joey led us over for a closer look. He reached into the grill and popped open the hood. Inside nestled a flathead V-8 with twin carburetors. "The speedometer stopped at a hundred and twenty-five, so I got the captain's buddy Bill to clock me with his radar thing. It stopped at one hundred and sixty, and I was still accelerating.

"I reinforced the front fenders and grill with iron." He pointed to long pipes crisscrossing behind the grill and running along the inside of the fenders. Then he walked to the passenger compartment and pointed out more steel inside. "I welded the doors shut and put more pipe from the firewall to the rear wheel wells. Heavy duty, near-solid rubber tires, police radio, racing transmission, and racing harnesses for protection. You should be able to run this thing into a brick building at one hundred miles per hour and knock the building down, and not hurt the car!"

I was in awe. It was exactly what I had asked him for three days ago, but hadn't really expected at all. I should have, though. As always, Joey could perform miracles!

Hays walked around the car, a forgotten unlit Lucky hanging from his mouth. "Just what the hell are you going to do, Steele?"

It was my turn to grin. "I'm gonna get us a sample of whatever it is they're shipping out of there every couple of days."

*   *   *   *   *

The moon had just crossed over the horizon, looking like a big silver eye. The sky was clear, and the white light it was casting gave the countryside an eerie glow. Joey and I were sitting in the Ford, just off the main highway on a revenuer's type stakeout. We were waiting for the station wagon from the hospital to come by. The troopers watching the place had informed us about twenty minutes earlier that they had started their run.

We picked a place far enough away that they wouldn't be on the lookout and would feel fairly safe. The plan was to pretty much do to them what they had done to Kate—follow them till we were ready, and then shove them off the road.

Being this close to the hospital and to where they were holding Kate left me empty and hurting. There was a tremble in my hands that had never been there before. I didn't know if she was still alive or not. All I could do was hope, and after all we'd been through this time, hope was growing pretty thin.

We'd all faced tough spots before, but this one just seemed endless. From day one Sharade had held the upper hand, and so far little that we had done had changed that.

Softly, like he thought somebody might hear him, Joey spoke my name, dragging me back out of the pits of my own mind. "Rick, here they come." He pointed down the road where a set of headlights were rapidly approaching.

"Let them get a good couple of miles ahead, and then take out after them. The moon's giving you enough light, isn't it?"

I could see the white of his grin. "Eyes of a cat, boss, eyes of a cat."

The station wagon flashed by without ever seeing us. As it receded into the distance, Joey turned the key on the Ford and stepped on the starter. A low rumble filled the passenger compartment. He slid the transmission smoothly into gear, and we rolled quickly onto the highway.

As he stepped down on the accelerator the rumble increased, and the back of the car slewed slightly to the side as it sought traction on the paving. "Don't get too close till we find the right spot. We want to push him off somewhere where it would be easy to dispose of the car."

Joey nodded without taking his eyes off the road and pushed down harder on the foot feed. The big car seemed to leap into the air as it rocketed down the highway, the hard rubber of the tires singing a tenor to the exhaust's bass.

The Ford sailed over the hill, and the hospital station wagon was visible up ahead. I wanted to holler over and tell Joey to "rig for silent night running," but I was afraid he wouldn't appreciate me calling him Kato. Instead, what I ended up with was Joey looking my way with a grin and a very bad Japanese accent saying, "We make silent running now, boss. No see us coming!"

All I could do was sit there and shake my head. He'd stolen my joke and he knew it. 'Course what was truly amazing was when he reached out and pulled a lever on the dashboard, and it became as quiet as a tomb inside. "What…?" I asked, a bit bewildered.

Joey nodded and grinned again. "Got the idea from the radio show. I added a set of super mufflers that I could cut in for silent running. Cuts down our top speed a bit, but I don't think that'll mater against the station wagon."

Speaking of which, we were about a hundred yards behind it now, and Joey let up on the gas. The big car slowed, and once we reached his speed we just maintained our distance. "Hold back till we find a nice, straight empty spot. Then we'll hit him. Okay?"

He nodded and hunched a little closer over the wheel, watching the road ahead.

It was late enough at night that the road belonged to just the two of us, and as far as the other driver knew it was just him.

We leaned into a small curve and topped another rise. As we did, I could see by the moon the next couple of miles were flat and straight. In the quiet of the passenger compartment, I whispered, "Now, Joey!"

The car leaped forward, and suddenly the sound of the exhaust filled the cabin again. Joey was grinning and yelling over the noise. "I want him to know we're coming. I want him good and scared!"

In mere seconds the distance between the two of us disappeared. As we got within ten feet of the car Joey flipped on the powerful head lamps, and suddenly it was like daytime in front of us. I could see every detail inside the other car.

The wagon's driver hadn't even known we were there till our lights came on. Once he did, he knew exactly what it meant. He stomped down on his own gas pedal, and for a brief second the wagon started to pull away. But Joey wasn't having any of that. He pushed down on his own accelerator and the gap between us disappeared.

The car jumped forward, and the heavily reinforced front end met with the rear of his car. Inside we felt nothing but a slight bump, but at the speed we were going his car took it like being hit by a Mack truck. Under the impact his rear crumpled, and the car fishtailed wildly. I do have to give him credit, though; he almost had it back under control when we hit him again.

Joey brought the Ford up beside him till my door was even with his already crushed bumper and jerked the wheel to the right. There was the screeching of metal tearing as our car melded with his, and he started to slide sideways. Just for good measure Joey hit him again, and then slammed on the brakes to stop from getting hit as the car spun sideways in the middle of the road.

The station wagon did a full spin in the middle of the road, smoke boiling up from the abused rubber tires. Inside by the light of our powerful headlamps, I could see the driver turn into a ping pong ball as the force bounced him around the inside. The instant the vehicle stopped moving, Joey and I were out of the Ford and racing across the hard concrete.

The driver was just righting himself when I jerked the door open and shoved the .45 in his face. "Ride's over, buddy. And I'd suggest if you want to see the sun come up you don't do anything stupid."

He looked like he was in his early thirties—close-cropped blonde hair, well-muscled, kind of a football player dressed in hospital whites. The name tag pinned to his breast read *Raymond*. The color drained out of his suntanned face faster than water out of a boot when he saw the gun.

Grabbing him by the collar of his white tunic with my left hand, I dragged his nearly limp body from the seat of the car and dropped him to his butt on the concrete. I waved Joey around to this side of the car with my gun. "We need to get this thing out of the middle of the road before somebody comes along. Good job of taking him out."

He grinned at me and started tying the driver's hands behind him as he sat there on the road. "I'll load him in the back of the wagon, and we can take it up the road and get rid of it."

I nodded in agreement and poked Raymond with my pistol. "You hear that, Raymond? We're gonna get rid of your car. And if you're not good, we just might get rid of you, too."

He was scared, but a defiant look was creeping into his eyes. "You guys don't know how much trouble you're in. When my boss finds out what you've done, he's gonna kill you both!"

261

I showed him my teeth. "He's been trying that for quite a while now, but it just won't stick! I don't think that's gonna change."

Joey was done tying him, and I dragged him around the car to the rear passenger door and muscled him up into the seat. "You wait here, sweetheart," I said as I slammed the door. Then I walked back around to Joey. I tucked the .45 back in its nest under my arm. "I'll drive the wagon down to someplace fairly secluded, and then we can question Junior and get rid of him and the car. We'll take as much of the stuff in the box as we need to find out what it is, and destroy the rest." I said it just loud enough that Raymond could hear me, too. If I could, I wanted to keep him scared.

"You want me to radio Hays?"

I shook my head. "Not yet. I want to question him first."

He nodded and walked back to the Ford as I climbed into the wagon.

\*    \*    \*    \*    \*

When the colonel dragged the illustrious Mr. Biddle back into the store and dropped him on the floor, he failed to see the spider's nest that he disturbed in the corner. To them, even the dead Mr. Biddle was an invader. The instant the colonel dropped his boot to the floor, they began to swarm. Within seconds they covered his body like a moving blanket, sinking their fangs into his cooling flesh.

Not much bigger than a dime and covered in soft, black hair, alone they were fairly safe. Their bite might raise a welt, cause an itch, or in extreme cases bring about a fever. The more bites, the worse the reaction. But in mass they could do some really strange things. The venom in a mass of bites could bring down a cow. But in just the right amount it could do something totally miraculous.

With their venom sacs empty, satisfied that the threat of invasion of their nest had been repelled, the mass of spiders crawled slowly back towards their hole, their faceted eyes neither seeing nor caring what was happening in their wake. The body of Elisha Biddle was changing.

The first thing that happened was the venom began to work on the blood beginning to clot in his veins and arteries. Like water in a pot it slowly began to heat, surging through the tiny line that connected it to the heart. It foamed and bubbled outward, expanding toward the brain. When it reached the nerves in his brain, it reignited the sparks to his neurons, and every so slowly his chest began to rise and fall again. And with it, the functions of his body came alive.

For a while more venom than blood raced through his arteries, but, slowing as it repaired the damage done to his body by the bullet, it became blood once more. Almost an hour after the bullet parted his brain like an axe splits a piece of wood, the pieces knitted back together, and Elisha Biddle lived once more.

He lay there on his back for a moment, trying to orient himself. His newly repaired gray matter was full of questions. What was he doing on the floor of his store? Why was he covered in itchy bites, and why did his head hurt? Must have hit it when he fell, he concluded, and then those damn spiders that were all over town must have attacked him! One of these days he was going to have to do something about them.

He rolled to his side, expecting to just stand up, but a wave of dizziness struck and he was forced to wait for it to pass on his hands and knees. There seemed to be some kind of ruckus going on outside. As a matter of fact he could have sworn he heard a shot fired as he was waking up. Using the pickle barrel for support he pulled himself to his feet.

There was something going on outside. Looked like the whole town was gathered in front of his store. Hopefully it wasn't because they were worried about him. Clutching anything he could find for support, he staggered his way to the door—or where it had been. It seemed now to be just an empty frame and a pile of glass. As he stepped through the opening, he said, "Does anybody know how my door got broken? And why are all you people in the streets?"

As the colonel turned, he nearly had a heart attack. The man he had sworn was dead was standing behind him covered in red bumps. The man seemed about to fall, and he quickly caught him and settled him in the chair he had been using before. Even the bullet hole was little more than a dent in his skull. There was something more to this than he had ever encountered before, but that was going to have to wait. He had a crowd to corral before he did anything else.

He let Biddle's wife come up to care for him, and he turned back to the crowd. "Here's the way it will work. I'll hold your families here, and you males, one at a time, will go with one of my men back to your house and give him what guns you have. Cause any trouble, and it's your family that will suffer. I will not hesitate to shoot someone if necessary. The better and sooner that you cooperate, the sooner this will all be over. Understand?"

A quiet mummer of yeses rose up out of the crowd, and one of the Carny brothers took the first of the townspeople back to his house to search for guns.

By the time the Carny brothers returned with the last of the guns, the colonel had worn out all his questions for Mr. Biddle, and worn out the newly resurrected storekeeper. The only positive piece of information he had uncovered was the part that the spiders had played.

So, as the crowd dispersed to try and catch what sleep they could, the colonel turned his newly fevered attention to the inside of the store. After finding an empty fruit jar and the lid, he located the nest of spiders and scooped as many as he could into the jar without getting bit himself. He held the jar up to the newly rising sun, studying the hairy-legged monsters crawling around inside it. "What secrets do you hold, little ones?" he whispered to himself.

\*    \*    \*    \*    \*

Joey and I pulled the two cars down into a field, out of sight from the road. I pulled the wagon's driver back out of the car and dropped him. Kneeling down in the dirt beside him, I showed him the .45 again. "Remember this? It's still looking for answers, and so am I. Since I'm a fair guy, I'm gonna give you a couple of options. Option number one: you can answer my questions, and I won't shoot you. Option number two—and I gotta tell ya, this is my favorite: answer all my questions and I won't shoot you. All sounds pretty simple to me. How about you?"

That defiance was creeping back into his eyes. I could see it reflected in the glow from the Ford's head lamps. "You guys are in big trouble, you know that? When my boss finds out about this, it's really gonna hit the fan!"

BOOM! The .45 went off in my hand, cutting a crease through the top of his shoulder and blowing a nice thumb-sized hole in the door behind him. "Wrong answer! And that's the only warning you get." I let him watch as I thumbed the hammer back for my next shot.

Suddenly Joey's hand was there covering my gun. "What the hell are you doing, Rick?"

I pulled my gun free and looked up into his eyes. "I think it's called *interrogation*. Now stay out of the way or I'll shoot you too!" I waved the gun at him, and he backed up closer to the Ford, shaking his head. Then I turned my attention back to the driver.

"Now, let's start over. Tell me about the women."

He started to hesitate, then he changed his mind. Looking down the barrel of any gun can be pretty scary, but one you could stick your finger in? Terror!

"You mean Thelma. She's working for the doctor as his chief aide, and living with her uncle. She seems to really like it."

I felt my lip curl up at that. Thelma gone over to the other side? I shook my head, and a glance at Joey said he was just as confused as I was. "And what about Doctor Gallagher? Where is she?"

He shook his head, scrunching his eyes shut and waiting for the bang that would mean the end of his short life. When it didn't come, he started talking. "Don't know nothin' about another doctor. There's just the prisoner with that funny mark on her face."

My ears perked up like a cat's. "What funny mark?"

"Some kind of big, purple mark around her mouth. She might be pretty if it wasn't for that."

Suddenly I was dancing! I was jumping up and down and yelling at the top of my lungs. Kate was alive!

It took me a couple of minutes before I settled down again. I wasn't the only one ready to celebrate. There was a big grin spread across Joey's face, and I could see a tear running down his cheek. We just might win this thing yet.

I had Joey get the box the driver had been carrying off the front seat and open it. Inside were one hundred little bottles, like the ones they fill syringes with in the hospital, all nestled in their own little compartments. I took one out and held it up to the light. It was full of a greenish yellow liquid, about as thick as blood.

I took it over and held it in front of the driver. "What is this?"

"You hijacked my car, and you don't even know what you're stealing?" he snorted in disgust.

I replaced the vial in front of his face with the .45. "Now again, what is this stuff?"

He squirmed, trying to get as far away from the gun as he could, but the station wagon stopped him. "Honest, I don't know. I make five different trips a week delivering this stuff to five different doctors. That's all I know."

"All?" I showed him my nice, straight pearly whites.

"Well, maybe one other thing, but I might be wrong about it."

"What?"

He was squirming again, so whatever he said I was tempted to disbelieve, but I was gonna listen. "I think it might be the same stuff he gives the townspeople once a month."

As I stood up I could hear my knees pop. Probably too much jumping around a couple of minutes ago. Not as young as I once was, and this caper had added a few unwanted years.

I walked over to where Joey was standing, and keeping my voice low I said, "Really nice job with that scene over there. I think knowing that I'd shoot even you to get what I wanted scared him more than the bullet."

He showed me his grin. "That's me, Mr. Academy Award! What now?"

"You get a hold of Hays on that police radio and tell him we've got a package to pick up. Better make it fairly evasive, just in case somebody else is listening. And while you do that I'm gonna go over and take care of Junior."

I grabbed the rest of the rope out of the car and went back to Raymond. Grabbing him by his collar, I dragged him over to the closest tree and propped him up against it. "Today's your lucky day. Looks like I don't get to shoot you after all."

I took the first loop of the rope and wrapped it around his neck, then proceeded to wind the rest of it around his body, tying him like a mummy, with one exception. "If you don't try to get out, that loop around your neck won't strangle you. If you do…." I shrugged my shoulders with indifference.

Joey was already in the car when I crawled through the window and into the other seat. "Do you think next time you could not weld the doors shut?" I complained.

"You wanted strong. Where to?"

"The first pay phone that you see. I want to call the doctor and see if he's got a good lab we can use to analyze this stuff we've got. Then back to the hospital. That's where you told Hays to meet us, right?"

He nodded and fired up the car, the rumble of the exhaust filling the night and cutting off any further conversation. As we pulled away I got one last look at Raymond tied to the tree, trying not to move.


Chapter 26


We found a roadhouse a couple of miles down the highway that had that pretty blue bell sign over the door, signifying a pay phone. I went in to make my call, but Joey said he felt safer waiting in the car. Something about drunken Louisiana country boys and pointy hats. I figured he knew what he was talking about and went in to make my call.

The bar was so thick with smoke that I nearly needed to use a foghorn and lantern to find my way up to the bar. I ordered a beer and asked the guy on the other side of the bar where the phone was. He pointed a grimy-looking finger towards the corner, and I set the glass back down. Somehow I just knew it was going to taste bad.

I scooped up my change and carefully worked my way over to the phone, trying not to disturb any of the boys at the bar who seemed to be having such a good time. I had almost made it when a bleached blonde with only half her teeth and one of her headlamps crawling out of her blouse decided she really liked the way I looked and stepped into my path. When I tried to go around her, she threw her blubbery arms around my neck and pulled me in close. I felt my head start to spin from the combination of her beery breath and the smell of stale sweat coming from her arm pits. More than another second or two and I knew they'd be picking me up out of my own puke on the floor.

As gently as I could I tried to pry her arms from around my neck, holding my breath all the time.

"What's the matter, honey? You shy?" she slurred into my ear, or something close to that. "I like shy guys! Hell, I like all guys!" Then she let out a cackle that made me want to go looking for eggs.

Finally I got one of her arms loose. "Sorry, ma'am, I just need to use the phone and call my wife," I lied. "I just want to let her know I'm headed home."

Two slobbery lips planted themselves on my cheek. "Cherry doesn't care about your wife, honey. She's at home, and Cherry's here now. Come on, honey, buy Cherry another drink."

It was like trying to escape from a python, but I made it and quickly tossed a buck on the counter and waved Grimy Finger down the bar. While she was busy with him, I ducked around her back and made my way to the phone, trying to grab a breath of fresh air as I did, but all I got was a double lungful of smoke.

I propped the receiver on my shoulder while I dialed, and my stomach did a couple more flip-flops. The phone smelled even worse than Cherry. Keeping it as far away from my mouth as I could, I dropped the rest of my change in the slot and dialed the doctor's number. Luckily he was there and I didn't have to go through his service. I don't know that I could have lasted that long.

I quickly told him what we needed, and he said he knew somebody that could help, and he'd have him waiting for us when we got there.

So with the address firmly etched in my mind, I fought my way back down the bar and out the door. When I stepped out into the night, I fell back against the building and filled my lungs with air. In the back of my mind I wondered if anybody in there would survive till morning.

As I climbed in the car, I noticed Joey already had it running, and his knuckles looked scuffed in the neon light of the beer sign. I raised an eyebrow at him suspiciously. "Somethin' happen while I was inside?"

He just shook his head and twisted in the seat to back out of the lot. As the headlights slid down the building, I caught a glimpse of two locals sitting in the dirt, their backs against the wall. I turned back to him and, suppressing a smile, shook my head. "You know, you keep up this unfriendly attitude and they're not going to invite us back!"

Joey just growled at me and stomped down on the gas.

*　　*　　*　　*　　*

The lab the doctor sent us to wasn't far off the highway. It sat among the factories and the warehouses that kept the local people working. It was a rather small, windowless building, whose brick had probably once been red but now was black from the dirt and soot of its neighbors. A half-lit neon sign, which used to read *Palmer Laboratories,* now just said *Pa m r La  rato ies.*

Joey took one quick look at the sign and asked, "Doesn't anything in this state work, or is that just the way they spell things here?"

"Sort of like the doors on this car?" I asked as I crawled out the window.

"I told you," he answered, crawling out the other side, "I welded them shut for strength. If you didn't eat so much...."

"And when have I had time to eat? The only place you can find to stop at is some hillbilly bar, where the people are dirtier than the ground outside."

"Well, they were your people!"

"Meaning what?"

He grinned and pushed me up to the door. "Meaning they were white!"

"Just because they were white doesn't mean they were my people!" I countered.

Then the door opened and all the conversation ceased. The man who opened the door couldn't have been more than four feet tall, and that was pushing it. A halo of stubby, wiry hair circled the back of his round head. Matter of fact, just about everything about him was round—his runny eyes behind his thick, round glasses, his pudgy hands, and his belly that looked like he was hiding a basketball under his lab coat. I wanted so bad to ask if his daddy was home, but for once I held my tongue.

"You must be Captain Steele. I'm Professor Palmer," he squeaked. "Doctor Redmond said you were coming. Please come in." He held open the door and waved us in with a tiny, doll-like arm.

The inside reminded me a lot of the outside: dirty, bare-brick walls with lots of junk piled up against them. In the center of the room were five or six long tables covered in stuff that looked like it was leftover from some old Karloff picture. Beakers were bubbling, with siphons and hoses going everywhere, blue going this way and red stuff going the other way. Bunsen burners were busy trying to keep stuff hot.

Professor Palmer walked over to the closest table and took one of the beakers off the fire. "Can I interest you gentlemen in a cup of coffee?" he asked, holding up the beaker. "It's my own special blend."

I was a little leery, but Mr. Cast Iron Gut was right there with his hand out. "Don't suppose you got any donuts to go with it?"

As he poured the coffee, Palmer slid a box across the table toward Joey. "Might be a little stale, but good enough for dunking."

Joey caught my look as he reached for one. "What?"

I held up my hands in a gesture of surrender. "Nothing. Not gonna say a word." Then I turned to the professor. Taking two of the vials out of my pocket, I handed them to him. "This is what we brought you to take a look at, Professor. I'm hoping you can tell me what it is."

He pushed his glasses up onto his forehead, and studied it with his eyes alone against the light. "Hmmm. Viscous, almost urine-colored." He wobbled his way over to a rather large microscope and, after making up a slide, stuck it under the lens.

For a long time he was quiet, just making notes on a pad and mumbling to himself. Finally after Joey's third donut, he turned away from the microscope. He held up the slide. "This," he said, "appears to be some form of spider toxin."

I was a little shocked to say the least. "Spider toxin? Are you sure?"

He nodded his ball of a head. "I'll know better once I run it through the centrifuge and spectrometer, but I'd stake my degree on it."

I wanted to ask where that degree was from, but I let it go. "Why would they be shipping spider toxin to doctors all around the state? Are they trying to kill everybody, or what?"

He looked thoughtful for a minute, then he took off his glasses and used them as a pointer at me. "You know, Captain, in some parts of the world the toxins of certain spiders are believed to have a regenerative quality."

Still seemed a little far-fetched to me. "You mean the fly never felt better than right before he died, right?"

He gave me a little laugh that sounded a lot like *ha ha*. "Very droll, Captain." He walked over to a tumbledown bookcase, searched for a minute, then slid out a dust-covered tome. Thumbing through the pages, he was back to talking to himself again. "Let's see, it should be here somewhere. No, that's not it. Nor is that. Eureka!"

His shout sent me two feet in the air, and Joey dropped his donut. Palmer hurried across the room, stabbing the book with a stubby forefinger. "I knew I'd seen it. Luckily my memory is almost total or I might have forgotten it."

He showed me a picture of a hairy-looking spider in the book that sent chills up and down my spine. It looked a lot like the one Joey had killed on the porch. Looking over my shoulder, Joey confirmed it. "Hey, I think I killed one of those!"

"Or at least its cousin," I added. "Kinda hard to tell without it being flat." Then I turned to the professor. "What's it say about the spider, Professor?"

He pulled the book back and, squinting, began to read. "In some cultures, the venom of the South American cave spider is considered to have regenerative properties. Some claim that in large doses, it can even revive the dead. Studies have been performed on the toxin, and although it does show very minute signs of cell regeneration, in the quantities necessary to show significant changes the toxicity would prove to be fatal."

"So you're saying that he's trying to kill everyone?"

Palmer shook his head. "No, more than anything I would think he's offering a false fountain of youth. I won't know more till I do a more thorough exam."

I figured that was all we were going to get for now, so I stuck out my hand to thank him. It felt a lot like shaking hands with a child, only his hands were calloused and worn by chemicals, like those of an old man. "Thank you, Professor Palmer. You can get hold of us through Doctor Redmond's office when you have the rest of the results."

Almost like we didn't exist, Palmer went back to work and we headed out to the car. All the way there, all I could do was shake my head. If it was a con, Sharade had been up to it way too long to have not gotten caught, and he had too many people in his pocket for that. I just didn't know yet. But soon it would all come together.

*   *   *   *

Dr. Katherine Gallagher never had a plan. She never had need of one. She lived a rather simple life, teaching a few classes here and there, identifying ancient artifacts, plotting the course

274

of ancient man, and every five years, if she were lucky, she went out on a dig for the summer. If she had a plan, it was to someday maybe get married and raise little anthropologists.

But *Kate* Gallagher had a plan! No mater what she always had a plan. Rick had taught her that. But until fate dropped him in her lap a couple of years back, she'd never needed one. Now, not a day went by that she didn't need one just to stay alive. So she had a plan.

She hadn't seen a clock since they tossed her into the cell, but from the growling of her stomach she had learned to tell when it was getting close to mealtime. And it was just starting to rumble, so she knew lunch couldn't be more than half an hour away. That meant it was time to put her plan in motion.

The first thing she did, and the scariest part of the plan, was to take the clamp off the port in her chest where they had been drawing out blood every couple of days. Immediately the dark red fluid spurted out and onto the floor. Careful not to let too much out but enough to make it look like a lot, she left little puddles on the floor and a trail leading back to her bunk. Just before sealing it up again she made a pool under the edge of her bunk and smeared some on the blanket. Then she lay facedown on the bed, one arm trailing limply to the floor, to wait.

It wasn't long before she heard the sound of the key in the lock, and the door swung open. Holding her breath and hoping that her growling stomach didn't give her away, she waited.

She sensed more than actually heard the man enter with her lunch tray. The roar of her heart in her ears was drowning out the sound of everything else. She dared to slightly open one eye.

The man entered cautiously, calling to her all the time. Then he saw the blood on the floor and dropped the tray and rushed to her side. He bent over her on the bunk and started to roll her over and onto her back. That was the moment she had been waiting for. Before all that had happened to her in the last weeks, her fist might have been enough to bring the guard down. But she was too weak for that. Instead, the leg from the small table that she had concealed under her body did the job for her.

She felt the chunk of wood bite into his skull, and could hear the crunch of his skull collapsing beneath her blow. The guard, now unconscious and possibly dead, tumbled down on top of her. Kate reached out with her other hand and pushed him to the floor. Then, as she rose to her wobbly feet, she delivered a second blow—an assurance that he wasn't going to give the alarm when she was gone.

The blood she had spilled to make her plan work had taken more out of her than she realized. Rising up off the bunk too quickly had left her dizzy. With a hand against the wall for support, she waited for the spell to pass. Once she felt stable again she headed for the door. Freedom was just a few steps away.

As Kate stepped through the door, she suddenly froze when she saw who was waiting there. Then her cracked and purple-stained lips broke into a smile. Today luck was on her side! "Thelma!"

Kate ran to the woman and threw her arms around her and hugged her tightly. But something was wrong. Thelma wasn't responding to her hug. And why was she dressed in a nurse's uniform? Kate backed up a step, confused. "Thelma? What's going on? Why are you dressed like that?"

Thelma tipped her head slightly to one side as she studied this scarecrow of a woman—a woman who seemed to know her, but who Thelma had no recollection of ever having seen before except in a quick glance through the door. Surely if she had met her before she would have remembered the mass of knotted auburn hair, the mad look in her eyes, and the skinny body in the bloody hospital gown. No doubt this woman was crazy.

Kate looked into the mousy brown eyes behind the thick lenses and saw no recognition. To Thelma she was a complete stranger. She reached out and clutched her shoulders, trying to shake some remembrance into her. "Thelma, it's me, Kate—your friend!"

Nothing seemed to work. All she got was a blank stare. Thelma had no idea who she was, and that meant Kate couldn't waste any more time. Looking deep into Thelma's eyes, she said, "I promise I'll come back for you just as soon as I can." Then she turned and fled down the hallway.

Behind Kate's fleeing form, Thelma began to scream at the top of her lungs.

\*     \*     \*     \*     \*

I was almost to the car when I thought of something and went back into Palmer's lab. When I reemerged I was carrying a battered copy of the local phone directory. I tossed it into the car and climbed in behind it.

"What's this?" Joey asked, holding up the book.

"Phonebook," I answered.

"Even in the dark I can see that. My question is *why*?"

"Got to thinking about that doctor that the kid, Raymond, told us about. I'd sure like to take a look at his records. And if we wait for Hays, it might be too late. Sooo, I thought you and I could take a little drive over there and take a look for ourselves."

Joey started the car and backed away from the curb. "Let me get this straight. You want me to drive you over there, and then the two of us are going to break into the doctor's office and steal his files?"

"Yep," I said, nodding.

Joey just shook his head as he shifted into first, all the while mumbling about his momma tellin' him I was gonna get him in trouble one day.

\*     \*     \*     \*     \*

Two weeks had passed since they had taken over the town. Everything had pretty much returned to normal. The two Carny boys had been good help around the town, an extra hand when needed. The corporal spent most of his time either drunk or working with the still he had built out back of the general store. The fat one they called Tucker liked to play sheriff, walking patrol through town and sticking his nose where it didn't belong.

On the second day, the colonel had sent the major to the capitol for news of the war. What he had brought back wasn't good.

The major had ridden hard the last few days, not stopping to eat or sleep. He knew the colonel would want the information he was carrying immediately, even though he'd rather not have to be the one who delivered it. It wasn't good. The war was officially over. Any combatants left in the field were asked to surrender, or would be declared outlaws. President Jefferson Davis had submitted to Yankee rule and betrayed the South. All was in ruins.

A man named Wilkes Booth had reportedly killed the tyrant from the North. But even with the North in mourning, the Confederacy hadn't risen up again. The people were tired of war, and sense said that Abraham Lincoln would have been fair with them. Now, who knew what was going to happen.

The major reined his tired horse to a halt behind the general store and slid from the saddle. Without even pausing to brush off the trail dust he pushed the back door open and stepped inside.

The colonel was there in the back room of the store where he had set up his "office." And like most of the days since that first night, he had one of the locals strapped to a kitchen table that he had brought in for just that purpose.

He would take his knife, slicing small cuts into one of the people, and then release the spiders. Within mere moments the spiders would bite, and shortly after that the cuts would begin to heal. It wasn't just one person; it was the whole town.

When he had questioned the residents, they all told the same story. None of them had been sick a day since they had come to town to live. Yes, they all had been bitten numerous times by the spiders—it was an accepted fact of life, like flies in the summer. No, no one in town had ever died from a spider's bite. And other than a man who had been crushed almost into paste by a runaway wagon full of hay, no one they could remember had died here. The cemetery contained only one grave.

The major stepped in the back door and stood at attention, waiting for the colonel to notice him. Finally the superior officer looked up from his experimenting and gave the major a weak smile. "Major. Good to have you back. What news have you for me?"

He hesitated, fumbling with his hat in his hands. "Well, sir, it isn't good."

Briefly the colonel looked up from what he was doing and met the major's eye. "No, I suspected as much. The Confederacy has fallen, hasn't it?"

The major was surprised at the colonel's attitude. "Yes, sir, it has. There is nothing left," he replied grimly. "The Yankees are everywhere."

The colonel brushed the thought away with a wave of his hand. "Never mind that, Major. There's nothing we can do about it now. But watch this." He took his knife and ran another long, jagged line down the local's arm, only to have it heal as he watched.

There was the excitement of a child at Christmas in the colonel's voice. He looked up at the major, his eyes bright with discovery. "Isn't it amazing, Major? It's the spiders! There's something in their venom that keeps the people alive. A few bites from a spider and you could virtually live forever, not our allotted two score and ten. Forever!"

"But the nation, sir—what about the nation? Isn't there something we can do?" the major fretted.

"What are nations when a man could outlive them all? If I wanted to, I could rule the nation! No one would ever be able to stop me." The colonel walked across the room and took the officer by his dusty shoulders. "We have found our nation, Major. From here we will someday rule the world!"

\*    \*    \*    \*    \*

Joey parked across the street from a building that looked like it belonged in Los Angeles. It was made from slabs of white stone, with a false balcony on each of the four upper stories and lots of windows. Fortunately for us all those windows were dark. The only light came from a dimly lit lobby behind big glass doors. As we crossed the street I could see the lone night elevator boy sitting outside his car on a stool, dozing.

"How do you want to work this, boss?" Joey asked as we crossed the street.

"You stay out of sight till I get him to unlock the door. Once he lets me in, we're good to go."

Joey nodded and disappeared into the gloom at the side of the building. Trying to look important, I walked up to the door and started to pound on the glass. The kid wasn't much of a watchman. I thought I was going to have to break the door just to wake him up. Finally, rubbing the sleep from his eyes, he came over to the door to see what all the noise was about.

"We're closed! Come back in the morning."

I ignored what he was saying and yelled right back. "Got a letter for Doctor Jackson. Has to be delivered tonight!"

"Dr. Jackson's not here! Come back in the morning."

I pointed to my ears like I couldn't hear him and yelled even louder. I held up an empty envelope I was writing a note on. "Got this letter for Doctor Jackson. It has to be there when he gets in in the morning."

At last he gave up yelling at me and tripped the lock on the door. Opening it just enough so he could speak through the crack, he said, "We're closed. You have to come back in the morning."

This time there was no conversation from my side. I just grabbed hold of the door and jerked it open, pulling him out onto the sidewalk.

He couldn't have been more than seventeen or eighteen, his face still pimpled with acne and his hair slicked back like Gable. That was almost my undoing. I was gonna slug him, but then I started feeling sorry for him, and he nearly got me. After all, who gives a kid a gun to watch an office building?

He was still fumbling to get it out of his coat pocket when Joey thumped him from behind. "What's up with you? You were gonna let that kid put a bullet in you."

I started dragging his limp form back inside. Joey picked up his feet, and we carried him to the open elevator car. "I wasn't gonna let him shoot me. I just started to feel a bit sorry for him is all."

"Well, the next time you wanna feel sorry for somebody, feel sorry for me. 'Cause I'm stuck with you for a partner!"

I propped the kid up in the back of the elevator and said snidely, "Life's rough all over. Now if you're done complaining, why don't you walk those big feet over there to that directory and see what floor the dishonorable Doctor Jackson has his office on. And maybe, just maybe, we can get out of here before he comes to work!"

Seems Jackson did his cosmetic work on the fifth floor. So after Joey got in, I took over the command post in the elevator and pulled the lever all the way to the right. It didn't move!

"Now what?"

"I think you have to close the door first," Joey snickered.

With a heavy sigh, I grabbed hold of the handle and pulled the door across. Then I moved the lever back to the right again. This time the elevator started up.

I watched the indicator, and when it hit five I pushed the lever back across and pulled open the door. The bottom of our elevator was sitting about ten inches below the floor. I just waved my hand at it in surrender and climbed out. "Close as it gets. Come on."

Joey made no attempt to hide his grin. "What about Sleeping Beauty there?"

I reached in and unscrewed the handle from the lift control. "He should be out for quite a while yet, but that'll stop him from stealing our elevator."

Quickly we made our way down the hall till we came to the frosted glass door with *Dr. Albert Jackson* painted on it in gold. I felt around the frame and under the door, but didn't find any trace of an alarm. I glanced over at Joey, and he knew what I wanted right away. He grabbed hold of the handle, and after one quick twist the handle and the lock pulled out of the wood frame.

"No sense in us wasting time being careful. They're going to know we were here anyway."

Inside it was a typical doctor's office—eight or nine cheap chairs for patients waiting, and a service window with a door next to it. I pushed open the door and Joey followed me through.

"Any idea what exactly we're looking for?"

I shrugged my shoulders. "Probably a filing cabinet set apart from the rest of the files. If this thing is as big as I think it is, I don't think he'd want his entire staff to know what's going on. Let's see if we can find his private office."

The first two doors I opened were exam rooms, but Joey got lucky. "Would you think his office might have a big, leather-topped maple desk, refrigerator, couch, and really nice chairs?"

"Possibly. Why?"

"'Cause that's what this one's got." He swung the door open and shone his flashlight into the gloom. That was it, or he was paying his nurses way too well. And in the corner by the desk there was a file cabinet.

The drawers on the cabinet were locked, but my knife took care of that. Funny how you could spend a fortune on a cabinet, but they never seemed to put any better locks in them. A quick twist and it was open.

I pulled out the drawers and rifled through the papers, but came up empty. Nothing but the kind of regular junk you would expect a doctor to have. Joey was on the other side of the room going through the desk. "Any luck?"

He shook his head. "Nah, just appointments and stuff. I did find a bottle of brandy in his bottom drawer for that extra hard doctor's day."

It was really starting to feel like we were wasting our time. Maybe he didn't keep his secret files in his office. Maybe they were at home. If that were the case, then we were out of luck.

I was about to give up on the search when I happened to glance back at the file cabinet. It was sitting just as I left it, drawers hanging open, files pulled out of place. Something about it struck me as wrong. I stood staring at it for the longest time before it finally hit me. The drawers weren't deep enough for the cabinet! The cabinet was almost three feet deep, but the drawers were less than two. "Joey, give me a hand with this."

Between the two of us we turned the heavy oak file cabinet sideways so I could get a look at the back. Then I took my knife and pried off the thin sheeting. There was probably some mechanism that swung it out of the way, but I didn't have time to look for it. It was getting late, and the elevator boy would be waking up soon.

Sure enough, behind the sheeting was another set of drawers. Without much more than a glance I knew that I had hit pay dirt. I grabbed up some of the folders and stuck them under my arm. The rest I handed to Joey.

"This all of it?" he asked.

I nodded. "Yep. Let's get the hell out of here. It's getting late."

As I followed Joey into the anteroom, I noticed the bulge in his back pocket. "What's in your pocket?" For an answer he gave me that big sheepish grin of his. Then I knew. He'd taken the doctor's brandy bottle.

When we got to the elevator it was empty. The kid had awakened and was gone. I held up a finger to my lips for silence, and Joey nodded his understanding. Then I gave him the control lever, pointed down, and showed him one finger. Again Joey nodded and started to screw the handle back on.

I plastered my back to the wall and inched my way over to the stairs. I figured if the kid hadn't taken off, that's where he'd be waiting. As I got to the stairs I heard the elevator start down.

The minute the sound of the lift filled the hallway he decided it was time to come out of his hole. Gun first, he peeked out. I didn't wait for the rest of him. I lashed out with my foot and sent his gun flying across the hallway to thud against the opposite wall. A scream of pain followed, but I never heard the scream. I leaped down on top of him to try and restrain him.

The kid surprised me. He was wiry and quick. He got in a couple good punches with his undamaged left hand to my side, looking for my kidneys. Fortunately for me I was twisted just far enough that they only landed on my ribs rather than the crippling place he was trying for.

I hit the hand I'd kicked and he cried out again, but it didn't slow him down. I took a short jab to the gut, and he got an openhanded blow to the side of his head that I hoped would make him see stars. Then suddenly we started rolling down the stairs. Me on top, then him. I was trying to keep my head from hitting and dodging his punches at the same time.

As we crashed to the landing there was a loud thump, and, as I watched, his eyes glazed over and his body went limp on top of me. He'd whacked his head against the wall as we landed. Instants later his weight was lifted off of me. Joey was standing there holding the kid up by his belt.

"You must be getting' old, boss. You almost let a punk kid take you."

Without saying a word I climbed to my feet, trying to rub the pain out of my ribs and my head.

## Chapter 27

Kate was panting as she ran down the hallway. The loss of the blood they had taken the last few days and the incident with Thelma in the hallway just moments ago had taken their toll. The slap of her bare feet against the concrete was growing less rhythmic. She was starting to stagger. If she didn't find someplace to hide and regain her strength soon, she'd never get away, nor would she have the power to if they took any more of her blood.

She leaned against the wall, head down, as she pushed herself forward. It was all she could do now just to stand up, let alone walk. Her vision blurred. Up ahead there was a big, wooden door set in the concrete wall. She focused her mind on that, and slowly she made her way forward. All she could hear was the pounding of her heart and the shuffle of her feet as she dragged herself down the hallway.

Then at last she was there. Kate fumbled with the latch for a few seconds. At first she thought it might have been locked, but it was only her sweaty hand slipping from the latch. She dried her hand on her gown and tried again. This time the latched clicked, and the door swung open.

On the other side it was cool and damp, a soft, almost undetectable breeze blowing towards her. She fell more than walked into the darkness, pushing the door shut with her body.

For a long time Kate Gallagher sat there, her back against the door, gathering her strength. She knew that on the other side of that door, Thelma's screams had by now sounded the alarm, and that Sharade and his people would be searching for her. But she hoped that in the maze of corridors downstairs, it would take them a while to get to this one door.

Thelma's screams echoed in her ears, worrying her already cluttered mind. What terrible thing had Sharade done to her to make her forget her best friend? If it were only a game she was playing, she would have never screamed. No, Thelma was definitely under someone else's control.

Feeling a bit stronger, Kate picked herself up off the dirt floor and took her first real look at her surroundings. She was standing inside a cave. She had made enough cave expeditions to know that this one was natural and very old. Someone had been nice enough to add electric lights, meaning that there was some purpose for them to be down here. And the draft that she was feeling meant that somewhere there was an outlet.

That brought new hope. If she could just follow that draft, there was a chance she could find her way out. So, revived with new energy, she made her way further into the underground cavern.

Kate walked till the lights went out, and then she walked further. With her hand on the wall to stop her from running into something, she just kept pushing her tired feet forward. Suddenly the sidewall beneath her hand disappeared, and she tumbled into the open hole.

After waiting a few minutes, in order to recover what little strength she had and to nurse a bang on her knee and elbow from the fall, she pushed her feet back under her and started forward again. Just a few yards ahead she found a spot where the tunnel turned again. Kate worked her way carefully in the darkness. After the surprise of the wall running out, she inched her feet forward to make sure there were no holes in the floor. Finding nothing but rock and dirt, she lay down on the floor and curled herself up into a ball. She was going to need to rest a bit before she went any further.

*     *     *     *     *

Dr. Sharade was comfortable. He was sitting in a deck chair out behind the hospital, watching the smoke rise lazily from his pipe. The temperature was perfect, there were no bugs to speak of—thanks in part to his pipe—and the stars were bright overhead. It had been a much better day than the last few.

He smiled as he thought about it. Steele was finally dead, the black man hadn't been seen, Thelma had become a real asset to the hospital, and the woman was providing sustenance for their friend in the tunnels. An almost perfect day.

He saw headlights approaching on the dirt road behind the hospital, and he rose and walked out to meet them. It would be the major returning from his nightly patrol. Army habits were hard for him to break, even after nearly one hundred years.

Seeing the doctor waiting, the major pulled up the jeep before he got to the hospital. As Sharade looked in the back, he felt his stomach sour. There were two bodies dressed in brown uniforms. Both were now stained with red.

The major shut off the jeep and climbed out, the night suddenly becoming so quiet he could hear the doctor sucking on his pipe. "They were just outside the property line, sir. They were watching every move we were making."

Sharade took his pipe from his mouth and sighed. His perfect day was rapidly becoming a nightmare. "And how, Major, am I to explain two dead state troopers?"

The major took off his broad-brimmed hat and ran his fingers through his thin hair. "I thought we could just dispose of the bodies in the tunnels like we have before, sir."

His pipe had gone out, and he stuck it in the pocket of his lab coat. "These are state troopers, not some vagrants who happened to stumble into town. They will be missed!"

The major was rapidly plumbing the depths of his mind, looking for a way out. "What about your friends? Can't they do something?"

Again Sharade sighed. His head was beginning to hurt. "We are nearly out of friends, Major. This struggle with Steele has brought us entirely too much publicity." He rubbed his hand across his eyes. "Dispose of the bodies, and I'll see what I can do." Then his voice hardened. "In the future, check with me before you take any drastic measures."

He may have had more to say on the subject, but the ringing of the emergency klaxon interrupted him. Sharade was heading toward the hospital with the major on his heels, when suddenly he stopped and turned on him. "Get rid of the bodies! You can't leave them there! We will handle whatever this is till you get there."

Chastised, the major turned and walked back to his jeep.

Inside the hospital was pandemonium. It looked like a beehive during an invasion, only with a klaxon ringing and the red lights above the doors blinking. It took a couple of minutes before he found Tucker. He was going down the hall toward the stairs at a half trot, trying to stop his gun from bouncing as he ran. Sharade called out to him as he went by.

"Tucker, what's going on?"

The fat chief of police, nearly out of breath from his short run, gave him a shrug and an empty hand gesture that said, "Don't know!" Wheezing, he said, "The alarm was sounded down by the cells. I'm guessing that doctor has escaped."

Sharade shook his head in resignation. "Can we at least shut off those damned alarms? I'm sure she already knows that she's escaped, so we don't need to go on reminding her!"

Tucker took a key from his belt and stuck it into the alarm slot and turned it. The result was silence.

"Much better," Sharade said. "Now let's go downstairs and see if we can find out what's going on."

Tucker drew his gun and started to lead the way down the stairs, but Sharade's patience got the best of him, and he shoved the portly police chief out of his way. "And put that gun away! You're most likely to shoot me or yourself. Even if she has gotten out, she isn't armed, and she's half dead from all the blood we've taken."

They made their way quickly down the steps, the pace leaving Tucker huffing behind him, and emerged into the lower hallway. Thelma had finally stopped screaming, but was standing against the wall with her face in her hands sobbing. Sharade put his arm around her shoulders to comfort her. "Now now, Thelma, it'll be alright. Tell me what happened."

She was still unable to speak through the sobs, but pointed to the half-open cell door.

The doctor motioned for Tucker to take a look, but when he drew his gun and started to push the door open cautiously with it, Sharade grabbed the gun and pushed him out of the way again.

The inside of the cell looked like a slaughterhouse. The blood that Kate had leaked out onto the floor was a sticky mess, and the guard who had brought her meal was lying near the cot, becoming a sticky mess of his own. Shaking his head disgustedly, he stepped around the blood, walked over and rolled the guard onto his back.

The guard was dead. When Kate had broken his nose, she probably smashed the cartilage up into his brain, killing him. Or possibly he choked on his own blood. An autopsy would determine that, but for now all that mattered was that he was dead. Behind him he heard Tucker whistle.

"For a half-dead girl she sure made a mess!" he chided.

Sharade wilted him with a glare and went back out into the hallway. Taking Thelma firmly by the shoulders, he shook her till she finally stopped sobbing. "Now, which way did she go?"

Thelma pulled herself together and pointed down the hall. "She came out and acted like she knew me. Why would she think that, Doctor? I've never seen her before."

The doctor just shook his head. "I don't know, Thelma. You say she went that way down the hall?" He pointed to his left.

Thelma nodded, and he started to walk away. Tucker was just coming out of the cell. "Get somebody down here to clean that mess up. Take her upstairs to my office. It looks like she might have gone into the tunnels. If she has, chances are we've already lost her and next week's supply. When the major gets down here, tell him where I've gone."

Tucker nodded in agreement, and as Sharade went one way down the hall, he took Thelma by the arm and directed her back toward the stairs.

*　　*　　*　　*　　*

Hays was waiting for us when we walked into the morgue, and he wasn't happy. "Where have you two been? You should have been here hours ago!"

I tossed the file down on the stainless steel table. "We've been out doing your job for you."

"What's this?" he asked, leafing through the pages.

I gave him my biggest grin of satisfaction. "Those are Doctor Albert Jackson's files on who he's been treating with the stuff we got from Raymond."

Shaking his head, he pushed it back across the table. "What do you expect me to do with this?"

I shrugged my shoulders. "I don't know, some kind of cop stuff, I guess. Investigate 'em, arrest 'em. Whatever it is you do."

He sighed and shook his head. "First of all, this is all inadmissible. It was taken without a warrant and without probable cause. And technically the people haven't done anything wrong. Do you expect me to arrest them for taking some kind of drug that's not on the market?" He walked over to the morgue attendant's chair and fell into it.

I followed him over and leaned down on the desk with my palms flat on the top. "That's not what's bothering you, Hays. What is it?"

He pulled a bent Lucky from his pack and tossed the rest down on the desk. He didn't say anything else till he got it lit. "That guy you left tied to the tree? He was dead when we got there."

I think my jaw dropped down to meet my hands on the desk. And when I looked over at Joey, he had the same expression   . "What do you mean *dead?*"

Hays blew a cloud of smoke into my face. "You know—dead. No breathing, no heartbeat."

I turned and walked across the room, shaking my head. "He was alive when we left him."

"Well, when my men got there they found him tied to a tree with a loop around his neck. And he had been strangled. That kind of points the finger at you."

He got up from the desk and walked over to where I was standing. His eyes were angry slits when they met mine. "I've been with you all the way on this thing, Steele, but this time I think you screwed up. Whether it was accidental or on purpose, he ended up dead from your carelessness."

I couldn't believe it. I scrubbed my face with my hands, trying to wipe it all away. "That loop could have never strangled him. It was way too loose for that. I just told him that to scare him. Somebody showed up in between and stopped him from talking."

Suddenly an idea hit me, and I grabbed Hays by the shoulders. "You've got to go arrest Jackson! If you don't, they're going to kill him, too. Don't you see? They're tying up loose ends."

It dawned on him that I was right, and he rushed over and picked up the phone. I could hear him giving commands to have Jackson picked up right away. I walked over to where Joey was standing. "We just can't get a step ahead. If they killed Raymond, then they probably know we're both alive."

Joey thought about it for a minute, then he shrugged. "They might think it was the patrol."

I shook my head this time. "Why would the patrol tie him to a tree? They'd just handcuff him and bring him in."

Hays hung up the phone and turned back to us. "They're on their way, but they're not supposed to move in till I get there. You two want to ride along?"

"Might as well. We don't seem to be getting anywhere here."

After a quick check of the parking lot, we walked out the back door and climbed into the squad. Joey got in up front, and I slid in back with Hays.

The drive over to Jackson's covered a piece of the city I hadn't seen yet. The further out we went the larger the houses got, and the lawns more sprawling with winding driveways. Some were hidden by great stone walls, and iron gates kept the riffraff out.

Well, there was a gate at Jackson's, but the riffraff, meaning me, got in anyway. And from the looks of the gate, so had somebody else. Somebody who was in a hurry. The gates were thrown back in the open position, both bent severely, right about the hood height of a car. A broken chain lay on the concrete of the drive.

Hays' driver didn't stop to ring the buzzer and announce us; he just accelerated up the drive to the house.

Without even thinking about it, the house pulled a whistle from my mouth. I didn't think I'd ever seen anything quite like it that didn't have a big, brass plaque by the door telling you what it was.

Greek columns, or maybe they were Roman (I flunked architecture), rose thirty feet into the air to support a great stone portico reaching out over the drive. Behind it stood more than just a house or a mansion. It was like one of the memorials in Washington for all the dead presidents.

We parked under the portico and climbed out, me looking up to make sure it wasn't going to come crashing down on our heads. Like I said, I flunked architecture and didn't really trust big, rocky things over my head. We walked up the steps to two giant doors with knockers bigger than my head. Hays picked one up, but before he could drop it a gunshot went off inside the house.

The .45 leaped into my hand, and my shoulder hit the door at almost the same time. Hays was just half a second slower, or he'd have beaten me to it. But speed was part of the problem this time, not an asset. The inside of the foyer was highly polished stone, and it was like glass underfoot. With my second step I slipped and slid all the way to the foot of the giant, winding staircase. Fortunately for the others they saw me hit the floor and were a little more careful. Hays stepped over me and headed up the stairs just as the second shot sounded.

I was just raising myself up when one of those giant black hands reached down and grabbed me by my shirt, half carrying me and half dragging me up the steps. When we got to the top, I wiggled free and went back to moving under my own power. "Thanks, but next time I'll take the lift."

Joey shrugged a shoulder. "Suit yourself. Getting' tired of picking you up anyway."

Hays tossed a dirty look at us over his shoulder and motioned for us to shut up.

There must have been twenty doors along the hallway. And behind each and every one all we could hear was silence. So with Hays and his aide on one side and Joey and I on the other, we started cautiously opening doors.

It was the fifth door we opened that nearly got Hays killed. All the rest had just been bedrooms—lights on, no one home. So by the time we got to number five, we might have been getting a bit sloppy.

Joey took up his position on the hinge side, and I took the handle side. After a count of three, I twisted the knob and pushed the door quickly open. The room was pitch black. Or at least it was till the two shots rang out. I followed them quickly with two of my own, aiming for the flashes I'd seen. In the confines of the hallway the .45 sounded like a cannon going off.

Over the ringing in my ears I heard somebody cursing behind me, and when I turned around I could see Hays up against the wall. One bullet hole was just about an inch from his head, and there was a rapidly growing red spot on the brown of his uniform. I told Joey to help him and motioned for Bill to take his place on the other side of the door. Then, crouching, I went in fast and rolled sideways into the darkness till I hit a piece of furniture.

I saw Bill look around the corner of the door, and I hoped he saw my hand signal motioning for him to stay. By then my eyes had started to adjust to the darkness, and my hearing was starting to come back. Straining it, I listened for the other man to breath or cough or even just shuffle his feet. When I didn't hear anything, I grabbed something from atop the dresser that had stopped my fall and tossed it across the room. When it hit the wall the gun went off again, and I had him.

I didn't really want to shoot him if I didn't have to. So, trying to place him, I tried to combine the quick glimpse I'd gotten when the door opened with what little I could make out now. The bed was between him and me, and from the shadows it looked like he was using a chair for cover.

Rolling another makeup jar to the door to get Bill's attention, I pointed up at the ceiling and made gun motions with my fingers. I saw him nod. "Now!" I yelled, and then, screaming at the top of my lungs as he fired at the ceiling to keep our gunman down, I leaped across the bed and onto the spot I thought he was hiding.

My left shoulder hit the chair, and my arm turned into a piece of cold sausage. I reached out with the other arm to try and stop my flight, but all I got was open air. The best I could do now was to try and do a roll and hope that it was enough to bring me down on top of the guy.

It brought me down alright, but not on top of him. I landed on his leg and I heard the bone crack, quickly followed by a curse. I reached out with my good hand, fishing in the dark for him, not knowing which end of him I was on.

My fingers felt something soft and warm, and I turned them into claws, digging in. Well, Mr. Bullets in the Dark had had enough abuse, and even with the broken leg he started to fight back. He slammed a fist into the ribs that the elevator boy had bruised earlier, and it was my turn to howl. I tightened my fingers even deeper and felt something warm spread under them. Whatever I was holding on to was flesh, and now it was bleeding.

Some of the feeling was coming back into my left arm. It wasn't up to precision work yet, but at least it made a handy club. I brought it down next to my other hand and got a couple grunts of pain. Then suddenly the room exploded with light, and a bullet crashed into the ceiling.

Bill had come to my rescue.

## Chapter 28

Sharade's perfect night had become a perfect disaster. Two dead troopers, a hijacked shipment of the serum, and now this—the escaped girl in the tunnels. He shook his head thinking about it. How could it all go so wrong? What was next? Steele still alive? He shuddered at the thought.

Unclipping the flashlight from the rack on the wall by the door, he pushed it open and stepped out into the tunnel. The air felt cool and damp against his skin. He wondered for a moment which way she had gone, then with a shrug set off. If he didn't find her alive in one tunnel, he'd find her desiccated corpse in another one.

No one but his closest associates knew what was down there. He was sure that even the townspeople who had grown used to the effects of the serum had no idea where it came from.

It was shortly after his discoveries in the back of Elisha Biddle's store that he had moved into the empty plantation house and set up his headquarters. He had been apologetic to the people of the town, pacifying them with promises of eternal health and life. Most thought he was a madman, but if he let them go back to their lives, no real harm was done. Besides, those that he had injured walked away with little more than a wispy memory of what had happened.

So, the colonel had moved into the great mansion on the hill, the Carny brothers had taken over operation of the farm, and Tucker got to swagger around the town pretending he was actually the law.

The major had become his chief confidant, much as he had been during the war. At first he hadn't wanted to stay, but with promises of an easy life, he had been persuaded. And as always, the corporal was at his side. For him the promise of all the liquor he could drink was enough incentive.

During the initial inspection they had found the old door beneath the house locked, double barred, and nailed shut. What could be so terrible on the other side to warrant such security? The major felt it was a mystery best left unsolved, but it ate at the colonel's mind like a sore tooth you just couldn't keep your tongue off of.

The door entered his dreams at night and occupied his thoughts during the day. It was becoming increasingly hard to accomplish anything at all as he obsessed with it. Finally he couldn't take it anymore. Armed with a pry bar, a torch, and his service revolver, he began his assault on the door. An hour later, sweat pouring from every part of his body, the last of the boards fell into the debris pile at his feet.

With trembling fingers he swung the thick door open. The slight breeze was cool, drying the perspiration from his face. It smelled of damp earth and something else, something animal. It made a chill run down his spine.

Taking a wooden match from the tin box in his pocket, he lit the oil-soaked rag at the end of his torch. The yellow light and the thick, black smoke it produced seemed somehow reassuring, and he stepped into the darkness.

The dust on the floor was inches deep, and each step he took sent clouds of it into the air, occasionally making him cough. In most places it remained undisturbed, but every now and then there were strange prints like none he had ever seen before. They were round and nearly as large as a horse's hoof, with two claws. Despite the trepidation he pushed forward into the darkness, the torch to guide his way in one hand and his cocked revolver in the other.

Suddenly ahead of him in the cave he heard a rustling sound and, as he raised his torch for a better look, a hissing like a cat's warning. The colonel raised the torch higher above his head for a better look. Just beyond his light he could see what appeared to be two red eyes staring back. They were as big around as the bottom of a mason jar, and nearly as far off the floor as his own.

As he watched they retreated back further into the cave and then, in a most amazing display, skittered up the sidewall and onto the ceiling!

For a moment the colonel nearly pulled the trigger on his revolver, but then instead he lowered the hammer and slipped it back into the holster at his side. At that instant something unsaid passed between him and the red-eyed monster. Suddenly they knew they were safe from each other.

The colonel turned his back on the creature and walked back up the tunnel. For a while he felt it following him, but then it stopped. He suspected that the creature he had just met there in the darkness was a larger version of the spiders that infested the town. And if that were the case, it might do to curry the beast's favor if that were possible. It might mean an even larger supply of the venom.

A plan began to form in his mind. Tomorrow he would tempt the beast with a sacrifice, possibly a sheep, and see how it reacted.

*     *     *     *     *

In the days that followed, the colonel tempted the beast. He knew now that it was what he had suspected—a giant version of the smaller spiders in town. Somehow, down here in the dark tunnels that honeycombed the ground below Cyprus Glen, it had grown to an enormous size, giving birth to thousands of tiny spiders in each egg sac. He suspected that the giant had sustained itself on the town's livestock and animals from the nearby swamp, possibly even the occasional resident. In one of the tomes from the days of the town's founding, he found mention of a beast that came in the night, and those first residents sacrificed animals and even people to it to keep it from killing them. Then suddenly, as the town started to grow even more, it became a myth and was forgotten.

The colonel guessed that the creature must have adapted to a new feeding schedule and seldom entered the town.

He spent hours below ground with the monster, learning its every move, studying, trying if possible to win its trust. He found that it preferred human blood to animal. The human blood acted almost like a treat to the creature. But his supply of human blood was very limited. If he began using the people of the town, they just might not be so forgiving this time.

That was when his most brilliant idea yet was born. He would open a hospital—a place for the old and the dying to come to and spend their last days. A place where if someone were to die, no one would question it.

Leaving the major in charge, he went off to study medicine and returned as Dr. Sharade. He remodeled the mansion, and it became the Hospital for the Care and Rehabilitation for the Aged. And while the patients upstairs were busy dying, he was busy downstairs perfecting the serum that would let them live forever.

Suddenly a scream echoed through the tunnels, tearing Sharade from his revelry. His face a grimace at the thought of what he might find, he moved a little faster through the caves.

\*     \*     \*     \*     \*

Kate felt something soft brush her face, and in her sleep she smiled. It was so nice here wrapped up in her bedclothes warm and safe, and with the soft finger of Rick's hand brushing her cheek to awaken her. She snuggled down further under the covers and felt something hard bite into her back. There shouldn't be anything hard in the....

Suddenly reality came crashing back to her. She wasn't home in bed with Rick, she was in a cave! And there weren't any bedclothes! So what was covering her? It was thick and sticky, almost like string, woven over her as she lay there on the ground. If only there were some light maybe she could see it. She was beginning to panic again. She tried to take control, to slow her breathing, to face her situation.

Out of the darkness came two glowing, red eyes like coals from a fire, and nearly as big as her fists. There was no stopping the panic now! Kate began to scream with madness. Those eyes there in the darkness had broken the last strand of her sanity!

\*     \*     \*     \*     \*

Thelma stood in the hallway, drying her tears and watching Sharade depart. When he rounded the corner out of sight, she dried her eyes one last time and headed up the steps. The encounter with the escaping woman had upset her more than it should have.

As she stepped through the door she called to one of the night orderlies, she couldn't remember his name, and told him to get some help and pick up the body in the cell downstairs and take it to the holding room. Then he was to get some mops and clean the room up, just in case the doctor brought the woman back.

She pushed open the door to the locker room, picked up her purse, and started for the back door. Then for a moment she hesitated. In the back of her mind it felt like she was leaving something very important behind. She stood there, staring blankly down the hall, trying to pry whatever secret it was her mind was holding from her loose. But no such luck. Finally she gave up, shaking her head, and went out into the night.

Thelma had hoped that the night air and all the stars overhead would help to clear her mind, like it did on most nights. Tonight it didn't. No matter what she tried, she just kept seeing that poor woman's face and hearing her ask, "Thelma, don't you know me? It's me, Kate!"

By the time she pulled open the storm door and stepped into the house, her thoughts were a whirlwind. This had happened a couple of times before, and the doctor had made it all right again. But he was busy chasing down the crazy woman, so she would just have to cope with it herself.

Vince and Sophie were already in bed, so rather than disturb them she climbed the stairs in the dark. Shadows made by the streetlights       cast eerie forms along the walls. She knew they were only shadows, but nonetheless she pulled in close to the banister, trying to stay at least an armlength away from them.

It seemed everywhere she looked the woman's face was there. Thelma had to stop in the middle of the steps and scrunch her eyes shut to make the visions go away. She pressed the palms of her hands against her temples, trying to drive the scene from her mind.

With plodding feet she forced herself to the top of the stairs and into the bathroom. Without turning on the light she jerked open the door to the medicine cabinet and fumbled for the bottle she sought. It had become so familiar to her that she could recognize it by feel alone. Dr. Sharade had said with the head injury she had suffered it might be necessary to use the drugs in the bottle to stop the nightmares she might have.

Thelma hastily pried off the top of the bottle and poured the pills into her hand. Greedily she swallowed them down, praying for the relief she knew should be coming. Then she staggered into the bedroom and fell fully dressed onto the bed. Within moments the drugs began their work, and her eyes grew heavy and she slipped away.

*    *    *    *    *

As the light came on, I unwound my fingers from the gunman's throat and climbed to my feet. I could see now that there was little doubt as to who he was. Unless, that is, assassins came in velvet smoking jackets with pencil-thin mustaches and fancy haircuts. The man I was trying so hard to kill was Dr. Albert Jackson.

I climbed to my feet sheepishly and offered him my hand, which he promptly slapped away. The anger in his face overshadowed his pain. "Get away from me, you ruffian! You've broken my leg."

I stepped back out of the way, and Bill helped him to his feet and into a chair. He noticed Bill's uniform. "Arrest this man. He tried to kill me, first by shooting at me earlier, and then by strangling me just now!"

I walked over, stood in front of the chair, reached out with my foot, and shoved the shoe of his broken leg just enough to send him halfway to agony. "No, that wasn't me who tried to shoot you. That was your old business partner Sharade tying up loose ends!"

He was about to deny it, but I tapped him again just to show I meant business. I was getting pretty good at this tough guy stuff. "Yeah," I said, "we know all about it. And we've got your records to prove it."

Jackson's complexion had suddenly gone gray under his tan. I wasn't sure whether it was from pain or from fear.

I was about to make sure it was from pain when Hays walked through the bedroom door and pulled me back with his good arm. There was a big, red stain on his shirt, and I could see what looked like a bed sheet crisscrossing his chest for a bandage. He looked a little wobbly, so I pulled over the chair from the vanity to sit on. He nodded his thanks and sunk into the seat.

"The ambulance is on its way, Doctor Jackson. But before it gets here you might want to tell me what happened tonight."

Jackson used his indignant face again and pointed at me. "That man, that ruffian, tried to kill me!"

Hays gave him a thin smile and held out his hand for the doctor's pearl-handled .32. Bill handed it to him, and he popped the clip free and ejected the shell from the chamber. Holding the copper-jacketed slug up for Jackson to see, he said, "I have a hole from one of these in my shoulder. So if I were you, I don't think I'd go pointing fingers at anybody. Now, do you want to tell me what happened before we got here? Or do you want me to turn Steele loose on you again?"

He panicked just a bit and tried to pull further back into the chair. "No, that's okay. I'll talk. I've done nothing wrong." I wish I could say he looked like he'd done nothing wrong, but he looked pretty guilty to me.

Jackson wiggled around in the chair to try and get more comfortable, but all that did was irritate his leg more. So finally he just settled in and started to talk. "I was up here working in my study across the hall when I heard the front door open. There have been a lot of break-ins in the neighborhood, so I've taken to keeping a gun in my desk drawer.

"When I didn't hear anything else, I got up and walked out into the hall to see what was going on. There was a man at the bottom of the steps. I called to him. 'Who are you, and what are you doing in my house?'

"Instead of answering, he fired a shot at me. Luckily for me it missed. I fired one back, then I ran down the hall and into the room when he found me and tried to kill me."

"What about the gunman? Do you know where he went?"

Jackson shook his head and winced. Must have made his leg hurt. "No. Until the lights came on I thought he was the same man." I should have broken his finger instead of his leg the way it kept pointing at me. "I'm guessing you people breaking in must have scared him off."

Hays was starting to match Jackson for color. He turned to Bill and said, "Tell the officers outside to scour the neighborhood and see if anybody saw anything."

As Bill left, Hays sighed and slumped a bit in the chair. My turn. I put my hand on his shoulder. "I'll take from here, Hays." He nodded and I stepped between him and the good doctor.

Putting my foot right next to his on the floor and making him wince, I said, "What was the stuff for that you were giving to your patients? What was it supposed to do for them?"

He was about to take a boat ride down that long river in Egypt, but my foot stopped him and he changed his mind. "It helped to keep them young. As long as they were taking it, they never seemed to grow any older."

I wanted to scoff at what he was telling me, but it matched up with what Palmer had told us earlier. I caught Joey's eye, and he shrugged one shoulder in kind of a "could be" gesture. Then I turned back to Jackson. "Where'd the stuff come from?"

He scrunched his face up in pain and tried whining at me. "Isn't that ambulance here yet? I need to see a doctor."

"It's on its way. Now answer my question. Where did the stuff come from?"

"Once a month Sharade would send me a case to use on my patients."

I looked around the room and whistled. "At a pretty big price, I'm guessing."

Some of that smug attitude crept back into his voice. "People will pay just about anything to stay young," he said matter-of-factly.

"And where did Sharade get the stuff?"

"I don't know."

I wasn't willing to accept that, and I bumped his foot with mine, making him howl. "Now where did Sharade get the stuff?" I demanded.

With tears of pain running down his cheeks, he held up his hands to try and ward me off. His voice was a squeal of fear. "Once when we were talking he said something about his friend in the tunnels! He said he got it from his friend in the tunnels."

My face was inches from his, and my voice was a low growl. I was finally getting somewhere. "What tunnels?"

"The whole town is undermined with caves. They run right under the hospital!"

"How do you know that?" I growled.

"I grew up there. Sharade sent me off to become a doctor."

I had a billion other questions, but the ambulance people were dragging their stretcher in the door, so he and I were done. I grabbed Joey, and we walked out into the hallway to talk.

"Well, what now?" he asked.

"We need to find somebody who knows about those caves. It sounded like a way to get into the hospital without being seen."

He nodded but still didn't look too reassured. "Where are we going to find somebody who knows about the caves?"

It was my turn to shrug. "We'll get Bill to take us back to the hospital, and maybe Redmond has an idea."

The ambulance crew wheeled Hays out into the hallway, and I stopped them before they headed downstairs. He looked pale, almost ghostly, from the loss of blood. "Don't worry about a thing, Hays. Joey and I can take it from here. By the time you're on your feet again, we'll have it all wrapped up." Then I gave him a smile I really didn't feel.

One of the ambulance crew looked at me and shook his head. "Wasting your breath, Mac. We sedated him, and he can't hear a thing you're saying."

Inside the room I could still hear Jackson yelling about all the injustices he was suffering. "Can't you give him something?"

The attendant shook his head. "Believe me, we tried. He keeps refusing, saying he has to be awake to protect himself."

I just shook my head and walked back into the room to find Bill. On my way, I stopped by the other gurney and leaned in close to Jackson. I let him see my teeth and the hard light in my eyes. "One last thing, Jackson, then these guys can take you someplace nice and safe. Do you remember if there was ever a geological study done on the town?"

His eyes said he was about to lie to me, but leaning down casually on his leg killed that idea. "1912. The state came out to have a look around," he gasped through the pain. "They were there about a week before we found out and sent them packing."

I stood up and nodded to the other two attendants. "I think he'll take that hypo now, won't you Doctor Jackson?"

He gulped out a soft yes, and the attendant sent the needle home. Seconds later the room was quiet and they wheeled him out. Bill was explaining to a couple of other cops what he wanted done when I finally finished crossing the room. I waited till he was done and then asked if he could take us back to the hospital. He said he was going that way anyway to check on Hays and would be glad to. He finished up what he was doing, and Joey and I followed him out into the night.

Chapter 29

Sharade followed the sounds of the screams, his flashlight forcing the darkness to retreat ahead of him. He knew that if she were still screaming, the spider may have her cornered but hadn't done any damage yet. And hopefully she hadn't done any to the spider.

The relationship between him and the beast had always been tentative at best. It didn't take him long to find out that if he overfed the monster he wouldn't see it for sometimes a month. So he kept the feeding light, drawing what blood he needed from his patients, but only what he needed.

Thinking about it now made him smile. After all these years of milking the spider for her venom, refining it, and then selling it to the people that could do him the most good, he had done quite well. The people in power in this state were at his beck and call. That was until the monster got out and went hunting on its own.

Even then, any other townsperson might have been fine, but it had to take the child of the town's only runaway and her outsider husband. That brought Steele and a whole wrath of trouble down on their heads. He shook his head. Maybe when the girl was gone it would all return to normal. Somehow he doubted it. It was beginning to feel just like it had before the end of the war.

He rounded a corner in the tunnel and saw something skittering ahead of him. The screaming had stopped a few minutes ago, and either she was out of breath or dead. Secretly he was hoping for the latter, but his flashlight beam bounced across the floor to reveal a mass of white webbing, pinning her wiggling body to the floor.

With a heavy sigh—he seemed to be doing that a lot these days—he knelt down beside her and began to cut her free. "The more you wiggle, Doctor Gallagher, the harder this is going to be to get off. Although I should just leave you here. You killed one of my people."

"What is that thing?" she gasped.

Sharade's knife made a smooth cut and the web pulled up from the floor, allowing her to sit up. "Unfortunately, Doctor, that is the only one of its kind, and the mother to all the smaller spiders in the village. Were I to leave you here she would come back and inject you with her venom, paralyzing you but leaving you conscious to all that was happening around you. Then she would come back and slowly draw the living blood from your system until you were nothing more than an empty husk."

Still partially wrapped in the webbing, Kate shuddered. "That's what you've been doing with my blood? Feeding that thing?" Her voice was almost a scream.

Sharade backhanded her, shutting her up. "Haven't you done enough yelling for one day?"

Kate's mind reeled from the blow, and she fought to maintain consciousness. Who knew what he would do with her. He might just leave her here.

He used his knife to cut her legs free of the webbing and jerked her to her feet. Then without a word he began dragging her down the tunnel. When she stumbled, he stopped and turned around. "If you fall, I will drag you the rest of the way back. So I suggest that for what little time you have left you try and stay on your feet, or your remaining days will be even more painful."

Stumbling and half running, Kate kept up with the mad doctor. The rocks on the floor of the cave tore at her feet. Biting her lip until it was bleeding, she found enough strength not to fall.

When Sharade pushed her through the door of her now-bare cell, she fell to the floor in relief. Like a dead woman she lay on the concrete, trying to catch her breath.

His face a mask of anger, he said, "You will not escape again. I'm going to make sure of that." Then he slammed the door and walked away.

In the cell, Kate pulled herself carefully into a sitting position. Her body was a mass of pain, but her keen mind was already blacking out the trauma and working on another plan!

\*     \*     \*     \*     \*

Dawn was just breaking as Bill dropped Joey and me off at the morgue door behind the hospital. I was starting to get used to going in and out of the door most people went through but never saw. And that had to be a bad thing.

Both of us were starting to look a bit like we belonged there or were escaping from there—bruised, beat up and just plain worn through. I don't think that there was a place on my body that didn't hurt anymore.

Joey yawned, grabbed a couple of sheets off the shelf, and stretched out on one of the stainless steel tables. Like always, within less than a minute he was snoring.

I was a little too keyed up for that, and I wasn't about to sleep on one of the autopsy tables. I might wake up to find somebody ready to slice me open!

I went into the attendant's office and sat down in the chair by the desk and pulled the phonebook across to look up the Hall of Records. If there was a study done on Cypress Glen, it should be on file someplace. Wasn't much I could do till it opened, but at least by then I'd know where I was going. I had to do something. Just sitting was going to drive me crazy.

The attendant, a bent-over old man with shaggy, gray hair and a mustache that went out of style fifty years ago, came in and sat down in the chair behind the desk. Without a word he pulled a bottle out of the bottom drawer and filled two glasses. He pushed one of them towards me.

I held up my hand in refusal, but he shook his head and said, "Drink it. It'll do you good. Right now you're whole life is in an uproar. This'll slow it down a bit." He waved a thumb toward Joey in the other room. I could hear his snores. "Don't we all wish we could be like him?"

I lifted the glass of amber liquor, the smell of charcoal thick in my nose. I started to sip it, but then just dumped it down my throat. I could feel the warmth spread all through my body. The attendant had already finished his and was refilling it by the time I sat my glass back down on the table. He didn't offer me a second one.

As he finished his second glass, he leaned back in his chair. "This thing with Cypress Glen's turned into quite a mess, hasn't it?" His voice was old, but firm.

I raised my eyebrows a bit in question. "You know about it?"

He gave me a half smile under his overgrown mustache. "Kind of hard not to with you guys running in and out of here. But I knew about it long before that." He paused while he poured another drink, and I waited.

He wiped off the back of his mouth with a hand. "You see, son, I was there when it all started. My name is Private Andre LuPon. I served in the Virginia Volunteers. I enlisted at the beginning of the war and was there with the colonel when it all ended."

Maybe it was the whiskey, but I didn't quite seem to be following him. "What war are we talking about?"

He smiled, showing me his slightly brown teeth amid all the gray hairs. "Why, the War of Northern Oppression, son—what you folks have come to call the Civil War."

I squinted at him in disbelief, and then it dawned on me. My hand flew for the gun under my arm, and before he could blink I had it out and pointed at him. "You're one of Sharade's men!"

He waved away my gun with the back of his hand. "Yes, I served under the colonel, but not under that name. I would have followed him through fire then, and often did. But that all changed one night on a hill above Cypress Glen."

He was totally ignoring me and my gun now as he poured another drink and sipped it. "We had just come out of the swamp with the Carny bothers, the corporal, the major, and of course the colonel. I was in the worst shape of the lot. I'd caught a case of the fever. When they made the assault on the town, they left me sitting on the ridge to die. I know that because for two days they didn't come back.

"And I would have died if not for those nasty little spiders everybody is so concerned about. Sometime in the night they swarmed over me, feeding and injecting me with their venom. I'm not real sure what happened then, but I think I might have died and been reborn. All I know is that God in all his wisdom decided he didn't want me yet.

"Awakening the next morning, I crawled off into the woods in search of food. I was close when they finally came back looking for me, and I heard what he said about being glad that I was gone. So I never went back.

It wasn't until some years later I realized that I was aging much slower than other people. It's been nearly one hundred years, but I'm only just starting to reach what would be my sixties."

I wanted to disbelieve everything he was telling me, but I knew it was true. Amazing as it was, it was true. "And you've kept this to yourself all these years?"

He held up his palms. "Who was going to believe me? And if they did, what little life I had was going to be over. It was bad enough every couple of years I had to change names and jobs when people started to notice. And I've watched my children grow old and die while I stayed young." His eyes grew far away. "'Times I would just as soon of died there on top of that hill."

"You never went back to Sharade?"

He shook his head. "No. I was tired of fighting, tired of causes. The war had taken all that from me. I knew that in the end no matter how much he professed loyalty to the South, the only person he was really concerned about was himself. If not, why didn't he use what he had to build an army of supermen and really pay back the North? Instead he set up that little empire of his."

I slid the .45 back under my arm. LuPon was bitter, but was he bitter enough to help me?

Under the mustache he smiled again. "I know what you're thinking, Captain. And the answer is yes. I've learned a lot in the long years I've lived. It's time he was stopped!"

So, for the next couple of hours I sat there and listened to the story of LuPon's life. By the time he was finished so was the bottle. His words were beginning to slur a bit and his eyelids had grown heavy. I thanked him and went upstairs to get a couple of breakfast trays. When I came back I woke the lumber mill in the other room.

As always Joey woke with a smile at the aroma of the food, even hospital food. He rolled off the dissection table, and I sat the breakfast down and found a couple of stools to sit on. While we ate I told him the story LuPon had told me.

"So you figure to use him to get us inside the back door of the hospital?" he asked around a mouthful of eggs.

I shrugged back my answer. "At least his information. I'm not about to risk anybody on this thing. Too many people have gotten hurt already."

He stabbed my toast with his fork and started to drag it across to his tray, but I snatched it back. "So what now then?"

I stuffed the toast into my mouth before he could try it again. "We'll need some stuff. I'll get a hold of Bill. He's probably still upstairs with Hays, or at least close."

Joey wiped up his plate with his last piece of toast. "And what about the spiders? The tunnels are bound to be full of them. What are you going to do about them?"

I tossed him my last piece of toast and got a grin. "Palmer. He should have some crazy idea about what will work."

So when we finished breakfast I went back in the office, and around the snoring form of LuPon I called upstairs and got hold of Redmond. He told me Hays was going to be down for a couple of days, but that he would make a full recovery. Then I had him put Bill on the line, and I gave him a list of the things we were going to need without really telling him what we were going to do. Like I told Joey earlier, I didn't want anybody else in any deeper than they had to be.

Palmer surprised me by being up, but then I wasn't real sure that he ever slept anyway. "I need something that will bring down spiders."

"Surely a little DDT will take care of that, won't it?"

I shook my head, even though he couldn't see me. "Well, Professor, I'm not really talking just one spider, I'm talking hundreds, maybe even thousands."

There was a pause on the other side of the line while the wheels in his head went round. "The same type you got the venom from before?"

"Yep, and more than likely in mass. Maybe some kind of spray or gas."

"Hmmmmm. And you need it how soon?"

"I'd like to have it before dark if I could."

"Stop by about five. I'll have something for you by then."

I broke the call, but for a couple of seconds I stood there holding the receiver. I'd really expected him to tell me that it was impossible, but yet he took it all in stride like it was nothing.

He reminded me a lot of Kate's father, Mr. Impossible himself. You ask for it and he'd build it. I guess that's where Kate got it from, her indomitable spirit. I just hoped that this time I wasn't too late!

*    *    *    *    *

Thelma was covered in a thin sheen of sweat, soaking her nightgown and the knotted-up bedclothes. It had been a long, painful night.

The drugs had done nothing this time to stop the nightmares. They had started from the moment her head had hit the pillow, and had not stopped all night.

She had visions of people she didn't know, trapped and screaming for her help—the woman in the hallway asking for her to help; a giant black man slipping away, his hand out for her to grasp and pull him to safety.

She swung her feet over the edge of the bed and sat there for a moment, her head in her hands and her elbows braced on her knees. For the first time in days she had awakened without pain. It was almost like sometime during the night a battle had been fought inside her mind, and that she had won.

She climbed to her feet, dropped her nightgown to the floor, and wrapped herself in her robe. Then she was off down the hall and to the shower. As she crossed to the bathroom she could hear her aunt downstairs in the kitchen. The smell of bacon cooking filtered upstairs, and for a moment her stomach somersaulted. She shuddered and raced away from the smell into the bathroom.

With the door closed and feeling safe, she opened the medicine cabinet and took out the bottle of pills that Dr. Sharade had given her. She poured them out into her hand, and then casually dumped them into the toilet. As she flushed them away she caught a glimpse of her face in the mirror. The Thelma of the last few days was gone. There was a sparkle in her eye and the beginnings of a plan in her mind.

\*     \*     \*     \*     \*

Sharade was sitting in his war room when the major found him. He was behind his desk, and there was an open bottle on the top. As the major entered, he held up one of the glasses in question. "Drink, Major? Seems it's been a long time since we shared a drink." Sharade's voice sounded tired and weary.

The major pulled up the other chair in the room and sat down across from him. "Yes, sir, it has been."

Sharade filled the two glasses, and they chinked them together in a salute. When they had both swallowed what was in their glasses he asked, "How bad is it?"

The major ran his thin fingers through his even thinner hair. "Not critical yet, but close. I sent the corporal after Doctor Jackson, but that state cop Hays showed up and got in the way. According to the hospital, he's there now with a broken leg. And we still have a missing shipment out there someplace."

Sharade leaned back in his chair, studying the tiny bit of amber fluid that remained in his glass, rolling it back and forth across the bottom. "The loss of the shipment is expensive, but replaceable. As is Raymond. Jackson is another matter entirely. I really wish you had made an attempt to get him out rather than kill him. It took me a long time to set that operation up. And if they have Jackson, more than likely they have his records.

"Before this I would have counted on that buffoon of a chief inspector to clean this mess up, but he's be compromised too. It looks like we may have to make a clean sweep of it and settle back down here at home for twenty or thirty years—then start over again."

The major raised his eyebrows in a question. "Will the town stand for that? They've grown pretty used to what the operation is providing for them."

"The town is not in charge here, Major—I am! And what I say goes. Besides, what have they really gotten from all of this besides a few trinkets and the rest of the state leaving them alone? I doubt they'll even notice."

Sharade leaned forward, reached for the bottle, and refilled his glass. But instead of picking it up, he picked up the old cavalry pistol. He broke it open and looked through the barrel for dust. Then he began filling the cylinder with loads of lead.

Snapping it closed, he spun the cylinder and pulled the hammer back. He sighted down the barrel at the major and squeezed the trigger. The sound of the hammer falling on the empty cylinder was like a cannon shot in the room. "Once it would have been so easy, just like that. Now I'm not even sure we can be killed." Laughing, he set the gun down and picked up his glass. "Get them men together. It's time we got ready to move undercover."

The major wiped the cold sweat off his upper lip with the back of his hand. He rose and picked up his hat and walked to the door. With his hand on the knob he turned to see that Sharade was pointing the gun at his back again. "If you're going to shoot me, go ahead and get it over with. Otherwise get yourself a new hobby." He stepped into the hallway and slammed the door. Sharade's laughter echoed from the room.

*    *    *    *    *

In a freshly starched uniform, her hat in hand, Thelma rushed into the kitchen where her aunt was busy making breakfast. Normally she would have spent nearly half an hour talking about the day to come and eating her breakfast. But this morning the smell of the bacon frying was almost more than she could handle.

Aunt Sophie noticed right away. "Are you taking the medicines that the doctor prescribed for you? You're looking a little pale." She held the back of her hand against Thelma's forehead.

Thelma backed away like she was afraid her aunt could read her mind with her hand. "I'm fine. I'm taking my pills just like he said to. I'm just in a hurry this morning. Lots to do." She scalded her tongue on a quick swallow of coffee, kissed her aunt on the cheek, and escaped into the living room and head for the front door.

Sophie came running after Thelma, a paper back clutched tightly in her hand. "Wait! Wait!! You forgot your lunch!"

Thelma paused with the screen half opened to take the bag, but before she could get her hand on it, Sophie opened it. "I used the rest of the pork chops to make you a sandwich."

The smell of the roast meat nearly made Thelma swoon. She had to grab Sophie's arm to stop from falling.

"See, I knew you weren't well. Come in here and sit on the couch, and I'll call the doctor."

320

Thelma forced a smile she didn't feel. "I'm fine, Aunt Sophie. Besides, seems kind of silly to have the doctor come look at me when that's where I'm going anyway. I just need some air this morning. I'll be fine, and I promise as soon as I get to the hospital I'll see the doctor."

Sophie pushed her hair back with her hand. "If you're sure. But I want you to call me as soon as you talk to the doctor."

Finally free of her grasp, Thelma stepped out on the porch and called back over her shoulder. "I'll call you just as soon as I talk to him." Then she was off and rushing up the street. She didn't slow down till she was sure she was out of Sophie's sight, and then only long enough to stuff her lunch in an already full trash can.

\*     \*     \*     \*     \*

Thelma made the walk to the hospital in half the time it usually took her. So quickly, in fact, that she was nearly out of breath when she got there. A wisp of her mousy brown hair had escaped from her bun, and a thin sheen of sweat had appeared on her upper lip. Hastily she wiped her face with a tissue from her purse, pushed the hair back into place, and put on her starched cap. She wrote her name in perfect script in the sign-in book and was ready for another day of work. But today, other thoughts were filling her mind instead of looking after the few patients the hospital had.

Fortunately there were only a couple. For the most part, the people of the village never got hurt or sick. If they did, all they had to do was wait a short while, and the serum in their blood would repair whatever the damage was or kill the virus that was threatening their body. So most of the patients the hospital got were outsiders sent here primarily to die, a task that Dr. Sharade was more than willing to help them with.

As a matter of fact, besides Uncle Vince, who had mysteriously taken ill, and Lou Anne recovering from her suicide attempt, there was only one old man she doubted would see sundown. He had been sent down from the city, suffering from a form of dementia and a rapidly failing body. But he had money, and that was why he was here. Sharade was after a piece of that inheritance, that and the plasma that he kept extracting from the man.

Thelma entered the old man's room. He looked almost ghostly under the sheet, his body frail with age, his chest barely rising and falling. She raised an eyelid and checked his pupil. There was no response from the milky blue-white of his eye. Whatever spark life had once given it had nearly burned out. Out of habit she wrapped her hand around his reed-thin wrist and felt for his thread pulse. Then she took his nearly nonexistent blood pressure. She wrote the numbers down on his chart and slipped quietly out the door.

Her next stop was her Cousin Lou Anne's room. There had been no response from her since the night of her wrist-slitting incident. Even though she hadn't known Lou Anne well these last few years, Thelma didn't really believe that she was capable of taking her own life. And then when she did it, she was nearly catatonic. What could have broken her spell long enough for her to do what she did? And even if she had done it on her own, why wasn't she regaining her strength? She was slipping away almost as fast as the old man in the other room. Gently she brushed her cheek. The flesh was dry like parchment and so pale you could see the blood circulating beneath it.

Her last stop was her Uncle Vince's room. He had suddenly fallen ill a couple of nights ago. They had brought him to the hospital complaining of chest pains and shortness of breath.

Sharade said it looked like a heart attack, and that the prognosis wasn't good. Now he lay in a hospital bed, his vitality wasting away into all the wires and tubes connected to him. Of all her patients, he was the only one that was conscious. But he was too weak to speak, and could only manage a smile now and then. Looking at him lying there, thin and pale, she had to turn away so he wouldn't see the tear that was forming in her eye.

Under control once more, she turned back and gave him her best smile. "And how are you this morning, Uncle Vince?"

Vince tipped his head to the side, and with grey lips formed a single word. "Sophie?"

Thelma puttered around fixing his bedclothes and plumping his pillow. "Sophie's fine. She asks about you every day," she lied. Not once since he had been brought here had she asked. It was almost as though he had ceased to exist in her mind. "Maybe today she will come and see you and Lou Anne."

Vince's eyes formed a question. "You remember. She came in the day before you did. She's right next door in the other room, getting better every day. Before you know it, she'll be in here helping you get your strength back," she lied again.

Vince just smiled weakly and tried to shake his head, knowing the truth. He was getting weaker with each passing moment, not stronger.

Thelma, with her plastered-on smile, leaned down to kiss him on the cheek. But instead, with her lips close to his ear, she whispered, "Don't worry, Vince. I have a feeling things are about to change."

\*   \*   \*   \*   \*

Kate lay on the floor of her bare cell. She pressed her cheek against the cool concrete, trying to draw strength that she no longer had. Her half-eaten breakfast was still where they had poured it out, rather than letting her have any utensils that could be used as a weapon. Despite her pain and her exhaustion, that brought a smile to her lips. They were afraid of her. And for the first real time in her life, she was afraid. Oh sure, there had been times when she'd suffered a quick fright, but this time she was really and truly afraid.

The death that she had defied so many times didn't seem too willing to take no for an answer this time. He was waiting here in this room for the moment when she gave up. Then he would swoop down on her, sucking her soul from her body and leaving only an empty husk.

She wondered what it would be like once she was gone. Not the crying part; that anybody could predict. No, the other side. She had never been much of a believer in a single creator. The study of too many ancient people had shown her the fallacy in that. People created gods for the things they didn't understand, and for situations they couldn't begin to comprehend. Kate was a scientist and knew the answers to all those questions they had asked so long ago.

And if there was a God, why had he permitted a man like Sharade to commit the atrocities that he had? Where was all that righteous power in the face of a tyrant or a murderer like Hitler or Sharade? Why let evil live and fester in the world? No. She had long ago stopped believing in God.

Dr. Katherine Gallagher believed in only herself—herself and Rick Steele, of course. But she was starting to have her doubts in him. If he didn't rescue her soon, there might not be anything to rescue.

Kate thought she heard somebody call her name and opened the eye that wasn't pressed to the floor. A few feet away stood a woman. Her hair and her dress were very distinct, but her face was fuzzy, almost like somebody took their thumb and smudged a painting before it was dry.

The woman seemed to know what Kate was thinking. "That's because you don't remember me very well, Katherine. You were very young when I died."

She tried harder to focus on the woman's face, and for second it was clear. Then it was smudged again. "Mom?"

The specter that was Sarah Gallagher gently caressed her daughter's face. "You poor child. You have been through so much!" Her voice was soft and sweet, almost like a song, the way Kate remembered it sounding when her mother would sing to her. "And now you've lost your faith. I suppose I could blame your father for that. He never was much of a church-goer."

The thought of her mother's ghost complaining about her father made Kate smile, despite the pain of her torn lips.

The woman shook her head. "I guess that's why I'm here. To remind you. I know what you've been thinking, and you're wrong. God gave us free will to do what we wanted. And when that goes astray against the rest of society, men like Rick Steel come along to set things right again."

"But why am I here? Why have I been tortured?"

"We learn lessons, Katherine, from everything that happens to us. It's like the old cliché, what doesn't kill us makes us stronger."

"I'm not sure, Mom, that I can take much more learning!" Kate said a bit snidely.

Her mom's mouth seemed to smile behind the fuzziness. "Katherine, you are the strongest woman I have ever seen, and I know for a fact that you're not going to give up and die. You're going to fight till there is no breath left in your lungs, no blood in your veins, or strength left in your limbs. I was taken from you to build that strength, that self-reliance. Now show me what Katherine Gallagher is made of!"

Kate pulled her tired and battered body from the concrete, and sat up. He mother reached out with ghostly arms and hugged her. "You can do this, Katherine. You can survive. Now I have to go." The specter of Kate's mom rose and walked slowly across the room. With each step she grew less distinct. Then suddenly she was gone.

Kate sat in the middle of the floor, staring at the spot where her mother had disappeared, thinking about the things she had said. She was still in pain, but now there was a new strength. She knew that she would survive!

Suddenly the quiet of the cell was broken by someone calling her name.

*     *     *     *     *

It was nearly lunchtime before Thelma could get away from her duties. The doctor was on some kind of tirade, and he sent everybody but his specials home. Unfortunately she fell into that category, so she had to make up for what the others were no longer doing. When she did finally get away it was almost too late, but she knew she couldn't wait another minute.

After carefully checking to make sure no one else was in the hallway, she opened the door to the stairs and slipped through. All the way down the concrete steps she kept looking over her shoulder to make sure she wasn't followed. Fortunately the lack of staff had helped as much as it had hurt. At least it meant no random people were going to be on the steps.

At the bottom she again checked the corridor before stepping through. It was hot and noisy from the machinery, but clear of people. When she got to the door to Sharade's war room, she crept quietly over and laid her ear against the wooden panel, listening for noises. For long moments she stood statue-like, listening. Finally hearing nothing, she decided she was alone and moved on through the basement.

With stealth she didn't even know she had, Thelma moved silently past the boiler room, with its hissing steam and whirling machinery, and around the turn in the corridor that led to the cells.

She put her face to the small, rectangular window in the door and looked in. She could see Kate sitting on the floor, facing away from the door. Softly she called to her. "Doctor Gallagher, it's me, Thelma." When she got no response she called again, this time louder. "Doctor Gallagher! It's me, Thelma." She saw Kate's shoulder start at the sound, finally, and knew this time she'd heard her.

Slowly she turned to face the door, and, involuntarily at the sight, Thelma sucked in her breath. She hadn't realized how badly she had been beaten.

Both of Kate's eyes were ringed with deep purple, and one was nearly closed. Her lips were swollen, and a tiny trickle of dried blood trailed down her chin. Her normally silky auburn hair was matted and tinged dark with dirt and blood.

Kate Gallagher lurched to her feet like a broken wind-up toy and limped across the room to the door. When she reached it she let her body weight fall against it, no energy left to move any further. She pushed her hand through the window, the nails torn and broken, the flesh stained rusty with dried blood. "Thelma, I knew you'd come... that you couldn't forget me for long."

Thelma touched Kate's fingers, tears streaming down her cheeks. "Doctor Gallagher, I'm so sorry. He did something to my mind, and I couldn't remember. But then last night it all became clear again!"

Thelma fumbled with the lock. "Let me get this open, and we can get you out of here."

Suddenly she heard Kate's intake of breath, and a hand clamped onto the back of her neck. "So, you've beaten my drugs and my hypnosis!"

Thelma flailed out with her feet, trying to kick free, but Sharade held her fast. Veins in his forehead were throbbing in anger, and his face was crimson. "I had such high hopes for you. I hoped that you would join us, but it appears I couldn't have been more wrong!"

Still holding her in one hand, he opened the door and hurled her inside. "Well, my friend in the tunnel can always use another guest for dinner!" Then he roared with laughter at his own joke and slammed the door and locked it again.

Chapter 30

I sent Joey off with Bill, Hays' aide, to get the stuff we needed while I hung around the morgue. After all, I was still technically dead. And besides, somebody had to wait for LuPon to sleep off the bottle he'd finished. I still wasn't sure whether he was what he said, but I really couldn't take the chance and let him get too far out of my sight. He just might be the only way I had of getting Kate out of there alive.

After a couple of hours of listening to him snore, I was about to lose what few marbles I still had. So to keep what sanity I had left, I decided that the human, whiskey-fueled buzz saw could look after himself for a while, and I'd take a trip up to see how Hays was doing. Even a conversation with his unconscious body would be better than what I was doing now.

I put on my hat, pulled it down low over my face till the brim was touching my ears, then I put on my jacket and turned the collar up. It wasn't much of a disguise, but since fake mustaches and glasses were in short supply in the morgue, it was the best I could do.

All I could do was hope that the bad guys had decided to take the day off and were out watching a ball game somewhere. Little did I know that one of them was just a little more dedicated than the rest.

By the time the elevator got to Hays' floor, I think I might actually have been whistling. I guess I was feeling pretty smug with myself at having snuck out of morgue without being seen.

I walked down the hallway like I owned the place, and without knocking I pushed open the door to Hays' room. It was probably just as well I hadn't. It would have been hard to say what Hays' visitor would have done in the short seconds I'd have wasted waiting for someone to answer the door. As it was my entry nearly threw him into a state of shock.

The man was about forty-ish and balding, hairy arms and hands sticking out of the top half of his stolen pair of scrubs. And his hairy hands were wrapped around the captain's throat, trying to throttle the life out of him.

A scream tore from my lips, and I threw myself in the air at him. He turned to see what was happening at just that moment, and my left shoulder caught him square across the chest. The two of us crashed across the hospital room and into the far wall.

I rolled quickly to my feet, and the .45 leaped into my hand. But the hairy assassin wasn't going anywhere. When the two of us hit the wall, his neck had been at the wrong angle. Now for the rest of eternity it was going to be at the wrong angle. He had broken his neck, and as I watched he drew his last breath and died.

I slid the automatic back under my arm and turned around to check on Hays. All I could do was hope that I had gotten there in time.

As I raised Hays back up onto his bed, his breathing was ragged but he was breathing. For a second his eyes opened, and he tried to smile. Then suddenly his eyes got big and wide, but I had already heard the click of a hammer being pulled back, so I was in flight over the bed, dragging him with me as the bullet pierced the spot that I had just vacated.

We hit the floor hard, and I could see that his shoulder was bleeding again, but I didn't have time to do anything about it. I reached up over the bed and snapped off two quick shots without looking. The roar of the .45 was like a cannon going off in the room. It was so loud I was surprised it didn't rattle the plaster off the walls. My ears were ringing like a fire truck, but amidst the din I heard a grunt from the other side of the room and ventured a careful look over the top of the bed.

The shooter was clutching at his left shoulder, and crimson was pouring out through the fingers and over the gun he was still holding. I'd gotten lucky, but just not lucky enough. As I watched and readied for another and better shot, he jerked open the door between us and fled into the hallway.

I wanted to stay and help Hays, but I knew that if this guy got back to his master's he was going to blow off whatever cover we still had going for us. A quick glance at Hays confirmed what I thought, and I was leaping over the bed again, hollering back as I went. "I'll send help!" I think he nodded, but I couldn't be sure. I was already moving too fast.

The corridor was total pandemonium. People were screaming and running back and forth, and at the far end I could see my quarry making for the stairs, leaving a trail of red behind him like a half-squashed snail. I screamed over the noise that Hays needed help, waved my gun in the air, and the Red Sea of people parted, screaming more and fleeing to the sides.

I crashed through the stair door with my shoulder, and without even thinking hurled myself over the rail and onto the switchback below. The guy was quick, even with a bullet in him—or maybe because there was a bullet in him he was trying to set the world's record for running down stairs.

Twice more I had to leap the rail, landing on the next switchback below before I started to catch him. By the time I was only half a flight behind, the bottoms of my feet and my knees were starting to feel like somebody had been pounding on them with a really big hammer. My lungs were full of fire, and I wasn't sure there was enough room left in them for air.

Targeting him as closely as I could, I threw myself over the rail one last time, pointing my feet. For a second I thought I was going to miss, but he was starting to slow down. Just as he looked up both my number tens caught him square in the back, and we both rolled down to the first floor landing.

Without waiting to catch my breath, I grabbed him by the greasy hair on top of his head and smacked his face down on the hard concrete. I felt his nose crunch and a couple of teeth splinter. But it was more than enough; his body went limp beneath me.

As I climbed off, the stairwell was suddenly full of people and I was looking down the shaking barrel of hospital security's gun. Rather than have it go off due to the vibrations of his hand, I grabbed it by the barrel and twisted it free from his hand. "It's okay, Pops. I'm one of the good guys."

I'm not real sure he believed me, but at least he was too scared to argue. "I need you to get all these people out of here and call the state police. And don't let anybody back in this stairway unless they're wearing a brown uniform."

He hurried to comply with my orders, and within a couple of minutes I was all alone on the landing with our bad boy.

I grabbed him by his collar and dragged him up into a sitting position against the wall so I could assess the damage I had done. He hadn't been pretty when this whole thing started, and he definitely wasn't going to win any beauty contest now. His nose was plastered up against the side of his face, and his upper two teeth had sliced through his lips before they jumped overboard. But ragged as it was he was still breathing, and the bullet hole in his shoulder was leaking less blood than his used-to-be nose. Or maybe he was just running out.

Trying to avoid the drips, I reached into his jacket pocket and pulled out his wallet. In the movies hit men never have anything that will identify them in their wallets. This guy must have never seen any of those movies, because his was stuffed with ID, all of it with different names. Guessing he must have had a side line as a pick pocket, or his mother just couldn't figure out what to call him. So a hell of a lot of good that did me. I did steal the twenty out of it though. I figured he owed me that for my trouble.

I sat back against the other wall, .45 in my lap in case he got rowdy, and listened to him breathe. After about five minutes or so his eyes flickered open, and before the pain had time to hit he tried to get up. I kind of discouraged that by waving the automatic at him, and he settled back down.

I tossed him my hanky to hold over his nose and asked, "Can you talk?"

He nodded and said in kind of a slurry voice, "Ya'll s'pposed to be dead."

Twain walked through my head for a minute, but I knew he'd never get it. "Maybe I am."

His eyes got a little rounder as he thought about that, then he shook his head. "No spook would need a cannon like that to stop me."

I just shrugged my shoulders. I was tired of the friendly small talk already. "So who paid you to kill Hays?"

"Who says I was tryin' to kill anybody. Maybe I was just visitin'."

"I've been places where they shoot at visitors, but this isn't one of them. Now who sent you to kill Captain Hays?"

He mopped some blood from his nose and winced at the pain as he touched it. "Ya gotta get me a doc! I might be bleedin' to death." It sounded more like acting than real fear in his voice. This one was a tough guy. He'd seen enough hard time to know the real score.

I acted like I was really considering what he'd said for a moment, then I shook my head and pointed the .45 at his other shoulder. "You're not bleeding to death yet, but you might be in a minute when I put the second bullet in you!"

"You wouldn't do that. You're one of the cops." But the look he gave me was more hopeful than confident.

I shook my head again. "You got me all wrong. I'm not a cop. As a matter of fact I think the city police referred to me as a kill-crazy maniac."

Fear's kind of a funny thing. It's a lot like water. If you watch real close you can see it rising. It was rising in him now, right from the toes of his fancy shoes to the whites of his eyes. Kind of a tiny shudder that if you didn't look close you might miss it. But you could never miss it in the eyes. They got beady and a bit glassy, and started to rock from side to side.

I clicked back the hammer on my gun, and a tremor took over his hand. "It's okay, mister, you don't have to shoot. I'll talk."

I felt a smile split my dry lips. "So let's start with something simple. Who sent you down here to kill Hays?"

By the time Bill and his troopers got there, I'd heard all the tawdry details of his misguided life. But somewhere along the way I'd also gotten the information that I wanted. I had a direct link now between him and the chief inspector, and maybe even a couple of the men over his head. Sharade's empire was crumbling fast.

Bill and his boys came into the stairwell with guns drawn, but I waved them down. "Hand him the killer's gun," I said. "He's more interested in seeing a doctor than he is making a run for it. Then when he's all patched up he'd like to talk to a nice stenographer. He's got a real good story to tell. Right, buddy?"

He nodded as the two troopers dragged him to his feet and snapped on the bracelets. There was a bit of panic in his voice. "Just get me to a doc!"

As they escorted him out, I told Bill what had happened both in Hays' room and in the stairs. When I finished, there was worried look on his face. "How's the captain? Was he hurt?"

I grinned at him. "Nah, unless I killed him dragging him off the bed and onto the floor. I'm headed up there next to see how he's doing."

Then suddenly it struck me that I was one black giant short on manpower. "Where's my sidekick?"

Bill grinned this time. "He said he'd seen you shoot guys before, so he went around back to unload the car."

I just shook my head and started back up the stairs, trying not to limp from smashing my feet into the concrete four times.

\*     \*     \*     \*     \*

Redmond was in the room with Hays when Bill and I walked in. Hays was sitting up in bed, and although he looked a little pale he was better than the last two times I saw him. The body against the wall was gone, and there was a white chalk outline where he'd fallen. A couple of photogs were busy taking pictures of the crime scene, and a trooper was taking down Hay's statement.

The doctor looked none too happy, and he wasn't holding anything back when he walked over to us. "Damn it, Steele, I should have thrown you out the minute you came through my door. Gun battles, chases, what's next?"

Pretty much all I could do was shrug a shoulder. "I wish just as much as you that none of this had happened, Doc. But I don't see how we could have done anything different. We're dealing with some really ruthless bad guys who'll stop at nothing to get what they want. But it's nearly over now."

I walked over to the bed and took a look at Hays. For a change he was smiling, but I could see the corners of his lips twitching for a cigarette. I reached in my jacket pocket and pulled out a brand new pack of Luckies. He took the pack in his good hand and tore the cellophane off with his teeth. Spitting it out he said, "I don't care what Redmond says about you, you're all right." He stuck one of the butts between his lips then held out his hand again.

I fumbled around in my jacket for a minute just to watch his expression change, and then I pulled out his gold lighter and handed it to him. His smile came back as he sucked the smoke deep into his lungs.

"So tell me where we are," he asked through the blue cloud surrounding his head.

I gave him the update on everything that had happened since the shootout at the doctor's. And speaking of him, I asked Redmond what the score was there, and he sent a nurse out to check.

When the nurse came back, her cute little smile was gone and she was wringing her hands. "He's gone, Doctor. Just like he was never there. His clothes, everything. Just up and gone."

I bit back the curse that was forming on my lips. I should have known better and had him watched. But then who would have figured a guy with a leg broken like his would get up and walk away? 'Course, he wasn't any ordinary guy.

Hays looked over at Bill a bit perturbed and said, "Get an APB out on him right away with a full description."

Bill started for the door, but I stopped him. "Not gonna make any difference, Hays. Sharade ordered him killed. So we know he's not going back there. If I were him, I wouldn't stop running for a long time. And as for us, we've got his records, so he was secondary to the case anyway."

Hays nodded and leaned over to stub his cigarette out in the ashtray on the bed stand. "So what now?"

I shrugged. "With the last two guys stopped, I think you and Redmond's hospital are safe enough." I gave the doctor the sweetest smile I could muster. He just scowled back at me, but I could see relief in his eyes. I knew how he felt. It seemed with every move we made we were drawing in more and more innocents. "All that is left is up to Joey and me." Then as an afterthought I added, "And if LuPon is what he says he is."

"And if he's not?" Bill asked.

My turn to scowl, and I was almost as good at it as Redmond. Why was there always one guy in the crowd that had to spoil it all with logic? "Then Joey and I will probably end up on Sharade's spit over an open fire. Either way we're out of your hair, and you probably won't see

Sharade again in this lifetime." I said it all with a smile, but I think we all knew that I was right. If I didn't bust Sharade's operation for good this time, he'd just hide out till the heat was off in forty or fifty years and start all over again.

"When do you leave?" Hays asked.

"We have to wait until five for the stuff Palmer's putting together for us. So once we get that, we're on our way."

He gave me kind of a quizzical look as he lit up another Lucky. "I know this may sound a bit stupid, but how are we going to know if you succeeded?"

"If we come back, we made it. If not, you might make a run into the village and make sure our heads aren't on a post someplace." Then I turned to Bill. "You said Joey was downstairs unloading. Did he get everything we wanted?"

Bill nodded and snickered a bit. "Everything and more. But you'll see what I mean when you go down there."

I checked my watch and it was well past noon, so I figured I'd better get my derrière in gear. I shook hands with Hays and Bill, and as I headed for the door, Redmond was standing there with his hand out. I grabbed it and shook it. His grip was firm and dry.

"Good luck, Steele. I've got a feeling you're going to need it before this night is over. If there's anything I can do…."

I shook my head. I couldn't think of a thing, then I suddenly changed my mind. "Could you get the cafeteria to send down a couple of lunches? This might be the last time Joey and I get to eat for a while."

Redmond's face split in a smile, and he gave my hand an extra squeeze. "I'll see what I can do."

I stepped out into the hallway and let out a big sigh. I wished I felt as confident as I made them think I did. There was a lot riding on Joey and me. Oh, I wasn't worried about him. He was a machine when it came to trouble. It was me—the little self doubts nagging at the back of my mind, the little mistakes that I might miss that could cost somebody else their life. That's what I was worrying about.

## Chapter 31

When I got downstairs LuPon was finally awake, having slept off the effects of the bottle. I grabbed some paper and a pen and shoved it in front of him before he either tried to get away or found another stashed bottle.

Raising an eyebrow, he asked, "What's this for? I'm not signing no confession!"

"I want a map of the caverns under the town. I want to go from the entrance to the hospital in the fastest way possible."

He rubbed his bloodshot eyes and started to object. "You don't need a map. You have me. I'll lead you through the caves."

I shook my head. "Sorry. As much as you want to even the score with Sharade, you're going to have to do it from here. Joey and I are going in alone."

I wasn't sure if he was really surprised, or if his mouth just hung open from the effects of the bottle. But it was gaping at me. "Do you realize how ruthless Sharade and his people can be? They wouldn't think twice about putting you two in the ground."

I felt my jaw set hard before I spoke. "That's exactly the reason we're going in alone. Nobody else is dying because of us."

I tapped the paper with my finger. "So draw me a map so I can find my way."

Without any more objections, LuPon picked up a pen and started to work on his map. I walked out to the other room, but he called me back. "You know, Steele, those caves are full of spiders."

"Yeah, I know. But hopefully I've got that covered."

\* \* \* \* \*

About a quarter to five Joey and I piled in the car and headed over to Palmer's lab. Not real sure what I expected, but it didn't look any better in the light. The brick was still crumbling and the garbage was still piled up around it. But at least you could read all the letters on the wall.

The door was unlocked, so we just made ourselves at home and walked in. As we went passed the receptionist's desk I wondered if anybody had ever sat there to greet customers, or for that matter were there ever any customers?

Palmer wasn't around out front or in his office, unless he was hiding behind the piles of paper and unopened mail on his desk. So we pushed through the door and into the lab.

Suddenly as the door closed behind us, what sounded like shots echoed from the back of the lab. Joey and I leaped behind one of the lab tables with guns drawn.

Carefully I stuck my head up over the edge for a look around. Seeing nothing, I called out. "Palmer, are you alright?"

Palmer came out of the back of the lab, his hair singed and still smoking in a couple of places, soot smeared all over his face. He had his hands raised in surrender. "Don't shoot, Captain. That was just an experiment that went a bit wrong."

Joey reached out with a damp thumb and forefinger and put out a couple of Palmer's hairs that were still burning. Palmer seemed not to notice. He took off his thick glasses and polished them with the tail of his shirt. "I guess I lost track of time. That's why I was still in back." Putting his glasses back on, he cracked a crooked smile. "I'll have to save that experiment till next time."

I looked at Joey to see if he knew what Palmer was talking about, but all I got was a shrug, so I just let it go and asked, "Did you manage to come up with anything for us?"

That seemed to set the professor beaming. He led us across the lab to a table covered with an old tarp. "Yes, I did. Yes, I did!"

With that crazy smile on his face, he reached out and jerked the tarp off the table. "Tada!" Underneath were all kinds of bits and pieces. Joey picked up something that looked a lot like a can of beans with a ring on the top, and Palmer snatched it away from him. "Careful. That might go off."

Joey looked at me with a *What?* look, and all I could do was shrug. How bad could an exploding can of beans be? But we just stood back and let him go.

Palmer picked up what looked like a water-filled fire extinguisher and held it out. It had straps like a backpack. "This," he said, "was just exactly what it looks like. It used to be a regular fire extinguisher. I gave it a better seal and increased the pump capabilities and filled it with a very deadly form of insecticide. If you spray it on the spiders, or anything else for that matter, it should kill them dead right away. There are two of them, and I put straps on them like backpacks so you can wear them."

He handed it to me for inspection and picked up one of the bean cans again. "I figured the sprayers for close-up work. These on the other hand," he held up the can for us to see, "I designed like tear gas canisters. Just pull the ring, throw it, leave it, whatever, and it should kill all the spiders within about two hundred feet. I worked up a dozen."

Professor Palmer sat that can back down and picked up another. This one was painted bright red, otherwise it looked the same. "This one I filled with a new high explosive, in case you need to blast your way through somewhere, or maybe want to close something up after you've gone through."

He seemed very pleased with what he'd done, and I had to admit that for no more time than we'd given him it was pretty fantastic. I slapped him on the shoulder. "Thanks, Professor. Looks like you've really come through."

His smile got bigger and turned into a full-blown grin. Holding up an index finger, he said, "I have one more neat little surprise for you." He reached into his pocket and pulled out a handful of .45 slugs.

"That's great, Professor, but I've got plenty of ammunition."

"Not like these." He held one out for me to see, but it looked just like any other .45 slug. "These are specially designed to explode on contact."

I was starting to think maybe he'd sniffed a bit too much of his bug spray, but the more he talked, the more sense he made. "I took and drilled the nose out, and filled it with the same explosive I used in the grenades. It won't be quite as powerful, but it should be more than enough to blow open a door."

I took one of them, and on close examination I could see where he drilled it out. It might work if it didn't blow up my gun in my hand.

There were a few more neat little trinkets of mass destruction on the table that he had to explain. When he was done we scooped it all up into the bags and took it out to the car.

He followed us out. "I hope that will be enough, Captain Steele. With more time...."

I gave him my big "thank you" grin. "I'm sure what you built for us will do just fine, Professor Palmer. I'm amazed you could get so much done in such a short time." I stuck out my hand. "Thank you so very much."

Professor Palmer shook my hand, and Joey and I climbed into the car. Moments later we were headed out of town on the highway, headed to Cypress Glen.

*   *   *   *   *

The ride down the highway was pretty much silent, except for the baffled roar of the exhaust and the click of shells into the clips for my .45. There wasn't much left of our conversation, so we were stuck with our own thoughts.

Joey's jaw was set in a grim, hard line, and I knew that if I looked in a mirror mine would have looked the same. We were headed into the breach again, and the odds were against us. But it seemed like that was just the way we worked. Nothing was ever easy. You come to a small town to help some people look for their lost daughter, and suddenly you find yourself in the middle of a century-old conspiracy by a bunch of near-immortals to try and take over the world. Well, maybe not the world yet, but you can bet it was on Sharade's list. A megalomaniac who ruled a town and wanted more. His mistake was when he took the wrong girl.

The only problem now was that he had both my girls. And I wasn't sure whether either of them were still alive. All I could do was hope—and plan for the revenge that burned in my soul if they weren't. Maybe Sharade thought that he had seen the worst of it during the Civil War, but he and his Yesterday Men hadn't seen anything till they saw me mad!

Suddenly I realized I was squeezing one of the Palmer slugs so tightly in my fingers that they hurt. Joey noticed too. He smiled and shook his head. "So what did that slug ever do to you?"

I smiled a thin smile back at him. "Just my head pretending it was somebody else."

He nodded and turned back to his driving. For a long time I sat there watching him. He was like a great, black idol carved from stone—the man who could sleep anywhere anytime, the man who never showed fear or confusion. He was like a force of nature once he started moving, and God help anybody who got in his way. "Hey Joey, can I ask you something?"

"Sure, boss. You can ask me anything."

"You ever get scared, doing what we do?"

Joey turned his big head in my direction, and a big grin slowly split across his face. "Nope, boss, I never do, 'cause I got you watching my back!"

I just shook my head and went back to watching the road and loading the clips. Just what I needed, another fan!

The route we took to the cave led out and around in a big circle, staying off the main roads and trying to avoid Tucker's patrols. I was hoping that if they were getting ready to go to ground the way the last gunman had said, they were as interested in the perimeter as they had been before. But either way, we managed to get to the cave entrance without being molested by anything bigger than a dog that liked to chase cars. It did slow us down some though. It was nearly dark by the time we got there.

As we unloaded, Joey looked off toward the setting sun. "Guess we won't be seein' that again for a while."

I shook my head. "Nope, not for a long time if LuPon's map is right. We've got almost ten miles of cave between us and the hospital, with the town sitting right on top of us."

LuPon said that the geologists figured that this must have been the outlet for an underground river that fed the swamp a gazillion years or so ago, and that the shifting of the earth had probably cut off its water supply leaving the cave. I didn't know if he was right or not, and really didn't care how it got here. I just knew it was the only option we had.

Sometime a while back, somebody had gotten busy and boarded over the entrance and let the bushes grow up around it. Without the map we'd have probably missed it. I'm guessing the only other people who knew that it was here were the geologists who did the survey, who with the exception of LuPon were all long gone, and the townspeople, and they weren't interested in it. So when I grabbed the first board and put my weight against it, it pulled loose with a groan. They were all old and pretty well rotten, so it didn't take me long to get the entrance of the cave open.

Behind the wood was a thick coating of spider webs covering the entrance, almost like lace curtains. In the failing light I could see hundreds of spiders fleeing before the board I was using to tear down their webs.

When I had the opening clear enough, I took a flashlight and stepped inside. Most of what I saw ahead of me was just like the entrance. Miles and miles of web covered virtually every inch of the cave. There were so many spiders moving over the webs at one time that I actually could hear them. I repressed a shudder as I stepped back outside and started to pick up my gear.

"What's it look like, Rick?" Joey asked.

I scrunched up one side of my face and closed an eye. "Well, you're not gonna like it, that's for sure. Got a few spiders between us and where we're going."

Joey drew his shoulders back and stuck out his chest. "Well, I ain't afraid of a few spiders." Then he thought about it for a second. Squinting suspiciously at me, he asked, "How many's a few?"

I picked up the sprayer and slipped my arms through the straps, and pulled the chest strap tight. I didn't look at him. When I answered him, I did it low so he'd have to strain to hear me. "Not more than a million or so."

He was just putting on his own sprayer when what I said hit him. I could tell it had the way his back got stiff, his head jumped up, and the sprayer slid right through his big fingers. "You said a million, right?"

I nodded in answer.

Joey closed his eyes, and I could see his lips moving as he said a silent prayer. When he was done, he picked up his sprayer and put it on. "So, let's get this thing rolling before I lose my nerve."

It didn't go quite that fast. We took the tape we'd brought and taped the cuffs of our pants and the sleeves of our shirts tight to the skin to stop any unwanted hitchhikers from climbing aboard. Then I took my sprayer and lightly sprayed down the legs of Joey's pants and had him do the same to mine.

We split up the grenades, each of us taking half the foggers and half the explosives. He'd managed to find two Thompsons someplace, and we each loaded up and slipped the sling over our shoulders, the butt of mine clanking against the sprayer tank. They wouldn't do much good against the eight-legged vermin we were facing, but would be a big help against the two-legged kind later.

Gas masks and miner's lights finished it off. Joey started to put his mask on, but then he jerked it back off. "Geeze, Rick, this thing smells like an old overshoe!"

"Here, take a whiff of this and that won't smell quite so bad." I held up the wand of my sprayer in his direction.

Reluctantly he pulled the mask back over his head and tightened the straps. If he complained any more after that, it was too muffled by the gas mask for me to hear him.

I put my hat back on and slid the headband of the miner's light over the crown. Then, following that single circle of light and with a board to beat down the webs, I led the way into the cave.

*    *    *    *    *

Trudging through the cave was like sitting in a dark theater watching a horror movie, and suddenly realizing you're living it.

The going was slow, and the floor was slick with the combination of dead and dying spiders and the spray we were using to kill them. Our shoes were sopping wet, and our pants were soaked clear to the knees. The only sounds we could hear clearly were the wheeze of our own breathing inside the masks and the occasional clank of something against our sprayer tank. Otherwise, the cavern was silent.

All around us was darkness. The only lights were the twin spotlights from our miner's lights arcing ahead of us and reflecting back off the webs.

At about half a mile in, I pulled the pin from one of Palmer's fogger grenades. Right away it began to spit sparks and hiss like a Black Cat on the Fourth of July. With a smooth, arcing toss I hurled it as far behind us as I could. It hit the floor with a clunk, and a second or so later thick, viscous smoke rolled out of the can. It filled the cave like a growing gray beast, devouring everything it came in contact with. All around the fog, spiders fell to the floor and writhed in their last seconds of life.

I looked over at Joey, but all I could see through his mask were his eyes, and they were two tiny points of light staring eerily at me from behind the glass. At last he nodded his approval, and we began moving again.

The trek became almost routine: spray the webs with bug killer, sweep them down with the board, and crunch through the mess to the next one.

The masks kept most of the bug killer out, but even they weren't perfect. They were hot, and sweat was constantly running down your face and into your eyes and mixing with the spray, giving your mouth a metallic taste and keeping your guts rolling over. The thick glass of the lenses was constantly fogging, and would only clear if you held your breath for a few seconds. But then just as soon as you exhaled it would begin to cloud over.

Whatever the poison was that Palmer had used itched against bare skin, so you were constantly trying to scratch where it had soaked through your clothes. And when you did scratch, it just got worse.

Because of the mess on the floor the going was slow, and it was hard to maintain your balance. The water that had carved the cave hadn't just traveled in a straight path; it twisted and turned its way through the hill. In the softer spots it had opened wide, but where the rocks were harder it narrowed down, sometimes barely big enough to squeeze or crawl through.

When the glowing dial said that we had been walking for almost three hours, I used my board to clear a spot for us to stand. Because of the spiders we couldn't sit or even lean, but we could rest. Slowly I lifted the bottom of my mask. The air tasted like bug killer, but it seemed clear enough not to kill us instantly.

I pulled off my mask and took a deep breath. Then I motioned for Joey to do the same. I started to wipe the sweat from my face with the sleeve of my shirt before I remembered that it, like everything else, was covered in bug juice. So it had to dry on my face rather than be wiped away.

Joey looked around and wrinkled up his nose. "You know, I'm startin' to wonder about this relationship. You never take me anywhere nice anymore."

I sniffed the air around him and said, "You ever think it might be because of the way you smell? You've got so much bug spray on you that people could just hang you in a corner and kill all the bugs in the house."

"Don't ever say 'hang' to a black man." He laughed, and then his face grew serious again. "Have you noticed that the webs have grown less the last half hour or so?"

I pulled a piece free off my pants. "Not only less, but they're thicker. You know, kind of ropier."

"And less spiders, right?"

"Yep."

In the light of my lamp I could see his tongue picking at something in his teeth, but he didn't say any more. I slipped the mask back over my head, but before I pulled it back down I said, "Saddle up. Standing around isn't getting us any closer to the other end."

Joey took a deep breath and let it out slowly. When he pulled his mask down, I could hear him mumbling his displeasure. I knew that for all his grumbling, he was every bit as dedicated to what we were doing as I was. The grumbling was just to make him feel good about it.

*     *     *     *     *

Another half hour of traveling and the webs in the cave had nearly disappeared. All we encountered were a few of the thicker ones every now and then, and the spiders were nearly gone. We stopped and I pulled my mask off again. "Joey, I'm thinking we can drop the masks. We seem to have run out of spiders to kill." I eased off the sprayer, and it clunked against the floor as I sat it down. Somewhere up the tunnel I thought I heard something move, but when I shone my light that way, all I saw was blackness.

Joey pulled off his own sprayer and settled to the floor of the cave. From somewhere inside his shirt he pulled out a couple of candy bars and offered one to me. "I'd have brought a sandwich if I could have figured out how to keep it dry. Figured the wrapper on the candy bar would do the job."

I hungrily tore the wrapper off the chocolate and savored the first bite. It was like heaven. With a mouthful of nougat I said, "I take back all the bad things I said about you." I washed the bite down with a swig of water and passed him the canteen.

He took a deep drink and said, "I wonder what happened to the spiders?"

I heard that noise again up the tunnel. This time he heard it too. "I don't know what that is, but I'm guessing it's your answer." I flashed the light into the dark again, straining my eyes to see something, but the only result I got were strained eyes.

"I think we can probably leave the sprayers and the rest of the bug grenades here. From what I can see with my light it looks pretty clear up ahead, and it will make traveling a whole lot easier."

He pulled his Thompson around in front and checked the drum. I did the same, and then I took the safety off and pulled back the bolt.

After we'd rested a few more minutes, I climbed to my feet. "You keep an eye out behind us. Don't hesitate to shoot. I'm guessing anything in here with us is hostile."

Walking slowly and listening after every step, we advanced about five hundred yards when we heard it again. It was just up ahead of us this time. We both froze in our tracks.

With the tommy gun tucked tight against my side to steady it and my finger on the trigger, I took the light off my hat with my left hand. I could hear Joey's slow breathing behind me, and the thundering of my own heart as I shone the light into the darkness ahead.

At first all I saw in the beam were rocks and dirt, but then as I started to raise the light towards the roof, I saw two ruby-like orbs staring back at me. At least I thought they were staring. I wasn't real sure they were even eyes. They looked like two blood-red gems, each facet glittering in the light.

I shifted the light a little more, and then I could see the long, dagger fangs dripping venom, and the eight hairy legs that were holding it fast to the ceiling. In the light, it shifted and chattered at me.

"Son of a—!" Joey gasped.

Then suddenly the giant spider moved! Fortunately for me, Joey was still on his toes. I was frozen to the spot with my mouth hanging open and my eyes playing saucers. He knocked me down and rolled on top of me as the spider shot by us on the ceiling of the cave.

The sound of his machine gun was deafening in the tunnel as he stitched a trail of bullets behind it as it ran past.

I pushed free of his weight and rolled into a sitting position to add my own ammo to his, but it was already out of range.

In the light of my dropped flash, Joey's eyes were wide now that the danger had passed. "I think we need to go back and get the spider stuff, boss. Looks like we're gonna need it!"

I shook my head as I checked the load in my gun. "We've got nothing strong enough, Joey, to even knock it down."

Still watching down the tunnel, he glanced at me out of the corners of his eyes. "You think there's more of 'em? And what do you figure it eats way down here?"

I thought about it for a minute before I spoke. When I did, there wasn't much confidence in the way I said it. "I'm guessing that way down here there's only one. And as to what it eats…." I pulled myself to my feet and walked a short way ahead in the cave. When I came back I was carrying what looked like a human femur. I tossed it down beside him, and he jumped away. "That's what I think it eats."

He was on his feet, rapidly brushing himself off like he'd touched something disgusting. "Is that human?"

I nodded in the half darkness. "I think so. I'd need Kate to tell you for sure."

Thinking about Kate put the urgency back in my soul again. I picked up my hat and reaffixed the lamp to it. "Let's go. We got places to be. Just keep an eye out behind us, and we'll be alright. We've probably scared it enough for now that it won't stop running for days!"

Joey just grunted and eyed the cave behind us with suspicion.

*  *  *  *  *

It wasn't long after our encounter with the spider that we rounded a slight bend in the cave, and we could see that up ahead it was lit up like a new sunrise by bulbs strung along the ceiling. But other than the lights, there was no sign of anything else. Not even our sneaky friend the spider wanted to put in an encore performance.

As we walked on, I noticed the floor of the cave was wetter than it had been. It wasn't much, but there was a constant trickle of water over against the wall. Joey noticed it too, because he said, "Must be pretty near where the old river came out."

"I was thinking that, too. Keep an eye out for the spot where it comes out of the wall. If we find it, I've got an idea."

Slowly a grin spread across Joey's dark face as he realized what I was thinking. "Gotcha, boss."

Just before we got to the heavy wooden door that led into the hospital's basement, we found what we were looking for. It wasn't much of a stream, but enough to let us know the river was somewhere back behind the rocks.

I took out the four Palmer grenades I was carrying, and Joey gave me his. Then using my knapsack and my knife, I made a sling to hang them on the wall just above the waterline. I was digging around in my pockets for some way to set them off when Joey reached into his bag and brought out a small black box with a button on it. In his other hand he held what looked like an oversized blasting cap.

I raised my eyebrows in question. "What's this?"

His grin got a little bigger. "Something I snatched off Palmer's bench. The papers said it was some kind of remote detonator. I thought maybe we could test it out for him."

"Did the papers say anything about not carrying the switch and the trigger in the same knapsack?"

He got a little sheepish then. "I didn't think of that."

I shook my head as I tucked the cap into the bag. "It either means that you're really lucky, or it doesn't work."

The grin was back. "Well my grandma always said I was born under a lucky star. So let's just go with that."

With the explosives set and the detonator box in my shirt, it was time to hit the door.

Chapter 32

It was just a wooden door. A bit heavier than most, but just a wooden door. Considering the horrors that lurked on the other side, it seemed a bit inadequate. And it was unlocked!

Carefully I searched the frame, looking for wires that might point to an alarm, but there was nothing. Sharade was so sure of his whole operation he didn't even lock his doors. 'Course there was the matter of fifty gazillion spiders between here and open air, but even so....

I motioned Joey to the other side of the door, and with my machine gun cocked and ready I turned the handle and pushed the door open. I waited. When nothing happened after almost a full minute, I leaped inside and rolled across the floor, ready to shoot anybody who got in my way. But there was nobody! Climbing to my feet, I motioned Joey inside and took stock of where we were.

Everything was painted white, with bright overhead lights exposing every corner. It was so bright after the crappy lighting in the dirt and rock of the cave that I was left almost blind and squinting. Through my slitted eyes I could see Joey having the same problem.

"Perfect spot for an ambush, and nobody's home?"

All I could do in answer to his question was shrug. I was as baffled to the response we were getting as he was.

My eyes had finally adjusted, and I could make out where we were. It was just an empty room with a hallway leading out of the other end. I re-tucked the gun against my side, and motioning Joey to follow I slipped quietly out of the room and into the hall.

Not much there either, just a bright white hallway with overhead lights. We inched carefully down it, my back to one wall and Joey's against the other. As we neared the turn up ahead, I could smell ozone and hear the constant thrum of machinery. "Boiler room," Joey whispered.

As I opened the door and stepped onto the steel steps leading down, Joey stood in the hall watching my back.

The big coal-fired boiler was rumbling like a freight train, vibrating the whole room and drowning out any sound that might be born there. Off to one side, giant pumps brought the condensate back to be used to make steam. I couldn't understand why such a small operation like the hospital needed anything this big. Then it suddenly hit me. He wasn't just supplying power for the hospital; he was supplying it for the whole town.

Suddenly another idea struck me. I wasn't sure that Palmer's remote detonator was going to work, but there might be another way to take this building off the map. With grease rags wrapped around my hands, I used the steam pipes to climb up the front of the boiler to the controls. Hanging by one slowly roasting hand, I reached in my pocket and took out a quarter. I jammed it into the high pressure cutoff, so when the pressure got too high it wouldn't open and shut the fire down. Satisfied that that would work, I finished my climb up and over the front of the boiler to the top.

Since the early days of steam power, all boilers have been equipped with a blow down or relief valve. So if the switch I had just jimmied didn't work, they would blow off the excess steam. It was sitting in the middle of the boiler—a big, pointy thing with a lever out the back. When it had to open, that lever would pop up, allowing the valve to blow off.

I took off my belt and wound it tightly around the lever, holding it from coming open. Then I climbed back down and picked up my gun. Sweat was pouring off me from the heat, and both my hands looked a bit like I'd laid them on a stove burner. But if it worked, it was worth it.

When the time came all I had to do was find an outlet and open it up fully to increase the demand, and boom!

When I came out, Joey was worried that it had taken me so long. "Where were you? I was about to come after you."

"I left the bad guys a little present," I answered.

"Well, come on. I got something to show you."

He anxiously led me up the corridor to the turn. After making sure nobody was around, he motioned me forward and pointed to a door. There was a massive bolt and a padlock on it. Pulling me back around the corner, he asked, "What's that look like to you?"

"Looks like a cell to me," I whispered back.

I felt the rhythm of my heart start to increase. If he had a cell, and it was locked, that more than likely meant prisoners. And prisoners could mean Kate and Thelma were still alive!

It was all I could do not to run up the hallway. When I got to the door, somebody inside my chest was using my heart for a snare drum. My mouth was dry and my hands were shaking. It took me two tries just to hit the padlock with the butt of my Thompson my hands were shaking so badly. But with the second swing I connected, and the lock fell away. I slammed the bolt back and reached out to push the door open.

At that instant I hesitated. What if she wasn't on the other side? What if the cell was empty? What would I do then? I wanted to take my hand and tear at my brain, shutting out that voice that was filling me with doubt. A scream lay unvoiced on my tongue as I finally found the courage and pushed against the door. Slowly the heavy door swung inward.

My vision was blurry with fear and the tears of hope that were streaming down my cheeks. She was there! Her head was nestled on Thelma's lap like a child's. On feet that belonged to someone else I crossed the room, dropping the Thompson to the floor somewhere behind me. I didn't even hear it fall. I dropped to my knees beside Thelma, trying to read her eyes. Like mine they were filled with tears.

Dark bruises ringed both of her eyes. Her lips beneath the purple stain were swollen and cracked. There was a trickle of dried blood from her nose and another from the corner of her mouth, trailing down her chin and onto the lovely throat I had kissed so many times. The port in her chest was slowly leaking blood that clotted on her breast. As I watched, I couldn't see her breathe.

My eyes begged Thelma to tell me, and when I asked, my voice trembled. "Is she…?"

At the sound of my voice, one of the purple, swollen eyes opened, and she tried to smile. "Hiya, Handsome."

I literally tore her from Thelma's grasp and crushed her to my chest, my tears falling onto her face, leaving trails in the blood and dirt. "Kate, I'm so sorry."

With what little strength she had, she raised her hand a brushed away my tears. "Hey Handsome, how come you're crying? Who died?"

I forced a smile. "Nobody, Beautiful, nobody!"

I scooped her up into my arms—she weighed nearly nothing—and climbed to my feet. Turning to Joey I said, "Let's get the girls up to the ambulance garage and get them out of here! Then I can clean up the rest."

We started toward the door, but Thelma stepped in between and dug her heals in. "No! I can't leave. Lou Anne and Uncle Vince are here. I can't go without them."

I sucked in a deep breath, held it for a long time, and then I slowly let it out. She was right. As worried as I was about Kate, she would never forgive me if I let the others die while I saved her.

I motioned to the submachine gun on the floor with my head. "Pick that up and try not to shoot me with it." Then I handed Kate to Joey. "Take her to the ambulance garage and wait for me. If I'm not there in twenty minutes, load her in a car and get out of here."

He handed me his Thompson and with Kate in his arms trotted off down the hallway to the steps.

I looked at Thelma and said, "Lead the way. Let's go get your family."

Despite it having been only a couple of seconds since they left, Joey and Kate were long gone. That easy, loping run of his could eat up a lot of ground very quickly.

We passed a couple more doors on our way to the stairs, but I wasn't interested in what was behind them anymore. I had found what I was looking for. Now as soon as everybody was safe and out of the way, it was payback time!          Even the steam lines seemed to be on my side now. They were running along the ceiling toward the stairs, which meant there was a good chance of finding a valve or a fitting ahead so I could send the boiler into high fire and the rest of the building with it.

Looking at Thelma marching along beside me, I had to smile. With Joey's knapsack slung over her shoulder like a bandoleer, her mousy hair sneaking out of her normally tight bun, and the machine gun, she reminded me a bit of a Mexican revolutionary: short and kind of squatty, armed to the teeth.

It was bothering me a lot that we hadn't seen anybody since Joey and I broke in from the cave. "Thelma, do you know what happened to all of Sharade's people?" I asked.

Her head bounced on her short neck. "I overheard him say before he stuffed me in the cell that he'd sent everybody away, except his close lieutenants—you know, Tucker, the major, and the corporal. He said he couldn't trust anybody else."

That explained it, but it didn't make me feel any more secure. I just had trouble believing that a smart guy like Sharade wouldn't have some kind of plan.

At the stairs I took the lead, and for once she managed to keep her big feet under control. I hardly heard a sound coming up the steps behind me. When we got to the top I eased the door open and peeked out into the corridor. It was as deserted as everywhere else we had been.

I pushed the door shut again and leaned my back against it. I knew I might have been beating a dead horse, but better it than me. It just didn't feel right. No alarms, no guards, just one big, empty building. But all I could do was shake my head and wonder.

I was going to have to play the game by their rules, and I didn't like that. When I played, I wanted to be the man in the know, the guy who wrote the rules and told the refs what to do. Now all I could do was move my piece on the board and wait for the trap to spring.

I looked at Thelma, and she was trying to stuff the hair back into her bun with the barrel of the gun. I thought I should warn her about shooting herself, but decided she was an adult and I wasn't her mother. "Do you know where Vince and Lou Anne are?"

She stopped playing with her hair and nodded, undoing all her gun work. "They're just a short way down the hall in side-by-side rooms."

"Can they walk?" I had my fingers crossed behind my back, but I had the feeling it wasn't going to do any good. And when she shook her head, I knew I was right. "Then we're going to need a way to wheel them out."

"Well, the beds have wheels. We can just push them out."

I knew how hard it was to move a hospital bed, even with wheels, so I shook my head. "We need wheelchairs. They'd be lighter, faster, and easier to control. Do you know where they keep them?"

She pointed the opposite direction down the hall. "There's a storage room jut down there full of all kinds of things."

I checked the hallway again, not that anything had changed. "I want you to go to Lou Anne's room and get her ready to go. I'll get the chairs and bring them to you."

Her eyes behind the thick lenses looked doubtful. "You sure you don't want my help?"

I shook my head. "No, I'll get the chairs      . You just get her ready." Then I opened the door and motioned her through. Once I was sure she was in the room and safe, I took off in the opposite direction after the chairs.

Everything was right where she said it was. The room was full of extra beds, commodes, and two wicker chairs with wheels.

It only took me a couple of steps to realize why she had tried to be so insistent over coming with me. Pushing one of the chairs with its four small wheels was hard enough. Trying to push two was like herding cattle. I tried putting one in front and pulling the back chair. That worked for about a second until all four wheels on the front chair decided to all turn at once, and it took off sideways.

The only alternative I could see was to push them side by side, but if I didn't do it from the armrest I had no control. Whoever designed the things was an idiot and put the armrest too low for me to walk upright and still hold on. By the time I got to Lou Anne's room, I was out of breath, my shoulders were stiffening up, and I was getting madder by the second. That little voice in the back of my head kept saying "Yep, this is his plan. All alone he intended to kill you with wheelchairs!"

I took a deep breath, told the voice to shut the hell up, and pushed open the door. Thelma had Lou Anne up and sitting on the edge of the bed. I helped transfer her to the chair. As Thelma went through the door, I said, "Whatever happens, don't come back. Just get Lou Anne in the car with Kate, and if I don't show up in a couple of minutes, the four of you take off. 'Cause if I don't get there right away with Vince, we're not coming."

She started to protest, but I didn't give her time. I slapped her on the butt and pushed her down the hall. This time I didn't wait. I was out of one room and into the next in an eye blink.

When I saw him lying there, I almost thought I was in the wrong room. The last time I'd seen Vince, he robust and full of life. What was lying in the bed now was something out of a tomb in Egypt. If you didn't look real close, you couldn't see him breathe.

Leaning in to whisper in his ear, I wasn't sure that I was in time. He had that musty smell of a dead body already. "Vince," I said softly, "I've come to get you out of here."

His eyes fluttered open, and in a raspy whisper he said, "Don't worry about me, Captain. The doc says I don't have much time left."

My voice took on a hard edge. "The doctor's the one that did this to you. If I get you out of here, you just might make it."

A glimmer of hope came into his tired eyes, and weakly he tried to push himself up off the bed. I slipped my arm under him, and helped get him into a sitting position.

"What about Lou Anne?" he gasped.

"Lou Anne's fine. She's with Thelma."

He tried to smile. "And Sophie? Is she there, too?"

I knew he was going to ask that. How do you tell a man who's wrapped his whole life up around a woman that she's the one that in the end betrayed him? I did my best to look reassuring. "Sophie's fine, too. Now let's get you into this chair and out of here so you can have a family reunion."

Thank God Vince didn't weigh any more than he did. Without him being able to help and the chair trying its best not to cooperate, I had a tough time getting him settled. But finally I managed it. Laying my machine gun across his lap, I fought the chair through the door and down the hall to the garage.

Joey was just finishing loading Lou Anne into Sharade's limo when I got there, and Thelma was watching the door with her Thompson cocked and ready. As I stepped through, I saw it come up, and my life started to pass before my eyes. But luckily she didn't pull the trigger. I stopped pushing the chair and walked over and, as gently as I could, jerked the machine gun out of her hands! "Try asking 'friend or foe' next time before you try to put a bullet in somebody. Now push Vince over here."

I laid the gun across the back of the car, and Joey and I lifted Vince and slid him in next to Lou Anne. Slamming the door shut, I looked at both of them. "When you leave here, you head straight for the hospital. Tell Hays and Bill what's going on. And if anybody gets in your way, shoot them."

It was Joey's turn to protest, and I had to bite my lip to stop from shouting. Didn't anybody take orders anymore? "Look, whether they survive or not is going to be because of you. I'm putting them in your charge and expecting you to do the right thing. I can take care of Sharade. I'm going to make sure one way or another he dies today, just like he should have a hundred years ago!"

Rather than stand there and let him argue with me, I walked around the big car to where Kate was. When I opened the door, her eyes opened, and she did her best to smile. "Joey says we're going for a car ride." The swelling made the words hard to form, and she slurred them.

"Joey's going to take you someplace safe."

"You goin' with us?"

I shook my head. "Nah, I got a couple of things to do first. I'll catch up."

She tried to force a smile. "Mom says you're okay, Rick. She says she likes you."

I could feel my brows knit together in confusion. "Your mom?" I asked.

Kate nodded, and, as dumb as it sounded, I was afraid her head might come off the way it lolled against her chest. "Yep, she came and visited with me while I was in there." She swung her thumb toward where she thought the building was. "She said you were coming to get me."

I could feel an empty hole in my chest at the thought of her leaving, and I knew if I stayed with her much longer I'd never let her leave. Taking her bruised face gently in my hands, I kissed her on the lips. "We'll talk about what your mom had to say later. Right now I just want you to remember that I love you!" Then I kissed her again.

A lone tear trickled her cheek. "I love you too, Rick."

I squeezed her hand and closed the door. Picking up my Thompson, I handed it to Joey. "Anybody tries to stop you, don't hesitate to use this."

Reluctantly he took the gun, and for a long time he stood there trying to say something. Finally I broke the silence. "Me too, Big Fella. I'll see you in the city."

His grin split his face. "You'd better, boss, you'd better." Then he climbed in the car and started the engine.

He was about to pull out when Thelma jumped out of the other side and ran over and kissed me on the cheek. "Thank you, Captain."

I gave her a two-finger salute as she climbed back in, and Joey slipped the car into gear.

I stood there watching until I couldn't see them anymore. Then, as I turned back toward the building, there was a dull thud to the back of my head, and the lights went out. The trap had just sprung shut.


Chapter 33


Sharade was drunk, or as drunk as he could get with his spider immune system. The bottle on the desk was empty, and he was face down on the pistol he had pointed at the major not long ago. The weight of his head was forcing the gun to leave its imprint on his cheek and temple.

His mind was far away from the once peaceful town of Cypress Glen, and was somewhere off in his past reliving his glory days as a gentleman and army officer, dashing in his fresh, crisp uniform, even his early days as the handsome, wonderful Dr. Sharade. But then the black cloud that was Rick Steele had invaded his Eden, which brought his heaven and all it provided him crashing down.

He stirred in his stupor, and his mouth drew back in a snarl. So many failures by the men he trusted most, men who had been at his side since the beginning. Did this eternal life they suffered from bring on a degeneration of the brain cells? In his dreams he made a note to himself that he would have to look into the brains of a few of the townspeople and see. It would give him something to do while he waited for the rest of the world to go by.

Something in his sleep disturbed him, and he stirred. Then it was no longer in his sleep, but a dull buzz on the corner of his desk. Slowly he raised his head and wiped the drool of sleep and alcohol from his mouth with the back of his hand. The noise was the alarm and flashing light on the corner of his desk. It was the alarm from the cave door.

Long ago he had removed the standard burglar alarm from the door and installed motion detectors inside in the hall. More than once the damp at the end of the tunnel had shorted out the alarm on the door and sent him and his men running in response. But with the motion detectors in the hall they were safe from the effect of the tunnel, and would still reveal anything happening around the door.

Rubbing his eyes, he slid open a desk drawer and flipped a switch. On the wall a small, round screen came to life. It was another amazing invention of the latter half of this century. A televisor screen, they called it. He had heard that they were even broadcasting pictures into the houses of people. For him, the only images he cared about were the two moving up his hallway.

As they came into focus through the interference, his breath caught in his throat. *Steele* and the black man were in his hallway!

Sharade scooped up the pistol off the desk top, but then another thought hit him and he returned to his chair. He knew exactly where they were going. Steele was going after the women, and possibly even the two patients upstairs. Well, let him. It just made him all that much more vulnerable.

Turning his chair to the radio transmitter behind him, he turned the dial and pushed down the speak button on the standing microphone. His lips close to the screen he said, "Major, we have intruders at the cave door. But I don't want them molested unless Steele himself tries to leave. Do you understand?

The major's voice came back through the speaker scratchily, but the question in it was still very clear. "Sir?"

Again, he was questioning Sharade's orders. Much more of this and something would have to be done! A new snarl filled Sharade's voice. "I said, unmolested unless Steele himself tries to leave! Watch them, but do not let them know you're there!" He didn't wait for a response before he shut the radio off. Thinking to himself, he was sure now something was going to have to be done!

*    *    *    *    *

The major set his walkie-talkie down on the counter of the nurse's station and shook his head. Sharade seemed to be losing it more everyday. If the two intruders were in the lower hallway, it was time to get the drop on them and pin them down. But no, he wanted them to wait until there was a chance of Steele getting away again. Whose side was Sharade really on?

He stuck two fingers under his tongue and whistled down the hall to where the corporal and Tucker were working. At his summons they stopped working and walked up to the nurse's station.

"What's up?" Tucker asked. There was dust from packing things all over his dark blue uniform.

"His majesty says Steele and his flunky are in the lower level, but he doesn't want us to do anything about it. Just stay out of sight and keep an eye on them. Only if Steele tries to escape are we supposed to do anything."

"And what then?"

The major shrugged his broad shoulders. "I guess do whatever is necessary to try and stop him. Now get out of here and find someplace where you can watch without being seen." As they walked away, he shook his head again. He just wished it were the old days again. Even fighting through the swamp was better than these cat-and-mouse games he was being forced to play.

So even though it irked the major to no end, he sent his men off to hide and found a spot for himself inside the nurse's station where he could watch through a crack.

With his cocked pistol in hand he watched as first the big, black man ran passed with the once-pretty, white doctor in his arms. Then he was forced to watch as Steele and the chubby girl rescued the other two from the rooms. It wasn't until they'd all moved into the garage that he called his men together, and they got ready to make their move.

But just as they were headed for the garage with guns drawn, Sharade put in his appearance and foiled them again. "Don't make a move unless he tries to get into the car with the rest of them. If that happens, open fire! Otherwise let them go, and we'll take Steele when they're gone."

"What makes you think Steele will stay?" the major asked, a little more harshly than he intended.

Sharade's face grew hard. "Remember who you're talking to, Major." Behind the eyes slightly reddened by the alcohol there was a fire burning. "Steele will stay, even after the others have gone, for me. He feels he owes it to the world to stop me for good. So when the others have gone, then we'll take our Captain Steele!"

Having been chastised enough for one day, and not trusting his mouth not to say what he was thinking, the major just nodded and went back to watching the garage from the cracked-open door.

He gritted his teeth as Steele put the old man and the girl in the car, and then shook hands with the black man. He wanted so badly to put a bullet in the giant's skull, but orders were orders.

Finally Steele said goodbye to his girlfriend, and the long, black car sped out of the garage. Turning to Tucker and the corporal, he had them move to either side of the doorway as he pulled it quietly open and slipped through.

It all went even easier than he could have ever dreamed. Steele was so entranced watching his friends leave that he never heard a single move the major made. He was able to sneak up quietly behind the man and bring the barrel of his revolver down, probably harder than necessary, on the back of Steele's skull and send him off into unconsciousness.

\*     \*     \*     \*     \*

There are four rules that should never be broken. Number one is Newton's first: if you throw an apple up in the air, get out of the way because it's going to come back down and hit you on the head. Number two is one of my favorites: girls should always smell good. Number three: water in no way should ever be associated with waking up. And number four: when you wake up, you should be in some semblance of lying down!

Well, they did a really good job of breaking the last two, and I was figuring they had a really bad-smelling girl hidden someplace to disprove the second one. And like an idiot I'd obviously broken the first one by walking under some unknown falling object.

Somebody tossed a bucket of cold water on me, and my senses slowly started to return. I wasn't lying down, I was standing up with my hands above my head, my toes barely touching the ground and a rough board trying to shove slivers into my face. I also noticed that my back felt a bit breezy. I found out why when I opened the eye that wasn't mashed into the board. Somebody had torn my shirt open from collar to waist.

Somewhere above me, my hands were manacled to the side of an old wooden building. Inside my head visions of pirates and slaves rushed through my thoughts. Sharade stepping into my line of vision did little to change that.

Sharade's mouth was in a half smile that made him look even more evil than a full one ever could, and his hands were clutched casually behind his back. "Ah, Captain Steele. Back with us again, are you?"

There was a crack on the tip of my tongue, but for probably the first time in my life I bit it back to wait and see what came next.

He turned his back toward me as he paced, and I wished I had a knife to stab into it. "Do you know where you are?" he asked.

"I'm guessing it's not Cleveland." There it was. If I had a hand free I would have beat myself in the head. Always do your best to antagonize the guy that wants to kill you!

"Very droll, Captain Steele." The smile faded from his face, and he nodded to somebody I couldn't see. The next instant there was a sharp crack, and my back exploded in pain.

While my head was swirling in pain and tears were filling my eyes, he went on talking as though nothing had happened. "You are in a very famous place, Steele. You are chained in the exact spot that this plantation used to punish their slaves. For nearly one hundred years this wall was used to show the cost of minor infractions committed by the black people who worked the fields."

His hand opened in a gesture of surrender. "Of course, there are much more severe punishments for more serious offenses, but I thought this one would be good enough for now."

"Lucky me. I don't suppose cake and tea was on that list anywhere?" There went that mouth again! Sharade nodded again, and once more my back screamed under the crack of the whip.

"That, good Captain, is a cat o' nine tails. Did you know that in the hands of a master, the person being whipped could be kept alive for an entire day? Of course when he was done, the offender wouldn't have even the smallest strip of skin left on his back. Fortunately for you, we're not going to take that much time."

"Am I not just the luckiest guy in the world?" I winced and waited, but this time there was no crack.

Sharade's face was close to mine as he shook his head. "You amaze me, Steele. Even in the face of uncertainty your bravado doesn't stop. Well, soon enough it will. You see, the major and his cat o' nine tails are going to beat you to death. And when we're sure that you are dead," he leaned in very close, bits of spittle hitting my face, "I'm going to use some of the spider serum to bring you back to life so I can do it all over again. I intend to keep doing that until I grow bored and find new atrocities to commit on your body." He laughed at the amusing thought of me dying again and again.

I myself didn't see much humor in it, but then as he said, I've always been kind of a droll guy.

Still chuckling, he turned and started to walk away. "I have other things to attend to, major. Call me when your little task is complete."

When I couldn't hear his footsteps anymore, the major lightly caressed my back with the cat, just enough to get my attention but not send me into agony. Nonetheless, sweat was beading out on my forehead, and a tiny trickle of blood was working its way down my chin from biting my lip.

"I want you to know, Steele, I don't agree entirely with his plans. Oh, I agree that you have to die. But you've proven yourself to be a brave and honorable man, and you deserve an honorable death, not to die like some darkie hanging from a chain."

I heard the rustle of cellophane, then the major spit, and with the rasp of a match I knew that I had gained a short reprieve while he smoked his cigar. It would give me a chance to weigh my options, if there were any.

He puffed the cigar to life, and I smelled the acrid smoke drifting my way. "It wasn't always like this, Steele," he continued. "Once we had a divine cause to fight for. But that cause ended, and so should have men like us. But we lived, nearly twice the lifetime we should have, and maybe forever according to the colonel—" he cleared his throat and corrected himself, "excuse me—the doctor.

"But the longer we lived, the further we got away from that cause. At first we worked to affect some kind of return of the Glorious South, but Sharade grew tired of that. He seemed to no longer care if we were forced to share our streets with darkies. Then it was his own personal rise to power, but he grew tired of that too. Oh he still maintained the control he had over the local politicians, but that was all.

"And where he had just been egotistical—all officers are a bit, anyway—he grew cruel. If we had been smart we would have left him then. If we had, the twins might still be alive. But out of habit we continued to follow him."

I could hear him puffing as he contemplated what he was saying. "Then you came along. For us, it was rather nice to have a real opponent to face, almost like a game. But then the things that he did, like letting the twins die, and the things he did to Doctor Gallagher and the others.... The rest of the boys were okay with it all, but it turned my stomach. We were supposed to be soldiers, even after all these years. Citizens were supposed to be left untouched." From his tone I could almost see him shaking his head in my mind, looking down at the ground ashamed.

"You and the black man—that was another story. You were soldiers, just like us. But not the girl and her father. They were townspeople, and we promised once we would stop any harm from ever coming to them. I think he could have explained it to them, and none of this would have needed to happen. But instead he took it as a personal offense, and he struck back!"

While he was busy talking, I was trying discreetly to explore my options for escape. It was looking pretty bleak this time. Chained to a wall like this, it looked like I might end up letting a lot of people down, not to mention myself.

As carefully as I could, I pulled against the manacles and the eye bolt that held them to the shed. Both were fast! But when I leaned against the wall, I felt the section give, like it might be rotten. I remembered that when the major had hit me both times, my weight collided with the wall and I felt it give. Maybe if I threw my weight against it every time he hit, maybe I could break something. Now the only question was could I last long enough to break free?

I heard what sounded like him checking his watch, then a couple of big puffs on his cigar. Next the butt landed by my feet, the smoke rising up and filling my lungs. Death by whip and cigar—could a guy ask for a more dignified death?

As I waited for the next strike against my back, I laid my forearms flat against the wall and pressed forward, testing for the best spot to slam my body into the rotting wood. Then I backed up as far away as the manacles would let me for the most momentum, waiting for the snap of the cat.

When it hit it was like a bolt of lightning tearing across my back, and I fought to maintain control through the pain. I threw my body forward with the strike, slamming my shoulder into the wall. I heard the soft crack of rotten wood behind the wall and felt it give another inch.

My eyes blurred with pain, and the blood ran like a tiny rivulet from my bitten lip. But against it all, I forced myself back and readied for the next blow.

The whip cracked, my back caught fire, and I hurled myself forward. The world was starting to spin around me, and I had to shake my head to stay conscious. Inside my mind it was a red cloud of screaming agony as the skin was being peeled from my back! Sweat poured down my face, mingling with the tears and the blood.

There was no breath left in my lungs, but from somewhere deep inside I found the last reserve of my strength and stepped back. I knew I was nearly done!

Again the whip cracked, and through the pain the words of a prayer left my lips and I threw my body forward one last time. Suddenly the air around me split with a loud crack, and I was tumbling forward with the pieces of the wall into the shed!

For a heartbeat I lay there, trying to find space in my burning lungs for a breath. I knew I didn't have more than a second. Already I could hear the major cussing and coming across the short distance to the shed.

I pushed myself up and to my knees, shaking free of the boards and debris. Only the eye bolt and the board it was bolted to remained. Holding it like a bat, I waited as the major pushed his head into the shed and then I swung, catching him full in the side of the face.

The major reeled backwards, and I was less than a step behind him, jabbing the jagged board into his face like a crude wooden sword. Blood was running from numerous wounds, and one eye was gone.

I didn't give him time to even swear. I just kept pressing forward and pressing him backward. He stumbled over a small stump and tumbled onto his back. I was on top of him in an instant, jabbing the board into the soft flesh of his face with both my hands.

His struggles grew less, and finally they stopped. I fell over onto him. I was bloody, and tears were streaming from my eyes as sobs racked my body. I was alive! Against all odds I had managed to survive!

Like a drunken sailor I climbed to my feet and weaved my way back to the shed. I didn't know how long it would take, but I knew if I didn't do something he wasn't going to stay dead. I rummaged around in the half dark until I found what I was looking for. It wasn't very sharp, but I figured it would do. Dragging the axe behind me, I staggered back out to where the major lay.

I put one foot on his chest, raised the axe over my head, and swung it down. There was a soft squishy sound as it hit his neck, cleaving through the flesh. Wiggling it free, I raised it again and smashed it down. This time it accomplished its task, and his head rolled away from his body. I pushed it further away with my foot like I was afraid it might reattach itself. "Grow that back, you son of a bitch!"

I dropped the axe beside his body and limped back to the side of the shed where my things were lying. Luckily for me there was a water hydrant there, and after letting the water run until it was nearly icy cold, I dropped to my knees and climbed under it, let the water wash the blood and the pain from my back.

## Chapter 34

She stood just outside the brightness in the cave. For many, many hatchings she had never advanced any further than this, until that time a few feedings ago when the wall of the bright section was open, and she went out into the world. Even in her dim memory it was not like she had discovered it to be. It took much hiding and much exploration before she found herself once more under the pull of the great eye in the sky. And then in the cloudy wet she had found food. But then he with the hurt had come and taken it from her. Then he had forced her back here and hurt her again and left her hungry.

Just when she had found fresh food invading her home, they had hurt her, too, and gotten away. But from the slight breeze that ruffled the tiny hairs on her forelegs, she knew that there, in the bright, it was open again. She raised her leg, testing the vibrations and feeling for the faintest movement. With just a lack of movement in the air, it meant that she was alone.

She sent out her chatter, listening. The echo came back, and she gauged the distance. The bright reflecting off the many facets of her eyes made it difficult to see, so she had to rely on her other senses until the shadows were gone.

Feeling safe at last, she skittered to the roof of the cave and approached the door. A sensitive leg went through first, testing, and then she followed through the door, up the wall, and across the ceiling. Then in the far corner she waited again. When no one came, still on the ceiling she started up the narrow hallway.

*     *     *     *     *

The icy water washed away the blood and helped to numb the pain, at least to the point where I could move again without screaming. And it helped to clear my head.

Still stiff and now half frozen, I climbed from under the water and let it run off me to dry. I tore the remainder of my shirt off, mostly just the sleeves and collar, and tossed them angrily away. I kind of liked that shirt.

Still limping a bit, the manacles and the bloody board they were chained to banged against my legs as I walked over to where they had tossed my things. My jacket was there, and luckily so was my automatic. I picked it up and made my way back over to the stump that the major had tripped over.

Dropping down to my knees like I was on a prayer bench, I stretched the chain across it, then laid the barrel of the .45 against one of the links. I'd seen them do this in the movies, but I really had the feeling it was going to be a lot tougher than it looked. With the gun held flat against the stump I closed my eyes and slowly squeezed the trigger.

The report was almost deafening, and the force of the shot tore the gun from my hand and furled it back to smack me like a fist in the chest. Slowly I opened my eyes, hoping that I would at least be half free, but the chair was still intact. The link was badly bent, but still welded shut.

I rubbed the new bruise forming on my chest and swore. Then I set the whole thing up again just like before. The only difference this time was I made sure the barrel was against the bent link, and I got a better grip on the gun.

Eyes closed again, I slowly squeezed. BOOM! The manacles tore against my wrists, the gun flipped out of my hand, and I rolled out of the way. But this time when I opened my eyes I could see a space in the link!

Now that it was open, I held my hands up and did the strongman thing with my wrists to pull it the rest of the way apart. Way harder than it looks! But I did manage to open it just enough so the other link would slide through, and the eye bolt and the board slid off when I raised my hand.

I was still wearing the manacles with about six or eight inches of chain hanging from each, but my hands weren't tied together anymore. I slipped my jacket on over the cuffs and chain, picked up my knapsack of goodies, and started for the hospital. As I walked by the major's body, I pick up his hat and put it on for half a disguise, and grabbed the axe. I might have some more chopping to do before I was done.

With the axe in my left hand and the .45 in my right, I started across the open green space that separated the outbuilding from the hospital. All I could do was hope that no one had heard the shots, or that they were too busy to look out the windows. There wasn't crap for cover, and the way I felt right now I wasn't sure I could duck and cover! So one foot in front of the other, I forced myself to keep plodding forward.

Above the hospital I could see dark, billowing clouds of smoke, and the boiler started to burn itself toward destruction. There wasn't a lot of time left!

I had heard stories from guys I knew about the marches the Japanese had forced their prisoners on, and could never understand how they had held on. I knew I wasn't suffering anything even close to what they went through, but I was beginning to understand. There were times when your mind just shut down parts of your body, like flicking a light switch and suddenly you could no longer feel the pain. All the energy in your body was being used to put one foot in front of the other.

By the time I got to the back of the building, I was nearly exhausted. My jacket had stuck to the drying blood on my back, forming a giant leather scab that tore free and re-stuck with every move. My chin was on my chest, and both hands were numb from carrying the gun and the axe. I slid down in a sheltered alcove to catch my breath.

I couldn't have been asleep more than a couple of minutes when I heard the back door of the hospital slam. Peeking out around the corner, I saw Sharade and the one they called the corporal talking.

"Go out there and see what the hell is taking him so long. Steele should have been dead a long time ago. If he isn't, put a bullet in him and the major, and then come get me."

"You mean shoot the major? But—"

"You heard my orders. Now go before I shoot *you*!"

As the corporal took off in the direction of the shed at a run, Sharade turned to go back inside, mumbling to himself. "Maybe I should just kill them all and start over." The door slammed shut behind him.

I took a deep breath and climbed to my feet. Time was starting to run out. It wouldn't be long until the corporal was back with the news of what I'd done to the major. I gathered up what strength I had and quietly opened the door and stepped inside.

The hospital had never been a bustle of activity, but now it was like a graveyard. Nothing moved. The only sound I could hear was the faint, far-off surging of the boiler.

Quietly, and as stealthily as a dying man could, I made my way down the hallway towards where I remembered Sharade's office was. I wasn't sure what my plan was, I just knew I had to confront him and keep him distracted till the boiler went up. That should take all of us out of the equation. I didn't see how any of them could survive an explosion like that.

I was almost there when I felt something cold and hard press up against the back of my neck. I turned my head just enough to see the grinning face of Tucker, his service revolver pressed against my flesh.

"You amaze me, Steele. You're as hard to kill as one of us. Only in your case, that's about to run out."

I forced a little half smile to my dry lips. I could almost hear them split. "You know how many times I've heard that today, Tucker? You guys need a new writer."

Tucker mumbled something in reply, but I had already stopped listening. I was standing with my left shoulder against the wall, and tucker was sort of centered on my right shoulder with his hand on my upper back and the gun against my neck.

Anybody with any smarts will tell you that to get out of a situation like this, you turn toward the gun. And that was just what Tucker was expecting. So instead I rolled to my left, ducking down as I did, making almost a full turn before he even knew I was moving.

As I did, I brought the .45 up and into his belly and started pulling the trigger. The first shots forced him back far enough that I could bring the axe into play. It caught him deep in the side, and as he fell backwards he nearly tore it from my hand. I dropped the .45 as he hit the floor and jerked the axe free. I was about to do to him the same thing I did to the major when the bullet chewed off the plaster next to my head.

I dropped my shoulder, scooped up the automatic, and holding the axe tight to my chest rolled across the hallway. The first turn onto my back tore the jacket free of the scab, and I think I screamed. I say "think" because I couldn't hear myself over the .45 spitting out death down the hall as I rolled.

Managing to make it without any new holes, I crawled behind the reception desk and dropped the clip out of my empty gun. I replaced it with one from my knapsack. There were four more clips in there and two of the Palmer grenades, but I wasn't sure just what the range on them was. It would be a shame to blow myself up this close to my goal.

I had a pretty good idea where the corporal was in the hallway, but I thought a couple of shots might draw him out. Carefully I slid around the corner of the desk and fired two shots in rapid succession. The first shot knocked a little plaster off the wall. The second shot knocked down the wall!

Professor Palmer would be pleased to know his explosive shells worked, if I ever got out of here to tell him.

When the dust finally settled, the hallway was a mess. The shell had taken out most of the wall and a good-sized piece of the ceiling. Light fixtures were hanging down, the loose wires were sparking like the Fourth of July, and water was spraying everywhere from the broken pipes. In the midst of all of that, under a pile of rubble was the body of the corporal, or what was left of the corporal.

One of his arms was gone, torn off at the shoulder, the blood pooling under him. His other hand searched the floor for some kind of purchase to pull himself free.

As I picked up my axe and started around the desk, I could see him watching me. He knew what was going to happen; he'd seen what I'd done to the major. His movements became almost frenzied, his one hand reaching and grasping for something just out of his reach. Then as I came the rest of the way around the desk, I could see what it was. His pistol was lying just beyond his fingers.

Slowly I limped over to where he lay. With my foot I slowly slid the pistol closer until he could get his hand around the grip.

I wasn't sure why I gave him the gun back. Maybe it was just a way to prove a point. Maybe I had to prove to myself that he was the cold-blooded killer I thought he was. Or maybe I wanted to see if he would use it on himself to relieve his pain. All I know is that the instant his hand closed around the butt of his revolver, the barrel turned in my direction, and he started to squeeze the trigger.

I didn't give him the chance to finish what he started. I brought my axe down on the back of his neck and finished the job the bullet had started. I knew from the churning of my stomach that it would be a long time, if I had a long time left, before I resolved what I had done to these three men. They were cold-blooded killers, and the notches on their guns were too numerous to count. All I had done was what should have been done nearly one hundred years ago. So as far as I was concerned, they were dead along time ago. Sharade was all that was left!

Chapter 35

Covered in the blood of three dead men and myself, the axe dragging behind me and my pistol hanging limply in my right hand, I staggered my way back down the hall.

I had barely enough strength left to put one foot in front of the other. The only chance I had of stopping Sharade now was one of Palmer's grenades. I was going to have to get close enough to pull the pin and stop him from getting away before it went off.

Not my favorite option. That meant that wherever he was when it went boom, I was going to be there too. Not much of a chance of walking away from that.

I wasn't afraid of dying, and never really had been. It's what happens in a war or when you're up against a guy like Sharade. As long as you win—you know, stop the bad guy—it made the dying okay.

Like I said, I wasn't afraid of dying, but I was disappointed. For the first time in my life, I actually had something to come home to. Maybe even a future. No chance of that now.

Yeah, if it wasn't Sharade, it would have been somebody else. That's what happens when you take some crazy oath to defend the helpless and protect your country and actually believe it. Or maybe I just didn't like the smug ass!

I got as far as the nurse's desk when the whole thing was taken out of my hands. That very instant the boiler decided to move from downstairs to the roof and fall back down again. Most of the first and second floors went out through the roof, and everything that was left burst into flames.

The explosion picked me up like an autumn leaf and tossed me and half the flaming rubble down the corridor. I'm pretty sure I hit the wall a couple of times and off the ceiling at least once before it ran out of power and dropped me facedown on what was left of the floor. But by then I really didn't care anymore. After the second time I hit the wall, I was having a little trouble staying conscious. So by the time I smacked down on the floor, the ref was already counting me out!

Coughing from the smoke, I slowly opened my eyes. At first I thought I was dead, but there was too much pain for that. I was lying spread-eagle on the hallway floor. Behind me I could hear the crackle of the flames as more of the building caught and the fire crept closer. All my parts were still there, but I couldn't get up!

By craning my neck just enough I could see why. All the junk that had been flung down the hall with me had picked the same place to land that I did. Only I landed first, and it all landed on top of me.

Cursing myself for getting caught in my own trap, I tried to raise myself free of the rubble, only to collapse back flat on the floor. Even on my best day I doubted I could lift all the junk on my back. And beat the way I was now, I was lucky to be able to lift a two by four!

Coughing, hacking, and nearly exasperated, I tried to crawl free. But that worked out just about as good as lifting the garbage off my back. Somewhere in the pile it felt like my leg was caught, and all I got for my troubles was more pain. As I slumped back to the floor, I found myself looking at the toe of a highly polished boot, and right next to it was another one. Between the two them, resting its tip against the floor was the blade of a sabre.

Slowly I raised my eyes, following the polished boots and the glittering blade. The boots ended at the knees and were replaced by blue-grey trousers, but the sabre blade just kept going. It rose right up to two hands crossed on the hilt, hands that belonged to Sharade, who was in a full-dress Confederate officer's uniform. Gold braiding gleamed on the sleeves of the tunic, and the stars sparkled on the collar. The whole uniform looked new.

As I looked up, the tip of his sword came up off the floor and drew a line down my face. I could feel the blood start to run. "What did you do that for?"

"To show you who's in charge." His accent had grown thicker with the addition of the uniform.

Suddenly the whole scene looked a little familiar, and I felt my stomach turn a bit. I figured the sword could do almost as much damage as the axe.

He must have read my mind, because his smile broadened. "Though you have vexed me sorely, boy, I am not of a mind to kill you yet. As a matter of fact, you did me a favor killing those three. They were becoming nearly as big a thorn in my side as you. I couldn't trust them to do as I asked anymore. They were relying too much on their own judgment." He snorted like a horse, and his eyes seemed to cloud a bit. "Can't have that in a military unit, you know. Could result in a mutiny. If you hadn't killed them I would have had to have brought them up on charges and court-martialed them."

My head was spinning, but I realized it wasn't spinning quite as fast as his. Colonel Sharade had turned the bend. His cheese had gone moldy. He was bedbug crazy!

Sharade paced back and forth in front of me, occasionally stopping to punctuate a point with his sabre. It was all I could do to keep my fingers and my head out of his way. Suddenly he stopped and swept the air with his blade. "All of this. It took me nearly one hundred years to build all of this! And in the course of a few short days you have reduced it to rubble! All for some snip of a girl that the world wouldn't miss." He stabbed the point down, and I tried to roll clear. It caught me on the left cheek.

He leaned down close, I thought to survey his handy work, but I was wrong. He got close to my face and lowered his voice to a whisper. "It's Richmond, isn't it? They're afraid I've grown too powerful, and they sent you to stop me!"

He jerked his sabre free of the floor and nearly took my nose off. "I will not stand that kind of treachery! President Davis will hear of this!"

When I had rolled the last time I felt something in the pile shift just a bit, and my leg felt freer. If I had the time I might have been able to crawl out. Behind me I could feel the fire getting closer, but it wasn't the only thing moving our way. What I saw just might have taken that choice away from all of us!

\*     \*     \*     \*     \*

Hundreds of scents floated to her as she hung suspended from the ravaged ceiling. She tasted each one, separating them, trying to identify them.

One she knew was familiar. It was the one who brought the hurt. He was like he was sometimes when he came to feed her, agitated almost like the hunger frenzy.

The other, too, she had encountered before. Earlier in the cave she had faced him and another. They had scared her with vibrations on her path across the ceiling. But now there was something different about him. Something that she always scented in her prey before she devoured them. He was trapped, helpless. Was he to be the prey of the one who brought the hurt? Was he going to eat this prey before him?

All caution was gone. The hunger frenzy was on her now, brought to a head by the scent of blood in the air. She skittered forward....

*    *    *    *    *

I lay pinned to the floor like a bug, watching another bug creep up behind a crazy man. I know I should have called out, but I lay there fascinated by what I was seeing. It was like watching one of those travelogue shorts in the theater where you know the tiger's going to eat the goat, but you just keep hoping not. And then when it happens, you can't turn away.

I had lost track of what was coming out of Sharade's mouth some time ago. It wasn't making much sense anyway, and even before the spider showed up I had concerns of my own. I had to decide which way I was going to die—fire, explosion or old age?

Pretty much figured by now the old age thing was out the window. The fire wasn't going to give me that long. So the only choice was probably explosion. I had wriggled around enough under the rubble that I had worked one of Palmer's grenades from my bag and was holding it with my finger through the ring.

At first I was worried that Sharade might see what I was doing and stop me, but he was long passed seeing what anybody was doing. So when the spider came up behind him and her forelegs reached out to pull him into a bear hug, or I guess in this case a spider hug, the look on his face was one of total surprise!

In a moment of clarity when he realized that his precocious pet was about to make him today's blue plate special, his eyes grew big and round, and a scream of terror tore from his throat. He looked at me there on the floor and begged, "Steele, save me! Help me!"

For a second or two as the spider started to drag him backward I actually thought about it. Then instead I pulled myself free of the rubble, jerked the pin from the grenade, and shoved it into his pants before he was beyond my reach.

A breath after that, the spider sank its fangs into him, and his struggles stopped and his screams ceased.

Like a child, the spider pulled him close to her abdomen with one of the front legs and started back down the hallway. As they disappeared into the flickering shadows, I rolled in behind the nurse's desk to find what little cover I could find against what I hoped was coming next.

I'm not even sure I had time to draw another breath before the explosion rocked the hallway, and bloody body parts, both human and spider, filled the air.

I pulled myself into a sitting position and tried to find enough oxygen in the smoke-filled air to fill my ravaged lungs. I got just enough to make me cough, spit a little blood, and know that somewhere there had to be a couple of newly broken ribs. The rest of me wasn't in much better shape. There was a major laceration on my thigh that every time my heart beat oozed what looked like catsup. My hands and face were blistered from the fire and cut from Sharade's sword. I was pretty sure that even if I had the energy left to stand up, I couldn't have gotten my legs to work. Not real positive that anything was still hooked up.

If I were a smoker, this would be the time for the last cigarette. You know, like in the movies where the two heroes are sitting side-by-side against the wall sharing one last cigarette before the final attack. Only problem here was I didn't smoke, and I was all alone. But I guess that if you're going to die in a burning building, that's the way it's supposed to be.

Only the guys in the movies are heroes. The rest of us are just dumbasses that didn't have enough sense to get out while we still could. They might give us posthumous medals, drape our coffins with flags, and some guy that never met us will be wiping tears and saying nice things about us. But the bottom line is still the same—we were too distracted to duck, too stupid to move, or dumb enough to think we were invulnerable.

Yep, we might have saved the world, but are you sure there wasn't a way we could have done it without getting shot? Stabbed? Set on fire? And if there was, why didn't somebody tell us?

I took another deep breath, coughed some more, and spit some more blood. Sitting here feeling sorry for myself wasn't going to finish this job.

I reached into my bag once more. It made me think a bit like Felix the Cat. In all those cartoons, he always had a way out in his bag of tricks. Me, I just had good ol' Professor Palmer's push-button remote detonator—a tiny black box with a big, red button!

I looked around the hospital at all the damage I had caused, and I think I smiled. I remembered my mother telling me when I was a kid that I was like a human tornado. Well, Ma, you were right! With my thumb I pushed the button down.

Deep inside the building I heard the faint sound of the explosion, and a moment later the shockwave rocked the building. The professor would be glad to know his thingy worked. Too bad there wasn't going to be anybody around to tell him. I closed my eyes and slowly drifted off.

## Epilogue

The feeling came back to my body slowly, and none of it was a good feeling. It was all pain. I don't think there was an inch of my body that didn't hurt. And that wasn't right. I was supposed to be dead. And if you believed all the gobbledygook they've printed about being dead, it's not supposed to hurt. So either I wasn't dead, or all those guys were wrong.

Carefully I opened one eye to a slit and tried to get a look at where I was, figuring that if I was still in pain I must still be lying in the hospital. Well, I was half right. Hospital—right. Sharade's hospital—wrong!

It was like the ending to the Wizard of Oz. People were all clustered around my bed, waiting to see if I was going to wake up. Any second I was going to get Ray Bolger looking at me and going, "You remember me, don't ya Honey? Your old pal, Hunk!"

But I knew it was no dream, because half a dozen of the guys in the room were in uniform. Some were state police, and some were army. Were we at war?

Suddenly I realized I wasn't dead! I tried to rise up in the bed, but my arms and legs were tied down. I struggled against them until that big, black face I knew so well put a giant hand in my chest and pushed me back. "Easy, boss. Those restraints were for your own safety. You kept trying to run away. If you promise to lie still, I'll untie you."

I nodded weakly, and Joey turned my hands and legs loose. When he finished, I looked at him and tried to speak. From all the smoke my voice was little more than a croak. "Kate?"

It must have made more sense to him than it did to me, because he stepped out of the way, and the most beautiful face in the world took his place. Sure it was still swollen, her one eye was still surrounded by a bruise, and that big, purple stain was still around her mouth. But her eyes were as clear as a summer morning. She reached out and took my bandaged hand in hers, and with just a hint of a smile she said, "Welcome back, Cowboy. There for a while we thought we'd lost you."

For just a moment the two of us were alone in the room, two people who had both been to hell and escaped. Our bodies hadn't remained unscathed, but our hearts had. We knew now that nothing short of death itself, and maybe not even that, could tear us away from each other.

If I had my way that moment would have lasted forever, but reality always finds a way to intrude, and this time it was Hays.

He was looking better than he had the last time I saw him. His arm was still in a sling, but he was back in command. "You stirred up quite the hornet's nest. Half the state's under martial law from the names on that list. Politics around here aren't going to be the same for a long time. And that suits me just fine."

He fumbled around in his pocket for a beat-up looking Lucky and a match, but just as he was about to light it he stopped and asked, "Do you mind?"

I raised the hand Kate wasn't holding and pointed the bandages at Redmond. Hays held up his cigarette and raised his eyebrows in question. Redmond simply nodded.

When he got it lit and was done blowing smoke at me he asked, "You feel up to telling me what happened up there? By the time my men got there, you were lying unconscious on the grass, the hospital was almost ashes, and there was a river where the town had been. There was no sign of Sharade and his people," he lowered his voice and leaned in close, "except that headless corpse up there by the shed. You do that?"

All I could do was nod. It looked pretty bad, but I couldn't take the chance of them coming back again. I motioned toward the water glass, and Kate held it up while I took a couple of sips. When I thought my throat would work again, I nodded, and she sat it back on the table.

I pushed myself up in the bed a bit. "You might want to find a chair, Hays. This is going to take

a while. And you might want to get somebody to write it down, 'cause I'm only going to tell it

once."

He waved to one of the troopers taking up air in the room, and he came over to the bed.

Hays sent him out into the hall, and he came back with a couple of folding chairs and a pad and

pen. When they were comfortable, I told him and everybody else in the room what had

happened since Joey and Thelma got away—the whipping, my escape, the final fate of Sharade

and his men. Twice in the middle I had to stop for water.

Hays looked at me a bit shocked as I finished up. "You're a mean one, Steele!" He

smiled, but behind it I could see he meant it. Then his face got a confused look. "But what I

don't get, then, is how you got out. To hear you tell it, you were almost dead."

That puzzled me a bit too. I pretty much figured I'd had it, and then I woke up here in

the hospital. Not that I'm complaining, mind you. I'd prefer being here with Kate to being dead

any day.

As I lay there looking around the room at Joey, Thelma, Hays, the doctor, and Kate, I

realized somebody was missing. Vince and Lou Anne were downstairs in rooms of their own.

That left only LuPon!

I called the doctor over and quietly asked him if he knew where his morgue attendant

was. He just shook his head and said that he hadn't seen him since the evening Joey and I left.

Even after I told him not to, he must have followed me down there to make sure that I

didn't fail. Then, after saving my life, he disappeared again. Hopefully wherever he was, he

could finally get a chance to live out the years he had left.

I had lots more questions, but to tell you truth I didn't care much if I got the answers or not. I was alive, Kate was alive, and I was holding her hand. The rest of the world could just wait.

End

8664381R00221

Made in the USA
San Bernardino, CA
19 February 2014